P9-CDM-474

Also by Edward Riche

Rare Birds

the nine planets

EDWARD RICHE

VIKING
CANADA

VIKING CANADA

Published by the Penguin Group

Penguin Group (Canada), 10 Alcorn Avenue, Toronto, Ontario, Canada M4V 3B2
(a division of Pearson Penguin Canada Inc.)

Penguin Group (USA) Inc., 375 Hudson Street, New York, New York 10014, U.S.A.
Penguin Books Ltd, 80 Strand, London WC2R 0RL, England
Penguin Ireland, 25 St Stephen's Green, Dublin 2, Ireland (a division of Penguin Books Ltd)
Penguin Group (Australia), 250 Camberwell Road, Camberwell, Victoria 3124, Australia
(a division of Pearson Australia Group Pty Ltd)
Penguin Books India Pvt Ltd, 11 Community Centre, Panchsheel Park,
New Delhi – 110 017, India
Penguin Group (NZ), Cnr Airborne and Rosedale Roads, Albany, Auckland, New Zealand
(a division of Pearson New Zealand Ltd)
Penguin Books (South Africa) (Pty) Ltd, 24 Sturdee Avenue, Rosebank, Johannesburg 2196,
South Africa

Penguin Books Ltd, Registered Offices: 80 Strand, London WC2R 0RL, England

First published 2004

(FR) 10 9 8 7 6 5 4 3 2 1

Editor: Cynthia Good

Printed and bound in Canada.

LIBRARY AND ARCHIVES CANADA CATALOGUING IN PUBLICATION

Riche, Edward
The nine planets / Edward Riche.

ISBN 0-670-04456-3

I. Title.

PS8585.I198N55 2004 C813'.54 C2004-902914-2

Visit Penguin Books' website at **www.penguin.ca**

For Frances

one

IT GAVE MARTY A START. He was stepping from his car, vision compromised in the twilight, when he caught sight of the stuff. For the sake of his new shoes he danced a jig to dodge it, setting the cuffs of his trousers to flapping like little wings.

A milky fluid was seeping from the expansive lawn of the vocational college, on which a number of snow sculptures—relics of a winter carnival—were surrendering to March drizzle. A Viking, Leif Ericson no doubt, was guarding the place with a sword blunt and soft as a stick of butter. His helmet was shy a horn. The same raggedy gales that had carried him to Newfoundland a thousand years earlier were now his undoing. To Leif's right a wedge once representing the old tricolour of the island, the standard of wishful thinking, resembled a melting block of Neapolitan ice cream. The opaque effluent pooling on the parking lot was pigmented, too. It had been necessary to dye the snow white.

He checked his black oxfords—conservative and upright, appropriate for a visiting vice principal—and was relieved to see they were unblemished. Tonight's was not a professional call, but a man with Marty Devereaux's profile in the community had to keep up appearances.

It was unlikely, unthinkable really, that any of the students from Marty's school, The Red Pines, a private school, would end up here, at a vocational college. The well-heeled parents of The Red Pines' students would send them, deservedly or not, to universities and professional schools.

No, Marty was here not for business, but to make a show of pleasure for a dinner prepared by students of French Cookery, 7:30 to 10:30 P.M., Winter Semester, Adult Continuing Education, Wonders of Learning Program. Marty's big brother, Rex—dramatist Rex; sad, fat Rex—was graduating.

Marty climbed the concrete steps to the front doors of the college, the largest of several brick boxes dominoed over the landscape. He stopped at the top to look back at the sodden lawn. It was a good thought for The Red Pines, a winter festival or carnival of some sort, another billable extracurricular activity. Marty, though, would have had the sense to hose the remains of the snow sculptures into the storm sewers before they became so unsightly. He went inside.

Why had Rex taken the course? Thirty years ago he might have put it to use, made it a proper trade. This was emasculating, dressing in an apron and pottering around a kitchen. Maybe it was a means of avoiding writing, of not getting around to that next play. As if anyone cared. As if anyone went to the theatre any more except out of some misplaced sense of duty. Yeah, the cooking course was busywork. Rex would claim it was self-improvement, part of the lifelong learning process, no different from the time (during his Sandinista period) he had signed up for Conversational Spanish. The very thought of adult education filled Marty with loathing.

Men were filing into the building, protesting the climate by noisily shaking coats and doffing hats before drifting toward an east wing. Marty reasoned these were the husbands of the wives who had taken French Cookery to spice up stale marriages. He joined their procession down the hallways of battered pea-green lockers.

☿

They were to dine in a classroom decorated in the manner of a bistro. Each of sixteen tables was set with red-checked cloth and a single emergency candle. Air France posters selling kissy Parisian boulevardiers and Provençal idylls had been taped to the walls, in some cases to mask signs of the room's usual function. Hidden behind the Eiffel Tower, Marty could make out an instructional diagram for pork butchery, dashed lines demarcating chops and trotters.

An unglazed window in the room's north wall revealed an institutional kitchen next door. The workspace was divided into stations by parallel rows of stainless steel counters. Big stoves were set to one side beneath an awning of exhaust-fan hoods. Crowns of blue flame, dancing on account of the commotion, kept a dozen or so pots the size of barrels steaming. The students wore professional whites, names embroidered over their hearts.

Marty saw that Rex's wife, Meredith, was already seated. She beckoned him to join her and another woman, a stranger.

Meredith was clad in pants and a loose-fitting collarless blouse that exposed the wishbone lines of her clavicle. Both garments were the colour and weave of shredded wheat. Her palette ranged through duns and earthy browns to beiges and buffs. Marty remembered her wedding dress being the ivory of worn piano keys. He supposed this was to bring her closer to the earth, to working people, to virtue—such was the nature of her vanity—but it succeeded only in making her look like some sort of POW. It had been years since Marty had seen Meredith in her one colourful piece, the vibrant sling in which she had schlepped her infant, Cathy. It was of indigenous Central American manufacture and meant, presumably, to signal solidarity with some guerrilla's struggle in the jungle.

Meredith's friend appeared to have mistaken the evening for a more swish affair. She wore an elegant, short black dress and lustrous silvery-grey stockings. Her hair, too, was black, shiny with gel, in a nervy flapperish cut. Next to Meredith the guest was almost zaftig, but with a muscular confidence. An inoculation cicatrix, a tortellini of fleshiness, visible just where the sleeve of her dress ended, dated her. She was of Marty's vintage.

"Jackie, this is Marty, Rex's brother. Jackie Spurell." Meredith tossed her hand in Marty's direction, not bothering to look up.

"Hello, Jackie," Marty said. He was searching for a place to hang his raincoat. The others had hung theirs over the backs of the chairs in which they were seated. Unhappily, Marty did likewise.

"They're running late. No surprise there." Meredith addressed both her tablemates at once by talking to the air between them.

"Jackie's husband, Ted, met Rex in AA."

Marty nodded to indicate that dealing with the alcoholism was a good thing, that there was no stigma, that he wasn't one to judge.

It had been long enough since Rex's first "meeting" that he was surely due a badge. Opening night of "Hello, I'm Rex and I'm an Alcoholic" found Rex at home, drinking as usual, thrashing away at a keyboard and watching over his sleeping daughter. Cathy was nine years old at the time. Meredith was off attending a meeting, Oxfam or something equally worthy. By eleven that evening, Rex, ego and id purring in sweet unison, was contentedly blotto. By quarter-past he was a kettle of words on the boil, in need of an ear, and a whisky-less sobriety risk. So he pocketed his smokes and made for his favourite beer parlour, The Spur, leaving his only child alone in the house. The front door was ajar when Meredith came home.

Rex later confessed to Meredith that he did not remember she was out, he was that drunk. What he told no one but his brother Marty was that he had—"sort of," he put it—"forgotten" his daughter, that he was married, that years and years had passed.

"What do you do, Jackie?" asked Marty.

"Was a nurse … back at it now, part time. You?"

"He's vice principal of a high school," Meredith could not resist answering for him. "The Red Pines. It's a private school."

"Meredith thinks," Marty tried to sound rehearsed, "that sending a child to a private school is an abrogation of one's civic responsibilities."

"Yes, I do. Yes, I do," Meredith said. "That's why the public system is going to shit, because people with some influence, the middle class, no longer participate."

"This is an old argument, Jackie," said Marty, "that goes on and on. I am sorry to say it's not a terribly interesting one."

"The principal there, Henry …?" Jackie searched for the name.

"Hank," said Marty. "Henry. Henry Lundrigan."

"He's involved in that thing … you know … that thing to save … what is it?"

"The Perroqueet Downs."

"Pair-Oh-Keet?"

"Like *parakeet,*" said Marty. "Old French mariners' misnomer for puffin, or so Hank tells me."

"I think that's great, what he's doing," said Jackie.

"Please! Optics. Spin," said Meredith. "It's just a show of ecological consciousness to … It's a decoy. Real politics have become too dirty. Yeah, the political has become dirtier than … dirt." She was too angry (always lately) to be coherent. "Ecology is a refuge for the gutless. Ecology and animal rights. What about human suffering? The condition of women?" It would be class struggle next, thought Marty, followed by a dose of lefty economic nostrums. Didn't these people know when they were beaten? "I mean it's all well and fine to be concerned about bogs and … and … frogs, but please, get in line! 'Preserve the Perroqueet Downs.' Like that would make any real difference. It's just spin."

Marty wished it were. Hank's conversion to the Green movement had started innocently enough: the abandonment of pesticide use on the pitch, slow food, a composting program, and then worm boxes for the cafeteria waste. Next it was the Gaia theory. If Meredith thought it an act, it was only because the change in Hank was so radical that it tested credulity.

Meredith was opening her mouth to send another blast Marty's way when his cell phone rang, cutting her off with a muffled trilling. The phone was deep in a side pocket of the raincoat. By the time he dug it out it was quiet.

"No matter, it bounces to my voice mail," Marty said.

Meredith huffed in disgust. Liberals of her sort could turn the delicate sensibilities on and off at will. They were easy to take inordinate offence (his cell had rung, he hadn't dropped his pants and shat), and when they chose, say in the matter of gay porn or the conduct of their favourite freedom fighter, be the very picture of tolerance.

Marty felt a mitt grip his shoulder and a mound of hot belly at his back. Enter Rex, he thought.

With Rex was another man who went around the table and took Jackie's hand. You could tell he was once handsome. Husband Ted/Sponsor Ted—or his ghost—looked tired.

Rex straightened to his considerable height and swept back a forelock the shape and size of a bunch of grapes that had fallen into his eyes. The younger Rex, aspiring artist in need of a look, had let the lid run wild until it was impossible to train. But this Rex wasn't far from fifty. Marty thought it looked undignified, even … the English had the word for it, was it *naff?* … and he wished Rex would cut it.

Both brothers' manes, black and now a little white, shared a slight Moorish kink, a consequence, the relatives said without foundation, of an eighteenth-century Portuguese sailor's seed, some wrecked captain in the mix. Fastidious grooming had toned down Marty's curls to a wave and perhaps thinned them a tad. The brothers didn't otherwise look at all Iberian. They were spawn of the Norman Conquest, if from opposite sides of the Channel. Rex's features were bolder and bulbous, more John Bull. Marty's finer, more Gallic. Rex said his brother looked like "a froggy functionaire."

From behind his back Rex produced a condensation-beaded bottle of Muscadet and set it in the centre of the table. "I thought with the first course, a simple fish soup, this." Since swearing off drink Rex made a show of not being tempted by its presence.

Rex was, thought Marty, a good, old-fashioned drunk. A fat guy who drank too much, so much that he lost control of his life and needed to stop. Looking at Ted you could tell he was one of those self-medicators for whom booze was a balm against head problems and who now reached for a bottle of tablets instead of spirits. Whatever worked. Everybody had their own problems. Miss Zwitzer, the music teacher at The Red Pines and Marty's lover, did nightly laps of white wine to reach her peace. Despite chronic sleeplessness, despite throbbing knees, Marty considered himself neither a drinker nor a pill-taker.

"Your main course will be hare wrapped in green cabbage leaves—it's a vamp on a sausage or a cabbage roll, both rustic and pretentious." Even for a playwright Rex was a poor actor, a mugger. "I call it 'A Farmer McGregor,' but nobody in the kitchen has the faintest what I'm on about. To accompany might I suggest a ..." Rex stopped and reached for the small of his back. He recovered and continued, but it was in pain that he croaked, "Beaune."

"I've been insisting that he get one of those chairs, those kneely chairs, the ergonomic ones." Meredith picked a paper napkin up from her place setting just to throw it back down. "You know, the type of chair where you're kneeling so the pressure is off your spine."

Meredith participated in the charade that Rex might actually still be working, that he might, one day, again write something and be paid for it. Two years earlier Marty had helped Rex land such a gig, convincing his old friend Lloyd Purcell to take "the brother" aboard a television series, a medical melodrama called *All Heart* for which Lloyd was head writer. Though Rex collected a fat cheque for writing an episode, his name never appeared in any credits and neither he nor Lloyd ever spoke of it to Marty.

"Everybody finds their back. It's normal. It's boring. And those chairs are a fad," said Rex.

"They are not. It makes sense," said Meredith.

"Eight or nine hundred dollars for a chair! Nonsense," Rex said. "And it's like you're praying. I cannot kneel before a computer."

Right, thought Marty, every act had to be an act.

Rex went back to the kitchen. Ted, who had not said a word, trailed him. The lights were dimmed and Jackie's eyes turned from chocolate brown to a burnt hue. Marty thought her gaze might be seeking his. What was she saying? Something about her spooky hubby? An apology? A plea? Meredith squirmed in her chair, already finding the evening a trial.

♀

The meal was good—or at least Marty thought it must be, as there were no complaints from Meredith, and Jackie even cooed. The guests at the other tables, looking cheerful and sated, had pushed back their chairs and were chatting.

Marty wasn't an eater. When he was still running middle and long distance, food became a simple fuel, a calculation of the calories required to carry him, and remained so. His road race ended during a sprint to the finish of a meaningless 10k. By then he was suffering nagging chondromalacia, and a small twist, a slight imbalance in his stride, tore his anterior cruciate ligament. So rudely did it cut him down that he couldn't even get his hands out to brace for the fall. The already damaged knee crashed into the pavement. The secondary trauma ripped into the posterior cruciate as well as the medial and lateral collateral ligaments. Marty could feel his knee blowing to pieces.

The doctors marvelled at the extent of the dislocation. It was over. So Marty, in an act of spite, of self-mutilation, turned to the butts. It was a complete capitulation, a statement that his will as much as his knee had failed. Thus his ambivalence toward smoking: he always sat in the non-smoking section of a restaurant, found the trappings and waste of the habit distasteful, was revolted by the stench of a full ashtray. He was aware of the hypocrisy in this and perfectly comfortable with it.

Rex came back to the table, kitchen steam and perspiration now tugging his whites closer, revealing blubbery dugs. In obvious need of a drink himself, he topped up everyone's wine.

"We've had a minor setback with the dessert. The pears were supposed to be poaching through the entrée but someone forgot … so … Dave, our instructor, well, he's in there now with a blowtorch and …"

"A break is nice anyway," said Jackie. "Gives everyone time to digest."

"Yeah," said Marty.

Rex, suppressing puffs and pants, whistling through his nose, was looking to Meredith for something.

"It was terrific, honey," she said.

"Just delicious. Fantastic," added Jackie. "Tell Ted."

"I will. He's on the pears. I should get back and give him a hand." Rex returned to the kitchen.

"Ted," Jackie took a breath, "just can't keep his mind on things. He's really preoccupied with …"

Marty patted his jacket pockets, frisking himself. Jackie watched and then, as if blowing a kiss, put two fingers to her lips. Marty found what he was looking for.

"I'm going to grab a smoke. Jackie?"

"I shouldn't leave. Meredith?"

"No, no, no, go on. Kill yourselves." Meredith sounded as though she meant it.

Disinclined to go out into the weather, Marty led Jackie through the halls in search of a hideaway. He caught himself towing the woman in his wake. He didn't mean to be discourteous, but familiar with the quadrangular way of the institution—girls' washroom here, auditorium there—he sensed in which direction they should head, where best to steal a drag. He slowed so that they might talk as they went.

"Preoccupied with?"

"Sorry?"

"You said your husband, Ted, was preoccupied with something."

"No, nothing. Just way too inside his head. Can't remember anything, can't concentrate, it's like he's got Alzheimer's."

"Oh."

"He's an airline pilot. He's on stress leave … the plane he was … well, it was just taxiing on the runway when it … it left the runway and went into some bushes. Nothing major. And, you know, things at Air Canada aren't good, so … I just know he screwed up … sorry … that he was the one responsible for the pears." She changed the subject. "You must like kids, hey?"

"Why?"

"Being in education."

"I'm primarily an administrator, some discipline, but with our student population it isn't often that I have to … do anything like that."

"So, no?"

"No?"

"Kids. Like them?"

"It's as though," Marty laughed, "I'm avoiding the question."

"Meredith and Rex have their hands full these days."

"With Cathy?"

"Yeah," said Jackie.

Marty knew all about it, knew how daughter Cathy was breaking their hearts. Rex and Meredith tried to be good parents, never too stern, never too accommodating, always encouraging and caring. But Cathy wouldn't be loved, was withdrawn and recalcitrant. One sensed in her reluctant words disdain for the world. It was different from the affected sullenness Marty saw in so many of the girls at The Pines. In Cathy it wasn't a pose, it was something real and unwelcome, a vandalous intruder. Nothing had been said about it of late, a sign that the situation continued to deteriorate.

"It's partly the school she's in." This was a misstep. Marty veered to diplomacy. "Not to knock Frank Moores High, good teachers, good principal … but the students. Different neighbourhoods, age of the kids there, simple demographics—sometimes there's problems. People think it's the boys that are all the trouble, but teenage girls … so difficult to reach. And where Rex and Meredith live downtown, the zone is very mixed."

"We live just around the corner, but … you know, no kids."

"So it's different."

"It's different."

"I have offered, many times now, to put Cathy in The Red Pines, gratis, but … well, you heard Meredith's view. And Rex, too. He thinks there's something snobbish about it."

They arrived at a remote corner at the rear of the college's main building. A set of metal steps screwed to the wall led to a lonely door. With what Marty took be an addict's urgency, Jackie strode ahead, taking the stairs two at a time. Her ankles were bound by the straps of heeled sandals. She trailed a tether of perfume, a potent sort. He thought she had been looking at him strangely back at the table, sending some signals he couldn't quite understand. He prided himself on being able to read people, to decipher subtleties of body language, to detect apprehension or authority, but Jackie was lost on him.

The door opened onto a vertiginous catwalk, a grillwork balcony overlooking an autoshop. A dozen or so cars, guts spilt, were spread across the greasy concrete. Amidst the steel and rubber and wires, a constellation of dials and LED displays from electronics and diagnostic computers flashed and blinked. There was a smell of gasoline.

At the room's centre was a freakish trophy, two front-ends from a couple of old Dodge Darts welded together pushmi-pullyu, each half-car pointing in the opposite direction, impaled on a ten-foot metal post. It was no doubt meant to be a bit of fun but had quite the opposite effect.

Jackie took a cigarette from Marty, keeping her eye on the outlandish assembly. "What was the point of that, do you suppose?" she wondered.

"Something to do. After class," Marty said, lighting her cigarette.

"That's what I need. Something to do after class."

Marty would have taken this for an invitation but that Jackie looked so forlorn saying it.

"I meant that earlier," she said, "about your friend Henry, the principal. Despite what Meredith said, I think it's brave."

Brave enough to make an impetuous pass, braver than me? wondered Marty.

"Brave?" he asked.

"Everybody's lining up behind the development. You know, business bigwigs and the city council and, like, board of trade types. And isn't … what's his name … putting it together?"

"Hayden, Gerry Hayden," said Marty, "or one of his companies, anyway. It seems small potatoes for them."

"Yeah? Like how much?"

"What are they talking about? However high-end, it's just a subdivision, two hundred units or so … they've got to run in the hydro and a new road and water and sewer … so I figure after costs they make maybe a couple of, three or four maybe, but say couple of hundred thousand a unit."

"That's forty million dollars."

"Maybe it's not so small." Marty was surprised by the calculation. Jackie was right, Gerry Hayden stood to make tens of millions on a project Marty had naïvely considered trivial. Perhaps that was why Gerald Hayden was rich and Martin Devereaux was not. "But for him, given all the aggravation … who knows? It isn't my league."

"The money might have something to do with it, don't you think? People are opposed to the development because they resent his success."

"Not my man Hank. He's a convert to the cause, to the planet. Have you ever been out there?"

"The Perroqueet Downs? No."

"Neither have I. It's close, just over the hills on the other side of the harbour. Can't be more than a ten-minute drive and then a twenty-minute hike, max."

"They say it's beautiful," said Jackie.

"Don't they, though?"

"What do you mean?"

"I wonder how many of the people demanding the Downs be preserved have actually been there," Marty answered.

"You're for the development?"

"I don't have feelings one way or the other. For much."

Jackie squinted, uncomprehending, at Marty.

"It's good, I think," she said, "for people to have strong feelings, to care. I've never been out there, to the Downs, but maybe I will some day."

"You're right," said Marty, trying to put an end to the discussion. Jackie was not warming to him; in fact, she seemed to be taking a dislike to his ambivalence. She was simply trying to make small talk, but Marty let his candour open a window to his character. More and more lately he thought of the wisdom of keeping his own counsel. What was ever to be gained by opening one's self up?

"We should probably head back," he said.

Jackie ground out her cigarette on the metal rail and tossed it below. Turning for the door to the stairs she staggered, her torso whipping forward.

"Shit!"

The heel of one of her sandals had found its way through the grillwork, twisting her leg slightly. She was yawing, caught in a lurch, her dress stretched tight to reveal the relief of her hips, its hem yanked up her thighs. She clutched the rail to steady herself.

"Shit."

Her leg tugged at the shoe, testing the strength of the heel. If she pulled any harder it would break.

"I'll do it," said Marty, getting down on his knees.

The heel was flared with wear at the bottom and was tightly wedged in the metal grille.

"Just unbuckle it," Jackie said.

"No. I have it." Marty put one hand beneath the sole of the shoe and grasped Jackie's ankle with the other. He gently turned her foot first one way then the other, inching the heel like a cork from a bottle. Jackie pulled in sympathy, guided by Marty's hand. Marty watched the sinews of her calf working through her stockings. The hosiery buzzed at his fingertips. His thumb slipped up under one of the straps and the buckle dug into his hand.

"There," said Marty. Jackie made the final effort to free herself, coming forward on the ball of her foot, straightening, and in doing so momentarily putting her full weight on Marty's hand. He could feel the pressure spreading the bones, opening them like a fan. He could feel his skin stretching. The shearing force became heat that ran up his arm, seized his chest, and then filled him from crotch to throat. He suppressed a gasp. The pain was pumping something into him. He was, to his genuine surprise, thrilled.

"Thanks," said Jackie, tiptoeing toward the door.

"Sure," Marty managed.

Jackie spoke to his back. "Okay?"

"Yeah," said Marty. "Blown knees. I used to run." He turned, uncertain whether any flushing in his face betrayed him.

"You don't look like an athlete." Realizing how this sounded Jackie added, "Not that you don't seem fit."

He'd given nothing away.

"I was always in the middle of the pack," he said.

♁

Outside, in a brick ravine formed by the rear face of the vocational college and a bowed retaining wall, Cathy Ford-Devereaux watched the shadows cast by Marty and Jackie play on the autoshop ceiling. The shapes were visible through smoked glass windows high in the bay doors. She had no idea that it was her uncle moving around in there. She was apprehensive that it might be a security guard whose rounds were taking him to the back of the building. They were usually creeps in cop costume for whom the harassment of the young was an obligation. It defined them.

Having not read the note left for her at home, Cathy was also unaware that her parents were inside the building she was passing. Her presence was entirely coincidental. She was forever afoot and could, at any time, be anywhere in St. John's, as far as its perimeter near the reservoir or the airport, at its centre, downtown on the harbour's apron. Cathy wasn't an ambler—she never tarried, always had a destination—but rather than take a bus, or bum a ride with someone's parents, or avail herself of the taxi account established by her fretting mother, she chose to walk. Walking ate up the hours. This was critical as Cathy privately held that time was passing more slowly for her than for the rest of the world. She knew of no way to test this thesis. It wasn't a time–space/physics thing. (Once, supposing it was, she tried and failed to read about that stuff, had actually gone into the library at Frank Moores High, looked up a book on the computer, found it on the shelf, opened it up, and tried, maybe for twenty minutes, to read it.) No, it was a question of how one experienced time. If you had a certain experience of an hour—Cathy, though she couldn't prove it, couldn't even think how you would prove it—Cathy had a more protracted experience. Her days were years, her months eons, her life an inconceivable eternity. She was on geological time, interstellar time.

Cathy was walking to Jeanette's house, where she would likely just sit around and watch while her friend yakked on the phone with boyfriend Scott. Jeanette imagined she included Cathy in this by making faces at things Scott said. Jeanette was crazy, but at least she lived eight kilometres from Cathy's place.

In her movements Cathy mapped the town, remembering and naming without words its alleys and lanes. There were four-hundred-year-old footpaths and secret passages out of dead ends. There was lately a shortcut across an incomplete expressway, the fragrant new blacktop still warm enough to melt the soles of your sneakers. Cathy knew of absent pickets and gashes in chain-link through which you could slip. She knew of motion sensors that would catch you in their invisible light and of dogs that would not bite.

The way behind the vocational college was the kind of place Cathy's mom worried about, hidden from the street, poorly lit. Cathy liked it because it was, by night, unknown. Cathy never met anyone here. If she did, she supposed it could be dangerous. Nothing much ever happened, though. Nothing much. Once, downtown, in the parking lot of the Colonial Building, some wheezing pervert pulled down his pants and started frantically jerking off. It was intensely scary for a moment and then more pathetic than anything. She always got sideways glances from men in cars, guys dreaming that she was some runaway who might fuck them to get out of the cold. But she'd gotten the same looks from some of her mother's friends and they were allegedly out to save the world. Feed Africa but first stick it in the sixteen-year-old.

Her pace and gait tonight were governed by the rhythm of the Patti Smith tune she had listened to before setting out, "Redondo Beach." *"Down by the ocean it was so dismal / Women all standing with shock on their faces / Sad description oh I was looking for you ... "* She loved that song—a tale or, actually, more a little movie of simple, everyday anxiety, so honestly told and with a bouncy reggae beach beat. It was mercifully without deeper meaning as far as she could tell, just saying something heartfelt, plainly. It was on a CD Scott had burned for Jeanette but which Jeanette had in turn given to Cathy, saying she totally couldn't stand the fucked-up mix of retro camp (there was even a song by Elvis, "[Marie's the Name] His Latest Flame," to which Cathy was partial) and indie noise. Jeanette said Scott made the CD that way to be "smart," something that, even after repeated listenings, Cathy did not get. Jeanette just played Alanis Morissette over and over and over these days and, though she wouldn't admit it, was growing her hair long like Alanis's, too. Cathy tried to get into it, and it was okay, but ... Alanis was way too good-looking for one thing, though at least of a sort of beauty that would age badly. She'd be fat and horsy some day, an old mare at pasture. Madonna could be the goat, Ricky Martin a pig, and Britney Spears, with those bovine peepers, she was Bessie! Yes, that girl was the real veal.

Alanis's whole act was suspiciously ready-made. You opened up the package and there was this fabulous thing inside, but after a moment you saw that someone had planned the whole thing, had planned Alanis. Probably Alanis planned Alanis. Cathy knew it was an unrealistic expectation, but she wanted stuff to be spontaneous. It seemed more trustworthy. It was stupid, like degrading, to be a "fan" anyway. There were songs by Björk and Hardship Post and Beck on Scott's CD that Cathy really loved, and a couple of other good ones by Patti Smith, including "Frederick," which was definitely the most romantic thing ever, but Cathy was nobody's fan.

"Desk clerk told me girl was washed up …" Cathy had not, until the other day, considered that Patti Smith was part of her mother's youth. The recordings were made during the vast indistinguishable past that was the time before her birth, so they were artefacts. But then in a moment of immeasurable embarrassment, her mother, passing Cathy's bedroom door and hearing familiar notes, had come in. Mom was excited that her girl was listening to music that she knew and actually sat at the foot of Cathy's bed bobbing her head in time like they were friends or something. Her mother—and this was the very worst part—sang along, the melody and rhythm calling back forgotten lyrics. "*Baby was a black sheep baby was a whore. / You know she got big. Well she's gonna get bigger …"* Cathy couldn't bear to think of it.

The service lane emptied onto a parking lot. Sleet and wind were coming on, shaking the streetlamps and giving the light an irritated quality. Cathy thought about strobe lights and how they could induce epileptic seizures. Why was that? On the far side of the asphalt field she spotted, on the lawn, weathered mounds of snow or ice, like memorials of a sort, headstones, or … what were they called? … she'd seen them in a *National Geographic* at the dentist's office … could it be *dolmens?* She wondered why they were there.

♂

All the way back to the classroom Marty yabbered on and on about his exploits on the track, about how he stayed in university, getting an English degree and then sleepwalking through some graduate work just to keep running. It was the same for Hank, a wrestler and history major whom inertia carried on to study education. They both realized soon after they were dropped from that last team roster that they had to do something, needed to make a living, and came up with the idea—not serious at first—of, shag-it-all, with the government getting out of the state, why not ride the privatization wave and open their own damn school? Actually, it was Hank thinking out loud, saying they should start a tutoring business, and Marty countering that—no, go the step further, a school.

"Hank, you know, he was just thinking out loud," said Marty, unsure whether he had already told her this. There existed in town a couple of private outfits, but they were parochial. A commercial opportunity was presenting itself, one made all the more attractive by the stultifying jobs they'd taken once out of college—Marty writing and proofing copy for the Newfoundland Department of Tourism, Hank teaching and riding herd at St. Matthews High.

He told her how well it had turned out.

Marty said all this to try and stop himself from thinking about his hand being crushed by Jackie's shoe. He was fully formed, knew exactly who he was, detested people who "discovered" things about themselves late in life.

"Though at first it was dicey."

"I guess, hey?" Jackie put little effort into feigning interest.

"It took a few years to even get the ownership of the building settled and then the financing and accreditation. We had to build a reputation. Then just a few years ago, there was this one boy, from an important family, you know, very well-to-do, who had a lot of trouble in the public system and ... well ... Hank, he rescued this kid and ... word got around." He was babbling. Shut-up! he thought. There was an unspoken pact between Marty and Hank to never mention the arduous one-on-one tutelage of various well-born underachievers that they'd been obliged to undertake in the early days, especially not the Malan kid—*the boy*—for his salvation had meant time that they could never again invest in individual students. To make young Russell Malan achieve, Hank coaxed and mollycoddled. When that failed Hank worked Russell like a ventriloquist's dummy. The boy appeared to think, to provide the right answers to the questions posed. Russell "got through." But always there was Hank looking on, leaning in, his lips never seeming to move. The job was done with the utmost discretion, and overnight, as if the Malans' circle had given benediction, The Red Pines was the premium private school in town. They were almost at full capacity, close enough anyway that Marty claimed there was a waiting list to gain admittance (and everybody loved being on the right side of a waiting list).

He told her how the timing had been perfect. After two full decades of decline the boards were off the shop windows in St. John's. (Unable to re-imagine itself after the collapse of the cod fishery from which it had sprung, rural Newfoundland was dying, with nobody much seeming to care. They and not the City had voted for Canada and Smallwood's vainglory in '48. Extinction was their final reward.) Offshore oil was buoying the urban economy and drawing itinerant petrochemical families from Texas and Norway, engineers from France and England. The Red Pines offered the lowest student–teacher ratio, the first computer lab, the safest environment. They did not offer an immersion stream, but their French-language program, with its *voyages* and *spectacles* and *monitrices enthousiastes,* was second to none.

"They didn't hesitate. They asked for the best private school in town and then enrolled their kids. For some of them it was a condition of their relocation."

"Right," said Jackie.

"And you know, it's just been a blur."

Shut up. She obviously doesn't care. Why should she? The woman didn't even have kids.

"A blur. We haven't stopped for ten years … it's been steady belt. Only lately it seems I even have time to think. It's been a ride."

Marty stopped short of saying that he was, in the quiet of a sleepless night, troubled that his and Hank's accomplishment might be nothing more than dumb luck, that if it weren't for a number of flukes, he and Hank could just have easily lost everything and ended up looking like fools. Their success fostered professional jealousy among those educators and administrators in town better qualified to have taken on the challenge but who, because of prudence or lack of initiative, had not. When Marty met them he could feel their envy like an arctic wind. They had, rightfully, considered Marty and Hank naïve and laughably ill equipped. Locals weren't to aim so high. But the two men were young and quick and bold as brass. You make your own luck, Marty said to himself. Fake it 'til you make it, right? Kismet, yeah? Marty put his suspicion that their good fortune was undeserved down to the creeping doubt that came with age.

"Sure," went Jackie. "Right."

What happened back there on the catwalk? Perhaps he had caught something, a virus, that had knocked him out of kilter. Something he ate? Game could do funny things with your head. Maybe the hare?

Rex and Ted were sitting at the table when Marty and Jackie returned. Ted was anxiously probing his poached pear with a spoon, as though looking for something within, a pit or poison. Rex, having polished off his own dessert, was running his index finger around the inside of Meredith's bowl. He collected the last traces of chocolate then sucked his finger clean.

Jackie slid her chair closer to Ted. She spooned some pear into her mouth and raised her eyebrows in approval.

"Jesus, Ted, this is delightful."

"You see the snow sculptures when you came in?" Rex asked Marty.

"What was left of them, yeah." Marty tried his pears. They were sweet and boozy.

"There was Leif Ericson." Ted finally spoke. He needed to work at it, as if drugged or head injured. Thank God he's not flying planes, thought Marty. "A caribou, I think, and something else. Stripes."

"Leif the Now-looking-rather-down-on-his-luck," said Marty. No one got the joke. "And the thing with stripes was supposed to be the flag, I think."

Marty lifted his glass. "To the graduates!"

Everybody drank, Rex and Ted cranberry cocktail.

"I really have to leave," said Marty.

Inasmuch as they would improve the bottom line, Marty was always on the lookout for ways to enrich the programs and physical plant at The Red Pines. The vocational college lobby was a study. Marty stopped to pull on his raincoat and lingered.

The nose was common to all educational institutions: chemical/lemony notes of cleansers and disinfectants, mint-masked urine, gag of chalk dust, the bodily pong of a thousand students.

A bronze bust of some ancient pol or territorial pedagogue, entry wounds for eyes, surveyed the space.

Celebrating Red Pines' living, breathing founders Marty Devereaux and Henry Lundrigan with sculptures, though conveniently secular, would run contrary to Marty's strategy of dressing and stressing the place to make it look like it had a lengthy history. The day The Red Pines had opened, students and parents filed past a display case replete with dented and tarnished trophies, never thinking to ask their provenance. At the inaugural assembly the gymnasium was redolent of liniment Marty had splashed about, fudging an olfactory echo of games that hadn't yet been played. All the pictures and fixtures, all the ornamentation was of such various or indeterminate age, anachronism on anachronism, that it was impossible to situate the place in time. The Red Pines' tenth year was an all-too-minor anniversary that Marty would let pass without celebration.

Marty's attention turned to the flags hanging high on the wall behind the bust: a Canadian Maple Leaf, Newfoundland's new dispassionate modernist banner, and a Union Jack. A fringed Jack would fit nicely at The Red Pines, evoking a colonial past (the Empire began here after all) and some, albeit spurious, connection to a venerable line of English schooling. It was the kind of thing the parents ate up.

Marty and Hank had toyed with the idea of a boarding school but questioned whether their largest market, newly moneyed parents, could jibe the convenience of being rid of their teenaged children with the cost and, no doubt, guilt of abandonment. In the end, The Red Pines' insurer settled the matter. The premiums on a round-the-clock operation would have been too high. It was a propitious call, for the media was lately making a meal of sexual shenanigans at Canada's most prestigious boarding institutions. The days of the discreet remedy for such indiscretions—blaming Walt Whitman and Oloroso, privately chiding the offender, sending him off to some bucolic rehab to dry out—were over, and the once-esteemed schools were about to be ravaged by litigation.

Still, Union Jack was a capital idea. He supposed there must be some kind of clearing-house for Imperial ephemera, some Raj surplus outfit where he could find the right one. Pushing at the heavy doors in leaving, he resolved to get on the Net and look.

Twice the Saab whispered a circle in Miss Zwitzer's cul-de-sac. Marty slowed on his second pass and saw her bedroom lamps were still on. Given the hour, he guessed Sophie would be nearing the end of a bottle of white and would be chatty, potentially amorous. He wasn't sure why he'd come. He steered toward his own bed.

Marty lived, by choice, in the suburbs. It wasn't a new development. His bungalow was twenty-seven years old, the trees in the yard only now taking shape. When he moved in he replaced a discoloured white shag carpet with a sandy-hued one of a tighter nap. He made no other significant changes. He kept the exterior painted the same slate blue as had the previous owner.

Michener Crescent provided him cover, deflected the questions asked of single men in their forties. Here he was seen mowing a lawn, returning with groceries, playing host, at the barbeque, to the comely Miss Zwitzer whose car would be conspicuously parked next to his some Sunday mornings. He was a reliable hetero bachelor, the vice principal of that private school who everybody knew would one day marry that music teacher, have kids, and make that house a home. But Sophie was barren and considered marriage an absurdity, and Marty, looking up and down the road, saw houses and only houses.

He entered and went to the living room, neglecting to remove his mist-slicked coat. There had been something wrong with the food, he thought again.

Marty cherished the ordered austerity, the tidiness, of his house. A cleaning service came once a week. The furnishings were mostly contemporary, modular. It was all quality stuff, functional and attractive. The one showy piece was a china cabinet made of curly birch. When he moved in he'd imagined what his place might look like and had taken his time getting it right. For his first four months the only substantial furniture in the place was his queen-sized bed.

He picked up the phone to check his voice mail. He had two new messages.

He thought about Jackie. "Spurell," wasn't it? He grabbed the phone book with his free hand and returned to the sofa.

"Hello, Mr. Devereaux." It was the school's secretary, Mrs. Norris. "Mr. Lundrigan called and he won't be able to attend a meeting tomorrow morning with a … Mr. and Mrs. Hayden, a Gerald Hayden, and he asked that you see them."

Peculiar that he should have just been speaking about Gerry Hayden to Jackie Spurell. It was as if he'd been overheard. But then the community was so small everybody could hear everything.

"It's for 11:30, so I've moved Mr. Summers to 10:00. Mr. Pitts is still at 10:30. If there's a problem, could you please call? Thank you."

Abraham Summers was an English teacher at The Red Pines, a pretentious closet case with a wet mouth and two failed novels. Summers, though aware of Marty's dislike for him, found a reason for a meeting at least once a month. Alan Pitts was the head of science.

Marty flipped through the phone book. There was a Ted Spurell at 16 Alderdice Street, just a block from Rex and Meredith.

The second message was from Hank.

"Marty, I was supposed to have a meeting tomorrow with Gerald Hayden. Gerald wants to enrol his daughter, but where he's fronting this Perroqueet Downs project, I thought it would be awkward and I was hoping you could take it. It was at 11:30. Call me if there's a problem. My flight to Toronto is at 1:00, so I doubt I'll be in at all. I'm back next Tuesday ..." Marty could hear Hank turning the pages of a calendar. "Second of April. Thanks for this, Marty."

The Haydens were money, so it was no surprise they would want to put their kid in The Red Pines with the rest of the money kids. Gerry Hayden could separate the dispute over the land from his family life. Not taking the meeting was unprofessional of Hank, he was reading too much into it. The fight, which Hank would surely lose, wasn't worth it. It was such small potatoes, just local stuff. Marty had forgotten about Hank's Toronto conference, something to do with ecology in education.

The night sky was clearing as Marty lay down in his bed. Clouds were taking to sea. Waking later, near dawn, he could see through his bedroom window, bright as a jewel, what he mistook for a star.

The Red Pines was originally a military hospital built by Americans stationed at St. John's during the Second World War. It was a two-storey H-block: long, twined north–south sections, joined at the middle with an east–west span. The front courtyard formed by the wings was closed with another wing that faced onto a crescent drive from the street. The U.S. army spared no expense in construction and the structure remained solid. The building was handed over to the Newfoundland government as a parting gift from the Yanks and used variously as offices and storage space, home to the wildlife division and mouldering criminal records. It was let go, closed up, and finally slated for demolition (the least complicated or costly of a number of options presented by consultants) when an unlikely alliance of veterans and local architects decided the building must stay. Promising to maintain its integrity wherever possible, Marty and Hank acquired it for a song. Right place, right time.

Within the front courtyard were two red pines—*pinus resinosa.* The trees had plates of scaly bark, which, at frequent breeches, revealed a sanguine layer of cambium beneath. Several other handsome specimens stood on the school grounds. A band of them ran up a hill behind the soccer pitch, eventually giving way to parkland of spruce and fir that fortified the city's most exclusive golf course. Marty and Hank occupied grand rooms that once served the ranking physicians, colonels. So well built and maintained were these offices that they had required almost no renovation. Marty made only one major modification: he removed the doors. This, as planned, created a sense of openness, of having nothing to hide, that comforted the parents. You could eavesdrop, but with difficulty. Marty also successfully argued to his insurer that it decreased the likelihood that a student could claim to have been struck or touched within the confines and so had his liability premiums reduced. Mrs. Norris's workspace—her desk, a nest of filing cabinets, photocopiers, and computers—separated the two men's offices. The school's records and automated billings were handled by a system originally designed to manage prison populations. It took the place of a second secretary. Marty called it, jokingly, "Deep Beige."

From his desk, Marty watched the smart cars arriving, depositing students, all of them puffy-eyed from inadequate sleep.

The girls were familiar with their new bodies, had limbs and curves under command, but few possessed what you could call grace. There was a line advanced by the pornographers of retail that these girls were sexual, but Marty saw enough of them, heard enough of them, to think this proposition questionable. They were, despite their protests and actions to the contrary, intellectually pre-sexual. It was Marty's view that anyone who fucked them should be obliged to listen to them.

The boys were simply unformed, enduring a hormonal purgatory. Glands on bust, they were spunk stupid, all knuckles and knees. They were pre-intellectual. Well he should be highly paid to care for them, thought Marty, taking the once-cherubic beauties from adoring parents, shielding their eyes, sparing them the shock as their dear little boys evolved into misshapen lumps of fury.

There were two contentious calls during the formulation of The Red Pines project. The first involved titles. Had Marty won the coin toss he would have called himself "head master" rather than "principal" as Hank—"tails"—had. The second, more difficult question was that of school uniforms. Marty had wanted something very traditional, with dandy Etonian or, failing that, Yankee preparatory school echoes. Hank thought they should be more casual and even briefly advocated eschewing uniforms altogether, feeling they would make the kids stand out in public, make them targets, work against the teenagers' deep need to conform to the standards of their peers. Marty rejected this suggestion out of hand. The uniforms were a gold mine. They sold four hundred new sets every September and more, as the teenagers grew, throughout the year. (The profits made up for those that had failed to materialize from books, from which, Marty learned, there was never money to be made.) Predictably, the designers Marty engaged did not want to knock something off but to make their own mark. With minor allowance for their creative impulse Marty's views prevailed. They went with blazers rather than a blazer-and-jacket requirement (but conceded to Marty's demand for wool), a scarlet-and-teal school tie, white shirt, and grey (in an uncommon light tone) flannel trousers. The girls had a choice of kilt or tunic (they bought several of each as well as the blazer and sweater). It was all made in Malaysia.

The parents loved, loved, *loved* it—loved the snob appeal, loved its conspicuousness. And the kids, to Hank's surprise, liked it, too. They couldn't get enough Red Pines' kit, buying all the extras, the sweats and team jackets and hats. They were, true to their school, perfect junior classists.

They customized, of course. Boys bought their blazers oversized. Despite complaints that the kilts drew the unbidden attention of men, hems were constantly being altered—up.

Less successful was Marty's attempt to fashion a coat of arms for the school. His effort featured a gryphon crest, stylized image of a pine tree on the pages of an open book, and abundant mantling. Below this was the Latin motto *Omnia suspicanda,* which Marty had taken to mean "question everything," an entreaty to intellectual curiosity. It was a graphic calamity: shapeless, disproportionate, tilting, and chunky. Reduced to letterhead dimensions it was squiggles and splat. And the motto should have been *Omnia dubitanda.* The words beneath the scrapped heraldry actually translated as "suspect everything." When he needed cloth crests for the uniforms Marty settled for something out of a catalogue. These, at least, included a sort of indeterminate coniferous tree, and Marty managed to have the words "The Red Pines" stitched beneath in a luxurious red thread.

As Marty could be seen in his office from outside, he made a point of arriving early and busying himself with paperwork. He might occasionally stand watch at the window and scowl at the young people arriving, something he knew helped flesh out his role. Marty watched the Malan boy, young Russell, arrive in his own car, a new Miata no less. He pulled up, as he did every day, in the "no parking" zone straight across the street from the school. He would get two tickets, one in the morning, another in the afternoon. At the end of the school day Russell would haul the tickets from beneath the wiper and throw them in the glove compartment or onto the floor of the passenger side. An accountant in the employ of his parents would deal with it later. It was a trivial cost of living. Marty detested the boy, on whom they had built their reputation. Marty could only think "Jack Russell" every time he saw him. There was something canine in his features. His looks stretched near the limit of his breed, a generation away from monstrosity. Should his eyes be a millimetre closer together, his ears a fraction smaller, he would be hideous.

His father, Dirk Malan, a South African (*Souff Efreeka,* was what Marty heard Mrs. Malan, the one parent he'd met, say), came to Newfoundland in 1993 to attend to a mine the family firm (Namibia) had acquired. The Malans set up house in St. John's to deflect accusations that they might be, like so many before them, carpetbaggers. They wanted to make Newfoundland their new home, they said. It was timely for people like the Malans to hightail it from the Cape, and needy Newfoundland was easy entrée to Canada. The mining and milling process (Marty forgot what it was they extracted) involved some pernicious leaching agent and left mountains of toxic tailings, a problem the Malans addressed with astute philanthropy—they gave good. They gave lots and they gave it to the tough causes, not to the merely halt and lame but to the infected, to the wasting diseases, to the otherwise unsaleable afflictions of the back passage. Rather than the Symphonia they contributed to new music and impenetrable avant-garde performance. They made little of their generosity, begging off the photo sessions with the oversized cheques and the plaques. Judicious and courageous community baksheesh put them beyond reproach. The mine closed, the tailings were sunk in fenced-off ponds in some remote corner of the island, and the Malans moved their money into money, where it still did its work. One would have expected that with their ostensible connection to Newfoundland behind them and a Canadian passport in their breast pocket they would have moved on to Toronto or Vancouver. But there, Marty suspected, they might encounter other ex-pats from the veldt, folks who knew better the family history. They stayed.

Girls were placing themselves in Russell Malan's path, levering their breasts upward and outward with their books clutched, cross-armed, against their ribs. When Marty was in high school, athletes, the stars of the hockey team, were most desirous. Now, he gathered, one needed only looks, the right clothes, and money. Money. Russell's grades were again slipping, he was spending too much time running his social network and luring pussy with the Miata. If he didn't straighten up, Hank would be obliged to put his hand back up the puppet.

It was Friday, a day six in the school's seven-day cycle. With Hank ducking, Marty would have to make the announcements this morning. He checked a sheet prepared by Mrs. Norris: the drama society was holding auditions for a play, *Voices,* by Audrey Caddigan; vegetarian fare—tofu this and TVP that—were now available in the cafeteria. The items were added to the menu in response to a student petition. They were to be offered at a premium and the margins were great. Marty thought he'd best read the play.

When they met privately Marty did not disguise his contempt for Abe Summers. On the basis of his two long-ago-published and little-read novels, Summers considered himself a cut above the other teachers and resented having to earn a living giving instruction to children of the almost rich. He asserted, when he took the job nine years ago, that work on a pending book prohibited him from taking a permanent, if initially less lucrative, sinecure at one of the pauperish regional universities. Marty knew that in truth Summers was avoiding the close scrutiny of doubting fellows on the university English faculty.

Summers spent his time away from the school being a writer and intellectual. He tried being a wit but couldn't pull it off. Sometimes he was a Newfoundland writer, sometimes a Canadian writer, sometimes a writer who didn't believe in those labels, all depending on the room. He gave readings, granted interviews, was a panellist on book-chat shows, attended literary festivals, weighed in on anything to do with the arts—cinema, dance, music—whether he knew anything of the discipline or not. There was a one-time flirtation with journalism, guesting a drinks column in, of all things, a men's magazine. Summers's poncey paean to the glories of the Vosne-Romanée was sandwiched between the similarly faint hopes of a Lamborghini road test and an illustrated guide to some new techniques for pleasuring the babes. It all left scarcely any time for "the book."

Summers continued to contend that part of his function at The Red Pines was as "writer in residence." Before his stint at The Pines, Summers secured—how, one could only imagine—just such a post at the achingly prestigious Philips Exeter Prep School in New Hampshire. There, Marty inferred, Summers was able to indulge his Cheeveresque vices and wax pretentious with like-minded New England poofs. The appointment gave Summers a pedigree Marty traded on.

The new novel—working title *The Anesthetist's Annual*—had yet to appear.

Summers always found something to gripe about and, in the supercilious way he addressed his complaints to Marty, seemed to be assigning blame. He was a tall man with a full head of dyed (Marty believed) black hair. An Anglophile, he tried to be donnish in his duds: tweed, worsted, and striped ties. (Marty loved to think Abe covetous of the Pines' school uniform.) This morning Abe had a folded cream handkerchief sticking out of his jacket's breast pocket. Marty put that portion of Abe's asperity, which could not be attributed to artistic failure, down to years of unfulfilled homosexual desire. In this day and age there was no excuse. Summers should just go on the knob and get over it.

Marty read a memo, wanting to give the impression he was being put upon. Some millenarian at the outfit from which he'd purchased The Red Pines' computers was telling him it was urgent they make the school's systems "Y2K ready."

"What now, Abe?"

"I've two matters." There was, incredibly—Summers was from Milltown—a trace of mid-Atlantic on his words, as if he'd caught a touch of it from books.

"And only twenty minutes to discuss them."

Summers huffed and took the kerchief from his pocket. He wiped his hands.

"It's to be expected that different students will perform at different levels," Summers began. "As it stands we have only one English lit. curriculum. The best of the students are being held back."

Something occurred to Marty.

"Audrey Caddigan?"

"Yes." Summers seemed surprised that Marty knew the name, that he was even listening. "Yes," said Summers, "she's a case in point."

"I was thinking of this play she's written. Have you read it?"

"Splendid, at least for a girl of her age. Promising talent, perhaps she'll be a new Rex Devereaux. Structurally, mind you …"

Marty stopped listening. Summers wasn't flattering; he and Rex got along, were both members of some "writers' league" in town. Marty understood they met monthly for sandwiches, cake, and regional pieties before breaking off into smaller groups to diminish each other's work. Rex was the sole dramatist of the gang. Experimentation in confessional short fiction was their métier—airy pieces without beginnings, middles, or ends.

When they were newly acquainted and he felt he had no choice, Marty attended some public readings to which Summers invited him. The works weren't so much read as they were intoned—a technique, Marty supposed, of lending them import.

The stuff was entertaining enough to those who could play the game of guessing which member of the literary circle was represented by which thinly disguised character, and occasionally titillating in its drop-by-drop accounting of seed spilled. (Though, if Rex were to be believed, they didn't fuck nearly so much as they wrote about it.)

"Full of teenaged angst," Summers continued. "Rather overwrought, but you'd expect that. Expressing themselves and all that hooey."

Full as he was of self-regard, Summers had a gift for condescension.

"But nothing to offend the parents?"

"I shouldn't say," Summers answered too quickly.

"*Voices*? Is it a musical?" asked Marty.

"No. About Joan of Arc. Actually about a play about Joan of Arc. Play within a play thing."

"I'd like to give it a look-over."

The name of the girl, Caddigan, was for some reason echoing in Marty's head. There was something else … a problem with her fees?

"Yes." Summers was anxious to move on. "So what I'm suggesting is two different streams, one for the more advanced students and another for—"

"For the dummies, Abe?"

"Not at all! You know that—"

Marty cut him off again. "Or *average*. You see what I'm saying? People pay to put their kids through here. They don't want to be told that their boy or girl is any less capable than another. Theirs are not *average* children. Most of them think the reason their child was underachieving was the way they were streamed in the public system." Marty enjoyed lecturing Summers. "Never forget, Abe, I'm in the hope business."

"But the best students are suffering. Some are bored."

Marty had to admit that there was risk in setting the beam low. If the smartest kids arrived at university and performed poorly, The Red Pines was in trouble.

"How advanced? What stuff? How big a class?"

"Some more Shakespeare, something other than *Romeo and Juliet,* maybe *The Tempest* ..."

"Not *The Tempest,* gives me the creeps."

"Some say the island in the play references Newfoundland. And if you think of the period it's not a totally mad proposition."

"More so, then."

"*Lear*?"

"Like *Lear*. Longish."

"It's only in works of that kind of scope and sweep that "

"Spare me. What else?"

"A Joyce story. More written work, essays, the beginnings of serious criticism. I haven't worked it all out. I'd guess fifteen students in both grades eleven and twelve."

"This class can't be identified as being any more 'advanced' than another."

"Special studies?"

"That's closer, don't like *special*—used to mean retarded."

"English A and English B?"

"Perhaps. But the advanced class would be identified as B. Or better, identified by the room number, English 223 and English 225. We could tell the parents it was simply to reduce class size. You're proposing introducing this when?"

"I suppose it would have to be next September," Summers said, sounding as though he had never before considered the question.

"And it would have to use existing staff. I'm not hiring anybody else. Let me give it some more thought," Marty said, turning again to his memo, signalling that Summers should leave.

"And … secondly," Summers said.

"Right." Marty lifted his head.

"It's a personal matter," Summers drew his ample lips into his mouth to moisten them, "but I think you should know. I've become a Catholic."

Marty wasn't ready for this.

"A Roman Catholic?"

"Yes."

"You were a …?" Marty didn't know or care.

"An Anglican. As I say, it's a personal matter, between me and my God, I suppose."

"This is a thing … an author thing, or something, isn't it?"

"No." Summers was discomfited. "It's nothing to do with my … practice."

Marty was pleased to hear Summers struggle with the word *practice*.

"How will this be manifested, Abe? I mean, where does it become my concern?"

Conversion was a Graham Greene thing, an Evelyn Waugh thing. Abe Summers probably thought it would suggest he was a man of depth, burdened by philosophical and theological concerns. There was no question of his motives being genuine. Marty supposed that Summers just wanted to move beyond his middle years, the tough ones with their unmet expectations and mortgages and incipient bewilderment. Summers would now try his hand playing the sage, putting his own failures down to mystery. Either that or he was looking to be forgiven the sort of sin best understood by a priest.

And Summers knew, surely it had come up in conversation, that Marty considered all religion bloody-minded nonsense, just disheartening evidence that the Enlightenment hadn't taken. Yes, it was a provocation. Summers must have heard about the incident with Dr. Abousaada at that PTA meeting. Marty had expressed his lack of faith in an effort to reassure the doctor, an Egyptian and a Muslim, that there would be no Christian proselytizing at The Red Pines. But the gent was devout and had reacted badly, had barked something at Marty in a foreign tongue—Arabic, Marty supposed—and stormed out.

"You're not planning on saying the rosary before class, are you?"

"Heavens no."

"Wearing less corduroy? Switching from Scotch to Irish whiskey? What?"

"Don't be flip, Martin. I just thought you should know."

"Sure, but don't mention it to the students, not even in passing."

"You're worried that it might be a problem."

"No. I'm guessing that at least forty percent of our kids are Catholic or come from Catholic families, whatever that means any more. But I'm sure that our secular environment gives no group more comfort. The Christian Brothers, remember? Stuff they would rather not think about."

"Yes," Summers said.

Alan Pitts appeared at the doorway, early.

"Oops, sorry. I ... I'll wait, sorry to interrupt," Pitts said, wanting to retreat but feeling the need to sputter an apology.

"No, we're through." Marty was relieved. "Aren't we, Abe?"

"Yes, we are," said Summers, standing. Three strides of his long legs took him past Alan Pitts and out the door.

Marty could tell he'd managed to offend Summers and was happy for it.

Pitts was a bright fellow with a boundless enthusiasm for science and education that perplexed Marty. He stayed after class with students, attended professional conferences on his own nickel, read the appropriate journals in an effort to stay current. He bore the heavy load of a teacher without complaint, setting high standards for his colleagues to begrudge. He was rounded, an accomplished singer, member of a couple of serious vocal ensembles, according to Sophie. Pitts told Marty that, after years of dilettantism—sod houses to rolfing—he found his calling as a teacher, and Marty believed it. So fit and otherwise youthful-looking was Pitts that one assumed his bristles prematurely grey. Alan Pitts loved kids, had three of his own from a late-in-life marriage to a woman many years his junior. It was sometimes the case with teachers that being so much in the company of kids kept them young. The cost, though, was a collateral stunting of emotional growth, a condition that presented in petulance and a quickness to hurt. It was the wiser tutor that kept distance from his charge. Alan Pitts, so far, seemed unscarred, which was perhaps why Marty liked him.

"Alan?"

"So." Pitts still hadn't sat down, was revving up in front of Marty's desk. "There are eight doors, eight classrooms, well … in fact … six classrooms and two labs, eight doors in lower northeast wing. Lockers opposite. Right?"

"I'll trust you. The science classes?"

"Yes, yes, exactly. The science classes. And the walls are bare … not now, there are some posters and a bulletin board, which I would move because we use the board."

Marty noticed that Pitts wasn't wearing a tie.

"So, what I'm proposing," Pitts continued, "is … is that we paint the solar system, on the wall."

"Paintings of the planets?"

"Eight doors makes nine panels, so it's perfect. Not 'we' like the school, but a project with students. They'd paint them. I suppose I'd ask you for the paint."

Marty leaned back in his chair, trying to look as though he were giving the proposal due consideration. He rocked.

"My one concern, Alan," Marty paused, "is that they'll be shitty."

"Shitty?"

"Shitty. Poor renderings. Hard to look at. And that I'll end up having to paint them over. And have you given any thought as to how long they'll last? Will I be painting the wall over come August?"

"Well..." Pitts was, momentarily, stumped. "I could ... promise you ... that they won't be shitty."

"If you can promise me that, I will say yes. But ..." Marty said, "if they are shitty, I will have them painted over and I will be unhappy."

"You won't be."

"And, Alan?"

"Yes?"

"You've got to wear a tie, okay?"

"Yes. Yes. Yes. I know. I'm sorry. There's one in my desk."

"The paintings are a great idea."

"Thanks," said Pitts. The audience had tired him.

"Aren't you teaching now?"

"Got a lab going. I knew this wouldn't take long."

"Well get back there. Liability issues. My insurance premiums would make your head spin."

"Sorry. I'm going."

It was quarter to eleven. Marty had time for a cigarette. Ten years ago, within a week of first opening, students divined that the copse of pines at the end of the soccer pitch was off school grounds and staked it out as their own, dashing there to share cigarettes during recess and lunch. They would do it somewhere, and Marty was just as happy they were out of sight. Having decided against allowing smoking in the staff room, Marty was forced to tool around in his car. This was an opportunity denied to, and coveted by, the couple of smokers on the teaching staff. Marty usually waited until he was several blocks from The Red Pines before lighting up, but today, his nerves tested by Summers, had his first of the day going soon after he left the parking lot. With no business to which to attend he navigated unconsciously, turning the car in the general direction of the downtown and the harbour. He was doing this more often lately, for after a decade of tinkering with its engines the school almost ran itself. Trial and error had given way to routine. The idle time had given Hank the opportunity to become entangled in the Perroqueet Downs issue. Marty rolled down his window so the cigarette smoke didn't too heavily scent his clothes. Onshore winds were imparting brininess to the air. He should have run Alan Pitts's plan past Cloris Foley, the art teacher. She wouldn't want to have anything to do with it but would make a fuss over not having been consulted.

Cloris was a graduate of the Ontario College of Art and so had the skills to produce both figurative and abstract images with technical precision. Unfortunately, she was utterly without talent. She made pictures that were, even to the untrained eye of someone like Marty, devoid of life and ugly. Inexplicably ugly. Apples in a pastel study were surely poisoned. A portrait caught nothing of the soul or spirit, but suggested that the sitter was riddled with cancer. Her forays into abstraction were similarly stricken, an interpretation of a disease's advance. She'd given Marty a derivatively Richterish piece some years ago, three young female heads—students probably—in soft focus, turning away from the viewer's gaze. He tried it first in his office and then in his house, but it sucked the light out of any room in which it hung. It now faced the back of the closet in Marty's extra bedroom. So unaware of her shortcomings was Cloris that she made perennial demands for a salary increase. After Marty's last refusal (she was the kind of person to whom you couldn't but say the wrong thing), Cloris protested by withdrawing extracurricular service, ending her tutelage of the failing Art Club and refusing to do chaperone duties at the dances. She was worth the grief. She had sapphire eyes; skin the colour of peach flesh; scent, fresh and malic to match; lips as red and wet as a fresh kill. She was leggy and taut, but curvaceous, with décolletage you wanted to dive in. She was an attractive and useless object, an ornament. She demonstrated a truth that nobody dared teach, that beauty was enough. And she gave Marty fabulous brochure.

Marty ventured into the warren of streets that made up the downtown's residential neighbourhood. The Victorian row houses here were slums when Marty was a boy but over the past thirty years had undergone a radical gentrification. All over, poverty was moving to the suburbs. A fair number of The Red Pines' students, children of doctors and lawyers and oil people, now lived here. Rex and Meredith bought their place in the seventies, were early settlers, and paradoxically for their efforts and those like them, would now never be able to afford it. They kept their house painted a rude pumpkin colour, a defiant announcement that they were among the bohemian pioneers, distinct from the yuppie interlopers. It was an island of audacity amidst the numbing (to Rex and Meredith's minds) teals and burgundies. Good taste had lately metastasized in St. John's. Marty didn't have time to stop and visit Rex. He wouldn't anyway. He swung the Saab up a steep hill, the grade so severe it slowed the vehicle to a near stop in front of a lemon cream–coloured three-storey, number 16, where Jackie Spurell lived. He gave the car some gas and continued on, heading back to the school.

☿

Gerry Hayden's skin was hard cured from a lifetime of sailing—"racing" his set called it to distinguish it from "cruising"—and, Marty guessed, golf. The tan was permanent, penetrating his deepest dermis. His hair and eyebrows were sandy. His wife, Sharon, was pallid, sniffly, and red-eyed allergic. She gamely tried to play the outdoorsy part, wearing for the meeting with Marty a two-piece nautical number bibbed like a sailor's suit.

"… Three senior Rose Bowl winners at the Kiwanis Music Festival, a testament to Miss Zwitzer's dedication. And we have a terrific athletics program, though given the school's small population we're not going to win any championships," Marty said, thinking it was what they wanted to hear.

"Bring in a few ringers," Gerry said.

Marty forced a chuckle. Gerry was indifferent.

"Listen, Mr. Devereaux, perhaps Sharon could have a look around."

"Of course."

"And you and I could talk."

Marty buzzed Mrs. Norris, asking her to take Sharon on the tour. Hayden looked to his wife and tossed his head toward the doorway, indicating she should leave. She complied silently, used to it.

"I was expecting," said Hayden, "to speak with Henry Lundrigan."

"He's leaving the province today. Business. Couldn't make it in."

"He owns the school, doesn't he?"

"We're partners."

"But he owns the majority."

"No. We are equal partners."

"Oh. Because I wanted to talk with him about my development, the Perroqueet Downs. He's causing me some problems. Do you know about this?"

"Yes. But before you go on, Mr. Hayden, I should tell you that Hank's involvement in any efforts to stop your project are on his own time. It's nothing to do with me or this school."

"Yeah. But you back him up. You agree with him?" Hayden asked. He was wringing his sportsman's watch, a conspicuous alpine piece, around the wrist of his right arm.

"I've no opinion one way or the other," said Marty.

"Okay. Then between you and me, in confidence, because this would really set your partner, Henry, and his friends off, it's just the beginning of a larger project to expand the city southward. People are flooding into the metropolitan area these days. They need somewhere to live. The Downs and some forest and a strip of agricultural land are already surrounded by the city. It's stupid to think that it's not going to be developed ... if not now, by us, then by somebody. It seems that people are getting upset over nothing."

"And between you and me, Mr. Hayden, I've thought as much. But then your argument is with Hank."

"Have you ever been on the Perroqueet Downs, Mr. Devereaux?"

"No."

"I wonder how many of the people protesting our development have."

Hearing Gerry Hayden say this, repeating the comment he'd made to Jackie Spurell the night before, was unsettling. There was a pushiness about Hayden, a sense of entitlement that was off-putting. Marty did not want to be of like mind.

"I'll confess something to you, Mr. Devereaux. We—by that I mean the firm, the family business—we don't need this project. By necessity we've become international. Smaller fish, bigger pond—that's the way things are these days. For tax reasons we operate out of the Bahamas and Ireland. We build everywhere, the States, Ecuador, even Southeast Asia. Sometimes building just means hiring other builders who subcontract to big fabricators. Different labour markets. We bridge and broker, you know. Pizza Huts in Lebanon, right? The nature of business has changed." Hayden drew a breath. "But this is home. My father is a very old man now. He's dying. He's taking his own sweet time about it, but he is dying. I tell him we're building six fish-processing facilities in Vietnam, it means nothing to him. But something in sight of the graves of his family ... and, truth be told, his old enemies ... it means everything ..."

"Do you have any other questions about our school, our programs?" Marty asked.

"Do you not want me to talk about this?"

"It doesn't bother me, but as I've said—"

"We, our group," Hayden cut in, "entertained the idea of getting into the private school business."

Marty thought this might be a threat if it hadn't been delivered with such disinterest.

"The Downs and the subsequent developments will be full of kids, and you know they're not going to bus into St. John's. It's a high-end development, at least the first phase." Hayden was so used to having underlings pay him heed that he never needed to cultivate charm. "And more and more of that is going to start falling to the private sector, worldwide. So, we thought, a franchise of private schools. We already build everywhere, just put all the fixtures in a box, cut volume discounts on books, national advertising ... international ... subcontract to existing state-run programs ... the whole deal. But, in the end, you know, it's not our business, and that's always a mistake—just because you see there's a pot of money in something you get involved, but you don't know the ins and outs and mistakes get made. Stick with what you know. It's more of an investment opportunity than anything we want to grow."

"Right," said Marty. The threat now sounded more like a bribe.

"Right," said Hayden, taking hold of the arms of his chair and pushing himself to his feet.

Marty followed his lead.

"I think your daughter," Marty glanced down at this desk, looking for the girl's name, "Sarah. I think she is an ideal candidate for The Red Pines."

Hayden stretched and hiked up his trousers.

"Sharon will take care of all that." Hayden gave his head a shake, fending off a yawn. He extended his hand.

"Thank you, Mr. Devereaux, and please mention to Mr. Lundrigan that I came calling. Tell my wife I'm in the car."

The bell for lunch rang.

♀

Some mornings, Cathy thought, when first waking and deciding to let herself slip again into dreams, some mornings she thought she could sleep for years as though under a spell. "Sleeping Ugly," she thought. This morning she came to briefly, saw her mother hovering over her bed, and without being fully conscious pled illness. Her mother accepted the claim. Whether she believed her or not Cathy couldn't say. These days her mother wasn't demanding Cathy do anything, was letting Cathy make her own decisions. It was a new approach to dealing with her daughter—treating her like an adult. Cathy knew this was a conscious strategy because her parents discussed it right in front of her, like she wasn't there or was too young, too infantile, to understand, like she was anything but an adult. They misdiagnosed her with teenage rebelliousness, of which Cathy had long ago grown desperately bored. Just the sound of the word, or the sight of it—*teen*—was enough to make her gag.

She piled her bed high with blankets and quilts and comforters, surrendering to their weight, fashioning a nest in which she could curl up and wait for the world outside to change to her liking. If need be she would wait forever. But she had to pee. She had already denied the call once, before falling back asleep, and now she was bursting.

The bathroom was downstairs on the second floor directly across from her father's "office." He was there again this morning, reading some tome. "Research," he called it. Cathy once challenged him, asked how one "researched" fiction, for wasn't that, after all, what he wrote? He snapped at her with some bullshit about "unstructured exploration" and "immersing" himself (in what she didn't know). She knew he wasn't doing anything, that the arts grant applications were, for the first time in his life, being turned down, that reading all those books was a way of not facing it. The worst of it was that he tortured everyone with the useless information he picked up in the process: history of the Moravian Church in Labrador, the physiology of thirst, the rhyme scheme of the villanelle.

It was an old attached house and the stairs from the second to the third floor sloped, on the horizontal, to one side. Cathy used the tilt to effect when descending, leaning into the wall with her shoulder and sliding against it.

Her dad looked up from his book.

"What are you doing home?" he asked.

"Sick," said Cathy, and then before he inquired further she added, "girl stuff."

Sitting on the toilet Cathy examined her legs and found them wanting. They were gangly and somewhat bandy. You'd say they were a filly's but only to be kind. Prone to getting away from her, they were forever covered in cuts and bruises. Her knees were hideous, bulbous things, matched in pure repulsiveness by her monstrous clodhopper feet. It was the bone structure that made them so horrible, the protrusions like rakes, tines, and broken ladders, leading in every case but one to the little doughy balls of flesh that were her toes. The exception was her aptly named big toe. It didn't belong to her. It belonged to a seven-foot ape, to a sasquatch. She wiped herself and, still in her pajamas, headed downstairs for a cup of coffee.

Only a year earlier—no, almost two now—Cathy purchased and consumed her first coffee, a cappuccino, to avoid being asked to leave a downtown café. The place was a hangout for young university types and even a couple of guys who were in bands. Cathy and some of her friends had, for a few months that winter, gone there after school to drink big lattes, smoke cigarettes, and enjoy proximity to these boys. Feeling they were too old to giggle behind their hands, they tried instead to engage the scruffy, deep-thinking cuties by looking wan and worldly. It was a failure, the objects of their desire were too self-absorbed to notice the girls' stagy disinterest. The frontier post was abandoned. Some of the girls, crushed, retreated to the mall. Cathy took from the experience two things: conclusive evidence that life for her was, and would forever be, a condition of constant humiliation, and a love of coffee.

She flirted with connoisseurship, getting money from her mother or father and going to a hippie-dippy health-food store downtown to mix her own esoteric blends of Yirgacheffe and Mandheling. Though the shop smelled wonderful, of spices, of cardamom and cinnamon, and of freshly ground coffee beans, and she loved going down there, she eventually settled for the supermarket stuff her parents bought. She realized that it wasn't a particular *coffeeness* that she loved, it was the comfort of the warm cup in her hands and, perhaps even more than that, it was the brew's adoring marriage with milk. This last factor was a conflict—Cathy had become a vegan.

This morning there was a carton of soy milk, purchased by her mother on request, in the fridge door, but Cathy opted for the real thing.

two

Hank was one of the few old friends that Marty still saw. Many of them were Newfoundland economic diaspora, scattered years ago, before the recovery, to Alberta, Ontario, and the States in search of work, vows to stay in touch forgotten. Others vanished in clouds of marriage and family, happy and otherwise. Some went mad in their way, craziness blossoming like dandelions as they entered their fourth decade. The same cellular telegraphs that thinned the hair and swelled the paunch also jangled the nerves, awakened them nightly for a ruminative hour of unravelling and a disappointing piss.

There was a drunk—a Derek, now indigent—whom Marty took pains to avoid, pretended not to notice jittering about the streets with his shopping cart of recyclables, until he became, after only a few years, a stranger. Schizophrenia and consequent institutionalization enervated a Fred. One coke-addled chum, a Pete, having put the mortgage up his nose, consumed the entire contents of the medicine cabinet—various pills and syrups, hydrogen peroxide, salves and mouthwash—to close his remaining accounts. There were successes. A Barry got rich manufacturing gewgaws, obscene novelty car deodorizers, and fishing lures, in Guangdong. Film-and-television Lloyd made a killing making killings. Kamal discovered a cure for a bone disease. Orv actually wrote a couple of top-forty hits, including "Nearer Forever," which was huge for what's-her-name.

There were the forsaken and the failures, not on a grand scale, but guys—Dougs, Harolds, Stans—who had not met, most painfully, even their own expectations. They chose to disappear, hiding in their cars, nursing inchoate rage, visors deployed against the revelatory sun, radios blasting some station that played Neil Young and The Eagles (because they could not fucking abide that hip-hop shit), which deafened them to the nagging background murmur of judgment. On the highways and the arterials and ring roads it was bumper to bumper.

Marty still had acquaintances but none were close. He didn't yearn for the company of the old gang but did, occasionally, on the sleepless nights, long to call someone other than Sophie and shoot the shit, just talk. He could call Hank, but it would wake his girls.

When Hank was fortunate enough to marry Beth Halliday, and soon after have children, the couple tried to include Marty, inviting him to dinner, coaching their two daughters to call him "uncle." The effort was awkward and soon abandoned. It was just as well; Marty found Hank's and Beth's pride of ownership in their children cloying.

Marty and Hank came to know one another through varsity athletics. At first merely nodding a greeting in passing at the phys. ed. building, as the years passed and they became the senior members of their respective teams, they would more frequently find themselves standing together at the bar during departmental functions, watching ever-younger competitors collect awards. They shared good-natured cracks about their diminishing athletic prowess, put down the callow newcomers' success to dumb luck or blue balls. Neither man was naïve enough to aspire to elite status, but both loved their sport. More precisely, each loved the state of grace they achieved in the midst of the game, when their hearts were tom-tomming and their blood rushing. Marty had always raced against the clock, paying little heed to the runners passing him along the way. He was too attuned to voices other than those spoken by the body, too aware of past and future tense to ever be a serious challenger.

Once The Red Pines was a success, Marty and Hank were members of a winning team. They shared a bond of victory. And though both men knew better, having witnessed so many champions fall to defeat, they could not help but revel in it.

♁

Marty thought it must have been nostalgia for locker-room fraternity that made him agree to join Hank for "a workout."

Owing to Hank's relentless schedule of public do-goodery, Marty and he hadn't spoken at length in three weeks. The salvation of rural library systems and the S.P.C.A. were Hank's latest commitments. Marty wished his partner would, just once, do something that might advance the interests of their business, like joining Rotary or the Liberal Party.

Marty asked for an informal lunch meeting, soup and a sandwich somewhere downtown, but Hank, cajoling in a collegial, backslapping way, suggested the gym. Since returning from his Ecology in Education conference, Hank was full of an aggravating brio, an evangelical enthusiasm that made him difficult to resist.

Hank's "fitness centre" was a nondescript sheet-metal box in a retail park, a bleak territory of building supply depots and discount electronics outlets near the airport. Inside it was resonant and airless. Changing into his shorts, Marty was reminded how long he had been away from the track. The meat on his thighs, once crisscrossed strands of muscle and sinew, had contracted and hung pendulously from the bone. The skin on his legs had blanched beneath a decade of cover. That they retained even trace pigment could only be determined in contrast with his bluish feet, which, it was clear, had not. His belly was slight, but loose.

Standing naked, Hank looked fit as ever. Though Marty would have once thought it impossible, Hank had grown hairier over the years. The pelt that ran from his shoulders to his ankles was now uninterrupted but for the rise of two pinkish nipples and the wrinkled flesh of his uncircumcised penis. Though Hank had prudently trimmed for middle age he remained ursine, with a squat, heavy trunk, thick neck, and a stealthiness at odds with his commanding physique. Hank dressed quickly, anxious to begin. His T-shirt testified to his participation in the past year's "RUN FOR THE CURE."

"Let's go," he said.

After three minutes on the stationary bicycle (part of an obligatory twenty-minute warm-up dictated by Hank), Marty began oozing what he would have thought was perspiration but for its profound sulphur and amine stink. Perhaps it was a by-product of the tar burning in his lungs, his rising temperature, and the forced introduction of all the oxygen turning him into a fleshy refinery.

Hank whirred away next to him, sitting upright, stretching his arms, shoulders, and chest while pedalling. He was limber for such a thick fellow, easily twisting himself into yogic knots. He appeared to have designed a regimen that maximized the exercise he could achieve in a limited time. Marty saw the twenty minutes differently. He saw it as an hour.

The line of stationary bikes was positioned below a stressed speaker. A radio was tuned to an FM station that crackled out rock music from the seventies. Marty could distinguish Led-Zeppelin—tectonic thunder and thwump à la Bonham and Jones, Jimmy Page's slurry of sparks and philtres, Robert Plant's quasi-quali caterwauling *"you need coolin'..."* This and a television opposite with a sports channel squawking out scores over pictures of endlessly colliding hockey players made conversation impossible. Nobody seemed to mind the din. In lieu of chitchat, Marty got Hank's encouraging smile and nodding head urging him on.

Marty surveyed the room, hoping to conjure a distracting sexual fantasy. It seemed a choice location to foster one. Excepting a couple of thugs grunting in a corner, the majority of the people here were lean, conditioned hausfraus. "Toned," thought Marty, was what they said these days. The gullies and canyons of their cleavage were mapped on their leotards with dark stains from the salty streams beneath. These passages should have marked the routes by which Marty's imagination explored the interior. It should have been an embarrassment of riches, but there was something uninviting about the firm buttocks and boobs heaving and bobbing all around him. The women were hungry, fighting against frames that wanted to be broad-arsed and buxom. They were licentious fat people trapped in sexless thin people's bodies. Try as he might, Marty was unable to picture them in the parts he scripted.

After warming up, Hank led Marty to the weights, not the dumbbells and barbells of Marty's university days, but machines with pulleys and levers, with padded benches that one lay or sit upon so as to push or pull a bar. Small anatomical diagrams were pasted onto the devices indicating which body part was employed in the exercise. The stylized figures in the illustrations were cartoonishly muscle-bound. Marty guessed this was the ideal to which most of the machine's users aspired. Not Hank, who was telling Marty how increasing his muscle mass would drive up his metabolic rate and burn fat.

"In concert with a cardio program, of course," said Hank.

"I smoke, Hank."

"You've got to quit." There was paternalism in Hank's words.

"Why? What'll happen if I don't, Hank? Will I die?"

Hank lay down and began a series of bench presses, two hundred pounds. He raised two bars (one for each pectoral, Marty supposed) from his chest, concentrating on each smooth, even stroke, conscious of his breathing. Even for a man of his size, Hank's strength was impressive.

Marty gestured to the anatomical diagram stuck to the machine. A faceless superman was shown with an enormous, sculpted chest. "You know, Hank," Marty said, "you would want an enormous dick to go with a chest like that."

Hank let the weight down with a jerky action and rolled from the bench. Marty thought he might be scowling. Saying "the bad thing," the worst thing, a sort of blue one-upmanship, was a game for Hank and Marty, an antidote for the long days of forced smiles and reassurances for the parents, a vent for constantly watched words. Lately Hank was disinclined to play. Marty lay down on the bench and, moving a pin, halved Hank's weight. Prone, the machine suggested to Marty a giant rat trap.

At first Marty felt that he wouldn't be able to budge the bars, but they eventually yielded.

"Good," said Hank, looking on.

At the top of the levers' path, with his reach extended, his arms like pillars, the weight seemed manageable, but on lowering it, unhurriedly, in accordance with Hank's direction, Marty felt as though his breastbone would cleave. He repeated the move twelve times, the weight growing ever heavier. His arms became tremulous. There was pressure in his sinuses behind his eyes. He was dizzy when he rose.

"Gerry Hayden mentioned something interesting when I met him," said Marty, steadying himself against an adjacent machine.

"Oh yeah, how did that go?" Hank asked, lying on the bench for his second set.

"All right. I gather that the old man, his father, is out of it. Gerald's running the shop. I think he really just wanted to talk to you about the Perroqueet Downs thing."

"I suspected as much."

"He said his wife ... Sharon, I think her name was ... would take care of registering their girl but she hasn't been back," Marty said.

"What was she like, the wife?"

"Oh, you know, three holes, two hands, no waiting."

Hank, as though overcome, let the weight drop like a hammer to an anvil. The sudden motion and the force of the impact caused the machine's cables to shimmy. Hank was quick off the bench and onto his feet. His face was florid.

"Stop that! Would you?" Hank said, looking over his shoulder to ensure Marty's crack had not been overheard.

"Relax, Hank. It's a joke."

"Not funny. It's vulgar, disgusting," Hank hissed. He turned his back to Marty and made for the next machine, one in which you sat and lifted a bar over your head. The pictogram indicated that this one built up the shoulders. The radio station was playing a second Steely Dan song in a row, *"And you could have a change of heart ..."*

Despite his entreaty to lift the weights with deliberation, Hank started pumping furiously. The veins in his neck were pronounced as he spoke. "You said Gerald Hayden mentioned something?"

"An idea. A good one." After Hank's rebuke Marty wasn't sure he wanted to continue the conversation—"vulgar and disgusting," yeah, like so much of life. "Worth exploring maybe. A franchise of private schools."

Hank stood, offering Marty the machine. Marty sat down. The bar was clasped in a position behind his head. It hurt before he even started to lift.

"What? Franchise The Pines?" asked Hank.

Marty nodded, sensing that if he tried to speak the words would be whimpered. With each repetition, ridges rose on either side of his spine.

"Like a chain?" asked Hank.

That was characterizing it unfairly, but Marty nodded again. "Maybe 'franchise' isn't the right word … a line."

"It's totally wrong-headed," said Hank. "People put their kids in private school because they get individual attention, because they're not sausages out of the mill. And I think of The Pines as being, despite the fact that it's serving an elite, I like to think of it as community-based. A chain of private schools is almost a contradiction in terms."

Marty could lift no more. He stood.

"No, it's not. There's nothing contradictory in the terms 'private' and 'chain.'"

"Semantics," said Hank.

"Each school would be unique … seem unique … appear to be a stand-alone operation," Marty struggled to catch his breath, "and quality controls … like assurances of a certain standard of instruction would be part of the deal. There would be a uniform curriculum, using the same texts and such."

"You've given this some thought, then?"

"No. Well, yes, some. A business has to continue to grow in order to survive," said Marty. "I mean, Newfoundland is a good enough place to start an operation like ours, to work the bugs out, but there just isn't the population base to … to expand … you think of Southern Ontario or out in B.C., the Eastern Seaboard …" The stale air and reverberant music were combining to make him nauseated.

"The Pines is something more than a business."

"Really?"

"Yes," said Hank firmly. "And you know it seems to me you would need a great deal of money, a big investment, to get that sort of thing off the ground. You know more about the money end of it than me. I don't know."

"You're sure you're not rejecting the idea because it came from Gerry Hayden?"

"Why were you talking business with him anyway?" Hank asked, walking away from Marty and on to the next machine. He gripped a dangling iron triangle and pulled downward from his upper chest toward his waist, his elbows pinned to his side. Marty watched Hank's triceps flex with each pull. It appeared something foreign was coiling beneath the skin at the back of his arm.

"It just came up in passing. And listen, Hank, I just said it was something worthy of discussion."

"And we have discussed it. Is that all you wanted to talk about?"

"Yeah, and the Malan boy."

"What about him?"

"His grades are slipping, precipitously. Staff have mentioned it."

"Who's really surprised?" Hank punctuated this with a derisive puff. He gave the iron triangle a final pull to his waist and then relaxed, letting the force yank his arms over his head.

"Do you think maybe you should talk to him?" asked Marty, stepping forward to take his turn.

"No."

"Why not?"

"The boy's got some hard lessons to learn. He has high self-esteem issues," said Hank. "Who's going to be there to bail him out later? The Malans can afford another tutor, a whole squad of them."

"You know another tutor won't work. Besides, he's only got one year left." Marty had completed three repetitions and his arms were burning.

"Why does it matter anyway, Marty? Stupidity doesn't have the stigma it used to. He'll do fine. Maybe they should send him to a military college. He'd make an excellent sadist."

"Give it up."

"And I think Malan's got money in the Perroqueet Downs development."

"Is that it? Don't you think that's unfair to the boy? Sins of the father?"

"It is impossible," Hank gave Marty one of his wrestler looks, a glare to intimidate, "to be unfair to the boy."

"I know it's your own time, Hank, but don't you think you've become preoccupied with this Downs thing?"

"No. Frankly I've never felt as committed to anything in my life."

"It's not the hole in the ozone layer or the desertification of Africa, is it?" asked Marty, letting go of the bar four repetitions short of the twelve demanded. "You just flew to Toronto, what did you see out the window of the plane? Nothing but trees and lakes and muskeg for days, it's like one of those endless Gordon Lightfoot songs! Realistically, is it that urgent a concern?"

To Marty's dismay, Hank was giving the question serious consideration.

"Yes," Hank answered. "It is. It's a whole earth problem, Marty. The latest thinking is that the earth, as a single organism, is at stake. Everything is connected. And that we share one planet defines our collectivity."

"Collectivity?" This term was worrisome for Marty.

"The symbolism is important, too, starting right here, at home. You know the line—think globally, act locally. The hole in the ozone layer is too abstract for most people." Hank paused. "With something this immediate, in our own backyard, you can see where people stand. This is *the* issue of our time. For my kids' sake I want to come down on the right side of this. Everyone will be held to account."

Hank smiled, though Marty couldn't think for the world why.

"You are scaring me, Hank. What is this? 'If you're not for us, you're agin us'? You can't tell me to have an opinion. And isn't it a bit grand to say, 'the earth itself is at stake'? It's a subdivision. If they don't build it there, they'll just build it somewhere else. Think locally for a change."

"I'm committed to this, Marty. You know, I've felt … and this …" Hank didn't finish. He planted his hands on his hips and looked past Marty, unfocused.

"So this franchise idea? Can't be convinced?"

Hank looked back toward Marty. "But nobody is stopping you."

Marty's head was hot. His scalp was itchy.

"I'm getting a shower. I gotta go eat," Marty said.

"You go on," said Hank. "I still have to do legs."

The speakers struggled with another Steely Dan number. *"Well I did not think the girl could be so cruel … "* Marty turned for the locker room.

♂

Marty went to a fast-food outlet he'd noticed during the drive to the fitness centre. Symbiotic enterprises, he thought. He ordered a burger, fries, and a Coke from the drive-through window. A girl in a gauzy mask of acne cream handed him a giant tub of liquid, heavy as a cinder block, and a bag that seemed by comparison to contain nothing but air. Because of an incomprehensible pricing scheme found only in fast-food and video rentals it cost less to order more, so Marty had, feeling there was little choice, "supersized." He parked the car in the lot facing a divided four-lane highway. He liked eating in the car.

Hank was being a prick. His Jesus act was growing tiresome. Who was he to grant Marty leave to proceed with the franchise on his own? They were partners. Together they were still into the banks for a million dollars. More. If Hank didn't care for the idea he could have simply left it at that. Prick.

It started to rain. There was a strip-mall across the road—hair, pizza, doctor, beds—and beyond a subdivision, a range of chimneys and siding. This part of town had been built up not fifteen years earlier and already it was starting to look rundown, the slipshod construction and second-rate materials—soggy, poorly seasoned lumber, crumbling brick—undone by the constant thunder of air and land traffic. It was the new way of the world, impermanence. The schools out here, overcrowded variants on the penitential panopticon, would empty as the broods moved away. The school board would face a population crisis elsewhere in its jurisdiction and propose busing the kids in. The parents wouldn't like it and there would be ructions. The schools, as shabbily made as the houses, would start falling apart, furnace boilers would burst, roofs would collapse under the weight of winter snow. They would be vandalized. Maintenance costs would forever climb. Because of the changes in the demographics, the land on which the schools stood would be undervalued and sold at a loss. They would be forced to build new schools and repeat the process. It was a lose–lose situation. Private schools never faced the problem because the parents had choice—they came *to* the school. The costs of education and health care were hobbling government, which was being forced to burgle taxpayers to pay the tab. Marty was beginning to believe, as he had not before, that an entirely private education system was a possible solution. Gerry Hayden was connected. His people hadn't considered getting in the school business for nothing, they knew where things were headed.

Despite the bag of food having seemed insubstantial, Marty was quickly and sickly full. He was unable to stomach the last of his fries. He belched up a bubble that tasted of sugar and grease.

Then he saw, walking down the median between the roaring lines of trucks and cars, his niece, Cathy. Her head was uncovered. Her coat was open. Marty could just make out a death head and some gothic lettering on her shrunken T-shirt, the logo of some band, no doubt. Her midriff was exposed, whitened by the damp wind. She was sopping wet and sucking the last drag from a cigarette.

She should have been in school.

Marty rolled down his car window and shouted her name, only once. Over the traffic she couldn't hear him. It was just as well, Marty thought, she was always tetchy with him. And being caught truant by her uncle, the vice principal, wouldn't seem like help. He would be obliged to deliver her back to Frank Moores High and there answer questions. He would have to call Rex and Meredith and tell them where he had found their daughter. And he was due for a meeting with Audrey Caddigan's parents in fifteen minutes.

By the time he pulled out of the parking lot and onto the road Cathy had already disappeared.

4

At The Pines lunch had ended and students were pouring back into their classrooms as if into drains. Miss Zwitzer's progress through the halls created an eddy in the flow.

Sophie ordered many of her clothes, particularly items she wore at school, from an Austrian catalogue service, and though modern and so international, something about their cut was unmistakably Teutonic. They were not formal but still too grand, suggestive of high country living, the kind of thing one wore for falconry on the estate. The corseting of the jacket she wore this day showed off her shape. Her mature femininity was a tool she used to advantage with the students, keeping the boys in line with a suggestion of sexual intimidation, the girls in awe of her worldliness.

The wooziness Marty felt leaving the gym had left him and he was now experiencing a lift from the exercise. His chest was full; his arms were hard. Though they made it a point never to reveal anything of their relationship in the school, Marty made straight for Sophie and, taking her by the arm just above the elbow, pulled her aside.

"Are you home tonight?" he asked.

"Why?" Sophie was startled to be touched with some intimacy by Marty in the hallway.

"I thought we might watch a video or something."

"Sure. You want to come for dinner?"

"No. You eat. I'm going to be stuck here." This wasn't true and Marty couldn't think why he had said it.

"Okay."

♄

Abe Summers still had not provided Marty a copy of Audrey Caddigan's play. Her name rang a bell because the cheque written to cover her tuition had bounced, an event unprecedented in The Red Pines' ten years of operation. Marty called the girl's parents expecting they would report a simple mistake, having written the cheque from an account that was closed, an error at the bank, something like that. But instead of dealing with it over the phone they asked to meet him.

They were already seated in his office when Marty arrived. Mrs. Caddigan looked to be in her late thirties or early forties. She made no effort to cover with makeup the bags under her eyes or the crow's feet, but had dyed her hair a funky orange, an unnatural metallic copper. She wore jeans and a grey sweater of the rough, homespun wool once favoured by seamen.

The father was a mess. His sports coat hung about him like a tarp. There was a two-finger gap between his buttoned shirt collar (though he did not wear a tie) and his neck, evidence of recent weight loss. His hair was thinning but in irregular patches like a bug-eaten lawn. His shoulders were up, gathering the fabric of his loose jacket into fallen loaves.

Shaking their hands in turn, Marty found them both bloodless. He knew this sort, knew what was going on. They would soon be divorced. Lots of the kids' parents were. It was no problem. From what Marty saw they enjoyed being single every second week or so. It was as much as their spent livers and genitals could handle. The matter of the children was always more complicated. That was the reason for the Caddigans' visit. The screw-up with the payment had to do with some new arrangement in raising the youngster, changes of address, fiduciary obligations as laid out in the terms of the custody and support agreements, that sort of thing.

"We're sorry about the money, Mr. Devereaux," said the father.

"And mortally embarrassed," added Mrs. Caddigan.

"Yes," said Marty. "It's not as though we have any mechanism to deal with it. It hasn't happened before. I mean … we have a waiting list …" Marty did not continue, leaving a window in the conversation, presenting the Caddigans with an opportunity to write a new cheque and have done with the matter.

Caddigan Pere swallowed audibly, gobbling air. "We still find ourselves …" he went wide-mouthed as a carp for another breath, "without the means to pay."

"At this time," added Mrs. Caddigan. "We have every intention of paying, as soon as possible. You see, Rick has had a …"

"I've had a few …" Rick took up the search, "reversals. I developed some remote-sensing technologies, stuff for the oil patch, pollution controls, but … just as I was getting a foothold, some big boys from Houston moved in and fucked me over." Hearing what he'd said, Caddigan apologized for the language. "Sorry. The matter is in litigation."

"What kind of technology?" asked Marty.

"I beg your pardon?"

Marty was sure Caddigan heard the question clearly. "What kind of remote-sensing technology?" he repeated.

"It has to do with bringing satellite images into focus. The ocean surface ..." Caddigan stopped, looked to his wife and then to Marty. "It's complex. I wouldn't want to bore you."

Marty could tell Caddigan smugly thought himself smarter. Even now, stating that he couldn't pay his bill, he held Marty—a high-school vice principal—in intellectual contempt.

"And on top of that my dad's been unwell," Mrs. Caddigan said, "and Rick had a car accident ..."

"Not a big accident or anything. I mean, Mr. Devereaux doesn't need to hear all the details, hon."

No, indeed he doesn't, thought Marty.

Trouble clustered. It was entropic and opportunistic. You never heard tell of someone with one simple, manageable problem. Strife sensed your weakness and shot into your cells like a retrovirus, putting a hitch in your helixes, making them breed predicament. What was that Shakespeare? "Sorrows came not as single spies, but in battalions"? Something like that, from *Hamlet,* he thought. But then, it had been so long ago that he'd read it, and he and Sophie had fallen asleep watching the video.

"It's all we can do now to keep the house. We're on Shaheen Crescent," Mrs. Caddigan said, reaching forward and laying her hand on Marty's desk. "This all happened quickly, we're not ... we've never had financial problems. It's embarrassing. I'm going back to nursing and there's hope of a settlement with Rick's suit, but our lawyer, he says that these civil proceedings, they take time."

Nursing. The neighbours on Shaheen Crescent would just love that, seeing Mrs. Caddigan dressed in her uniform, heading off for the night shift. Marty wondered if she knew Jackie Spurell. He'd thought about Jackie often since they'd met at the vocational college and one morning woke to a receding dream in which something, something he wouldn't let himself recall, happened between them.

"We might have moved if it weren't for Audrey," said Rick.

"It's the same with the school," said Mrs. Caddigan. "It would be so disruptive, and the year is almost over. It would be such a shame to put her back in the public system. We've had some horrible experiences. Her brother, our eldest, he had such trouble ..."

"He's a casualty, is what he is," Mr. Caddigan erupted.

"He had such promise, but now ..." Mrs. Caddigan's voice trailed off for a moment. "He has no ambition and he got involved with a bad crowd."

Yes, in battalions. Marty divined the details: their first-born, the son that they'd imagined a tax lawyer or a cardiologist, was now, in his late teens or early twenties, a pot-stupid mouth-breather taking up space on a mildewed sofa in front of a television in the basement. They would kick him out but for a lingering sense—that the son exploited—that they, through bad parenting, were to blame. And moving to a more modest home would bring the matter to a head: they would have to tell the realtor whether they were looking for a place with two bedrooms or three. The address on Shaheen Crescent would have, not fifteen years earlier, unfairly entitled the Caddigan kids to a superior education within the public system. But with the end of denominational schooling there came a reckoning, a balancing that liberals like the Caddigans had clamoured for. Now, after the perestroika, one public school wasn't much different than another. They were all overcrowded, understaffed, and falling to pieces.

"But our son's not the issue here, is he," Mrs. Caddigan continued. "It's Audrey. She's an exceptional child."

Marty gave a nod of affirmation. He'd taken years to perfect this gesture, a double dip of the head with the eyes closed for solemnity. It said "by our silence we acknowledge that your child is special." In refining this pseudo-Montessorian shtick, Marty tired of it.

"We will pay," said Mrs. Caddigan again.

Mister quaked. Convulsions, originating in his diaphragm, rolled up his torso, into his neck, and finally his jaw, which flapped despite his every effort to bite down against it. The bastard was weeping. "I'm sorry," he went.

Marty shouldn't have been surprised; men now had liberty to cry. It was a rare occasion when Marty was a boy, a privilege reserved for war heroes and the like, fellows who had witnessed the unspeakable. Now lads were bawling at every turn, professional athletes, statesmen, gang bosses, and business bigwigs, and they did so without compunction. They were heralded for their sensitivity. The blame, Marty supposed, could be laid on the advance of evangelical movements, the Pentecostal wailers and charismatic chest thumpers who had streamed into the cities from the hills, from the bays and backwaters, to encourage these naked and, to Marty's mind, untoward displays of emotion. Weren't enough tears shed by women and children and old men? Surely another salty drop and the world was at risk of floating away.

"Audrey is everything to us," Mrs. Caddigan said, ignoring her husband and trying to look Marty in the eye. "She's such a bright girl. Her friends are here. She's so excited about her play. It would be devastating."

"I'm sorry," Mr. Caddigan said again.

Why did they do it? Marty wondered. Why did all these people, these parents who brought their woes to him, why did they have children in the first place? His latest thinking was that they did it to block out the interior voices, their thoughts, that on ceaseless repetition were becoming noxiously boring, that would, unchecked, drive them mad. Whatever the reason, they bet their hearts, never giving a thought to losing the wager. The genetic admixture proved sour and a son disappointed them or a daughter reviled them. Or studying, as they compulsively did, their issue for inherited traits they saw things, tics and tendencies to conceit or cruelty that shocked them and brought them to unflattering reflection. A marriage fell apart, or a beloved spouse died, and someone was left to raise the children on their own. Plans and hopes were sunk. The price was their soul. In Marty's experience nothing caused more suffering than love.

Mr. Caddigan was struggling to get a hold of himself, sniffing back snot, wiping tears with his knuckles. Marty wanted rid of him.

"We can wait," Marty said, "but I won't be able to release her marks until any outstanding fees are paid."

"Thank you," said Mrs. Caddigan. "It won't be long."

ψ

Somehow Chuck Curtis always found a way to sit close to Cathy. Today in Donnelly's physics class Chuck was in the seat directly in front of hers, providing a close-up view of the weeping zits on his chunky, perfectly Chuck neck. She could smell him, too, exhaust from the biological cauldron that was turning all those Corn Flakes and potatoes and ground beef into his meat. Chuck roast. When in the company of his friends (his locker was close to Cathy's) Chuck never missed an opportunity to say something derogatory about her as she passed. Alone with her Chuck flushed, tried and failed to be pleasant. The poor brute obviously had a thing for her. Dream fucking Chucking on. And her mother forever asking whether she had a boyfriend. Be serious.

The class was mostly boys. They thought physics a manly subject, to do with mechanics, high voltage and such. They were disappointed to discover it was studied, in the main, with pen and paper and much math. Thus Donnelly's tired jibe that one befuddled student or another must have confused physics with phys. ed. when they had selected their courses. Cathy chose physics randomly, one class being the same as the next to her.

Cathy liked Donnelly and despite her efforts to tune him out found some of the stuff he talked about interesting. It wasn't because of any effort on Donnelly's part.

"When you were looking at the newspapers this weekend," Donnelly said, "did any of you happen to read about the new comet?" He never expected them to answer his snide questions and continued straight away. "It was discovered by an amateur astronomer using a very simple instrument. That's not uncommon, you know, for transient objects like comets or asteroids to be first seen by an amateur astronomer."

Donnelly walked to the dirt-speckled classroom window and looked out into the fog.

"The comet will, as tradition dictates, be named after her. Comet Gomez." He turned to face them again. "Imagine that. Imagine having your name on part of the heavens. You would be of the ages." Indeed Donnelly looked to be thinking of the stars, his eyes far away. Maybe he was just bored.

"Miss Gomez, by the way, is sixteen years old. She's a paraplegic." Donnelly paused for a moment and then reached for a book on his desk. "I believe we have stumbled through the first law of thermodynamics. The second law, or why the mountains fall into the sea ..."

Cathy raised her hand.

"Yes?" said Donnelly.

"Will the comet crash into the earth, sir, and destroy us like the dinosaurs?"

There were snickers from the class. Donnelly's eyelids dropped.

"The ancients thought of them as portents—you can look that up later, Palmer," he said, pointing peremptorily to a curly headed lad about to crack wise. "But it's a ball of frozen gas, Miss Ford-Devereaux, not an avenging angel. Regrettably, it will pass no closer than the orbit of the planet Neptune."

The thought of the Caddigans still rankled as Marty left his office for the day. Why were they burdening him with their sob story? He was a businessman, providing a service. Had they gone to the phone company or hydro and made the same plea? Did the bank care? It wasn't that much money—twelve thousand bucks. They could find that. This was such small stakes.

In the corridor Darcy Slocom, an overqualified math teacher (picked up at a discount after some unspecified, though surely egregious, misconduct landed him on a dean's shit-list), called to Marty from the door to the staff room.

"Marty, you'd better come and see this."

Slocum, Cloris Foley, and Mrs. Norris were watching a breaking news story on the small television that sat atop the fridge. There were killings. Frantic circuits of police and paramedics were at the sight of the bloodletting. An institutional building. Suburban setting. Heaping damage. Corralled teens tore at one another in ecstatic distress. Maybe they were burying their Ayatollah. A text message scrolled laterally across the bottom of the screen: Mass Shooting Columbine High School.

As if opening a hatch Cloris took a cupped hand from her mouth to speak. "Some kids did it," she said. "Students."

There was more carnage on the tube. Dead kid at the bottom of some stairs. Sniper taking a position on a rooftop. Cop in body armour using a mirror mounted on the barrel of his automatic weapon to view around a corner. Crafty, that.

"They say there's like ... twenty shot or something," said Slocom, who, Marty noticed, was eating a bag of cheesies.

Mrs. Norris couldn't take her eyes from the television. She recognized the kids.

"Colorado?" asked Marty.

"Yeah, place called Littleton, near Denver," said Slocum.

The picture cut from the scene to a ready expert being interviewed at a news desk.

"It's a cult of the Apocalypse down there in the States," said Marty.

"What about the victims?" said Cloris, taking Marty's comment to be heartless.

"I don't know. What about them, Cloris?" What he did know was that this was going to have "repercussions." There would be "aftermath." People would be taking the time to "heal" until they found "closure." And, most immediately, thought Marty with regret, it was going to necessitate the calling of a Red Pines PTA meeting.

"Public school or private, Darce?"

"Jeez, I'm not sure … public, I think."

Marty left. He so hated PTA things. A columbine, he knew, was a sort of flower.

Sophie liked to say she lived on the lake. It was no more than a pond, the boundary of a municipal park. As the sylvan setting was near the city centre it was one of the more desirable addresses in town. Her home was forty-odd years older, on a considerably smaller scale than the massive dwellings of her neighbours and unique among them in that it was oriented toward the water. The windows one saw from the street were of the dining room, kitchen, and bedroom.

Sophie had parked diagonally across the driveway so there was no room for Marty's car. He pulled up at the curb, worried that Sophie had been drinking and driving.

The back door was unlocked. Marty entered through the kitchen to the muted sound of sloshing water and a melody of Schubert's.

Sophie was in the bath humming to herself, a certain sign she'd been to the well.

"Hello," Marty called.

"Maaaah-ten," Sophie sang in answer.

The walls of her house were covered with photographs of generations of musical Zwitzers—a jug-eared cousin with an oboe, an aunt posed in song next to a piano, framed playbills. There was a picture from the earliest days of photography, her great-grandfather in the faltering court of Sultan Abdulhamid II of Turkey where he had created a Western orchestra, a gift at the behest of Kaiser Wilhelm. Sophie's ancestor sat stiffly, alone in crisp focus, surrounded by a blurry guard of swarthy men in fezzes.

Sophie kept rearranging the photos, so it was hard to keep relationships and chronology straight. The gallery followed the peripatetic clan about the world: to Germany in 1917, her grandfather as director of The Bavarian Opera in the thirties, her maternal grandmother in folk costume in the company of Cosima Wagner at Bayreuth. There was a scandalous nude of a notorious auntie from Vienna, surname of Neuzil, by a supposedly famous painter, surname of whom Marty could never remember. There was a photo of Mahler, *that* Mahler—a distant relative. Sophie owned several of the composer's letters (probably written by his wife Alma, she said), simple courtesies, best wishes on the occasion of a marriage, and so on. Some uncle had once been a close friend and musical associate of Kurt Weill, but there'd been a split.

Later pictures showed Sophie's father and mother in Buenos Aires, then young Sophie herself at the piano, which by the demanding standards of the Zwitzers she never truly mastered. Sophie was born there, so Argentina was always deemed, without much affection and no pride, "home." The family moved to Santiago in the early seventies and then to Canada. Sophie's brother Dieter called Sydney, Australia, home but toured the world as a concert pianist. Her sister Anna was first violin with the Los Angeles Symphony. No matter where they scattered, though, no matter what passport they held, something in their expression—a melancholy and wariness—testified they remained European.

"You should really lock the door," Marty shouted. It wasn't a dangerous town, but for a woman living alone, it was imprudent. There was an open bottle on the dining-room table. Vodka.

"Yes, or something might happen," Sophie called. Then she laughed.

Marty sat on the living-room couch. His gaze fell on a familiar photograph, an image with the agency of a riddle. Grandfather Zwitzer and another man stood side by side, a set of stone steps behind them led to a building fronted by Roman columns and a portico, detail obscured by bright sunlight and consequent overexposure. The men were laughing at or cheering for something just out of frame. There was nothing unusual about the content; it was simply the shape of the frame, its aspect ratio, too tall and thin. Had it been trimmed?

Vodka. Sophie shouldn't drink spirits, thought Marty. She was too fond of wine, but it was a private and minor vice. It never interfered with her work. Keeping it together after a night with the hard liquor was more difficult. Marty heard the water draining from the tub.

He dared not make a comment about the booze. Sophie led her own life. That was their deal.

She entered wearing a bathrobe and a towel turban, her bare feet stepping silently from one Persian or Afghani rug to the next. The carpets were a passing pursuit of hers, along with antiques. She had acquired the best of these things while travelling, always buying cautiously and wisely. There wasn't a whole lot to be had locally, though it was fun to look on a rainy, childless Saturday afternoon.

On those occasions Marty accompanied her, he often picked up something with which to dress The Pines—battered bookcases for the library, the occasional wooden desk for a teacher. He once found, and paid too much for, a big, old (too big, too old) tabletop orrery, a clockwork model of the solar system. The dealer said it had come to Newfoundland from England sometime in the late nineteenth century. It featured only seven planets, ending with Uranus, so was likely built sometime after the 1780s and before the 1850s. (Had Alan Pitts seen it? Was that where he'd got his idea?) You turned a crank and the planets circled the sun. But there was something wrong with the spoke attached to the earth's moon, the only moon on the model, so that it collided with its host every third rotation, jamming the works and consigning the apparatus to basement storage. Most recently Marty purchased a map of the world printed a century earlier, in 1899. It was a gorgeous thing, thick rag paper velvety with wear, stippling and cross-hatching showing topographic features beneath nations in a shocking colour palette, cobalt-blue and chrome-yellow inks now considered too vivid or too costly, perhaps toxic. The British Empire appeared to be painting the world pink.

Sophie had accumulated more furnishings than her small house could properly accommodate. Her greatest find was a mint Biedermeier secretary. The most peculiar was a teapoy, possessed of an unsettling odour and with dentils that looked suspiciously like some creature's actual teeth. Atop it all, anywhere they could be put on display, were old musical instruments: a couple of violins, strangely bent horns, a balalaika. She couldn't or didn't care to play them, sticking to the piano. They simply took up space.

Sophie's complexion was daguerreotype. In dim light her skin was pewter. She applied the relief, brought out her thin nose, cheekbones, and eyes in a long, refined unction with particular creams and powders. She moved through the living room, smiling coyly, continuing into the dining room and then the kitchen. The house was a music box, thought Marty, with Sophie, her fine mechanisms growing shaky like those of the old orrery, taking a wobbly turn whenever the top was lifted.

"I'm having martinis," she called, her mongrel accent adding an *h, mahrtinis.* "Can I offer you one?"

"Sure," said Marty. "When did you start drinking martinis?"

"I had a couple last fall, at the hotel during those meetings for Canada Music Week. And today when I was at the liquor store I thought of it. They're all the rage now. 'It's cocktail time again!' I read that on a poster." Sophie laughed at this, as if her following a trend was comically unlikely. Marty heard a cocktail shaker. "I also bought a set of martini glasses. I love the look of them."

She returned with two martinis in oversized glasses. She handed one to Marty and then sat on the couch next to him, pulling up her legs and tucking her heels in against her bottom, the position causing the top of the robe to fan open. The drinks each had two large olives bobbing around in them. They should have been run through with a swizzle stick, thought Marty. They were like strange eggs or the mossy droppings of a forest ruminant.

"On the news, Martin, on the radio, they were talking about a massacre, in a high school in the U.S."

"Yeah, I saw some stuff on the television at The Pines and then at home."

"What's that about?"

"Another rapturous ending to some disappointed American's *issues,* Sophie. Instead of prayer or *Oprah* they took the express line. You would think someone would have been aware of the perils of letting spoiled, narcissistic teenage boys tote machine guns." The thought of it was making Marty weary. "It's going to have to be addressed, though, since it's been continually on the news. The parents will be freaking out. It's a Hank kind of thing, sensitivity and all that. I wonder, would sending home a memo or a letter of some sort do?"

"I'm sure it will all be explained in a movie some day. The killers will be famous," Sophie said. "So, *Maahten,* are we going to take that holiday?"

She had heard all she wanted to about the grisly affair in Colorado. For all her years in Canada she still seemed slightly embarrassed for North Americans, perplexed by the lives they misled.

"If we are, I'm going to have to call."

The two-week Easter break was approaching and Sophie had been on Marty to travel with her to Tuscany. While the place looked attractive in the glossy spreads he'd been shown—all vineyards, poplars, and crumbling beauty under a perpetual sunset—Marty realized he didn't much like the people he knew who'd been there, couldn't stand their pushy "you must go, you must" enthusiasm. The Tuscan proposal was just the latest of Sophie's beseechments that Marty "lighten up" so they could have "some fun for once." Fun. By their repetition these small disputes, these minor disagreements, were becoming as familiar as those with family.

"These last-minute deals the travel agencies offer, Martin, they're not literally last minute."

"I still can't say."

"You seem to have more time these days."

"I guess, hey?"

"Come off it, you're a workaholic. That's avoidance of some sort."

"No. No, it's work. It's being responsible."

"Come on. Italy."

"I'll try. I'm trying."

"Maybe I'll just go myself."

"You could do that."

"Piss off, *Maahten*."

"Do you know a student named Audrey Caddigan?" Marty asked, needing to change the subject.

"There are so many. It's exhausting keeping up with them all."

"Don't know her?"

"Actually, I do."

"And?"

"Exceptional student. No, that's not true—almost exceptional?" she chuckled. "Like us all, I suppose. Bit of a misfit, I gather. Doesn't seem to fit in. I see her leaving class alone, or showing up early by herself. But then, you know this is often the case with the bright girls."

"Her parents were in my office this afternoon. The father cried."

"That's sad," Sophie said dispassionately, holding her drink at arm's length, admiring the look of it in one of her new glasses.

"I hate that. I really do," said Marty. "It's an imposition."

"What was the matter?"

"Money. Just money. No, more than that. Unfulfilled dreams or something."

Sophie laughed again. She's getting drunk, thought Marty.

"That's very philosophical of you, Martin," Sophie observed. She relished a sip of her drink.

"I don't know why I brought it up. It's not like I'm paid to take this stuff home. I should just forget about it," said Marty.

"You always bring everything home."

"Then I've been an asshole."

"Yes, for years. What film did you get for us?" asked Sophie.

"I went to the video store," said Marty, "but I couldn't find anything."

This happened to Marty occasionally—he'd look over the thousands of video-cassette boxes on display and find nothing of interest. It was an experience he found dispiriting, as if the lack of an hour-and-a-half's diversion signalled an essential emptiness at the centre of the universe. Marty tasted his drink. It was so cold it felt like aspic in his mouth.

Sophie stuck her fingers into her glass and fished out an olive. Drops of the vermouth-scented vodka fell from her hands onto her chest. She had seven years on Marty and joked about being an older woman. Her age was just starting to show in her neck, where tendons were raising a tent of skin. Her exquisite, full breasts were beginning to relax.

She chewed the flesh off the olive and removed the pit from her mouth, laying it in an ashtray on the side table.

"What will we do, *Maahten?*" she asked. As if that might be in doubt. There was an inevitability to their congress: it would take place in bed, Sophie would be noisy, panting and puffing, Marty would be silent. Marty would feel like coming after about five or six minutes but would hold off for a couple more. Lying underneath her spent partner, Sophie would continue to rub her pelvis against his weight for another two minutes before achieving orgasm. So it had been for almost nine years.

"Whatever you like, Sophie," he answered. The martini's action was rapid. Marty already felt it.

"Whatever you like," he repeated so he could hear himself saying the words. He felt them in his throat, as though they had undergone a transubstantiation. It was unlike him, but he had, of late, started feeling quite unlike himself.

Sophie stood and walked across the room to the stereo, her nail hitting the plastic "play" button with a percussive click—a conductor rapping her baton on a music stand. The wheezing and buzzing of a bandoneon filled the room: Astor Piazzolla. The tango master, for whom Marty had never acquired a taste, was a favourite of Sophie's. Marty found the music flirted with cacophony, and there was something in the sliding step and sudden halt of its rhythm that set his stomach fluttering as though he had tripped and caught himself falling.

Sophie returned to the couch, sitting closer to Marty. Her heat was acting on the aromatic essences in the booze and the soaps and salts from her bath—bergamot, wormwood, citrus. Impulsively, without a thought, Marty reached for the lapel of the robe and drew it open, exposing Sophie's left breast. He watched himself doing this, and the actions were those of a stranger for whom he was ashamed. It was uncharacteristic behaviour. Despite their many years together Marty remained timid. Sophie appeared grateful for the rare spontaneity. She looked down at her naked flesh and back to Marty with a smile of surprise. Her nipple darkened as it hardened with a suddenness that almost made it jump. Marty put down his drink.

A giggle escaped Sophie as she surrendered to Marty's weight and let herself spread over the couch. The towel wrapping her head came undone, gathered strands of hair, still wet, spilling out. Marty moved on top of her.

His face pressed to her skin, the colognes of Sophie's bath were stronger. Sophie's fingers wove a glove of his hair to pull him closer. If only she would give a tug. He could feel her breath deepening, could feel her heartbeat against his brow. He squeezed her two breasts together, pushing them against his cheeks. Drawing his tongue across the flesh, pushing hard enough to feel the breastbone beneath, he tasted soap. Wash your mouth out, he thought.

Sophie's legs were sliding up around him. She dug her heels into Marty's ass.

The knot in the robe's belt was slack and he easily pulled it loose. His fingertips sought out the smooth flesh of Sophie's thighs, his knuckles brushed her pubic hair. He pushed a loose fist in against her.

Sophie said something Marty couldn't make out, the words were throaty, not English or Spanish, but German. He sat up and began hurriedly loosening his tie, unbuttoning his shirt. The seam at the crotch of his trousers was cutting into him, but rather than constricting it, called up his blood. Sophie sat up, too, her robe falling from her shoulders as she slid from the sofa to the rug where, to Marty's dismay, she lay on her back.

This was not how he had imagined it. He had been entertaining the thought of Sophie on top. And more than that. His head was growing sick with it, but the truth was he wanted to be taken by Sophie, and roughly. He wanted to see her grinding away above him, hear her making demands as, no doubt, Jackie Spurell would do.

"Come on, *Maahten,* fuck me," said Sophie, but it was more an invitation than a command. Her knees were up, her legs languorously swaying. Sophie was accommodating, liked a little adventure, but Marty could not bring himself to ask that she … what? He wasn't even sure what he would ask.

He stepped out of his trousers, pulled off his briefs and socks so that he was naked. He lay on top of her and pressed the length of his cock against her. Sophie took his head in her hands and all too gently pulled his mouth to a deep kiss, her tongue searching his mouth with disappointing silken delicacy. Her back was rippling against the rug, her hips rising and falling.

She was becoming wetter, opening up. The reach of her thrusts could now almost grasp him and take him inside. There was a glandular animal funkiness in the air, the exalted salt of cum and cunt. He slid a leg beneath hers and levered her upward and to the side as he rolled over on his back. It was no use. Sophie rolled in the opposite direction an extra turn, coming to rest on her knees, her face pressed to the rug and her ass up in the air. Fucking vodka, fucking tango music. This was where it led, to the floor with your rear end submissively waving in the wind. Marty was about to stretch out and grab her, drag her toward and lift her on top of him, but she said urgently, "Get inside me, Martin."

Perhaps he imagined Jackie saying the same words, perhaps with more insistence—even a command or a taunt, surely more coarsely—but he felt as though he would burst. He got up. The ripe curves of Sophie's buttocks begged to be licked or bitten, but his impatient cock was tugging him toward the glistening mound rising in their shadow. She was in flood. He easily pushed far inside her and began to pound. Sophie rocked into his thrusts, bucked against them, all the while softly and unconsciously humming along with the music on the stereo, metronomically governing the rhythm of their coupling, accenting the beat, keeping Marty in the difficult time.

Marty drove with increasing furor, his pelvis slapping noisily against Sophie's ass. He shuddered and came. It was not as though a star had exploded, merely as if clouds had parted to allow a short moment in the sun, like coming briefly awake, except in the opposite direction and with distressing torpor: falling asleep. He lay on the carpet. Sophie slid forward and let her belly rest on the floor.

Marty said nothing until a song ended.

"Do you ever have any fantasies, Sophie?" Marty asked. "Something you've never said? Something you wish I'd do?"

"There is one I have, where I imagine you love me," she said.

"Jesus, Sophie. You know I love you."

"In my fantasy you scream the words at me. And I believe you. We're different people, easier to make happy. But it's a fantasy. They say it's perfectly normal and healthy to have them."

The music started again.

three

THE DAILY TOING AND FROING of students across the soccer pitch, distressed and doughy from the heaving of frost, was recorded in deepening shit-brown tracks. Marty sized up the problem from the window of an empty classroom on the school's second floor. If it got any worse he would have to have the most seriously damaged patches re-sodded. Couple of grand—minimum. The scars in the turf wound east in a lazy arc, running from the school's rear exit and terminating in the grove of pines where the kids went to smoke. Marty was wondering whether a short, obstructive stretch of fencing altering the traffic pattern might be an economical solution when he noticed that the trees at the trail's end were thinner, their branches providing less cover than formerly, so that he could see into the tiny wood. Marty went downstairs to his office, pulled on his overcoat, and set out to investigate, leaving the building via the front doors.

Halfway across the field the water had already penetrated his shoes and his socks felt mealy against his feet. There was a pair of galoshes in his office, but Marty was reluctant to wear them. They made him feel old.

The damage to the lawn was worse than he first thought. Off the worn path there were abundant pits and divots that would require professional attention. He knew that the students, as a matter of course, did as much casual injury to school property as they could get away with, so an entreaty to avoid walking on the pitch would backfire. Maybe he should fence the whole thing.

Drawing closer to the stand of pines at the perimeter he could see that the trees were indeed losing needles and that the bark was peeling off in curlicues to reveal more of the blood-coloured layer beneath. He coughed loudly so that any students lingering in the bushes would hear him coming and make themselves scarce.

There was a breeze and yet the area stank of stale tobacco smoke. The ground was carpeted with a pus-yellow foam, trampled thousands of cigarette filters. Marty saw the cause of the trees' distress: their trunks had been carved up. Using pocketknives and keys, he supposed, the smokers were scratching their marks into the bark. Names and dates. Solitary oaths—"cunt," "fuck," "shit." One enterprising young Michelangelo had taken the time to render the five-point leaf of a cannabis plant. Marty and Hank were celebrated as inveterate cocksuckers. A primitive stick figure rendering had Hank nailing Marty in the ass, their identities "Dev" and "Luggy" cut into their balloon heads. No one was spared. Abe Summers was a fairy. Ms. Foley was a whore. Pitts was a tool. Marty was shown in another drawing to possess an oversized organ, hungrily detained in the outlandish maw of an unnamed, though anatomically specified, female kneeling before him. As if her skin had erupted in a blistering pox, the woman's form was covered with dozens of tiny swastikas. Surely Sophie, Marty thought.

Some students were goats. Barry Myers, a morbidly obese lad who graduated three years ago, was immortalized in cellulose. For some reason Dorothy Chan, a brilliant, virtually blind Chinese girl who passed through the school five or six years earlier, was singled out for scorn. Audrey Caddigan was said, in a dispatch so recent as to be still oozing sap, to "eat cum" and was depicted, with a few deft strokes, lying legs upward in a receptive V. There were strange symbols, stylized stars and lightning bolts and swirls, accompanied by one of two names, "Blags" or "Exks." There was, to Marty's knowledge, no youth gang activity in town, and even if there were it would unlikely be part of the bourgeois lives of his fold. They must be some loosely bound cliques, their names a cryptic pop reference, something lifted from street argot, or that version of it translated by black middle-class entertainment industry hucksters, the bejewelled Puff Doggy licence holders, and sold to white kids like so much breakfast cereal. Still Marty worried what the glyphs meant. You could find trouble anywhere. He'd read that one of the Columbine killers had shown up at the school that day in his BMW. He felt rising in himself a sentiment he consciously and daily gnawed against like a bit in his teeth: a disgust for teenagers.

Further into the grove circles of seating had been fashioned by dragging fallen tree trunks together to work as benches under the cover of the largest pines. Marty stepped on something that splintered under his weight. It appeared to be a bottle for prescription medicine. Looking at the shards of plastic he noticed that here, mixed with the cigarette butts and rusty pine needles, were small phials, no doubt once containing drugs, what sort he couldn't guess. The air was sour and charred. A burnt mattress, springs strung with ribbons of melted plastic like candy floss, was tossed into the bushes.

Beyond the pines, spruce and fir took over. The forest wasn't open, but Marty could see trails, almost tunnels, leading away toward the golf course. There was, no doubt, evidence of other, more sinister goings-on up there, things he was better off not knowing.

This wasn't school property so there was little Marty could do. There was someone at City Hall he could call, though he would want to make sure that the police didn't get involved. He'd discuss it with Hank.

The damp air was making his bum knee throb.

Marty returned to the school along the mud track, which led to the rear entrance. He was about to pull the heavy door open when he saw, stuck to the heel of his shoe, looking like a beached squid, a used condom. He scraped it off against a concrete step.

The door closed behind him. Marty was buffeted by heady fumes and wrapped in darkness. He instinctively reached for a switch. His fingers ran across a wall that was tacky to the touch and found that the lights were already on. He blinked to hasten his eyes' adjustment and saw the first stage in Alan Pitts's planetary project.

Marty had been informed of the schedule but had forgotten that the Science Club had painted the corridor completely black the night before. Fluorescent lights ran the length of the ceiling but the walls were sucking in every ray sent them. The paint job did nothing to evoke the cold infinity of space, rather it coiled and closed in on you, scat hot and stifling, a devilish bowel.

As Marty padded down the passage, soft sounds escaped the rooms off the hall: lecture rhubarb, the scratchy advance of chalk across a blackboard, the bubble and clink of students conducting their labs. He would ask Alan to hurry the project along.

Entering the front office area Marty saw that Hank was holding court. He was sitting on the edge of his desk, shirt sleeves rolled up, speaking to a group of six or seven men and women. Marty could tell by their dress, their aura of righteousness, that they were some of Hank's environmental acolytes. Marty and Hank needed to talk about the pine grove. It was now more than a question of the propriety of Hank holding these sorts of meetings at work; this shit was getting in the way of the orderly operation of the school.

Mrs. Norris was at her desk, holding the handset of the phone out toward Marty, her hand cupping the mouthpiece. "Gerry Hayden for you," she said.

"I'll take it in my office."

Marty picked up the phone without bothering to remove his overcoat. "Hello," he said.

Hayden was talking to someone in his office, his phone was obviously held away from his mouth. He hadn't heard Marty.

"It's just fucking zoning, okay? Who do we know at the airport authority?"

Through his office window Marty spied Russell Malan pulling up across the street. Marty glanced at his watch. The boy was forty-five minutes late returning from lunch.

Hayden returned to the phone. "Hello?"

"Hello," answered Marty.

"Mr. Devereaux, Gerald Hayden. Sorry about that ... but it's always something, you know?"

"Yes."

"How have you been?"

"Well."

"So, I'm wondering. You never got back to me."

"I didn't know I was supposed to," said Marty, watching Russell Malan step from his car. A girl Marty did not recognize was exiting the passenger side. Her artificially orange hair was held up with what seemed to be chopsticks or knitting needles.

"Sure. We talked about you establishing a school as part of our new housing development."

"No. We talked about private schools in the abstract, Mr. Hayden. As I recall our meeting concerned your daughter. I take it you have decided not to enrol her at The Red Pines."

The girl from the car looked to be crying. She stopped before crossing the street, buckled at the waist, and retched on the pavement. Russell, ambling toward the front doors of the school, either hadn't noticed or didn't care.

"Well, not this late in the school year." Hayden was making it up as he went along. "But we're still thinking about next September."

"We limit our class size, Mr. Hayden. There's a waiting list. I wouldn't put it off too long."

Hayden must have blown air into the phone for there was a rough pulse of distortion. He thought Marty brazen. If he wanted to enrol his daughter they would damn well make space.

"Oh, well, I'm sure we'll be all right," Hayden said. "As for helping us establishing a school, are you, personally, interested? I know your partner couldn't be involved, and if it would cause any friction between you two …"

"I'm sure it would," said Marty. A button on his phone lit up. Someone else was calling.

"Even a consultative role?"

"What would that entail?" Marty asked.

"Look, I want to say something. I disagree with your friend Mr. Lundrigan about the Perroqueet Downs, but I respect his right to an opinion. Okay?"

"Okay," said Marty.

"So you think it over. If you can come up with some way that you can work with us on this without jeopardizing your relationship with Mr. Lundrigan, call me. You know if there were anyone else in this community I could make this proposal to, I would."

"I don't see that there is any way I could work on it."

"Think about it. That's all I'm asking."

"I will."

"Great. I have to go, Marty."

"Goodbye, Mr. Hayden."

Through his window Marty could see the girl wiping vomit from her mouth with the sleeve of her sweater, an oversized boys' navy with Red Pines crest, $85. Being sick only made her more upset; the muscle spasms that had tossed out the contents of her stomach were now a motor for sobs.

Marty headed for the front doors. As he stepped from his office

Mrs. Norris handed him, in passing, one of the small slips of blue paper they used for telephone messages. At the threshold of Hank's office Marty saw that things were winding up, they were congratulating one another, shaking hands and hugging in a manner entirely inappropriate for people conducting business. They'll be singing "Kumbaya" next, thought Marty.

Marty was in search of the girl but saw Russell Malan down the hall, closing his locker. Marty shouted.

"Russell!"

The Malan lad stopped and looked skyward with exasperation, being caught coming in late by Mr. Devereaux was evidently a bore. Marty marched on him.

"Where were you, Russell?"

"Out, sir," said the boy.

How Marty longed to swat Russell, to let his arm swing wide and bring the flat of his hand crashing into one of the boy's freakishly small ears.

"Yes, that's evident, Russell. But you're late. You're supposed to go by the office and get a late slip from Mrs. Norris."

Russell rolled his eyes. He shuffled toward the office, making a point of ever-so-slightly brushing against Marty as he passed.

"Wait," said Marty. "Who was the girl in the car?"

"I don't know what girl you're talking about, sir," Russell answered without turning around to face him. Marty knew it would be useless to pursue the matter.

"Your grades are slipping, Russell. Exams are three weeks away. Watch it."

This brought Russell around. His lower jaw was moving from side to side, stretching the skin on his face. A vein on his temple stood out.

"Yes, sir," he said, looking Marty in the eye. "I'll watch it."

Marty waited for the boy to walk the length of the corridor and turn the corner toward the office before setting off again to find the girl.

He bound upstairs, scanned both wings, and saw not a trace.

She was not lingering outside the school's front door.

From the exterior corner of the building Marty looked toward the pine grove but could see no sign. He walked across the street to Russell Malan's car. There, near the front fender on the passenger side, was the pool of the girl's issue, bile and french fries and something else vegetal. Some had splashed on a headlight.

Because the blue slip of paper Mrs. Norris had handed him was crumpled and moist, Marty realized his hands were clenched. He unfolded and read the note. He and Sophie were invited to supper at his brother's that night. It was short notice. Hadn't he just attended Rex's graduation dinner? Marty was thinking it through, realizing that the event at the vocational college had been a full two months earlier, when he saw, coming through the front doors of the school and heading toward him, Russell, his coat on.

"Where the fuck do you think you're going, Russell?" Marty immediately regretted the profanity—he was seething and needed to reign himself in.

"Home," said Russell carelessly. "Mr. Lundrigan told me to go home." The boy noticed the vomit on his car and winced.

☿

"When did we start sending kids home, Hank?" Marty asked.

"He was insolent." Hank, preoccupied with some documents on his desk, didn't seem to think it was of much consequence. "He wasn't listening to a word I said. Just giving me the 'Yes, sir. No, sir. Three bags full, sir' routine."

"We are paid to deal with the problems, Hank. Not to send them home. This is a private school."

"We've done all we can for Russell. More. I've got better things to do with my time."

"Like holding meetings about the Downs?"

"What meetings?"

"Just then, those people here in your office."

"That was the Downtown Neighbourhoods Association, Marty."

"Same thing."

Hank huffed in disbelief. "You're all sweaty."

"'Cause I haven't stopped for the past hour, Hank. The trees out back are dying. The students have hacked up the bark."

"Yes, and …?"

"Trees, Hank! Trees!"

Hank knew he was being mocked. "Call the City."

"No." Marty sounded defeated. "You can tell there's been drugs and, besides, it's … it's just a stinking mess. It would reflect terribly on The Pines."

"Then what do you propose we do?"

"I don't know," said Marty.

"Jesus, Marty," said Hank. "I thought you knew it all."

♀

Marty called Rex planning to beg off dinner but before he had time to offer an excuse, Rex ran down the elaborate menu he was preparing. Marty said he'd be there by seven and, though he hadn't spoken to her, offered Sophie's regrets.

The May days were finally beginning to feel longer. Walking from his car to Rex and Meredith's house, Marty could feel heat from the setting sun on his face.

He entered Rex's without knocking and found himself crowded into the porch with Jackie Spurell. She was in well-worn jeans and a nylon windbreaker. Her cheeks were pink from the out-of-doors and she carried a draft of spring air. Her hair was longer and wilder than when last they'd met.

"Oh, hello," she said. Marty could tell she had forgotten his name.

"Marty," he volunteered.

"Right," she said, "Principal Marty, saviour of the Perroqueet Downs."

"No. That's my partner, Henry Lundrigan. I ..."

Jackie began to nod her head; it was coming back to her.

"Right, right, right. Sorry! I remember now. You hadn't been out there ... to the Downs," she said.

While Jackie did not recall Marty, he had been unable to forget her. She was tormenting his dreams almost every night, engaging in acts that Marty, only months ago, would have found unforgivably degrading. Perhaps it was because she was a stranger, and so cipher, that her image had taken its particular role in his malady (that was how Marty thought of it, as an illness from which he would eventually recover). Even the subconscious had rules, if less rigorous than those of the waking life, which did not allow people doing certain things. The fact that Marty did not know Jackie and was unlikely to encounter her in the course of daily business made it possible to leave his shameful REMs at his bedside, forgotten by breakfast. Indeed because Marty knew his nocturnal visions were merely symptoms of some virus or brain-heat, he almost found it funny to be pressed up against the woman whose phantom, the night before, had for their mutual pleasure drenched him in scalding streams of some unknown liquid. *Almost* found it funny.

Meredith was coming down the hall waving a five-dollar bill like a toy flag.

"Are you staying for supper?" Marty asked Jackie.

"No, no," said Jackie. "No such luck. I'm collecting. For mental health."

Meredith handed her contribution to Jackie, who began writing out a receipt.

"Come on now, Marty, you're made of money," said Meredith. "Make a contribution."

"Sure," said Marty. He took out his wallet. There was a twenty- and a fifty-dollar bill inside. He handed the red fifty-dollar note, nutty old Mackenzie King glowering out of it, to Jackie.

"How much?" asked Jackie.

"Fifty," said Marty.

Meredith looked to Jackie. Both women seemed embarrassed.

"That's generous," said Jackie.

Marty felt awkward. It was too much to give, especially with Meredith having offered up only five bucks. Did it look like he was trying to impress or put on a show of being better off than his sister-in-law?

"It's … you know, something I'm concerned with … personally." Was he saying that he was mentally ill? "I … had serious problems with insomnia and, well … lately I've been sleeping, but I have these terrible … well, not terrible, but profound, dreams, you know, and I wake up feeling just awful."

"Yeah, Rex said that even when you were a teenager, hey?" Meredith spoke up, saving him, giving his gesture legitimacy. Marty supposed she was so long defending or advocating for the disadvantaged and downtrodden that only in his weakness could she warm to him. "Up padding around the house half the night," she said.

"Drove our father crazy," Marty said. "Mom worried, too."

"I must go on," Jackie said. Marty stepped into the front hall to make way for her.

"What we talked about before, during the dinner thing at the vocational college, about the Downs," he said. "I am going up there some day."

Jackie was already on the sidewalk but the door was still open. For a moment it seemed she hadn't the slightest idea what Marty was talking about.

Then she said, "Call me. I'll go," and closed the door.

"Rex is in the kitchen," Meredith said.

"When we were teenagers …" Marty said.

"Yeah?" answered Meredith.

"Rex slept like a log."

♁

But tonight Rex was out of sorts. His agitation was manifested in his drinking heavily—vicariously—through Marty. With the hand of a master alkie, popping the bottle's cork with the index finger and thumb of the same hand by which he clutched the neck, Rex poured his little brother a succession of tall whiskies. He was preparing risotto and was obliged to stand next to the stove so that he could stir. His timing was off because Cathy was late. Marty sat at the small kitchen table, his eyes level with Rex's belly.

"We've reconsidered your offer," Rex said.

"Offer?" Marty was getting hammered.

"To take Cathy at The Red Pines. Next September. We were going to discuss it with you tonight, as a family."

"Great," Marty said, though it wasn't. He realized that he had only made the offer assuming Meredith would not accept. Though it would inevitably sometimes be so, The Pines wasn't supposed to be a dumping ground for troubled students. Russell Malan had been a project they'd taken on of necessity. Cathy, Marty supposed, would be the first case of obligation.

"She's just screwing up royally at Frank Moores. When she goes. Have another drink." He poured Marty his third triple. "Good, hey? Islay."

"Yeah," said Marty, though he could scarcely tell one Scotch from another.

"MEREDITH!" Rex bellowed over Marty's head. "ANY SIGN OF THAT GIRL?"

"No." Meredith's voice came from the second floor. "Just start without her!"

♂

The whisky had dulled Marty's palate and now, at the table, Rex was plying him with some Italian red wine. The risotto, which to him looked like some wet, undercooked rice, was unaccountably rich for something that had so little taste. He hadn't yet tackled his daunting serving of gluey osso bucco—what was all the fuss about Northern Italian cuisine?—and was already full.

Rex and Meredith's consternation over Cathy's tardiness was evident in the way they went at their meals: Rex, with uncharacteristic care, picking off tiny morsels, and Meredith trowelling hers around the plate.

"She does it on purpose," said Rex, laying down his fork.

"She's a teenager. They're scatterbrained. She forgot," countered Meredith.

"My thinking is that if she's driven a little harder, academically, she'll focus." Rex addressed this remark to Marty but it was meant for Meredith.

"The risk being, of course," said Meredith, "that she'll become frustrated and rebel even more."

"School's just one part of it," Marty said, feeling he should reduce their expectations. "The program at The Pines will help but she's got to want to ..." but Marty wasn't sure what Cathy would have to want and was relieved to be interrupted by Meredith.

"While it's fine to have hopes, I don't think there's anything to be gained by setting some ... standard or goal."

"What is the difference?" Rex responded, and they were off, picking up the argument they'd been having before Marty arrived, likely one that had been raging for days. The booze made it easy for Marty to tune them out.

In the dining room was a fireplace. The mantel was crowded with framed photographs. There was a picture of Meredith, scarf wrapped about her head, in a baked Ethiopian landscape during the famine. Another, taken in the aftermath of some demonstration against the World Bank, showed her against a savaged storefront. In both photos, which had pride of place to the front of the display, she was beaming. Rex's snaps had to do with the theatre. He, droopy-eyed and toothy, in the company of the fruits and fellow alcoholics who performed his interminable Newfoundland social histories. His two-and-a-half-hour ten-hander about a strike in the lumber woods. His bladder-torturing three-act sealing disaster. The shows had made his name at home and then in Toronto but were not broad enough to have been popular and made any money. It was a shame that Rex didn't do comedy. They loved a funny Newfie on the mainland.

Here was Rex standing before a show poster; here trying and failing to affect glamour at an awards dinner. The most recent family photos of Rex, Meredith, and Cathy together were five or six years old, and were shouldered out of the way by those of Mom and Dad at their business. Even as a toddler Cathy appeared joyless. At the back of the mantel, obscured by the others, was a larger black-and-white photograph. Marty needed only to see a corner of the image, the sun on the tips of the rods, a coniferous forest in the background, an aerosol of black flies thick enough to diffuse the light, to know it showed him and Rex as boys during a fishing trip on the Gander River. Rex, then at six feet, was four inches shy of his final, towering height, but was already the widest, stretching his hip-waders to their limit, looking there on the pebbly beach like a bath toy. Marty, if his grin was an indication, was the happiest. That holiday was an idyll of big, plentiful pink-bellied trout. Marty had not so much forgotten about the trip, only not thought of it lately, as though it was leaving the range of memory. He couldn't now fathom what in the world would make him smile like that.

Marty suddenly wanted to interrupt the argument and ask Rex whether he missed their parents. They had died in a highway accident fourteen years earlier. Based on the skid marks—two abrupt black crescents—the police concluded that their father may have swerved to avoid something, an approaching vehicle drifting into their lane or an animal, or perhaps nodded off and lost control of the vehicle. On that moonless night the car left the road at 130 km/h and smashed into a boulder the size of a house, an "erratic," a random geological hazard, dumped there by a receding glacier.

The front door of the house opened and then closed heavily.

"Cathy?" Rex called.

"Yeaaaah?" she answered, already shuffling up the stairs.

"Dinner's on the table. Remember, Uncle Marty was coming."

There was a considered moment of silence followed by a theatrical sigh. She entered the dining room, the doleful rhythm of her step that of a pallbearer. She went to her seat and dropped into it, letting her limbs and head hang limp. She squinted at Marty's plate, trying to make out what was on it.

"Is that meat?" she whined.

"Oh, *jaysus,*" said Rex. "Yes, it is meat."

"Cow," said Cathy.

"There's risotto," Meredith offered, her tone to Marty's ear uncharacteristically diplomatic. "You love risotto."

Cathy sneered at her mother. She took no notice of her uncle. "Does it have cheese in it?"

"Yes, it has cheese in it. It has Parmesan cheese in it … it's risotto," said Rex.

"That's dairy," Cathy said triumphantly. "I don't eat dairy. It's cheese. It's cow."

"It's a bit of cheese. You can eat a little bit," Rex said, reaching for the zone of pain in his lower back.

"She has said," Meredith was intent on defending Cathy, "that she isn't eating dairy."

"You do it on purpose, Dad."

"Coke and Pepsi and chips evidently don't have any cow in them. How about pot—is there any cow in pot, or in beer?"

"I didn't ask you to cook me supper," Cathy said.

"You live here, don't you?"

"I DON'T EAT COW!" The shriek cut a path in the air through which she escaped, running to her room.

These teen years were difficult ones, Marty would tell distressed parents, suggesting that they would, by some arbitrary date, come to an end. But, of course, they did not. Unhappiness was an unending condition in some. One needed only to look around to realize that, in fact, things didn't necessarily get any better. They often got worse. The depressed, the angry, the lonely rarely recalled their happy childhood. If Marty weren't such a hypocrite he would tell the parents instead, "That sadistic prick at the office whose career is in permanent advance, the moron running the department, the bitch who banged your husband for sport … imagine them as children."

Cathy was punishing her parents for her being among the unhappy many. Meredith's face and neck looked slapped. Rex was holding both hands against his back, as if thwarting a leak sprung in his guts. He pushed to arch his spine and inch himself out of his chair. He stood.

"And to think, Marty, that girl is one of the few things holding this marriage together," he said. "I'm not hungry."

4

Yvette: It was after Matins. The door was ajar. I heard every word.
Mariette: It was wrong of you to listen.
Simone: What was said?
Yvette: The Abbess strictly forbade Sister from staging the play.
Simone: But we have worked so hard.
Yvette: The Abbess said Saint Joan defiled the Church.

This last bit was inflected almost as a question, the word *Church* emphasized in the manner of the Valley talk they learned from television. Marty looked down at the copy of the script Abe Summers had provided him. The line was to have read "defamed" not "defiled." He turned again to the action, such as it was. Summers and he were seated in a line of folding chairs, probably where the seventh or eighth row would be. Marty craned his neck to see up over the stubby thrust at the front of the stage.

A big-boned girl in a nun's costume stood waiting, in shadow, stage left. They'd perhaps got the idea of what a nun should look like from *The Bells of St. Mary's,* for she was not at all French but Irish, like one of the Presentation or Mercy Sisters that had peppered the St. John's streets of Marty's youth.

For a moment lights came up backstage. Marty thought he glimpsed in the flash, above startled stagehands, a sprite or leggy monkey shinnying up a pole. The missed cue struck the actors upstage mute.

Abe Summers leaned into Marty, his breath lactic. "Arch in spots but rather sophisticated, don't you think?"

"Too clever by half," said Marty.

The nun, regaining her composure, moved—performing each step—toward the girls at centre stage. The girls, though supposedly attending a convent school (as represented by crafty *trompe l'oeil* stone walls separating them from the business backstage), were dressed in short skirts more appropriate to cheerleaders.

Simone: Is it true, Sister?
Sister: The Abbess says we may not perform the play.

The convent girls groaned in choral despair.

Sister: But as our Maid of Orleans heard voices calling her to battle I have heard yours upon the stage.

So the title *Voices,* thought Marty. The voice of God was the voice of children was the voice of the artist, et cetera, et cetera. Altogether too grand a theme but a welcome relief from teen suicide, that of at least half of the Drama Society's previous productions.

The lights dimmed upstage as backstage was revealed, this time on cue, the final scene of the play—the play within the play—that the girls would perform in defiance of the Abbess. The figure Marty had seen scaling the pole was now lashed to it with ropes.

"That's the Caddigan girl," whispered Summers.

She had the temerity to cast herself as Joan of Arc. Electric fans below, obscured by the fake stone wall, set crepe flames to licking the writhing saint. Amber lamps playing on the paper contributed to the effect.

Shaving one's head clean for the part was obviously asking too much. Miss Caddigan had teased her orange locks into a blossom echoing the pyre. Marty had seen the hair before, on her mother and on the hitherto nameless girl he'd witnessed being sick on Russell Malan's car. The roasting Joan was wearing only a beige body stocking. Her nipples and pubis masked by her rope halter, she appeared nude. The struggle against her bonds was a choreographed rolling of hips and shoulders. Her head was back. Her mouth was open.

"What's going on here, Abe?" Marty asked.

"I believe that Joan is overcome with religious ecstasy."

"Is that what it is? You learn about that in confirmation class?" Marty could feel Abe bristle. "I'd like to see more God and less of the girl."

"You're proposing making changes?"

"Why else would I have come down here? To give you a Tony Award?"

"They open in three days."

"It's a high-school play, Abe. It doesn't 'open,' it just happens." Marty didn't appreciate Summers bothering to volunteer an opinion. "Another thing, in the public system, because every kid has to get their turn, these 'entertainments' are interminable. This is a private school. I own it. I expect that every kid will get a star turn and I expect it will be shortened considerably."

Rising from his seat Marty noticed that the young performers had finished the scene and were standing on stage looking out at him and Summers. Miss Caddigan was now hanging from the post, letting the ropes take her weight. They were waiting for some comment, desperate for approbation.

"It was very good," Marty said. "Mr. Summers has suggested some minor changes and I agree with them. Just tremendous work. I'm impressed."

four

THE AIR OF THE SCHOOL was transformed in June. The sun coming through the windows catalyzed a reaction in the trapped exhalations of the students that, containing as they did elemental boredom (Bm^{11}) and dread (Dx^{283}), filled the place with dire vapours. Drawing one's breath seemed more a labour. There were pending exams but most of The Red Pines kids knew they would do well. The graduates' anxiety was more to do with the dawning realization that they must soon make the first consequential decisions of their lives. They, upper-middle-class chosen that they were, had next to pick a career path. Marty knew there might be a European interlude, a couple of the more earnest might do a stint of good works in some Third World shit-hole. Some would blow a few semesters on liberal arts, big thoughts, and serious fucking. But they would eventually have to choose. And this caused them to feel that they were now adults. It wasn't at all true. Their education would drag on for many more years. An equally specious profundity would overtake them again when they graduated from university, then when they completed a professional or graduate school, when they got their first significant position, when they got their first promotion, when they got married, when they got married again (feeling that their feelings the first time had, in retrospect, been false), when they saw their first big money, when their parents died. The only event that would truly change them was when they themselves had children and began anew the cycle of expectation.

Marty enjoyed preying on the graduating students' vulnerability. He would affect seriousness when speaking with them, as though they were now grown men and women, not boys and girls. He would leer knowingly at any young bucks who had given him grief, implying that their day of reckoning was nigh, that they now had no choice but to smarten up. This wasn't true either. Marty watched thousands of them move on and knew that charm and charisma or family connections would suffice. Hank had buckets of charm and it served The Pines enterprise better than Marty's business acumen or doggedness. Marty's contribution, his design for the school, was by its nature invisible and unacknowledged. It was just as well. Nobody saw past Hank's smile.

For Marty the most baneful manifestations of this misplaced gravitas were found at the graduation dance. Decked out in gowns and evening jackets the kids would sniffle their saccharine goodbyes to all their old friends, most of whom they'd see within the week, and, maudlin from booze and drugs, tear around town risking the seemingly meaningless later chapters of their lives. (To Marty's dismay even elementary schools had started holding graduation ceremonies. Ever-younger kids were getting a disproportionate sense of self-importance, learning that lesser and lesser accomplishments deserved praise.) So mawkish did Marty find the scene at The Red Pines grad that he managed, in his division of labour with Hank, to no longer make even a ceremonial appearance.

In return Marty took on the always too long concerts and recitals, the schedules of which more often interfered with Hank's family life. (Sophie, who was usually present at these events, laughed at Marty's impatience, telling him that duration was an aesthetic of the school concert.)

So it was the previous evening that Marty had endured two acts of *Voices*. Summers had heeded Marty's admonition to better cover the cast but not to more equitably share the limelight. He was flirting with insubordination. Parents who had come to measure their child's beauty and talent against that of the others didn't get the dog and pony show they wanted but something approximating a real play. Approximating. Marty could hear Rex in his ear pointing up the expository dialogue and speechifying. The cast and crew were happy enough, all hugs and kisses backstage, but Marty, grinding his teeth through the long second half, was going to insist on a production of *Grease* next year.

Pitts finally responded to Marty's memo asking that Pitts expedite the painting of the hallway by the science classes with an apology and an excuse. Exams meant the project would be delayed. Pitts would resume work in the summer, supervising student volunteers during his vacation. He reported that his team of keeners had so far only completed "some of the star fields" and the first of the panels, the planet Mercury. Pitts didn't have a class during the last period of the day so Marty scheduled a meeting.

It wasn't like Pitts to shit him, so Marty was disappointed when, standing before the wall, he saw swirling constellations, a stencil outline of the word *Mercury,* but no planet.

It was no wonder they were behind schedule. On this single panel there must have been several hundred stars. This worked against the gloominess of the pitch-coloured walls but induced in the viewer a dizziness or vertigo.

Pitts was short of breath when he arrived, late. He was becoming more scattered, thought Marty.

"Sorry," said Pitts.

"No tie, Alan."

Pitts reached to his neck.

"Sorry."

"Excellent job here, Alan," said Marty.

"Thank you."

"It's like … 3-D?"

"It's painting technique. *Chiaroscuro and Sfumato*. Italian. Anne Hopkins and Jim Cahill did it. Talented kids. They did the sets for *Voices,* too."

"Right. You told me you'd finished the planet."

"We did. It's there."

Pitts pointed to a dot at the centre of the panel, one only slightly bigger than its neighbours.

"You're kidding me, right?"

"No. It's Mercury. It's a tiny planet, only got a diameter of three thousand miles. The paintings will be to scale. Obviously it makes the point."

Marty squinted and saw that it was rendered more painstakingly than the stars, with a crater-pocked charcoal and silver skin. Brief rises on the planet's surface threw shadows. There were blast marks, fissures screaming outward from blisters. Recent collisions or volcanic activity, Marty supposed.

"It looks like the moon."

"Yeah, it does. Hotter, though. This was a miniature. It'll be easier to paint the larger planets. They won't take nearly as much time. Although Earth will be demanding. "

"I'm finding it a trial."

"What?"

"Nothing, a bad joke."

"It's all mathematical. We're just figuring out Mars now."

"All the stars here, Alan? Tell me you're not taking the trouble to …"

"Oh yeah, they're in the right position. That," Alan indicated a streak of white, "is Gomez, the comet. The degree of precision isn't great … well, actually it's terrible, but …"

"It's on your own time, Alan."

"I'm loving it, Marty. I didn't know half this stuff. Mercury's orbit is extremely eccentric, so they thought for a while there was another, inner planet, Vulcan."

"Fascinating."

"We're going there again."

"I don't follow," said Marty.

"We're going back to Mercury."

"Who's 'we,' Alan?"

"Us. Humans. The Earth. Earthlings, I guess." Pitts laughed. "Earthlings! On *Messenger*. It will launch in 2004. NASA."

"Well, that is … a good thing, I guess." Marty looked back at the wall. "What did you call it? *Sfumato?*"

"Yeah, *Sfumato*. Means 'dark smoke.'"

The bell sounded.

"I got my homeroom, Marty."

"Of course," said Marty, his words lost as up and down the hallway classroom doors opened to belch out students. The swelling mass swept Pitts away. Marty briefly had the sensation that he was sinking in the tide before, as quickly as they'd come, the kids were gone.

Walking away Marty thought that Alan might be going a little potty. Marty's affection for the man may have blinded him to the signs. It was easy to mistake an unhealthy obsession for enthusiasm. Maybe there was trouble at home and Alan was just making work for himself to get away from it. Regardless, Marty would now have to keep an eye on Mr. Pitts. Marty realized he had fooled himself into thinking The Pines was beginning to run itself. He would always have to be there watching over things, forever the steward. If it wasn't the conduct of a teacher it would be a toilet overflowing or kids cutting up the trees out back. Marty was a designer, a builder, not a manager. This day-to-day aggravation was a waste of his time and it would never end.

He made for Miss Zwitzer's class. He needed to talk, to test the clarity of his thoughts by hearing them said aloud. Sophie didn't have a homeroom so would be free. But when he got there he saw, through the window in the door, that she was with a student, the Caddigan girl. They were seated quite close together, leaning in as if to share a confidence, their legs touching. Audrey Caddigan was speaking, Sophie listening.

The Red Pines didn't, couldn't, have a guidance counsellor. It would be admitting that some of the kids had problems or that their course in life might be in doubt. And the position would have been a nonproductive salary unit.

Marty turned for his office. It was just as well Sophie was otherwise occupied. She didn't give a damn about his problems, or was smart enough not to let herself care until she and Marty had invested more in one another. In answer to his woes she would simply suggest he quit, try something new. Like that was even remotely possible.

Hank's voice came over the PA making the end-of-day announcements. The school year was winding down, band instruments were to be returned or alternative arrangements made (Marty wondered whether they charged a summer rental fee—the damn things had cost him over fifty thousand dollars, and that was from a bankruptcy auction!), the exam schedule was to be posted tomorrow. Hank droned on. Orders were being taken for the yearbook (Marty made a mental note to have a last-minute editorial glance), and congratulations were extended to three Red Pines students who had garnered medals in a national math olympics. You couldn't buy advertising like that. Marty would thank and commend their teacher, Mr. Pope. A small bonus, a few hundred bucks, was warranted. Mr. Devereaux was asked to come to the office for a message.

"Finally," said Hank, "there will be a gathering today at four o'clock outside City Hall to protest municipal development policy, in particular the plan to build a subdivision on the Perroqueet Downs."

The last words, cranky with distortion, bounced off the hard walls. A low-pitched, wet *phthump*—Hank's thumb leaving the microphone's fat "talk" button—punctuated the insult. How *could* he? The speakers sizzled as the system powered down. Marty ran.

When he reached the office the pressure radiating from within his knee was excruciating. Mrs. Norris was waiting for him, but Marty held his hand up to her face to stop her from speaking and went directly for Hank.

Hank was in his office, pulling on a sports coat. He'd already removed his tie. Marty wished he'd wait until he was home, wouldn't walk past the parents waiting outside with an open collar. It was from this cavalier attitude to dress that Pitts no doubt took his cue.

"What the hell was that?" asked Marty.

"Was what?"

"The announcement. Encouraging the students to join some protest at City Hall."

"Encourage? No."

"Totally out of order, Hank. Nothing to do with the school."

"Becoming politically conscious and involved is educational. Being engaged in the democracy. Civics. They're learning to—"

"It's not a debate. You can't do this."

"Let's vote on it, Marty. Hey, whaddaya know? It's a draw."

"No, no, no, Hank. Doesn't the bank get a vote? Last I checked they owned more of this joint than you or I. Funny thing about it is, when the operation goes up the spout, they're still going to want their money back."

Hank appeared to be giving this last point some consideration.

"Marty," he said, "I'm thinking about trying to make the school paperless."

"What?"

"Paper is the biggest constituent of landfills. Most people think it's biodegradable, but it can take forever. With the technology we have available maybe we could make some courses paperless."

Marty could not think what to say. Mrs. Norris tiptoed up behind him.

"A Jackie Spurell called," she said. "Left a number. Said it was urgent. That's why I asked Mr. Lundrigan to page you."

When Marty turned around Mrs. Norris was holding out the message slip at arm's length, as though Marty might be dangerous, might snap like a dog. He took the note from her hand. On it was Rex's phone number.

"Meredith had Rex call me. I couldn't think what to do so I phoned you," Jackie said. She had answered when Marty telephoned his brother's place. As she spoke he could hear, in the background, Rex storming and roaring, Meredith keening. "Rex was going to call the police, but I persuaded him to wait until you got here."

"The police?"

"Well ... Rex keeps saying that Cathy stabbed Meredith."

"Stabbed?"

"She hit her with a knife. A slash more than a stab."

"When did this happen?"

"Half-hour, forty-five minutes ago."

"Is she going to need stitches?"

"I thought so at first—there was a fair bit of blood—but it doesn't look as bad now."

"Blood?"

"You're coming down here, right?"

All he could say was, "Of course. Right away."

♆

Marty went inside without knocking and immediately sensed discord. There was fault in the atmosphere. As if the building had capsized and its contents been tossed about, the front hallway was littered with mail, an errant rubber boot, and, inexplicably, scraps of bread crust. It was quiet, as if unoccupied, but in the slanting columns of afternoon light Marty saw lively twisters of dust motes, a trail left in the air by recent tumult. Marty turned his head. Rex was standing in the middle of the living room. Fingers knotted into sclerotic fists, he was kneading the small of his back, rooting at a nub of pain.

"Meredith's in the kitchen," he said.

This seemed to be a request that Marty proceed there immediately and not discuss the matter with him.

There was blood on the kitchen floor, more than he expected, splattered and smeared over mismatched brightly coloured tiles. It was so like Rex and Meredith to do the floor in such a manic pattern. Now with the blood, inky against the dark, the clownish checkerboard turned his stomach.

Stepping into the room he saw Meredith seated at the rough wooden kitchen table, her hand wrapped in a dishtowel. Jackie was standing over her, hands on her friend's shoulders. Meredith had been crying.

"Where's Cathy?" Marty asked.

"Up in her room," said Jackie.

"I'm sorry we called you, Marty," said Meredith.

"No, it's fine."

"It's unfair of us to ask that …"

"Look, I see this kind of problem all the time," Marty lied. "Don't worry."

"Rex thinks we have to call someone, a professional, like a social worker or a family counsellor."

"Don't," said Marty. "They might be obliged to call the police. It'll make things worse. There's no saying where that will end."

"We're at a loss, Marty."

Marty looked down and saw at his feet the serrated breadknife with its egg-yolk yellow plastic handle. There were beads of blood on the scalloped teeth of the cutting edge. On the flat of the blade retracting pools were drying in whorls.

"Let me talk to her," Marty said.

Cathy's room was on the third floor. Climbing the steps, Marty was guiltily preoccupied with the thought that he would not have come to Meredith and Rex's aid if it hadn't been Jackie calling. He felt ridiculous being in thrall with a woman who viewed him as the most casual of acquaintances, as no more than her neighbour's brother-in-law. His foolishness had landed him in the middle of a grave situation for which he was totally unprepared. But Jackie *had* called, hadn't she? She remembered him. Off the top landing all the doors were ajar but one. He knocked.

"Don't come in, please." Cathy had not a hint of distress in her voice.

"It's your uncle Martin."

"So?"

"Your parents phoned me."

"I don't care. Why does it matter who called you?"

She was right, Marty realized. Theirs was not a close relationship. She had, only minutes earlier, stabbed her mother. That her parents called hardly recommended him.

"I'm coming in," said Marty, unable to imagine what else to do.

Cathy was seated on her bed, legs hugged against her chest, looking over her knees at Marty. On the wall, posters—girl singers, Britneys or Christinas with their bare bellies and depilated mons Veneris; and muscular (but scarcely more mannish) boy bands—sagged and bowed under their own weight, push-pins at their corners tearing the glossy paper. On the dresser a collection of horse figurines of substantive manufacture had lost their brushed chestnut lustre beneath a deposit of dust. The bedspread had pinkish fringes. Garlands of candy-coloured costume jewellery were strung around the bedposts. A wall-mounted shelf, perhaps a yard long, held a dozen or so volumes of well-meant, tepid literature for young people, local product written by friends of her parents, the kind of pseudo-medieval fantasy and nonpenetrative adventure beloved of school librarians and read by lonely girls. It took Marty a moment to realize what was wrong. The room belonged to a twelve-year-old. In a show of nihilistic lethargy, Cathy hadn't touched a thing in years. The pictures and objects were to be read ironically. It was an intent Marty found mordant in one so young.

"What happened?" asked Marty.

"She was driving me crazy."

"So you stabbed her?"

"I didn't stab her. The knife hit her knuckles. I was cutting a bagel in half. Everybody is, like, so overreacting. They overreact to everything. They're professional overreactors, that's what they do for a living. And she hit me first."

"She hit you?"

"She slapped me in the face. Hard."

"That doesn't seem like your mother."

"I swore at her. She slapped me. She was washing dishes so her hands were all wet and soapy. It really hurt."

"What were you fighting about?"

"Comet Gomez."

"How's that?" asked Marty. He vaguely remembered Alan Pitts saying something about a comet.

"I was just getting a bagel and she starts in again about the girl and the comet, about like how amazing it is that this crippled girl can discover a comet. Like that really happened! Like her parents didn't actually find it. Like her dad doesn't like work in like an observatory or something. And Mom, she's been going on about this comet for like weeks or months. So like now besides getting good marks so I can go to med school so I can join Médecins Sans Frontières and get a boyfriend that she'd fuck, on top of all that, like in my spare time, I'm supposed to go out and discover a new supernova or something!"

Cathy could tell the crack about getting a boyfriend that her mother found fuckable really freaked him out. He like *locked* or something, his jaw waggled before clenching, and he straightened up with a start like someone put a finger up his ass. Uncle Marty was such an unbelievable tool. And this was who her parents turned to! Better than the cops, like her father was screaming. She thought Dad was seriously coming unhinged lately, and that maybe he was capable of calling the police on her.

It seemed impossible that those two, Uncle Marty and her dad, were brothers, unalike in every respect but that they were so obviously damaged. Didn't Marty smoke, though? Her father had quit years ago, soon after giving up the booze.

"Do you have a cigarette?" she asked.

"Are you allowed to smoke?"

"I do all the time. I just lean out the window."

He was obviously badly in need himself, going directly to the window and opening it. She accepted an offered cigarette, though to smoke it she was obliged to squeeze through the window, shoulder to shoulder with her creepy uncle. Even in the breeze and over the cigarette smoke she could smell his cologne or aftershave, maybe deodorant.

♇

Leaning out over the window ledge Marty's head was surrounded by maple leaves, the crown of a volunteer, now crowding the tiny yard below and the air above. He remembered that years earlier there had been a fuss made about the tree, Rex saying he would cut it down before it grew to shade the garden and house—to "etiolate the lot" is what he'd actually said; Cathy, fresh from environmental indoctrination in school, demanding that it be saved so that it could continue to produce oxygen for the planet; Meredith, predictably, siding with her daughter.

But Rex was right. The garden was all but dead. What grass remained was scraggly and pale, almost completely overtaken by moss. A round metal table and chairs beneath the tree went unused because of the constant precipitation of gum, bugs, bird shit, and keys. It was as though some beast large and horrible had sneezed on the place. Removal of what had so quickly become a sprawling, light-seeking giant was now prohibitively expensive.

From the maple might be hewn the bows of a yoke for Rex's shoulders. Then he could better pull the load of petty domestic troubles, the small packages that together became tonnage, through his fat life: the kittens born inside a new sofa, the money lent to the brother-in-law, the Barbies flushed down the toilet, even the tiny head lice and the immeasurable weight of indelible ink on the fabric of your best trousers. Now this.

Seeing his niece with the cigarette in her mouth made Marty regret having given it to her. She was jammed up against the window frame, trying to avoid physical contact.

"So ..." he said, searching. "I don't think ... you should hit your mother with a knife or swear at her. I think, and I know this is the last thing you want to hear, but I think in my time if you struck your mother then your father had licence to beat you within an inch of your life."

"Times change, hey?" she said.

"Don't be saucy with me."

"Sure."

"And don't—" He paused for a moment and Cathy thought she saw him bare his teeth, flash them like a cornered crackie. "Don't *sure* me."

His cigarette was disappearing twice as fast as hers. She was toying with the idea of quitting, coming to the realization that she didn't much enjoy smoking. Watching Uncle Marty was watching a true junkie, a devoted slave. He sucked them back with such fury you could hear them crackle.

"Maybe," Marty said, "things might improve if, next year, you came to The Red Pines."

Cathy grimaced. She couldn't stand those smug, rich snots from The Red Pines.

"I'm only doing this for your parents. I offered it once and they're now thinking it's a good idea."

Cathy had expected platitudes from her uncle the emissary—"everybody loves you," "why are you so angry?"—maybe an invitation to take an extended, clammy hand, or even, God forbid, hugs. Lately Cathy's father wouldn't stop hugging people. She could see, and was deeply relieved, that embrace, perhaps even simple touch, was not an emotional instrument at Uncle Marty's disposal. Cathy realized she didn't know Uncle Marty at all.

"You'd have to smarten up," he continued, "and I haven't got the time or the inclination to baby you. In fact, I, and I'm sure you feel the same way, would like nothing better than for you to stay at Frank

Moores, with your friends. For that to happen you're just going to have to change. For a start, you're going to have to go downstairs and apologize. You're going to have to show some remorse."

He returned her gaze for the first time since coming into the room. The flesh around his eyes was folding into canyons and wadis in which wisps of smoke from his cigarette lingered. He looked older and more exhausted than should a man in his … what? Forties, Cathy guessed.

"I don't care if you mean a word of it," he said. "But your parents had better buy it."

"I can do that," Cathy said.

"Thank you."

He tried to smile at her but it came off as a wince.

"I didn't mean to cut her," Cathy said. "I just … like … when she slapped me … It was just a reflex."

♅

Bless the little bitch for making this easy, thought Marty. But "a reflex"? Maybe if you're a crocodile. He had encountered the reptilian brain in kids before—in *the boy* for one, amoral and automatic. This couldn't be the case with Cathy. She was a mess, but Marty sensed a beating heart and, in doing so, felt the sudden need to leave the room.

"I'm going back downstairs," he said. "I think you should come down in ten minutes or so."

"Okay."

Marty turned for the door. A thought occurred.

"Jackie Spurell," he said. "What's the story with her?"

"I dunno. Lives around the corner. Friends with Mom and Dad," said Cathy. "Bet she's loving this."

"Yeah," Marty said. "Is there something about her husband?"

"Mr. Spurell? Oh yeah, he like drove a plane off a runway. He's a real zombie. He's worse than Dad."

♀

"She feels terrible about it," Marty said. Rex had joined Meredith and Jackie in the kitchen. The three of them waited on his words as if they were wise. Rex looked grateful and beholden. Meredith, he could tell, was completely re-evaluating him. And Jackie … Jackie saw valiance, had the kind of look in her eyes usually reserved for firemen and paediatric surgeons. Such adoration was, in Marty's experience, always short-lived and so to be exploited with haste.

"A lot of stuff has built up, maybe it just had to come out." That sounded right, thought Marty. "Parents have such high expectations. So it's hard for a teenager today. There's peer stuff, too. And feeling that you're not yet an adult but no longer a child, not wanting to give up the security of childhood, not wanting to face responsibilities. The pressure is … lots. Lots of pressure." He was saying too much now, he could hear the bullshit coming through. "Probably the best thing to do now is … forget about it, forget it ever happened."

To illustrate his point Marty bent down, picked the bloodied knife from the floor, carried it to sink, and tossed it among the pots soaking in the fading suds.

This, gauging by the nonplussed mugs of his audience, was the wrong approach. And well Marty should have known. Rex and Meredith were inveterate dealers-with-*it,* talkers about *it,* sharers of *it.* They could never stomach the immediate solution of simple avoidance.

"For a period." Marty corrected his course. "Put it on the back burner for a couple of weeks. Get on with living."

Rex groaned. It was a low-frequency pulse from the bottom of his gut, belched sour.

"Rex?" said Meredith.

"My back," said Rex.

From upstairs came tentative footsteps. The quartet looked toward the ceiling as if they expected it to come crashing down.

"I've got to get back to the school," Marty said.

♁

Pulling into The Pines parking lot Marty saw Sophie striding for her car, chin thrust haughtily forward. Her eyes were needlessly shaded by large oval panes. Two ends of a scarf tailed her. She dared boots to the knee. So thoroughbred was her confirmation that she could get away with all of it.

Marty parked in a space that allowed him to intercept her.

"I went by your classroom earlier but you were with a student," he said.

"Yes."

"Did you hear the announcements?"

"What announcements?"

"On the PA, during homeroom."

"I suppose I must have," she said.

"Hank? Inviting the kids to join in some protest?"

"I didn't notice."

"We had a huge row about it."

"That's terrible." Growing restive, glancing toward her car, Sophie made no effort to sound sincere.

"I don't know how much longer I can put up with it," said Marty. "He just doesn't seem to care what I think. He's become reckless."

"Relationships end. You and Hank have been boyfriends for almost fifteen years."

"Come off it."

"Seriously, though, maybe it's over. Maybe it's no one's fault. If people didn't change ..." Sophie lost the thought.

"What are you doing tonight?" asked Marty.

"I've been asked to adjudicate a national piano competition in Montreal next November and a preliminary round in Vancouver in July. We're meeting for drinks and then dinner to talk it over."

"Who's 'we'?"

"Some people from the festival," Sophie said. "Some people from the music school. Heather, Kika, Clive. I introduced you to them at my annual, but I'm sure you don't remember."

Sophie's "annual" was a do she threw every August on the eve of the Royal St. John's Regatta, the venerable amateur sculls known locally as "The Races." She was right, he didn't really remember. He could summon faces, young new faculty from the university's School of Music, but put no names to them.

"I remember," he said.

Marty assumed he would be spending the evening with Sophie, that having not spoken with her earlier he now deserved her attention. He needed to talk about the scene at Rex and Meredith's, about Cathy slicing her mother. He'd leave Jackie out of his account. He waited for Sophie to invite him along or to suggest they meet later, but she said nothing. He had nowhere to go.

"I have to go to the office," he said.

"Don't work too hard," Sophie said. She started again for her car.

"Don't drive if you've been drinking," Marty called.

She looked back over her shoulder. It was none of his business.

♂

Strict limits on caffeine, nicotine, booze, and exercise were critical defences against insomnia, so Marty's nocturnal routine at home rarely varied: two smokes while watching the first half of late-night news on television and then to the bedroom. Eight-ounce glass of water on the night table. Once under the covers he would read twenty or thirty pages of an anodyne novel, espionage thrillers (ideally featuring the comforting certainties of the Cold War) or mysteries, something easily digested, before turning in. Contemporary literary fiction was more and more a feminine province, for and about women even when written by men, and of little use to Marty.

In the basement there was perhaps five hundred pounds of boxed-up English lit. Marty was granted (gifted, actually) his English degree just as the PoMo armies were advancing. Two years later the deconstructionist flag flew over the department. Marty made a few half-hearted efforts to read the new scholarship but found its abstruse formulations incomprehensible. He suspected imposture, but having faked and guessed his way through the academy wasn't confident enough in his own mind to level an accusation. Soon after graduating, and to his relief, he forgot most everything he had been taught about literature. Though now, because of the times or having finally "gotten it," the skeptical relativism of postmodernism was beginning to have some resonance. Like he needed that.

His rage at Hank ran adrenal. Tonight he sensed, dreaded really, that sleep might be elusive and delayed turning off the television once the national and international portion of the news was over. He lit a fourth cigarette. An adenoidal barker from the CBC came on with the local news. Because of years of "high grading," the shrimp being caught off the Funk Islands were too small and too few, and fishermen were taking their boats off the water.

Who was Clive? Sophie said she was meeting a "Clive," to whom he had allegedly been introduced, for drinks. He'd have remembered a "Clive." Maybe not.

A wolf was killing dogs in a community on the Labrador Coast. The reporter, a severe young woman, delivered her script to the camera. The shot was framed to show a desperate collection of shacks over her shoulder. Why, thought Marty, didn't the creature merely huff and puff and blow the houses down?

Would Marty be jealous if Sophie was getting some strange, from a Clive or even a Kika, on the side? Who was he to judge, an oneiric pervert in the service of Mistress Jackie?

And then it was Hank. Coverage of that afternoon's protest showed him standing in front of City Hall, speaking into a megaphone. "… A new way of looking at land, at our earth, our only earth … looking at it not necessarily as a tradable commodity like any other …"

Lofty nonsense, thought Marty. The people on the Labrador coast would take new housing over their hectares of tundra. The television showed a fair crowd, in the hundreds. Another reporter spoke. The group—a coalition of groups, they asserted—standing against the Perroqueet Downs project would next investigate legal avenues, pursue an injunction to forestall the bulldozers. Others took the megaphone. A portly city councillor opposed to the development was cheered when he proposed a park. Hank was interviewed by the reporter and clarified that he was not in favour of a park, that a park too was intrusive. As the reporter clewed up they showed file footage of the Perroqueet Downs, a slow pan revealed a windswept headland that fanned into the sea, inaccessible cliff-faced islands beyond. In the long shot, the video image pasty, it appeared almost featureless.

Marty turned off the television and went to the kitchen. He needed a drink and there was gin in the freezer. Opening the fridge he saw that its contents had been reorganized, bottles and jars wiped and put in laboratory-like order. The house cleaners must have been in.

He poured three fingers of gin into a tumbler and topped it up with orange juice, the only mix available.

Parks! Hank was against parks!

4

The pencils ceased scratching. Exams ended. The students slipped the confines of The Red Pines for the sun, and the building sighed at their leaving.

The marks were in and only three students had failed, among them, *the boy*. Abe Summers had given Russell Malan 30% in English. The young monster managed a 50% in math. Marty figured the teacher, Mr. Pope, hadn't the stomach to keep anyone back or, more likely, would do anything to be clear of Master Malan.

Three fat envelopes, so full that they tested the elastic band binding them, were waiting for Marty on his desk. The top envelope had his name written on it. It held a note of apology from Mrs. Caddigan and a wad of cash. The other envelopes were likewise stuffed—her daughter's tuition for the past year and the next—in mixed bills of various denominations. It was mostly hundreds, but there were fifties and twenties and even a few fives and tens. The bills were supple and downy, well circulated. From whence had they come? Marty was disgusted. Jesus Christ, it was like a dope deal. He put the envelopes in a drawer. Mrs. Norris would have to take it to the bank later.

Hank appeared in the doorway. Since their confrontation the two men kept contact to a minimum. They spoke daily but in the curt, businesslike nature of these exchanges they were both acknowledging that, as Sophie had suggested, their relationship had changed. Hank wore this with some sadness. Marty resolved that he no longer cared.

"Nothing we need worry about?" Hank asked.

"In what regard?" said Marty.

"Marks."

"Nope."

Hank walked away looking as if he longed to say more. Marty waited a moment before setting off in search of Abe Summers.

Marty found him clearing his desk.

"I was just about to come and see you," said Summers.

"Oh?" said Marty.

"Yes. I have a proposed curriculum for the new English class."

"Right."

Marty's expression must have conveyed his befuddlement, for Summers elaborated.

"The advanced English class. We spoke about it a few months ago."

"Yes," said Marty, remembering, "of course."

Summers handed Marty a sheet of paper with a lengthy paragraph of dense type—the proposed syllabus. Marty scanned the page for titles or names he might recognize. *Araby. Othello*. He was careful not to react to the inclusion of a post-colonial title. He knew it would be there: a novel of South Asia (whither the North?) or the immigrant experience penned by some Oxbridge Brahmin or, as in this case to force Marty's hand, a very fine new book by a hip cinnamon beauty. Abe would like nothing better than to record Marty's rolling eyes as evidence of racism or sexism when they were merely signs of boredom at the predictability of it. Maybe the Newfoundlander in Marty just envied his Imperial cousins being first past the "post-."

Marty knew a recent novel by a local hack on the list and pointed it out.

"I've read that book, aren't there dirty bits? And narcotics feature in the plot, if I recall."

"Right. I'd forgotten. I wanted something local, and it's easygoing, faintly amusing."

"Fluff. Get something else. A coming-of-age story, or better something historical," said Marty.

"Historical fiction?" Summers scowled.

"Sure. That would be nice."

Marty was aware of Abe's abhorrence for the genre. In his withering, if simple, criticism Abe deemed historical novels glorified book reports, history lite for those who couldn't be bothered with all those dates and poorly reproduced maps, who grew bored with *longueurs*. It all demonstrated, in Summers's view, a failure of imagination and a deplorable presumptuousness in speaking for the dead.

But Marty had a natural affinity for the craft. Intellectually dishonest though they might be, folks took comfort in tales of yore. It was of the present that no one could agree on the facts. Fiction with a contemporary setting could hold nasty surprises and so imbued the reader with a constant background dread. These were not books with which one wanted to curl up. People, these days, needed to know that the puppy didn't die before they started reading the damn book. And why not? thought Marty.

Marty once read a rather far-fetched evolutionary explanation for fiction claiming that its readers were "selected" because their taste for make-believe made them more conscious of the possible. They were consequently warier, better equipped to deal with the always startling exigencies of the future. (Marty supposed then that authors, scenarists of any sort really, Rex and his anxious ilk, had evolved into nature's great worriers.) By the same argument historical fiction was self-defeating, making life's dangers blissfully remote and so inuring its readers to risk. Summers's theory had it arse-foremost. It wasn't history that historical fiction's fans found difficult, it was fiction.

Marty never went into it with Summers because he knew that the real cause of Abe's disdain was that historical novels, unlike his own po-pomo wankfests, sold.

"Yeah. But nothing too recent. Period I mean. Nineteenth-century back is always safe."

Summers shrugged his acquiescence.

"I see you've failed Russell Malan," said Marty.

"Happily. I don't think I have ever encountered a student more contemptuous of learning."

"So the grade may have been prejudiced by your feelings for him?"

"Rather the opposite in fact. Being conscious of my bias I've always gone easy."

"Gee, that's big of you, Abe. But I regret not easy enough."

"I'm sorry?"

"I want you to pass him."

"I think not."

"Why?"

Summers gripped the edge of his desk with both hands.

"It's dishonest. Fraudulent."

"It's stage management," said Marty, his meaning lost on Summers.

"And … it isn't fair to other students who passed legitimately," Summers said.

"He's got deficits."

"Phhhhttt!"

"Dyslexia, then. Dysgraphia. ADD. Take your pick."

"You are fast, Marty. Dose him, then."

"If we Ritalin'd the boy … he'd probably kill someone." Marty pointed at Summers. "You, perhaps."

"Understand that passing Russell would simply prove to him that he needn't do the work, that someone will always intercede on his behalf."

"He's correct in that observation. Maybe he's smarter than you give him credit."

"I've no doubt he has some kind of calculating, predatory cunning." Wrestling a tremor of anger, Summers forced himself to speak with deliberation. "But there is no question that he did not score adequately on tests designed to assess his understanding of the material he was assigned. He failed the course. He did not make an effort. It's galling to suggest—"

"What purpose is served by keeping him back? The Malans will simply move him to another school, blaming his lack of achievement on us, no doubt. On you." Marty tried sounding conciliatory. "Abe, it's not as though he's going on to an English degree at university. Let the little monster get his high-school diploma. It won't hurt anyone."

"Why isn't Hank dealing with this? When he was tutoring the boy there were no problems."

Abe would prefer it were Hank standing before him, wouldn't he, thought Marty. Hank would act on principle, thoughtless of the consequences. Abe could take the opportunity to say how impressed he was by Hank's position on the Perroqueet Downs. Hank could commiserate with Abe over the dreadful state of arts funding, agreeing it was tragedy that Abe had to stoop to teaching to make ends meet. That he must suffer the added indignity of ungrateful, inattentive students! Insupportable! They could congratulate one another on their integrity, pat one another on the back for being paragons of social, cultural, and environmental high-mindedness.

"Hank doesn't know about it," said Marty. "I want you to pass Russell."

"I won't do it," said Summers.

"The sooner we pass him, Abe, the sooner we'll be rid of him. One more year. And is this really the place to stake out your moral terrain? Surely a man has only so many stands, so many battles in him. Why do you want to get exercised over this … piffle? It's a rich kid's mark in high-school English, it's not Munich."

"I won't do it," Summers said again.

"Then I will."

Summers looked away.

"Just don't act surprised when he shows up next September for grade twelve," said Marty. "And don't worry, he won't be in your precious advanced class."

Two hours earlier Cathy dropped her first hit of acid, a paper square smaller than a postage stamp featuring an image of Pikachu. Cathy would usually accept a drag off a joint, had done ecstasy five or six times (half of it shitty), and drank a little, less than most kids. Drugs weren't a big thing with her. Tonight there was this party and boyfriend Scott arrived at Jeanette's place with the LSD. Jeanette refused to take it. Cathy thought about it for a moment and then, out of curiosity and boredom, to provoke Jeanette, said she would. Absurdly, she felt reluctant to chew it and swallowed hurriedly. It was dry and she wondered if it stuck to the side of her throat. Would it work then?

She knew that there was something wilful and defiant in her decision, that part of her was doing something "bad" because this was the grad season and she felt resentment at being excluded. There were a bunch of graduation dances tonight. Her grade eleven affair had been last Friday. She had stayed home and listened to music. If she'd been asked to attend, if someone wanted to be her *daaate,* she would have scoffed at the notion. It was beneath her. The thought of her classmates in their gowns heading off to some Holiday Inn ballroom looking like circus animals, like performing monkeys or dogs, made her sick with embarrassment. Her so-called friends, Tanis and Colleen, who claimed to share her disgust for the ritual, abandoned their ideals and, once invited by guys from grade twelve they said they couldn't stand, had quickly accepted. It was disloyal and cruel of them to go. Cathy realized now that though she sometimes hung out with Tanis and Colleen, she didn't really like them that much. Jeanette, for all her weirdness, was always straight with her.

Cathy knew that somewhere within herself there was a need, a deep need, to have been asked to one of those dances. More distressing still was self-awareness of this need. She never questioned herself. Until now she had been sure of everything, had divided the world neatly into that which was "the decent" and, the overwhelming majority of all people and concepts, "the stupid." If those definitions slipped away, if you spent time analyzing your motives with self-knowledge, then you'd be paralyzed with indecision.

Scott swore it wasn't supposed to be a strong dose. About an hour after taking it he said he was starting to get off and wanted out of Jeanette's place for fear that he would have trouble dealing with her parents while stoned. Something was definitely up with him, his eyes were wild and his hair was swept and pasted over his head like it was greasy or wet. He yapped laughter at a couple of things that weren't in the least funny. Cathy had yet to feel any effect.

The plan was to get a bus, but at the stop Cathy said that with the night so warm she would walk. Jeanette whined and complained, probably not wanting to be alone with Scott, who was now unable to contain fits of hysterical giggling and making totally nonsensical observations: the pole marking the bus stop was, he reported, "like gum."

Cathy wasn't long gone when the bus carrying Jeanette and Scott passed her. Though it was almost empty and there were plenty of available seats she could see Scott standing inside. He looked crazed.

The light from inside the bus was pouring out its windows as a heavy phosphorescent gas, automotive ectoplasm, and possessed for Cathy a new beauty.

The bus would snake all over the east end on its way. Cathy's route was almost a straight line to the subdivision containing the house in which the party was being held. She would pass through three rings of the city's growth at their narrowest points, starting in a suburb built in the mid-sixties, its flat bungalows diminutive beneath the trees rising around them, then through a band of boxy vinyl two-storey affairs erected on seemingly infertile ground in the seventies, and finally she would arrive in a new development, so recently built that she had walked it only once before.

The acid took hold as she cut through a playground she knew, a shunt across the years, out the arsehole of one burb and up another. The hidden park's location was ill considered, a concession to some requirement by the municipality. So piss-stained and littered with broken glass was the tract of weeds that it was never used. A see-saw had not survived continual vandalism. There was a slide and swing set. Cathy sat in a plastic sling-seat, walked herself backward and pushed off. The chain in her hands was cool and then synaesthetically wet. She was conscious of the saliva in her mouth and couldn't stop swallowing. She looked up and saw the metal links streaming toward her, confirming she was hanging from strands of water. Something had happened to render the universe liquid, the rising swing brought her up toward a firmament not of a billion hydrogen/helium infernos but of spume. The stars were bubbles at the surface of the world. She surprised herself by letting go, and flying through the air she was swimming. She landed on her feet, letting the momentum set her scudding over the hard ground. She found a lane between two high-fenced properties accessing the park. Spilling from it she saw a fanned alluvial delta of sand, gravel, and litter. Suburban geophysical forces were at work. The rains that would have been thirstily consumed by the forests and marshes now ran freely off roofs and pavement, becoming torrents. Overwhelmed sewers blew geysers, the land erupting in spots to become new mountains, soft mountains. What was the study of the characteristic of being soft called? What was the science of softness?

The streets of the new subdivision were bulging, the slope to the rain gutters exaggerated. Town was swollen; town might burst.

Having neglected to get the street address from Jeanette, Cathy spent some minutes winding through the crescents and cul-de-sacs before finding her destination. Among lifeless neighbours it stood out, a demonic jack-o-lantern of a house, which, as she drew nearer, throbbed.

The front door, glass pane fractured, swung open. The carpet in the front hallway was mud-trodden and peppered with cigarette burns. The place was packed wall-to-wall with kids from all over, many of them too old to be at a high-school grad party. Cathy knew what was happening. Parents out of town, some kid decided to party with a few friends, word got out, turned virulent and spread, the kid was overwhelmed, unable to stem the tide of opportunistic crashers, of beery goofs and hooligans, of resentful hard tickets from poor neighbourhoods. The situation was out of control. The house was being trashed.

The music was earsplitting, so loud that, coupled with all the shouts and crashes, its source was impossible to determine. It could have been coming from the basement or the unseen opposite side of the living room. To Cathy it seemed to be coming from walls and floor itself. The house was in seizure.

Cathy thought she recognized some faces but needed to find Jeanette, even Scott. The atmosphere was poisonous and she felt as though she were getting more and more stoned by the minute. A towering jock swayed and collided with her, shoving her into a wall.

The air was like bread, like doughy white bread. She looked down. With every step a collar of bilious lather rose from the carpet to surround her sneakers. A bottle flew overhead, tumbling end over end, a bird full of shot, and exploded against a wall. Nobody paid it any mind.

The hallways were too long for a house, almost institutional. A line of boys was sitting on a long bathroom counter like it was a bench. They were passing a joint and hooting at a girl in her grad dress being sick in the toilet.

As Cathy plumbed deeper into the house the gowns and tuxes grew more numerous. Clouds of crinoline and bombazine gas were enveloping her. The young graduates had seized the master bedroom for their headquarters. There might have been twenty or thirty of them in there, passing around bottles of champagne and joints. Someone was doing lines of cocaine from an enormous dresser. The dresses and dinner jackets didn't look as cheap or gaudy as those of her friends, they looked good. These were kids from The Red Pines. Attention was focused on one boy, he seemed their leader, with a narrow face. His head turned one way and he was beautiful, another he was hideous. Clinging to or, more properly, swinging from his arm was a carrot-topped girl, her eyes drugged and unable to focus, swirling like those of a porcelain doll. The boy said something that made the other boys laugh and the girls squirm. He yanked his red-headed date upward, thrust his tongue into her gaping mouth, and pawed roughly at her breast.

Cathy backed out of the bedroom. She was in the wrong house.

five

Marty had eaten at La Perdrix before. He'd taken Sophie on her birthday last year, but had never been for lunch. Though half the diners were women, the daytime atmosphere was masculine, clubby.

A waitress showed Marty to a table near the rear, negotiating a bumper course of woollen backs. Marty knew some of them: small pond peddlers and jurists, ranking colonial administrators, oil folk—parents of Red Pines students. If they recognized him they would probably be displeased with his presence. Someone who educated their children was *the help* and had no business fraternizing with the movers and shakers. Marty felt this prejudice justified.

Hayden was with a Punjabi fellow, younger than he or Marty perhaps but showing the beginnings of the middle-year's battle with weight. Both of the men wore a smart suit. Hayden's blue, almost veering to indigo, pinstriped with crimson threads. The darker-skinned fellow's was an oyster grey, paned, but with much brasher candy-coloured lines of tangerine and cherry. By fit and richness of fabric he could see they were bespoke. Marty's charcoal-grey suit was well enough made but off the rack. Now, in this company, the thin gap round his collar where the jacket didn't hang properly and the sleeves, too high on the wrist, were letting in gusts. The man in the light suit stood to shake Marty's hand. French cuffs.

"Marty Devereaux, this is Kulvinder Singh, Ken around the office. He handles a lot of logistics for us. Jesus!" Something occurred to Hayden. "Do you have a title, Ken?"

"President of ARPEC Construction, I suppose, but we haven't put anything through ARPEC in years." Ken spoke with a faint townie accent, the island's least tuneful, flattened vowels and a nasal buzz, more east end than East India.

"I just tell people to 'see Kenny.' If we ever go ahead with the Downs thing and you do the school, you'll see a lot of Ken."

The proposition didn't seem to especially excite Ken. Marty sat down.

"We were just talking about Celebration, the Disney town. Ken was just there."

"In April, actually," Ken said. "Florida vacation with the family. We have a place in Marathon. I just drove up to Orlando to get away from them. Had to have a look."

"You familiar with Celebration, Marty?" Hayden asked.

A development like Celebration—a sterile, gated, suburban fantasia—was just what Hank and his people feared Hayden envisaged for the Perroqueet Downs. While Marty hadn't imagined that Hayden's group would do anything inventive or daring, he had not let himself think the worst. Still, business was business. If Celebration was the model then so be it.

"Somewhat," Marty answered.

"Place gave me the willies," said Ken.

"Yeah, it's creepy," agreed Hayden. "It's all controlled by Disney. They dictate the architecture, the colour palette, everything. Planned community."

"Still, there are things we can learn from any development," said Ken.

"Naturally," said Marty.

"Ken, can we show Marty ..."

Ken reached to the floor beneath his seat and retrieved a worn leather folder. Hayden didn't carry papers. Ken took a file from the case and handed it to Marty.

"These aren't final, just reductions of preliminary architectural sketches and some possible site plans," Hayden said.

The drawings showed, page after page in a loose, playful hand, houses with charm. They were large structures but not ostentatious. The site plans showed the structures lining crescents and streets that wrapped around, rather than intruded on, the landscape. It was no doubt a trick of the line, a sleight of the draftsman's hand, but the houses, whether angular blocks emerging from their surroundings like stone outcroppings or sweeping sculptural curves, seemed organically related to the lots on which they sat. It was as if they'd grown there, like the mature oaks and chestnuts drawn on their grounds. The artist's ploy of casually ending off the drawings before they were complete left parts of the buildings afloat, letting you imagine a weightless life, never once confessing, graphically, to the existence of retaining walls, fill, stanchions.

"The designs are not," Hayden continued, sounding as if he were reading from a speech he'd commissioned, "knock-off Newfoundland Victorian. The architects say that they have 'cited' certain aspects of that style as well as some vernacular." He stopped for a breath. "I can't see it. Frankly, it's a lot of artsy-fartsy gobbledegook to me. These people 'talk' a great building, Marty. I'm waiting for the hissyfits when the homeowners start adding on the two-car garages. Still, on paper anyway, they are attractive."

"They are 'new' buildings," said Ken. "A conscious departure from the old 'heritage' notions. Some of these structures will be using modern materials like sheet metals and fibreglass. There's a term they use ... *transgressional?* Could that be it?"

"That heritage shit drives me nuts," said Hayden. "Like time doesn't pass."

"I agree," said Marty, having really only formed an opinion on the matter for the first time. "It's a provincial attitude."

"That's just what it is," said Ken. "It's provincial. Conservative in the worst sense of the word. Backward looking. Shows a lack of confidence in contemporary thinking."

"Like the old buildings weren't new once," said Hayden. "I hate that, when there are stretches of a town with nothing but these meticulously restored places. They all look the same. You can just tell there is some self-appointed group of taste-police bullying the neighbourhood, telling people what building materials they can use, what colour paint. So anal."

"Like Celebration," Marty said.

"Yeah, exactly." Hayden was smiling.

A handsome young waitress arrived. Though they had not consulted the menus in front of them, both Hayden and Ken went ahead and ordered. Hayden requested the freshest fish they had. Ken asked for lamb chops. When told the kitchen offered rack of lamb, Ken suggested, with impatience, they simply cut the rack into chops before cooking them. It would be done. Marty said he would have the fish as well. The men sitting across from him were used to being waited on. They paid top dollar, why shouldn't they get what they wanted?

"Porter Furlong are the consulting architects," said Ken. "They're probably the best outfit on the east coast and local to boot. They gave a bunch of the work on this project to the newest partners—some exciting young talent in that group. They just won a bunch of awards for designing some crazy stuff in … in … I think it was … São Paulo, Brazil?"

"And they don't come cheap," Hayden said with both derision and resignation.

"It's another bone we can throw them," Ken said, leaving Marty to assume who "them" was. "We anticipate that the very sorts of people opposed to the development will live there. Those demographics share sets."

"They're beautiful homes," said Marty, honestly.

"Show him the sewage," said Hayden.

Ken withdrew another set of drawings, pencil pastorals of a marshland. These drawings were even more accomplished (or artful?) than those of the houses, delicate scratches and swirls of graphite suggesting small birds, even butterflies, filling the air over rangy bulrushes and cutlasses of tall grass. You could hear hot-weather insects buzzing to the sun. On the saltwater beyond a couple of sea kayaks were caught passing.

"We're building in an environmentally friendly waste water disposal project. Bio-remediation. We'll be taking the sludge and using it to fertilize a large greenbelt, for recreation. We won't be asking St. John's to hook us up to the municipal system and we won't be contributing to the waste stream."

"Doing a damn sight better than the City," Hayden observed.

Marty looked again at the drawing. In the background you could see low-slung buildings, the actual treatment plants, hiding in the topography.

"It seems the very model of development. I don't understand why anyone should oppose it." Marty's tone was deliberately dispassionate. He did not want his genuine view that the proposal was a good one to be misunderstood as sycophancy.

Their conversation had been racing. There was a need to pause, to be silent in acknowledgment of their agreement on the facts, on the fundamentals. Ken rubbed his eyes.

"To be fair to the opponents of the development, we will be building on what is now a relatively pristine piece of country."

"There are a couple of guys, Chamber of Commerce types, on

City Council who are behind it a hundred percent." Hayden steered the talk away from opposition to the development. "Dirk Malan owns another two and says he'll deliver them. We just need to get two more councillors on side and it will be approved."

"Is Dirk Malan somehow involved in the development?" asked Marty. In truth he really wanted to know how it was that Dirk Malan "owned" two city councillors, but thought better of asking.

"Yeah," said Hayden. "That's not a problem, is it?"

"No, not at all," said Marty, thinking how Hank had guessed that Malan was involved. "Just … just that his boy, Russell, attends The Red Pines."

Neither Hayden nor Ken seemed to fathom the relevance of Marty's information.

"Bruce St. Croix, the Ward 6 councillor—remember last year he got the City's recreation department to buy those pedal boats from his brother?—anyway, Bruce is up to his neck in shit over this minor hockey thing," Ken said. "Borrowed some money from the organization to take a short-term position on a sure thing. And, well … you know, Marty, as is so often the case in these affairs … short-term position of it is … he's fucked." Ken turned to Hayden. "We can bail him out and then …"

"Then it'll be just one, Marty," said Hayden.

"Sure. One." Marty couldn't think what else to say.

"If you were with us on this … We just have to swing one vote," said Hayden, waving to and winking at someone across the room.

Marty resisted the urge to turn and see whom.

"We'll swing one. There's no doubt about it," said Ken.

"I don't think it would be appropriate for me to come out and endorse the development any more than I think it's appropriate my partner Hank opposes it."

"No, never. We would never expect you to make a statement," Hayden said.

"Nothing that anyone could clearly interpret as having any meaning one way or another," said Ken.

"Exactly, exactly," said Hayden. "No position. Kenny here has an expression … what is it?"

"Deliberately vague to provide latitude."

"That's it. Never paint yourself into a corner."

"But if you," Ken jumped in, "… if you were to apply to City Council for the permits to build a school …"

"It would be obvious," said Hayden.

"So you want me to do something sooner rather than later?"

"What are we now?" said Hayden. "July second. They'll put off voting on it as long as possible. With summer holidays that means September or October, November at the latest. I'll tell you something else, in strict confidence now, Marty, but … the mayor is not a well man."

"No?"

"He's very volatile now, very unpredictable," said Ken.

"There was," said Hayden, "what they called 'an emotional emergency,' involving His Worship. Nobody knows about it. We have his support now, but …"

"There's some urgency," said Ken. "And you'll keep working on your partner, try to bring him around."

"Yes, let's not forget that," agreed Hayden. "Bring him around to our way of thinking. That would make life much easier."

Marty nodded affirmatively, though he knew he needn't waste any more time with Hank. No one spoke for a moment. The waitress arrived with their meals. Marty's halibut looked delicious, crusted and smoky from the grill, flecked with herbs and granules of salt the size and shade of beach sand.

So the mayor was flipping out. He looked a bag of nerves the last few times Marty had seen him on the news, skittish. What was it about running a city that took such a toll? Provincial and federal politicians were predictably ineffectual or corrupt, took their lumps from the press and the public and moved on, none the worse for wear. The city brought down its ringmasters. Mayors and ward councillors could not hide behind the abstraction of policy. For them politics was a fallen fence, slubby ice on the rink, rats. If you could walk it, or look over it, if you knew that the people down there were real, the sense of responsibility, the guilt over your mistakes, was too easily felt, too hard to forget. If you weren't a psychopath you had no business in municipal politics.

The scent of preserved lemon rose from Marty's warm plate. He tucked into his fish, moist below its delicately charred exterior.

"If this were to go ahead, what would be your part of the school?" asked Marty. "Are you willing to take an equity position?"

The query appeared to disturb Hayden's digestion. Marty realized that talking actual dollar figures over lunch was gauche.

"The land itself, naturally," Hayden said. "The land the school was built on … beyond that …?"

"Early days, Marty, early days," said Ken. He moved the conversation on to spare Marty any discomfiture over the faux pas. "I don't know whether Gerry has mentioned that we considered running our own school."

"He did," said Marty, looking to Gerry.

"It seemed not a bad business. So we looked at several different operations. The Red Pines was easily one of the best. I'm not bullshitting you. We looked—I mean we had someone look—at private schools right across Canada and a couple of the top ones on the eastern seaboard of the States, even looked at operations in England and Scotland. Hundreds, Marty. And taking everything into consideration, from a business point of view, The Red Pines is among the very best."

"Thank you."

"And," said Ken, "it's pretty obvious, what with the lack of investment by government—I'm talking about here in Canada—it's pretty obvious which way things are going. Health care, same thing, right?"

"Right," said Marty.

"Then think of the States. Biggest single operator of private schools down there is the Catholic Church. You've got to ask yourself how long that's going to last."

"You can see the tort lawyers circling," said Hayden.

"There are six million private school students in the U.S., Marty," said Ken.

"Six million. I think I'd heard that number," Marty said, though he wasn't sure where he'd heard it. It seemed a lot.

"Average tuition is around $20,000 U.S. a year and that's exclusive of merch or food concessions. Do the math."

Marty needed to pipe up, to demonstrate that he knew his trade, that he too knew the lay of land. "Yeah, hey," he said.

"I mean the very, very rich, they're going to keep sending their kids to the same old schools, the prestige places. Status thing. It's not that the kids can go to those places, Marty, but that they can't *not* go." Ken was more animated now. Talk, particularly his own, stimulated him.

"That crowd," Hayden shook his head, "with the prep schools and the kids with the stupid pet names, 'Whiffy' and 'Pinks' and 'Plucky.' I race with these people, Marty. It's unbelievable. If great-granddad hadn't invented the Oreo cookie or patented the Pneumatic Whatnot, most of 'em would be bagging groceries."

Hayden seemed not to connect his own fortune with this indictment.

"But the larger market—" Ken said, "it's not being served."

"Wrap your package in red, white, and blue, you know, go all out. Use the word 'American' a lot. It's a prayer for them down there, a dumb-tit." Hayden stopped for a moment. Using his fingers he removed from his fish and scrutinized a pearly white bone the size of a finishing nail. "Call your school like a … The Red Pines American School or The American Pines School—that sounds all right, hey? Is there an American pine? I mean, like an actual tree? When it comes to American patriotism there's no such thing as good taste. All out."

"Jingoism, I guess, rather than patriotism," Ken corrected.

"Sure, Kenny, whatever," said Hayden with some irritation. "The other thing for them, for the Americans? God. Big God." Hayden stopped to think, looking out across the restaurant. "But I guess you can't go there," he said and turned back to his plate.

"And hire a lobbyist to tell you the how and when of the school voucher issue. Be ready, it's a … well, you know …" said Kenny.

"Sure," said Marty, not knowing at all.

"At this point, what with this cum-stained dress, Marty," Hayden said, "there's a chance the Republicans will be elected next year and these Bush people, they mean to dismantle government. How far they get, who knows?"

"The U.K., that's different," said Ken. "Places like Eton, they're bound up in the history of the State and the Church. It's a world unto itself, foxhunting and appeasement. It's not an example that translates to another setting."

"Fox … Don't hold back, Kenny," Hayden was laughing. "You're such a bitter Newf. Have some pity. These are people who still have a queen. A queen!"

"She's on our money, too," observed Ken.

Hayden chose not to hear him. "Those British schools, Marty … there was one in Scotland, very expensive. We saw pictures and it was like being sent up the river, just miserable. They're very competitive in their unhappiness, the Brits. So mean, so mortgaged. But then, they like it to hurt."

"Who?"

"The English, they say that about them, they're into a little pain, turns them on."

Marty felt his neck reddening.

"I don't know," he said.

"The English vice," said Ken.

"They really want to be Americans, you know. They envy Americans—that's why they hate them."

"I think," said Ken, "they confuse American democracy with classlessness and … and American freedom, licence. Of course the situation is quite the opposite."

"What are you getting on with, Kenny? You have this tendency to needlessly complicate things. You do. It's much simpler than all that. The English? They just want to stop being so self-conscious, they want that American … unconsciousness … that's not the right word for it but you know what I mean."

A further thought occurred to Hayden. "Shit, Marty, you should open an American school, your *American Pines,* over there. Teach the English kids how to be Americans. That would be a twist, hey?"

"Great time to be growing your kind of business, Marty," said Ken. "If you look at children as a commodity—and you know I'm not suggesting that anyone would, you know that—but if you did, they become more valuable as they get scarcer. If people were still having three and four kids, it would actually decrease your market because fewer people would even consider private schooling. With one or two offspring, it becomes a possibility. In fact the demographic situation is forcing government's hand. The high end of the market just keeps getting bigger and the older schools, the boarding schools, are in trouble. When we looked for an operator, some sort of transnational education provider, we found that there wasn't one. There's a need for a new model."

"You got that right," said Marty.

"Paradigm shift equals market opportunity. Always. And …" Ken studied the chop held in his pudgy fingers, a lollipop of lamb, before taking a dainty bite. He chewed and wiped his fingertips in his napkin. He swallowed and continued. "I understand the kids at The Red Pines get an excellent education to boot."

"An excellent education," Hayden parroted, forking through his fish.

"You've created a great brand," Ken concluded before focusing more intently on his meat.

That, in fact, was just what he had done, thought Marty. He'd never been able to articulate what it was that he, and not Hank, had contributed to The Red Pines. It was "brand." It was his concern that things look or seem right that created an overall effect that provided the consumer, in this case the parents, with a level of comfort with and confidence in their purchase. It kept them coming back. Marty had given the school its identity. The Red Pines brand was his.

"I saw on the news," Marty said, "where the groups opposed to your plan are going to seek an injunction or something."

Hayden, his mouth full, waved his hand, brushing off the idea.

Ken spoke. "Non-starter."

"Oh?" said Marty.

"They have no grounds," Ken elaborated. "You see, there's already been a community on the site."

"There are deeds, my friend," said Hayden, "deeds."

"Really?" said Marty.

"Called Dunchy Head. Abandoned … when was it, Ken?" Hayden asked.

"Middle of the eighteen hundreds, something like that. It was just a tiny fishing settlement. There was no road in, and being so close to town …" Ken answered.

"Not ten miles away by sea and completely isolated. Imagine the torment, being able to smell the coal smoke, hear the city," said Hayden.

"So what we are, in fact, doing," Ken offered a rare smile, "is de-resettlement."

Resettlement was a widely aggrieved piece of social engineering from the Smallwood era, a bungled effort to concentrate the dispersed coastal population so as to foster industry, a mid-twentieth century project to drag Newfoundland from the seventeenth century into the nineteenth. Ken was pleased with his crack, thinking it cleverer than it was.

"How can you *not* get behind that?"

"You know, Marty," said Hayden, "you know what I hate the most? It's when they refer to the Downs as 'unspoiled,' as though building there, like making use of it, letting people live in it, would spoil it. That's such bullshit, Marty, 'cause this place is about commerce. They didn't cross the pond in leaky boats for a theatre festival or to watch whales, they came to this place to make money, to kill whales and sell their fat. North America is about capitalism, and it got its start here, right here. Money means vitality, money means movement. That's our lost tradition, Marty, not running the fucking goat. There should be a fucking museum. Men have been doing business in Newfoundland for five hundred years. We've traded with Lisbon and London and Havana and Genoa from the get-go, and there are those that would have us all gamekeepers and actors. Build, baby, or wait tables."

♆

Once in his car Marty resolved to go to the office and start work immediately. Promptly putting together a compelling package for City Council would demonstrate his seriousness to Hayden and Ken, show that he wasn't vacillating. The Perroqueet Downs school would be the first in the franchise, the prototype. The plan would essentially be the manual for operation of future outlets, a document laying it all out, from principles of design to curriculum. Marty was to work on a bible.

No such guide had existed for The Red Pines so they'd improvised. Part of the problem between him and Hank was the absence of rules or protocols. No one knew what was expected of them. The new business would have a code of conduct, a list of causes principals and vice principals were allowed to publicly support—safe bets like the Y.

Marty would no longer be burdened with trivialities. Those would be the concern of his appointed operatives, men and women—department heads—who took direction from the book.

Before anyone paid attention to those essential things that separated his brand of school from the others, they would want to see the dollars and cents, the business plan. There would be several approaches to plant—the re-purposing of standing structures, even existing schools, and, as was the case with the project at hand, building anew. A trip to the Perroqueet Downs was required to view the site.

The Red Pines was shut for the summer. The heavy exterior doors should have been locked but were not. Perhaps the head custodian, Mr. MacNaughton, was in. He was conscientious and might be checking in and giving the place the once-over. MacNaughton was the sort of fellow Marty would take with him, appoint head of custodial services. Once there were enough schools operating you could cut volume discounts with suppliers of cleansers and detergents, of mops and brooms. You never knew how things might turn out. Perhaps you would develop efficiencies in the cleaning of your buildings and end up contracting that service out to other institutions. You never knew, you had to continually expand, to keep moving, that's how you discovered your strengths, your competitive edge, and became one of the big players—unless, of course, like Gerry Hayden, you simply started with vast supplies of family capital.

The place reeked of paint. It wasn't MacNaughton, but Pitts.

Atypically empty, the hallways were resonant. By their absence Marty was aware of the noises that normally filled the school, the tin-can clatter of lockers, trebly squeaks of sneakers on the hardwood of the gym, the roiling tides of chatter. Illumination from distant windows reflected weakly in streaks down the burnished floors. The gloom exaggerated the boom of Marty's steps.

"Alan?" Marty called as he neared the wing with the science classrooms.

"Hey! Marty!" Alan, unseen, sounded happy to hear Marty's voice. He came to greet his boss, meeting Marty at the corner. He was wearing oil-stained overalls. He held a bouquet of paintbrushes in his hand, the colours running between them and down their stems. "Marty. You're goin' to love it."

But Marty did not. He walked down the hall, as would a visitor to a gallery, and in the presence of the artist made an effort to look as though he were carefully assessing each panel. But he was not. He was heading, as quickly as courtesy would allow, for the last completed panel of the series, the fifth. It captured his attention the moment he'd rounded the corner. It was not, like the others were, a dot or small circle in the centre of a field of pitch. It was a huge, floor-to-ceiling, swirling, orange-and-yellow vortex with a gory heart. Every step he drew closer the more ominous it became. He passed the other planets. Earth, azure and white, seemed right. Mars—red—yes, The Red Planet. Then.

"Jupiter, Marty. The Romans' Zeus. When Zeus became an adult he had Cronus poisoned so that Cronus would vomit out the other children he'd eaten," said Alan.

"What?"

"Some mythology."

"What am I looking at here, Alan?"

The picture was not as well realized as the others, was rougher, with visible strokes, even the occasional gob of paint and, in one spot, a dribble that ran all the way to the floor. It lacked depth, was, unlike its partners on the wall, flat and naïve. The larger part of it resembled nothing so much as a well-marbled rib-eye.

"The great red spot. It's a storm that's been raging on Jupiter for hundreds of years."

"So this is Jupiter?"

"Yeah, part of it. Remember, Marty, everything is to scale. Considering the size of the other planets this is all of Jupiter that would fit on a panel. It's a gas giant. You could fit three Earths in the great red spot alone."

Marty looked back at the painting of Earth. The relative sizes were as Alan stated, but now on further examination Marty saw, below a veil of cloud, something wrong with the third planet. He stepped closer to get a better view.

Where one expected to see the blue North Atlantic, framed by North America and Europe, there was only a square-topped peninsula jutting into the south of an empty ocean. To what should have been the southeast there was another small stretch of coast off which was a large island. The only substantial landmass was antipodal, to the erstwhile south. This vast unknown continent covered the entire bottom third of the globe.

"I was wondering when you'd notice," said Pitts.

"What's wrong with the world, Alan?"

"It's merely a question of perspective, Marty. I mean, if you were approaching from space why would north necessarily be the top? I've depoliticized the depiction, taken away the western/northern geocentric notion. This view is of the Indian Ocean from the south." Alan pointed to the island. "That's Madagascar."

Marty began to see it. The triangular territory spiking into the sea was India. Sumatra and Java hooked up toward northwest Australia.

"The world is upside down?"

"There is no top or bottom to the universe. It's an endless expanse in every direction."

"I suppose you're right," said Marty.

"You're not sold?"

"I've got to think about it." It occurred to Marty that Alan was unassisted. "You alone, Alan?"

"Yeah, the kids have been in to help a few times, but … it's their summer vacation. They stuck around right up to Mars. I know when they volunteered they were sincere, but …"

"I'll be in my office," Marty said, turning to leave. He hadn't gone far when Alan called after him.

"You don't like the paintings, do you, Marty."

"I like them, Alan. It's only that I expected something more, I don't know, conventional."

"What? Like God, in the sky?"

It was such a peculiar question, and judging from Alan's tone not a sarcastic one. Marty was puzzled. "No, of course not," he said.

"Because he's not up there, Marty," Alan said.

"I haven't really got time for a big philosophical discussion, Alan."

"Right. Sorry," Alan said and turned to his cans of paint.

♅

Marty began to have problems when he arrived at the section of the proposal describing his principles of design, the part of the brand most dear to his heart. *Design* or *décor* didn't seem the right term. It was more than mere surfaces, more than *a look. Mise en scène* was pretentious, perhaps a little fruity, and wrongly suggested that the created environment was only show. Marty was building a space where a certain kind of education could take place. The appropriate *platform? Crucible?* He couldn't find the right word, even the right context in which to discuss it. What was the section heading, the title, the name? What was his theory called? He couldn't think expansively in the confines of his office at the school. He needed to be more contemplative. He needed a smoke. With only Alan in the building, who would know? He threw open a window.

The taxonomic wand did its usual magic and the conceptual nitty-gritty fell from the theory's baptism. Marty typed it in, centred it, and underlined it. He tried all caps and then making the font bold, but neither looked right:

<u>A Common Sense of Tradition</u>

It suggested a sound, rational approach. No, more. It said plainly *common sense*. This was critical, for there would be those who worried about those aspects of "tradition" in education they had suffered in youth and wanted to spare their own children. It wasn't a blind fealty to the old school but a reasoned retention or recovery of its desirable points. It was no accident that Marty avoided the definite article in the title, for he was referring to tradition not as what was, but as what could be.

And as "common," it was something shared. It included only those parts of tradition everyone could stand behind: honour, respect, manners, high standards. It didn't exclude anyone on the basis of race or religion or (supposing they could pay) class. Love of country and faith were out.

This led to the conceptual nub, that this was "sense." Marty wasn't claiming he could invent tradition, but by evoking its "sense" he was employing its pungent effect. This was in every way superior to an actual tradition. It came without baggage, there were no dark chapters to later be discovered, dooming it to revisionist re-interpretation.

Marty's plan also skilfully masked its own genealogy, being from and of nowhere it avoided being from Newfoundland. Though the island meant nothing to a greater part of humanity, just a lost and empty northern expanse, it occupied a singular place in the Canadian imagination. Their quiet bigotry could prove an impediment to the initial phase of expansion to the mainland. They enjoyed the yokels' singing and dancing, their antic faux-Irish chimping, could stomach them as toothless ghosts, the stoic rickety sea-serfs of yesteryear, but no self-respecting Canuck would think of sending their child to a "Newfie" school. The island people were at heart still savages, born devils on whose nature nurture never stuck—a race born of contempt.

The Upper Canadians, deeply insecure in their newly minted cosmopolitanism, were forever measuring themselves against the great metropolises of London, New York, and Paris to find themselves wanting. They needed someone to play the hick. The fit was perfect. Newfoundlanders were now shamefaced over it, but for many years their Toronto masters could not have found more willing monkeys.

An operation somewhere more benign, maybe somewhere in Nova Scotia (of which were held—and by the Americans, too—vague but positive views), might do to stand in for the "first" of The Red Pines line.

The middle class of North America was, as never before, transient—following the economy from northeast to southwest. St. John's was flourishing now but in twenty years … who knew? It made sense to operate schools that could be disassembled, loaded into semis, and hauled to the next market, be it Arizona or British Columbia, or for that matter packed into a container and shipped to the U.A.E. or New Zealand. You could roll up the Astroturf playing fields and take them with you to Japan. Japan!

The vaunted customs of the Upper Canada Colleges, Andovers, and Harrows were a burden as much as anything, a weight of expectations and dictates that fucked up as many as it served. Marty would give it to them in a box. When they were done with it they could throw it away, keeping perhaps a necktie as a souvenir. Portable tradition! "EXCLUSIVITY FOR ALL!" Wasn't there something to that effect in the American Constitution, in the later articles?

He began to type furiously—his past for the future.

Marty gave himself five or six days to write a first draft. With Sophie in Vancouver for her precious little piano competition (she'd simply left, not even bothering to call and say goodbye), he might even put in a few all-nighters.

After two weeks Marty still hadn't completed the proposal. Costing the construction of the two schools consumed much of the time and many of the figures were no more than informed guesses.

Presuming Hayden gave him a serviced lot for nothing, Marty still needed about six million dollars. Together his share of The Red Pines, his house, and his RRSPs and savings represented scarcely more than a million dollars in equity. Peanuts. Until there were more schools in the chain and consequent economies of scale, the margins were terrible (this was precisely why the small independent private schools were vulnerable, why Marty could prey on them). There was a cap on pricing; the fees had to stay at the limit of affordability for the upper middle class—expensive but not impossible. (Though, as the banks well demonstrated, there were fortunes to be made from people living beyond their means.) The old established schools didn't charge a hell of a lot more but expected donations to their bulimic endowments, and then from named or connected families. They turned away ten kids for every one they accepted. That kind of marketplace was far too disorderly.

No matter how many times he shuffled and re-jigged the figures he couldn't see how the schools would be profitable in less than nine or ten years. Things started looking up soon after that. Even if Marty asked the bank to go deep he would need Hayden to take a large position, too large. There was government, but Marty hadn't invested enough in party politics to finagle one of those dubious private/public partnerships. If only Hank had joined the Liberals. And where the project involved the privatization of education, nobody—short of those fringe right-wingers in Ontario and Alberta—would touch it. The alternative was to put together a consortium of investors. This would take time, but as the project was under the aegis of the Haydens, Marty was confident of success. Business in the small city—who was he kidding?—business the world over was conducted not so much with contracts and tenders as it was with the winks and nods of the burghers. Gerry Hayden would let it be known that Marty was one of them.

♀

Money worries were always bad for his insomnia and Marty experienced a few rough nights.

His old companions on television had abandoned him. The chat shows' jollity was forced. The guest comics always seemed shiny with flop sweat. News had become a steady stream of unmediated disaster. Bad or very bad stuff happened some place, Marty saw it live, and then watched a commercial. Contemporary dramas and comedies meant nothing to him. Despite the welling music and agitated laugh tracks telling him how to respond, he did not understand the stakes or get the jokes. Shows from the seventies, fading or colour balance skewed to magenta, dated him and so left him disconsolate. Music videos were nothing but hooligans and rude stooges pointing and shoving, their coteries of whores in lordosis, asses quaking like paint shakers.

The narcotic wave that once reliably ran through his frame after masturbation was being denied him by Jackie Spurell. Doing a star turn in his fantasies she was reluctant to take direction. Marty would try to picture a normal erotic encounter between them but she, snarling and bitchy, had darker stuff in mind. He could not resist, and after coming found not peace but a thudding heart and shame.

There was, he understood, a new generation of sedatives in the pharmacopoeia, pills with fewer side effects. If things didn't soon improve he would call the doctor.

This day waking at dawn and unable to get back to sleep, he decided to go to the school early. There wasn't any more he could do. He'd print a copy of the proposal and call it done.

Sunlight was filling The Pines, giving it an uncommon airiness, even something like buoyancy. He went to the staff room, intending to make himself a cup of coffee.

Marty actually smelled Alan Pitts before he saw him asleep on the couch. It was an odour Marty knew, reminding him of his uncle Desmond's room at his grandparents' house. Des was the brother of Marty's mother who, because of myriad dysfunctions (some spoken of, some not), never moved out of his parents' house. Marty didn't know what eventually became of Uncle Des, hadn't thought of him in years, not until walking into the staff room and once again getting a whiff of man-funk and unwashed loneliness.

Alan was getting to his feet, having been awakened by Marty's entry. He was tentative; there was rust in the joints.

"Did you sleep here, Alan?"

"Hmmm? Yeah." Alan rubbed his head roughly with the heels of his palms.

"Why?"

"I was just working late. On the paintings. And I … I was planning, you know, to start early. So …"

Marty didn't want to hear any more, certainly not the truth.

"I don't know about that, Alan."

"Oh," Alan was barely awake, "… it's a problem?"

The star boarder! Of course it's a problem, thought Marty. Alan was smart enough to know it was.

"My insurance," said Marty.

"Right, of course." Alan, standing and sensing his infraction, tried a peace offering, making himself smile as a sign of amicability. "I should put on some coffee. Want some?"

"No," said Marty, turning away. "I'll be in the office."

How was it, Marty wondered, that one so unsympathetic, so uninterested in the problems of others as he, should be so beset by the woeful? People were mistaking him for some sort of emotional Mother Teresa. He did not present a kindly visage and had no history of altruism. Perhaps, given the human condition, it was a simple matter of statistical certainty that you would spend much of your life colliding with or stepping over the fallen.

Alan was coming undone at an alarming rate. The years he'd avoided were rushing in, mugging him in quantum chunks. Three years from his twenties showed up suddenly in his lower back. He took a brain-rattling blow of five years to the jaw. Maybe the paintings themselves or the act of making them might be to blame. Marty didn't know much about it, but were not painters, image-makers of all kinds, particularly susceptible to madness? Van Gogh to Rothko, there was an uncommonly high percentage of head cases among their ranks. It was even more so among his brother Rex's thespian crowd. Rex regaled him with tales of their hysterics, the tantrums and unfounded jealousies, their rages and wailing despair. Perhaps mortals had no business trying to capture or render life, doing so offended the vengeful gods. Maybe the strange business violated some fundamental principle, a rule that prohibited life from seeing or knowing itself. What was it Rex said, "Nature mocked art"?

He was standing near Mrs. Norris's desk, dumbly watching the repetitive mechanical action of the printer, when he heard a familiar sound that he couldn't quite place. It was coming from outside, like the occasional shuffling of a deck of cards, an intermittent *shushing*. He went to the window, looked out, and saw a flash of colour leave his field of vision. The sound was gone. Marty knew what it was.

He walked down to the street and watched the runners coming. The leaders, the first two or three, had already passed, but close on their heels were other serious racers. Marty could tell by their faraway eyes, their focus on a point beyond, by the way the line of the road seemed to pass through them, that they were contenders. They were running *to*. They didn't even see Marty standing there.

Marty wished he were among them, even in the approaching middle ranks. This bunch saw Marty, saw the trees, the school, the sky, saw every inch of pavement before them. These were the runners *from*. Their startled faces evinced every hurt, the mash inside the knees, the chest filling with hot chip fat. They forced a smile for Marty as they went by, mistakenly assuming that his standing there watching them was encouragement. A few of the old guys and gals—late thirties in this case—might place in their age category but there were no cups or even ribbons here.

There were a goodly number of them filling the road, the multitude of heavier feet sounding now like a rock fall. Time was when Marty knew all the races, their distance, sponsor, specific characteristics, like an imperceptible incline or an absence of shade in the stretch. The flapping paper numbers pinned to the shirts going by showed that this event was sponsored by BCN 520, an old local radio station to which nobody listened.

Then, through the stroboscopic fence of trunks and limbs, Marty noticed a man standing on the opposite side of the street.

He hadn't been there when Marty first came down and so must have approached behind the cover of the rushing pack. He was tall, straight, white-headed and was staring at Marty. He looked, thought Marty, like a farmer. No, a rancher.

Only the occasional straggler was left to cripple past. The man crossed and offered his hand.

"Dirk Malan," he said.

"Martin Devereaux."

"I went by your home. You're a hard-working man, Mr. Devereaux."

"I'm busy these days."

"I wouldn't have thought, not in the summer," said Malan.

"What can I do for you?" asked Marty.

"It's about my boy."

"Russell."

"His grades."

"Yes, he barely scraped through this year."

"He's not academically inclined, Mr. Devereaux. We realize that. It was never a strength of my own either, and I don't mind saying I've done well." Malan looked about before continuing. "We are grateful for everything you people have done to help, especially Mr. Lundrigan."

Marty supposed by "we" Malan meant he and his wife, and not some corporate or regal entity. Malan kept going as though he had planned what he was going to say.

"I pleaded with Mr. Lundrigan to continue tutoring Russell, but he … he refused."

"He takes issue with your involvement in the Perroqueet Downs development," said Marty.

Malan drew his head back. His eyes fluttered in a way that was oddly fem. "What's that got to do with Russell?"

"I've no idea, Mr. Malan."

"I knew he'd become some sort of Green."

"Yes," said Marty. "He's that."

The news that his business affairs had somehow become entangled with the burdens of family threw Malan for a loop. He now seemed to stray from the speech he'd rehearsed.

"Short of it is, Mr. Devereaux, the grades Russell got this year will never do."

"I can assure you that the marks were, in fact, generous. Russell is not a gifted student."

"But if he's to go to college, they'll be an impediment."

"Do you think," asked Marty, "that Russell will go to college?"

"I'm certain of it, sir,'" Malan said, taking umbrage. "Yale. Yale seems suited to our purpose."

Dirk Malan was serious.

"Isn't Yale better suited to one more ..." Marty considered his words, "as you put it, academically inclined?"

Malan waved a hand dismissively. "That's just marketing. Did you know they adjust the marks, fix it so they're higher? Suggests they get a better class of student. All the best schools do it. It doesn't do Harvard any good to graduate C students. It would damage the brand, if you take my meaning."

"Indeed I do. And I've heard those stories about the grades. I'm not sure I believe them," said Marty. "You are aware Russell will be required to take a standardized test before he's granted admittance?"

"We've already signed him up with a service in the United States, in Albany, New York, that prepares young people for the test. Russell will go next June, the moment he's finished here. They guarantee success."

"Then they're very bold."

"It's comprehensive. They charge thirty thousand dollars." Malan drew his hand up, bringing his fingers to his temples but not quite touching the skin, as if coaxing a thought from within his skull. "The admission tests are not our immediate concern. Having these bad marks on his record, however … it would draw attention. He'd be subject to unfair scrutiny."

Marty started to see it. It was for Russell's sake the Malans were hiding in Newfoundland. They'd hoped to educate him here, out of sight, until such time as he shed his scaly skin.

"What do you propose I do?"

"Re-test him. Or at least go through the motions."

Marty knew what he was suggesting, had already done it, but without Malan's gall. The half measure, upping the grades so that Russell might simply pass, not going all the way and giving him an A, now struck Marty as the coward's choice.

"I don't know what to say here, Mr. Malan."

"Then I will leave you to think about it." Malan started to go but stopped and turned back. "It's not as though Russell is going to go on to great things in university. He's not going to discover a vaccine or a new galaxy, we know that. It's just that these days, if he's going to continue on in business, even if it is the family business, it's helpful to have a degree from a top school. It looks good." Malan paused. "And I don't think they can teach you how to run a business in university anyway. You're a business man, you know what I mean."

"I studied English literature, Mr. Malan."

"There. You make my point. Perhaps that could be Russell's major, English literature."

♁

The day turned out to be a scorcher. The runners were lucky to have raced in the early morning. When Marty returned home that afternoon the air was soggy and ungiving, failing to satisfy the lungs, every third or fourth breath wanting another. Near and far was the infernal drone of lawnmowers. The guy across the street, Something Murphy, waved to Marty as he pushed his machine in a calculated series of intersecting diagonals that gave his turf a smart checkerboard nap. Shit, thought Marty, Murphy's got an argyle lawn. Marty looked at his own patch. It required a trim.

Inside, on the kitchen counter, was a note. It was written in a careful, even strained, hand on a sheet from a small tear-away pad, a promotional freebie from Floronax Cleansers and Strippers of Markham, Ontario.

Dear Mr. Devereaux,

We came on schedule. There was not much work for Debbie and me to do. We changed the sheets and the floors where not to bad but we did vaccum. There was some dust but not a lot. You need cleaning only two weeks. Call you call Oswald at the office if this is ok for you.

Trina

He wasn't leaving any footprints. Hank would love that.

Next to the note Marty dropped the hard copy of his proposal. It read differently on the page than on the screen. The printed version made no less compelling a case than that which he composed on the computer. It was straightforward. It was comprehensive. The difficulty was in the section with which Marty was most pleased—his treatise on the uses of tradition. The perfect critical reader, the nonexistent ideal, would realize, as Marty had now, that the power of tradition was in its temporal weight. It was thus a brake or anchor against the headlong tumble into the unknowns of the future. But there was a danger, not for the students, but for the handlers, of becoming entangled in the works. They could become fettered to a period of Marty's invention, one that had never been. Or worse. The rope lashed to the rock hove overboard could snake around your leg and pull you with it into the deeps.

Time was not, as he'd previously thought, a medium in which events happened or a dimension in which they were measured, but a reagent, a cause. Tradition was a function of time. It could probably be expressed as an equation:

Tradition = (Conduct/Mores) × Time
or
Time/Memory = Melancholy/Nostalgia

Wait, that didn't make sense. Did it? Fuck sake, he was confusing himself. Maybe he was becoming as nutty as Alan Pitts.

Marty fixed himself a drink. He was almost finished a bottle of gin purchased three days earlier. Stress. Maybe the booze was responsible for his recent weight gain. After plateauing for the last eleven or twelve years, he was again starting to pack on a few pounds. He took his tumbler out to the backyard.

He sat at a wooden picnic table, one made in a workshop at the local mental hospital. The gas barbeque was still wrapped for the winter in its grey vinyl cover, tied down tight with twine. He hadn't had occasion to fire it up yet this summer. Sophie loved barbeques, found they summoned some of the rare good associations, of *asados* with the family, from her childhood. She collected bbq kitsch when she travelled, novelty and souvenir bibs and aprons, ones with cartoon drawings of grill-bound pigs or steers and attached holsters for cans of beer.

Sophie once showed up in a cowboy hat she'd been given as a gift for adjudicating a competition in Calgary. Later that evening, drunk, she pretended to forget about it and, after shedding every other stitch of clothing, climbed into bed with the thing still on. She stood up and struck a pose, one hand on her cocked hip, the other tugging the Stetson's brim down to hide her eyes. It was just horsing around and they'd both laughed—and Marty felt as hard and long as a policeman's nightstick and they'd gone at it like mink.

Sophie hadn't called once this trip. He didn't want to face it, didn't want to expend the emotional resources to deal with it, but Marty knew, or knew that he should know, that things were changing between them.

The neighbour backing onto his property turned on his sprinkler. A fusillade of water pellets cut across their shared wooden fence, receded, and returned. Marty, sitting still, felt a bead of sweat rolling down his temple and over his cheek. It must be over thirty degrees, he thought.

♂

St. John's is walled in hills, verdant bridges to the wild. The presence of fox in the heart of the city is not unheard of. Night people have been startled by an owl plucking a pigeon from the air. Until ten or twelve years ago it was not uncommon to hear tell of a flummoxed young moose showing up in town, shitting on cosmopolitan pretensions as it went.

It was late June before the days were long and warm enough for Cathy to walk the seaward face of the rocky keep. Even now, in July, the ocean breeze brought up goose flesh on her bare arms.

An advance guard of soldiers and mercenaries—Englishmen, French with Iroquois, Irish confederates, the Yanks—had cut her trails along the coastal boundary. Cathy made balance beams from the remnants of their stone fortifications, the collapsed bastions, the footings of ramparts. Her strides measured a powder house and a fever hospital.

Having been force-fed the history not only at school but at

home, Cathy knew why they'd held the post. But both the fish and the Warsaw Pact were gone. Let it fall, she thought.

Though the city's electric aura was beginning to appear in the near sky, as day failed it became harder to make out the footpaths and rabbit runs renting the blueberry and azalea of the hills. A misstep could mean a deadly fall. Sensing the slip to dusk, Cathy turned up over the ridge, toward town.

Her original route was to have been a shortcut from Jeanette's, an arc around the built-up areas, on a whim going home via downtown, going farther than her family's house and doubling back. This would have taken her past a plaza outside a government office tower used by skaters. Then maybe the music store. She might see someone, most likely kids her own age wandering aimlessly about. Anything was better than nothing.

Since school closed Cathy's long days stretched even further. Time tired, the moments oozed. Her report card was all Bs and a C. Not bad, she thought, given the effort—like none. Her teachers were less pleased, insisting in the attached comments that she could do better, much better. Yeah and …? The notes triggered a hiccup in the parentals' pretense of disinterest. Her mother leaked a few tears. Her father railed, convincing himself that the remedy to Cathy was a summer job, something about responsibility and understanding the meaning of a day's work, *blah blah blah.* Coming from him! Besides, she'd take a job in an instant, anything to eat up the hours.

If night had not fallen so quickly Cathy would have descended a mottled baize slope at the east end of the harbour, passed through a spooky margin of dockyards, and gone on into the heart of the city. Stuff was happening there, people were going to restaurants, bands were lugging gear into clubs, actors were sick with dread in their dressing rooms, there was the giddy lift of anticipation as the curtain rose. The thing adults least appreciated about their world was the comfort of social ritual, that their behaviour was prescribed:

a waiter handed a couple their menus and someone said, "What are you having, sweetheart?"; a former lover was greeted with knowing looks, a loaded kiss on the cheek, and not a shred of embarrassment; it started to rain and you confidently whistled down a taxi. Cathy never quite knew what to do. Everything she tried felt awkward and false, as though she was always pretending. She studied the world so that she might one day know how to be in it.

As it stood, her abbreviated route through a golf course put her in a wood behind the place her uncle Marty worked, The Red Pines. Her father's suggestion that she transfer here seemed, thankfully, to have been dropped.

An empty school, gold and salmon in the setting sun on a warm night in July was, she thought, the perfect monument to nothingness, to apathy and having nowhere interesting to go.

She walked past the building and on to a wide boulevard, the air weary of cut grass and barbeque smoke, coming to a trail alongside a choking brook. Ribbons of plastic, shopping bags and industrial strapping from the lands upstream, the new subdivisions and malls swayed in its flow like logy polyethylene eels. The stream was not of water, she thought, but of cough syrup, sweet and gooey and laced with codeine.

The houses backing on the shallow valley were larger as she went. She came to a small pond in a park. The homes here were the most overblown. They were trophy dwellings. There was one exception, a tiny place alone in facing the water. It belonged elsewhere, in a fairy tale? No, an English novel perhaps, one of those books they turned into a television series, the sort her parents watched, even as Dad slagged every line.

She walked on to a busy avenue that reached for the city's centre and continued past the street on which she lived.

The last daylight left the sky. There was a rising blare, clatter fast as a kitten's purr. She was downtown.

A trace of perfume—grapefruit and roses—was on the air as a woman rushed by. There was the bitter scent of coffee, diesel exhaust from the buses, fried onions and tandoor smoke from an Indian restaurant, shit and tidal backwash from the harbour, and something high and saline, a smatchiness peculiar to St. John's, like the city was corned.

Head down, shoulders up, hair a veil, Cathy was invisible to much of the world. If she drew the gaze of an adult on the street she judged it predatory and moved along more swiftly.

Her physics teacher, Mr. Donnelly—rumpled, his eyes rheumy—approached without seeing her. Checking his pockets he strode into a seamy pub from which escaped the sound of hillbilly music and laughter like the croup.

Five chattering girls from a tribe unknown stepped from an expensive clothing boutique, their booty in shiny bags with braided cord handles. Their circle tightened, their shoulders rubbing together. They fell mute as she neared them and snickered at her back as she passed.

Mrs. Spurell bound out of a drugstore on the other side of the street to a car left idling at the curb, its hazards flashing. She climbed behind the wheel and disappeared into traffic.

Place was a village, she thought, a claustrophobic village. No, it was less and worse, something tighter and more suffocating. It was a clan of apes picking nits from one another.

Ahead, Chuck Curtis emerged from the music store and started in her direction. Their paths would meet. Chuck had changed. His acne had subsided; he stood taller and seemed better to know what to do with his hair. He was better washed. Toward the end of the semester he stopped ragging her, and even tried to make polite conversation. Now she could see, as she had never before, that his eyes were blue and tranquil. He was close enough that she could feel them falling on her. Chuck had a milk-chocolate tan, a bit of a burn marking his cheekbones. His hair was sun-bleached blond. The summer was good to him. His hands were big and hard, the skin of his knuckles with a texture like that of a pebble or stone, chalky white lines cutting the rough surface, a man's and not a boy's. He was wearing a white T-shirt and jeans, with a worn belt. It was ridiculous, but the thought that he was almost handsome spontaneously came into Cathy's head and she had to put it away. Chuck smiled. She could not help herself and smiled back.

"Hey?" he said.

"Hey," she said. It was a moronic way to greet someone.

"How's your summer going?" he asked.

"Pretty good," said Cathy.

"You got a summer job or anything?"

"Nah. You?"

"Finished today. With the city parks, working with the grounds. Planting and stuff. Pretty cool."

She realized she had nothing whatsoever to say or rather, though filled with ideas and feelings, could not for the life of her think how to express them. Her choices were to sputter like a jerk or continue to pretend she disliked Chuck and didn't want to speak with him, to let on she had better places to go, more interesting and better-looking people with whom to talk.

"What are you doing?" he asked.

How could she answer this? She couldn't very well confess that she was simply walking around town because she had nothing to do. She couldn't, in fairness, tell him it was none of his business. He was, after all, trying to be pleasant. She tried, but couldn't so quickly fabricate a wonderful, strange destination, some event at which her attendance was critically required—a performance, surgery.

"Nothing," she said.

"Let me show you something."

Cathy was disinclined to follow, but then it was, he promised, "something."

He led her up a steep side street off which was a narrow alley servicing the buildings of the main drag. Set as they were into the side of a hill, it was the buildings' second floors that were on a level with the lane. The storefronts below were mostly retail outfits or, as evidenced by the stench of grease and the cabbagey ferment of food waste, restaurants.

"Do you remember the fire?" Chuck asked.

"No," Cathy said, though truthfully she did faintly recall some news of a fire down here, four months ago, five?

"It was in that bookstore," Chuck said. Cathy remembered now. "The guy that owned it, Rosenkrantz, lived upstairs," he added.

They'd come to a boarded-up doorway, its frame marked by sooty fangs where the smoke had forced its way out. Chuck grinned. With two hands he picked up the barrier and lifted it easily away.

"Go on in," he said.

Cathy stepped into an open loft apartment. It was decorated in an Oriental theme, Turkish or maybe Egyptian—what did she know?—with beautiful rugs, overstuffed chairs, and humpties. An aspect of authenticity prevented it all from being kitschy, but it was close. The walls were lined with swollen bookcases. The lampshades were fringed. The tables were low. No, she decided, it was gaudy, intended to evoke the East but coming off more like a whorehouse in an old Western movie. That was the two-thirds of the apartment closest the door they had entered. The wall opposite was a sheer face of flaking charcoal interrupted at intervals by sheets of new plywood, pale like the flesh beneath a bandage, covering the holes where once there were windows. Between this charred vertical plane and that of the floor on which she stood there was an eight- or ten-foot gap. The ceiling was completely black.

Chuck was fitting the barricade back in place, a fussier task than removing it. Cathy walked cautiously to the end of the floor. She guessed the missing section had either burnt or collapsed under the weight of the water used to fight the blaze. She dared to let her toes out over the edge and looked down. It was like a swimming pool filled with ink in which, bobbing sleepily, were innumerable books.

"The guy," Chuck was now ensconced in a leather chair, his feet up on one of the ottomans, "collected these rare books. He tried to rescue some of them from the fire downstairs. He got so much smoke in his lungs he died a couple of days later."

"What kind of rare books?" Cathy asked, stepping back from the brink.

"Some old science books. An old Koran, which is like the Islamic Bible …"

"Yeah, I know what it is."

"Right. And also … signed first editions … which are like a big deal … by … by … famous writers anyway … can't remember their names."

"How do you know all this?"

"My dad's an insurance adjuster. He's handling the claim. It's all going to relatives in Chicago."

Cathy sat down in another opulent chair. Everything was covered with a fine dark dust, like cocoa powder. One usually became accustomed to smells, not so the acrid scent of the building's interior, which continued clawing at her lungs.

"I bet that can be interesting," said Cathy.

"Insurance? Yeah, I guess."

"How long have you been coming here?"

"Couple of months. I love it. I don't know why. It's like it's mine. It's like it's my … office or fort or something? I'd spend the rest of the summer here, but … I'm goin' away tomorrow."

"Where?"

"The Muskokas. It's cottage country in Ontario. My mother is from there. We go every summer."

"Must be nice."

"Nah. It sucks. Everybody else, my cousins and uncles and stuff, are like really rich, and we're not. And my mom just hates it and my dad just hates it. I don't get why they go. And people are always calling me Newfie and shit. It's horrible."

"That's racist," said Cathy. She wasn't sure it was. She was echoing a sentiment she'd frequently heard voiced by her father in an effort to boost Chuck. One of the few things she knew about boys and men was how fragile their egos were, how in need of constant support.

"It is, you know," said Chuck, then, "Do you want a drink?"

"What? Like liquor?"

"Yeah," said Chuck, "there's a whole bar." He was excitedly out of his chair and into a kitchenette near where they'd come in. He opened a cupboard and withdrew some bottles, laying them one after the other on the countertop. She thought Chuck was charming, in a way, behaving as though he owned the place, being the debonair gent offering the lady a drink. "I don't even know what half of this stuff is, like vermouth? What do you mix with vermouth? There was some Kahlua, but I drank that."

With whom? Cathy wondered.

"Do you think maybe that chemicals from the fire might have affected it somehow?" asked Cathy.

"Nah," Chuck said. "Chartreuse? Ever heard of that?" He was holding a bottle of green fluid at arm's length. The label looked like it belonged on some bad-tasting medicine.

"I like the colour," Cathy said.

"Glasses?" wondered Chuck.

"What did you drink the Kahlua in?"

"I drank it out of the bottle," said Chuck grinning.

Cathy couldn't help herself. She was laughing.

"Listen," said Chuck, "later … like now … now soon, like tonight, what are you doing?"

4

The club was close with boy sweat, animal and unclean. It was slapped together like a shack, with ersatz wooden panelling, queasy hue of green on the walls, and enough cigarette scars on the bubbly linoleum floor to make a pattern like the measles. The works was tacked on the back of some tumbledown shit heap, an old metal shop, in the arse-end of downtown. It had taken Cathy and Chuck at least half an hour to walk there. The club was packed with kids older than her, though mostly still underage. The girls were dressed to go out, to go to a club, to dance, and Cathy felt self-conscious about her dull clothes. There were friends of Chuck's there, but he didn't go to them. He stayed with her pressed to the wall, occasionally pushed up against her by the crowd. To be heard over the racket he had to bring his mouth next to her ear and his lips had brushed her like a kiss and she sensed heat at once sparkling and molten. They'd been there for almost two hours (Cathy would be crucified when she got home), and the band, a newly constituted punk/country outfit of heroic nobodies from other local bands, a perverse anti-supergroup of fucked-up refuse-to-be-knowns calling itself Nay Cindy, were only now mounting the stage. They were underfed, lacking certain vitamins essential to life. Their skin was the colour of a shaved dog. The guy slinging the bass, heavier than he, round his neck was surely dying from the drubbing he'd looked to have taken. Oblivious to his surroundings the drummer, dropping to the stool behind his kit, shoved a hand down the front of his trousers, adjusted his cock and balls, and done, studiously sniffed his fingers. The guitarist, made of smoke, was in a murderous rage about something—the sound, the light, the venue, the life. The lead singer played guitar, too. She was a black-haired girl, shoulder length, in neglected chains, sleeveless, pants dirty with something like motor oil, fat belt with a big honking buckle.

She wore workingman's boots and squinted as though sixty watts were the sun. She smirked, sardonic and doubtful. Girl in a band.

They plugged in. An electronic hum crawled across the room like running wax, like spiders, provoking hoots and cheers. The girl at the microphone swung a claw at the guitar on her hip and brought it back against the strings like she was drawing a six-gun and there was an avalanche, there was blizzard of cinders. And now there were drums and bass, a horse she was riding, and steady hammering like twelve tons of clock, and then the second guitar and the girl singer like a monster chewing rocks and the floor was a storm at sea and the horse was charging and Cathy was dancing.

six

THIS SUN BURNED with unusual dedication. The worry for the Royal St. John's Regatta Committee was not whether the races would go ahead but how many cases of heat prostration there might be among the oarsmen and the lakeside throng. The august body of former greats and municipal muckety-mucks would make the official call early next morning, but Sophie, putting her trust in the weatherman and providence, announced the holiday and her party preceding it at three in the afternoon.

"You'll come?" she asked Marty.

"When did you get back?" he replied.

"Two days ago."

"You might have called."

"So might have you, *Maahten*."

"I didn't know you were in town."

"Then you weren't listening when I told you my dates."

Had she said anything? Perhaps. He couldn't argue the point.

"Besides," Sophie continued, "I was jet-lagged."

Jet-lagged? Though it was Vancouver, a day's flying against the sun, surely she meant *hungover*.

"What are you doing for the rest of the afternoon?" he asked. A

Pavlovian response to Sophie's voice had him aroused.

"Phoning people, running around getting stuff."

"Oh."

"Why?"

"I thought I might come over."

"No."

No? Was Sophie telling him that she did not want to see him? "No?"

"Not 'no' like that, *Maahten,*" Sophie said impatiently. "You could really help me by picking up some glasses at the rental place."

"Did you book them?"

"Yes."

"Okay, I'll see you later."

Marty was surprised to find Sophie had reserved thirty glasses for wine and another twenty tumblers for spirits. Her party was never so well attended. Marty was wearing, as he had done for the last six or seven years at least, a cream linen jacket and matching pants. The garment was of fine quality but suited for warmer climes. Sophie's regatta shindig was the only event that regularly occasioned putting it on. He'd found the trousers snug when he first buttoned them in his bedroom, but when he climbed into the car they cut into his belly. When he'd attempted to close his jacket before walking into the rental agency to pick up the glasses he found he didn't have sufficient slack in the fabric and left it open.

By the time he'd entered Sophie's kitchen it was too late to return home to change. The waistband of the pants was under such strain that the top edge was rolling outward. Sizes too small, the outfit was not loose and airy as intended, but constrictive and hot.

He'd come a few minutes early in the expectation that Sophie would be alone. There was a need for them to talk. Marty didn't exactly know where this tête-à-tête might go; there was a risk it could get heavy, so the pending arrival of guests provided an escape route, a means of capping it. But he found her assembling hors d'oeuvres in the company of two youngish men, younger than Marty in any case.

Sophie had a new hairdo, its length split and twirled up in two cockeyed buns that stuck off the back of her head. She was wearing a tank top and shorts with a bibbed front, like cut-off overalls. Marty couldn't decide whether she looked like a milkmaid, one of those virginal jug bearers you would see smiling up at you from the label of a cheese, or one of the Jetsons.

One of her gentleman callers had a shorn head, the scalp just losing its sheen beneath stubble. The other lad's locks were sculpted with glossy gel into peaks like a meringue. The trio was giggly. Marty detected the candied pepper-and-sage smoke of a hash spliff.

"Whatcha makin'?" Marty asked.

"Snacks," said Sophie. She and the two men tried to contain themselves but broke into fits of laughter.

Did he look that silly? Marty wondered.

"Sorry, honey," Sophie said. "It's Clive's fault, he made me smoke hash."

"I did not make you do anything of the sort," replied the man with the buzz cut. He posed, irritatingly snapshot-ready, when speaking.

"I'm Marty." He briefly considered adding "Sophie's boyfriend" just to make her uncomfortable, returning the favour. Sophie and he eschewed such labels by unspoken, mutual consent. None were satisfactory or meaningful, not "partner" nor "close friend." You couldn't beg off an invitation by saying "I'll have to check with my partner." Why did it matter what a partner was doing? What authority did a close friend have? "Lover" wasn't on, definitely not "occasional fuck." Every option really only said "not husband," "not wife."

"Clive."

"And this is Derek," said Sophie. The oily-headed one nodded and showed prodigious white teeth. The two of them were svelte, even pinched, with flat tummies like teenaged girls. Clive wore a clingy grey T-shirt that exaggerated his thinness. Derek, more tastefully, chose a somewhat oversized short-sleeved button-up silk shirt, buttercup yellow checks on white. Both of them were in billowy trousers. "You've met Clive, Martin."

Both Clive and Marty shook their heads.

"Sure you have, last year," Sophie insisted.

"I came late last year," said Clive. "We must have missed each other."

"You rented enough glasses," said Marty.

"We're having a crowd tonight," said Sophie. "Some Hollywood glamour."

"Hollywood?"

"Actually, they're only from Toronto, but they are in the film business. My uncle, Kaspar Berg, is involved with the score and some songs. He got on my flight when I connected. He was going to surprise me," Sophie answered. "Uncle is fantastic, you're going to love him. They begin shooting the movie in a couple of weeks."

"It's a big Newfoundland musical," said Derek.

Marty shivered at the thought.

"I told Uncle to bring along as many of his film friends as he likes. The more the merrier," Sophie said, turning her attention to the preparations. The glitterati must have their delightful antipasti.

Marty did not pitch in. After watching them for a few moments—Sophie rolling prosciutto cigarillos, Clive running raw, blue-grey shrimp onto bamboo skewers, and Derek actually carving radishes into flowers with a paring knife—he sensed he was intruding, getting in the way of their chummy, stoned banter. He mixed himself a gin and tonic, tall enough to last, and announced he was going out into the front yard for a smoke.

The long stretch of heat had reduced the pond. The shoals were clogged with reeds and cattails. Grasses that would normally be gently waving below the surface were on top of the water, reminding Marty of Sophie's hair floating in the bath. A rank felt of algae was forming in patches on the still waters. The stereo started inside and Marty could hear muffled music, dancey electronic pop, not the kind of the thing one found in Sophie's collection. He walked onto the trail skirting the pond and carried his drink away from the noise.

It was becoming obvious to Marty that Sophie was in some sort of denial about her age—how else to explain her behaviour, her new friends, and her capricious coif? She was distancing herself from his seriousness, his rectitude, because of the shadow they cast. She was having what should have been *his* mid-life crisis (and he'd been saving it). His sense of purpose pointed up her fecklessness. Sophie was satisfied to be a music teacher, had deliberately turned away from the sadistic rigours of the concert stage. She lacked the discipline. Marty wasn't one to settle for anything. He wouldn't be surprised if they were in there now, blowing another joint, laughing at him, laughing at the vice principal.

Perhaps Sophie was bored with him, tired of his preoccupation with work. Fine.

Marty'd never met "movie people." There was Lloyd Purcell, he supposed, but Lloyd was in television and a writer, about as glam as an orthodontist. Proper film folk, the "lights, camera, action" sort, would probably be big-headed flounce-abouts, not unlike brother Rex's theatrical set, but rich and better to look at. They said it was a growth industry in these parts, producers attracted by suspect tax credit schemes and semi-skilled workers paid in lowly Canadian dollars—"snow niggers" the L.A. people called them. Despite the many millions of dollars thrown at them, Marty never heard of any of the pictures turning a profit and suspected the whole enterprise was run by charlatans. Marty never got in on any of the good scams.

He soon heard the first revellers squealing and bellowing above the music. He wanted to wait outside a while longer, until a crowd large enough to hide within had arrived. Only then could he avoid having to swap seasonal banalities—lawn care and holiday plans—with the people from the school Sophie was obliged to invite or, worse still, meeting anybody new. But his glass was empty.

Marty needn't have worried. Word of the movie people's prospective appearance must have gotten around, for every possible guest, including what looked at first glance to be the entire faculty of The Red Pines, had come. The names of the picture's stars were murmured, Canadian "celebrities" Marty had never heard of, and Lauren Walker, once an above-the-title "A-lister" in Hollywood. No longer girlish, Walker was reduced to chasing parts that forced her to use her talents as an actress and ply them in locations as far-flung as Newfoundland.

Marty was pouring himself a third or possibly fourth drink when Hank and his wife, Beth, arrived. Beth carried an unruly spray of wildflowers, a gift for Sophie, and wore similar blossoms in her hair. Hank had become, in the five weeks since school closed, heavily bearded—maybe shaving was bad for the environment, chlorofluorocarbons in the foamy cream, ducks eating discarded razors; maybe he was going for an ascetic look, eco-Sufi. Whatever his and Beth's intentions, they just ended up looking like a couple of aging hippies. To avoid them Marty was forced to converse with the nearest familiar, Abe Summers. Abe was nattily attired for the English country—blue blazer, eggshell cotton trousers, candy-cane-striped shirt. All he needed was a Pimm's and an ascot. Then Marty could murder him with impunity.

"I've just begun dramaturging Shanawdithit," Summers said with pleasure.

Marty thought one of them must be tight, for Abe made absolutely no sense. "You're whatting what?"

"Shanawdithit, the last of the Beothucks."

"Right. What about her? Dead, isn't she?"

"Your brother's written a play ... a draft in any event ... based upon her life, another of his social histories. You must know about it, he's been hard at it now for ... at least four years."

"Haven't heard of it." This was true. "You're making it up."

"Sorry?"

"You're making it up." Marty found tormenting Abe irresistible. He knew now that it was he who was drunk. "You're a lying cunt. You don't even know my brother."

Summers was aghast and, if Marty judged it rightly, spooked. Marty was having his first fun of the evening.

"I'm kidding, Abe," Marty said. "You're doing what?"

"Dramaturge, working through the play with him." Marty's feint of aggression seemed to have raised the temperature, a gloss of perspiration bloomed on Summers's forehead and upper lip. "Helping him ready it for the stage. Rex is determined it have 'dramatic truth,' beating himself up over it if you ask me. He's developed a tremendous aversion, almost pathological, to theatrical or narrative contrivance."

"Right," said Marty, not actually sure what Summers meant. It was probably just more of his usual bullshit, but so confident was Summers in his pronouncements that they demanded to be heard. It was having an unwelcome sobering effect.

"And that's all well and fine in theory, but ... the thing is, no matter how serious, if people are going to sit and watch it, it has to, you know, at some level, entertain. There's a tyranny of gratification. Audiences have developed this sense of entitlement to easy epiphanies." Summers lowered his voice. "They get it from movies and television, I suppose. I'm realizing that stories that work as entertainment are always contrived. Rex's piece is a big piece, too big now. We're concentrating on the ending, the third act."

"Always a great place to start," said Marty.

So Rex's next opus would be about the extinction of a people. That would have 'em rolling in the aisles. By "a big piece" Abe no doubt meant "a much too long piece," which, given the duration of Rex's earlier works, meant it was over three hours. And what, in the name of God, was wrong with an epiphany, of any description? wondered Marty. He'd gladly take one.

"Do you remember Lauren Walker in *The Chief*?" Abe asked. "She was remarkable."

♄

The film people arrived in a convoy of three identical minivans, the famous and surprisingly diminutive Lauren Walker among them. Marty, and he supposed the other guests, just assumed they would all be actors and actresses, but they were, with the exception of Ms. Walker and a leggy protégé, mostly technicians and handlers—high-falutin carnies. This Marty gathered from their gadgets. Having come directly from set they all had tools and electronic jigamarandies manacled to their belts. What part these devices played in the making of movies, Marty could not guess. There was a telltale scruffiness about them, the rumples and wrinkles of the itinerant worker. Despite having a genuine movie star in tow, the group was Kaspar Berg's entourage; he was its engine. He was a commanding figure, broad, over six feet, his gleaming bald head with a deep cleft, possibly a scar, up the middle, a plum-coloured turtleneck gathered beneath his chin. Though his hands were mammoth, as large as Marty had ever seen, a ring with a yellow gem-setting on one of his long fat fingers still seemed outrageously proportioned. Man was big.

Kaspar's boisterous gang found their own way, easily making themselves at home, fixing drinks, juicing up the celebration, a gust of gaiety through the rooms. Once they found a moment, Kaspar took his niece aside. They talked softly in German. He stroked her head like she was a child.

When Kaspar rejoined the party his movement created a vacuum sucking up bodies in his wake as he barrelled past. It wasn't long before he sat at the piano and began to play.

The man possessed what Marty supposed to be complete faculty with the instrument, his fingers an unmediated extension of his mind, conductive tendrils streaming from his imagination. Like a conjurer's trick requests for songs were answered as they were called out. A show tune became lieder became a pop hit became a standard in seamless progression. As Uncle Kaspar would have it the instrument was either a roaring train or a toy. Marty had heard Sophie play this same piano, a large-lunged upright Bösendorfer, many times and it seemed to be quite fond of her, and she, in turn, spoke highly of it, but the thing just loved this guy, was giving as good as it got, thrilled to be played this way.

Between numbers Kaspar would free his right hand from the keyboard to take a drink or theatrically mop his brow, always keeping a bottom-end rhythm going, a jazz club heard from the street, with his left. He would toss out a gracious compliment, tell a joke or a scurrilous story about some screen legend, and provide his own incidental music. After a cracking Weill medley he summoned Lauren Walker to join him. She feigned reluctance, fished for and got pleas, drawing applause when finally relenting.

She took hold of the piano with one hand, cocking her head just so, instinctively finding her light, letting her curls unfurl, signalling that she was ready. Kaspar pulled loquacious ornaments from the keyboard, nothing at all melodic, just sugary harmonic chatter to flatter the woman's presence.

Lauren Walker turned and, it appeared, began to talk to Cloris Foley, who was sitting on the arm of the nearest chair. *"Someone told someone and someone told you …"* she said, her last words almost sung. Kasper smiled as if someone were whispering a secret in his ear. A tune, first an unrecognizable tease, emerged.

"... but they wouldn't hurt you that much. Since everyone spreads a story with his own little personal touch." Lauren Walker stopped, her final note riding the diminishing sustain from the piano. She and Kaspar waited a moment in the silence and then commenced in earnest, *"Do nothin' till you hear from me, pay no attention to what's said ..."*

Lauren Walker sang for their sins. Suspecting rapture, she looked from Cloris Foley to the heavens. Marty thought he might have heard the song before, the words were pleading the case of another of love's lost causes. *"If you should take the word of others you've heard ..."*

She brought her gaze earthward to meet Marty's. *"But does that mean that I'm untrue?"* She was looking right at him, putting on the hex. Stars, they called them, and indeed they were, gliding, evanescent spurs that filled your eyes when you were sent so high, so fast. *"Reveal how I feel about you."*

Lauren Walker had every creature in earshot spellbound. Her rhythms governed their blood. She held their breath. *"Some kiss may cloud my memory,"* she sang, *"And other arms may hold a thrill. But please do nothing till you hear it from me. And you never will."*

The final notes filled the room and faded. The audience sat for a moment, transfixed, then erupted in gratitude. Marty saw by the radiance in everyone's eyes that they all had the experience that Ms. Walker had been singing just for them. "How I feel about *you,*" she had said. She had made it plain.

And who had not been transported, taken? It was almost laughable. He was sure no one else caught it, but the supposedly impromptu performance was a crafted, rehearsed act, a gift for Sophie from Uncle. Lauren Walker and he had likely grabbed a few minutes at a piano somewhere, a rehearsal room or even a hotel bar, run through the changes and bridges, maybe the first verse and the chorus, nodded in agreement and gone on their way. That performers did this wasn't a revelation, and Marty didn't feel as though he'd been deceived; rather, seeing it pulled off by such professionals up close, he was fascinated by the method. It was the sincerity of it. It wasn't hollow, was even reciprocal, serving as it did every showman's deep need for need. Masters knew that there was never any faking it, that they must, as Marty never could, stand before the crowd, breast bared, offering up their hearts for the taking.

A gift for Sophie. Marty thought about his own niece, Cathy. She was in some kind of need. What did Marty have to give her?

Taking advantage of the jubilation rocking the room, Kaspar rose from the bench, swept his tall, rattling tumbler of bourbon off the piano, and to duck compliments made for the door. Marty topped up his G&T and followed.

Kaspar was looking over the pond, taking his air in the form of a cigarette, a foreign make smelling oddly like figs and, more faintly, horses and tack.

"That was wonderful in there," said Marty, noticing that he was beginning to slur his words. He would switch to water.

"Nothing, a bit of a lark," said Kaspar. Courtesy failed to mask his discomfort. They never talked about it.

"It was very … polished."

"I've played those songs many times."

"They're terrific."

"Yes, they are."

"How often do you have to practise, to be able to …?"

"I don't practise any more. I'm too old and wouldn't get any better. And you know some of that repertoire, those old tunes, don't really benefit from too much rehearsal."

"No?"

"Best they are played by someone young and talented who doesn't really know them and has to make it up as they go along … or so we like to believe."

"You're being hard on yourself."

"Nah. For me it's of little consequence. I no longer perform."

"Oh. What do you do?"

"This and that. Entertainment industry. Why all these questions?"

"Just curious. It was … like a show."

"I have been in that business for years. After a while everything is a bit of a show."

"Yeah," said Marty.

"I should return to the party," Kaspar said. He wished to conclude the conversation.

♆

The night was offering no relief, if anything the air was closer than it had been in the day. Going back into Sophie's, Marty caught his reflection wobbling in the Plexiglas of the storm door as it jerked to a close. Busting out of his wrinkled linen suit he looked like a pimp run to seed.

Inside Hank had taken centre stage. Instead of levity he brought gravity to the proceedings, talking to a nodding cluster of suckers. Marty caught snippets on his way to the gin: "sustainable development," "carbon dioxide dumps," "addicted to cheap oil," blah fucking blah. Hank was giving a lecture, no, worse—a sermon. Among those in thrall to his Rasputin-like presence was Lauren Walker. Only natural, thought Marty, refilling his drink. These actors and actresses were common marks for good causers. Their presence at a protest, picture in an advertisement, lent legitimacy to the crusade. Beauty was enough. Brigitte Bardot and that other bimbo … that other skag, what was her name? … Tanya Tucker! They'd done the local seal hunt serious damage a few years earlier, snuggling white-coated pups for the cameras. Now the corpulent harps and hoods covered the ice floes in the millions, the unchecked population taking its turn wreaking havoc on the seas.

Surrounded by sycophants for years, telling them their every idea was genius, show people lost their critical faculties. They shared, with politicians, distended vanity but were even less equipped to make policy, somehow misconstruing that people were cheering their cockamamie views on cruelty to lobsters or guns for babies when in fact it was their funny walk or their hard little tush that drew the applause. Hadn't dabbling in government by various Bonos and Bonzos made a Heaven's Gate of California's infrastructure?

Marty couldn't help himself, it was like picking a scab, he had to go back in there and hear the bullshit.

"We're shooting in that area," Lauren Walker weighed in. "Set's a reproduction eighteenth-century fishing village. So primitive! I don't know how your ancestors survived. It's really just fantastic. And the landscape! That harsh, rugged beauty."

"Rugged beauty"? No wonder they needed writers. If I were a rugged beauty would you blow me? thought Marty.

"It's a treasure for all humanity," she said. "It's much more than a local issue." One visit and she was an expert.

"You really have to see it up close to fully appreciate it," said Hank. "It's subtle, mosses and lichen. It doesn't really photograph well. I know that sounds trivial, but it makes our case a lot harder. The people trying to preserve grasslands have a similar problem. It's not as sensational as the rainforest."

This wasn't real talk. The two of them were voicing a fucking filmstrip! Everyone nodded in agreement. Marty could no longer hold his tongue.

"What happened to the ice age? I thought we were supposed to have an ice age. I'm sure when I was growing up we were all worried about things cooling down. Now we're worried about it heating up. Am I right?"

No one answered.

"Surely if the planet gets too warm we could set off a nuke somewhere in the desert and blow dust into the atmosphere, right? Like nuclear winter, only it would be controlled, like a kind of nuclear autumn. Has anyone looked into that? Technological solution there. Nuclear remediation!" Marty thought this quite clever.

"And! And! It seems to me," Marty said, "that the problem you have can simply be reduced to humans. We're spreading like weeds, building everywhere, eating everything."

"Weeds aren't a bad analogy," said Hank, scratching the itchy skin beneath his new beard.

"Thank you," said Marty, giving a slight bow. He could tell Hank was worried what he might say next. "So, if you want to do the planet a real favour, you should let the Third World starve, right? Let Africa roast and everyone there die, you should just kill yourself. Better yet, murder/suicide killing spree. Use that opposable thumb to cock the hammer and spray some fast-food joint with bullets and then turn the gun on yourself, blow your *Homo sapiens* brains out. Smokey the Bear, or Donald the Dolphin, or whoever the fucking animalpersonguy ... what's that called? ... ANTHROPOMORPH! ... whatever the anthropo ..." he was having trouble saying it now, a second time, "mascot for the environment is ... they'll thank you." Now Marty made a staccato clicking noise, *eh-net eh-net eh-net,* through his nose, his attempt at a dolphin's "thank you, go fuck yourself," but nobody had a clue what he was doing or found him in the least amusing. The silence that met him cleared his senses and he could feel that he was swaying unsteadily.

"Who the hell are you?" asked Lauren Walker.

"I'm the boyfriend," said Marty.

The girlfriend (the ex?) soon corralled him out the back door and up against the side of one of the film production's minivans.

"What is wrong with you? Why are you being so hostile?" Sophie demanded.

"It's not hostility. It's the truth. Hank is full of shit."

"So what if he is?"

"People should know." Marty noticed a silhouette in a neighbour's window, someone taking in the show.

"And it's not just Hank. I saw you harassing Abe."

"Yeah, you see the thing is ... he's full of shit, too ... I don't play favourites."

"Don't ruin my party ... please, Martin."

"Am I embarrassing you in front of your showbiz friends?"

"You're drunk."

"Not too drunk to fuck."

"No? But too drunk to drive. I'm calling you a taxi." She turned away and walked back to the house.

Marty could hear her muttering to herself in Kraut.

As he lay in bed the next morning, Marty wasn't in the least contrite. Maybe, feeling out of sorts as he did, aching behind his eyes—clot-mouthed, cold-headed, hot-bodied—maybe he would have had less to drink. Once home he had unwisely fixed himself another tall one, something to accompany three critical cigarettes. Yes, a few too many gins, but that was all. And despite the poisoning he was, this morning, showing a shocking vitality beneath the sheets. A surprisingly hefty tumescence was making its presence felt. It didn't yet rage but was so primed that just the slightest touch, a feathery glance, would turn it into lumber. Marty knew it was not in a state to be talked to, it wasn't a listener, this chubby, it was a bully and a thug.

Coming to grips with the problem was made easier by his determination to call Jackie today. She'd been on his mind as he'd fallen into the dumb sleep of the drunk and was waiting for him in the morning. In fact, dream girl was all over him. Possessed of invisible wings she was atop him, riding hard, and in an instant on her hands and knees. She had him in her mouth her hands her sex her ass so that the imagined act, at its sudden wet resolution, was simultaneously many.

He dozed briefly. When he finally rose and padded to the kitchen for coffee he felt worse. He was an untrained drinker, hadn't the skills for holding his liquor or coping with the consequences. After drinking half a cup he was asleep on the couch.

He woke again an hour later. His arms and legs were freezing. A shower provided momentary relief. As soon as he'd towelled off, more waste oozed from his pores. His stomach was empty and sour, urgently calling for sausage, toast, and runny egg yolk. He dressed, anticipating climbing into his car and going to a diner, MacNamara's, but realized as his swollen fingers tied his shoes that the Saab was parked on Bristol Close, in front of Sophie's. The back of his neck reddened at the thought of it. Sophie would soon be awake. Marty had to move swiftly lest he be seen by her and called inside for a dressing-down, obliged to revisit last night. He had to retrieve his car now, get in, get out, perhaps never to return. He called a cab.

☿

The food, the papers, and the anonymity of the restaurant did him good. His body chemistry, while still shaky, was struggling toward an electrolytic balance. Some internal regulator wanted and got chocolate milk. It worked wonders. The local rag, usually no more than a vehicle for ads and sports scores, today had six or seven pages of regional coverage. The movie was mentioned in a fluff piece about Lauren Walker. She claimed to have fallen in love with Newfoundland and was considering buying a summer retreat here. The item featured several photographs. One showed her on set between takes costumed for the musical, dowdy dress and bonnet—the well-meaning school marm or the thoughtful spinster aunt—with the mayor on her arm. Marty supposed they'd give her the key to the city, if anyone ever really did that, for simply being famous and having bothered to come. St. John's, despite its old fortifications, was not a place one could consider gated. It was, as a colonial port, open, louche. And Town wasn't, in recent history, a place people clamoured to enter. With its variable economic fortunes it was a place you left. Better they should give notable visitors passage on the next ship out. If they were bound and determined it be a ceremonial key, it should be made clear that it was for the back door and slipping away in the night. Below the recent photo was a publicity snap from Ms. Walker's heyday, something out of the files, tits high, teeth big.

Most of the rest of the paper was dedicated to the Regatta, controversy about a new shell, arguments that the schedule favoured one squad or another, general sporting life, and history lite.

Marty needed a cigarette but smoking was prohibited in the restaurant. He paid and left.

♀

At his house Marty looked up Jackie Spurell's number but did not call right away. He wanted to rehearse, in his head, what he would say. It occurred to him that there was a possibility that her husband, Ted, might answer. Marty knew not to hang up. Ted could then just use the *69 feature and find out who had rung. And Ted calling back asking *what that was about?* wouldn't do. No, Marty would, if Ted answered, ask for ... what was a good name? An ordinary name? Harry? Bob? Ted? No, of course not Ted. Then John, he'd ask for John Smith, and then Ted would say *wrong number* and hang up and think nothing more of it. John Smith. But John Smith was so ordinary as to be too ordinary and sound suspicious. You couldn't trust a John Smith because you knew that wasn't his real name. And anyway, wasn't John Smith that pilgrim-banging Pocahontas? "Is John Smith, there?" "No, he's out screwing Pocahontas." Better a name so loaded as to be forgettably normal ... like something Einstein or Picasso ... no, those would stick ... Felix Breshnev. No, but Felix was excellent. Felix Smith. So Marty was Felix Smith.

But what if Ted was standing in the room when Jackie answered, inhibiting her ability to speak freely? He could, when and if Jackie answered, ask straight out whether Ted was there. Jackie probably wouldn't recognize his voice immediately. If she said "yes," Marty could say, "It's Marty Devereaux. Should I call back later?" Jackie's answer would tell Marty how responsive she would be to his proposition. If she slyly exhorted him to call again at a time her husband wasn't about then Marty knew he had a chance. A chance of what? Of fucking her, of course. Of bringing their flirtation to its inevitable conclusion, of luring her into an adulterous affair? He hadn't thought of it in those terms before. It was tawdry and predictably middle class, something out of Updike. And it was predatory. He was only going for it because having seen the state of poor Ted he figured he had an opportunity. Still ...

If Ted wasn't around and Jackie answered, Marty would be totally exposed, would have to put the question to Jackie baldly and live or die by her reply. It was this prospect that gave Marty the jitters so that he hesitated, pacing tracks around his bungalow. Would he eventually ask Jackie here, to his bed, the bed he'd shared with Sophie? He was cheating on Sophie, too. Wasn't he? No. No, it was ending. He went for the phone.

After three rings he sensed that the call would go unanswered, that he would get a brief reprieve, an opportunity to reconsider.

"Hello?" It was Jackie.

"Jackie?" he said, realizing immediately that he was to have asked if Ted was there.

"Yes."

"Hi, Marty Devereaux." A feverish collar was constricting his neck, making speech an effort.

"Oh. Hello, Marty."

"Hello," he said again.

"Yes?"

"Remember I mentioned … I mentioned before … we talked about going out to the Perroqueet Downs."

"I do."

"Well … thing is, I … for business, I have to … to have a viewing of the site, the site of the development."

"Yes."

"And I said, or you said, you might be interested in going along."

"Right, yeah."

Marty could tell she was puzzled, there was that tone in her voice.

"So, I'm going tomorrow, and do you want to come?"

She didn't say anything for a moment. Maybe Ted was there, maybe he was standing right next to her and Marty had put her in a difficult position, dangerous even. Marty could hear her breathing. No, it wasn't Ted. She was thinking it over. What Marty was really asking was dawning on her and she was wondering whether she could, whether she would, whether she'd come to that place, whether she would betray not so much Ted as herself.

"What time?" she said.

Marty hadn't thought that far ahead. "Oh, like … the afternoon, around three."

"That would be … difficult for me."

"The morning, eleven in the morning?"

"Sure, that's good. Ted's at group in the morning."

♁

The Regretta was such a dumb-ass holiday. Cathy knew girls who rowed, big-boned jocks from school, and her mother, on one of her occasional health kicks, participated a few years ago, rowing for some women's shelter. Cathy, like most of the bodies wandering around the side of the lake, couldn't be bothered with the races. When she used to come with her father they would buy tickets on the raffle wheels or toss rings or lay down coins on the Crown and Anchor. The cries were the same today as they had been then. "One for a nickel, two for a dime, three for a quarter." "Can't win if you don't spin." "One ticket holding up the wheel." She would have liked to play but was, for no reason, no reason at all, mortified at the thought, at the potential for embarrassment, at the possibility she might win and that one of the barkers would point out "the lovely lady," "the pretty girl in the black T-shirt," "the morose, lonely one, with the big ugly knees," "the one over there without the boyfriend." She needed the cover of her dad's towering presence, but she was too old for that. Besides, Dad wouldn't come to the Regretta any more, it had bad associations for him, landing as he always did in the confines of a beer tent. There, soused, he would work his nationalist act, preaching "Free Newfoundland" nonsense—"the ultimate expression of a people," "the Terms of Union were terms of surrender," "the example of Iceland"—to the converted. Failing to stir his rum buddies to action he would fall into a maudlin funk, muttering that the people of Newfoundland, beggars amidst bounty, servants in their own house, were getting their due. So hopeless, so hopeless.

Cathy threaded the crowd. The petitions to bet were only the foundation of the din. It was augmented by wailing children, roaring generators, starter pistols and air horns, chattering pinwheels, pennants and flags spanking in the wind.

Torches of cotton candy reached for hair and clothes. Punchy wasps bounced around the overflowing garbage bins. All you could smell was deep fat and horseshit from the pony rides. She ate a tofu hot dog, drank a piss-warm Coke, and left.

The holiday shut the town down. Cathy ambled across streets that would normally be choked with cars. The absence of activity made her feel exposed, took from her the ability to hide behind the more bumptious citizenry, and sent her to the cover of the alleys and lanes and then, as if by accident, to the boarded rear entrance of Rosenkrantz's bookstore.

This wasn't the first time Cathy had passed this way since Chuck's family had dragged him away to Ontario. The burnt-out building exerted pull. If she was to be completely honest with herself she'd admit she was a touch drunk with that boy, an affliction that made her cringe when she saw it in other girls.

Cathy took the barred door in her hands and pulled it open. She couldn't quite believe she'd done it again, that she had the guts.

Sheer beams of light pierced gaps in the boarded windows. The glass panes in the rear wall were so soot-stained that they afforded scant illumination to the interior. More fine particles had settled, but not enough to cover evidence of the earlier visit, the footprints and smudges, impressions on the furniture. Where the place seemed exotic then, it was gloomy now. With her attention focused on Chuck she had failed to appreciate the dimension of the destruction. The exposed beams had been charred and shrunken with violence. Creeping stains on the rugs showed where the blackened ceiling, bowing in spots, was leaking and would eventually succumb.

How would she approach Chuck in September, when school re-opened? It wasn't as though they were close friends; they'd only hung out that one night. She couldn't stop thinking about him. It was crushing, but her thoughts returned again and again to his near presence, to his pushing up against her, the bulk and heat of him. Up in her dreams Chuck was champion and baby, confidant and charmer, chaste-ravisher boy-man pirate. She wanted.

She was wasting her time. Chuck would ignore her. He hadn't sought her out that day, called her, they just happened to meet in the street. There was no reason why he should have given her a second thought since.

There was a bedroom off the main living area, the door to which was open. Cathy looked inside but felt that she should not enter. The bed was unmade, blankets tossed aside as the poor man, old Rosenkrantz, must have left it when he sprang to his feet in the middle of the night, smoke detectors squealing, the air poisonous, his racing thoughts turning to the fuel, the bomb of books, one floor below.

She walked to the other side of the main living area. This wall was entirely covered with shelves, or rather one rambling hand-built bookcase that looked to have been extended and extended until there was no more room. Rosenkrantz's collection was completely different from the one that cluttered her parents' home. Theirs was willy-nilly. Slight paperbacks, novels, plays, political tracts with mauled covers and broken spines, ignorantly defaced with meaningless marginalia, with phone numbers, doodles, and to-do lists, used and then carelessly discarded, stuffed wherever they might fit. Here Cathy was looking at a temple of books, an ordered and tended private library, a wall of leather, of straight, sometimes ribbed, spines. Why an original or older copy of something so easily reproduced as a book should be so valued she could not understand. These were all esteemed but not equally so. A couple of volumes were singled out, standing alone from the others, set apart by heavy sculpted bookends. Cathy reached for one. It was a tall book, its chestnut leather cover was coarser to the touch than she would have imagined. She opened it. A title page was filled with text in a foreign language—she guessed after a minute it must be Latin—and a small square illustration of a woman blowing some sort of horn. On the top of the page were the words *Ioannis Keppleri* and then below what looked to be the title.

HARMONICES

MVNDI

LIBRI V. QVORVM

It was surely an antique—if you used that term for books—but given the suppleness of the paper, not a terrifically old one. Cathy flipped through the pages, text interspersed with tables, diagrams, and geometric drawings. It was something to do with math or science. What if it were a hundred, two hundred years old? Was that really old for a book? When was the printing press invented? She'd learned that in school but forgotten or, she realized now, had not tried very hard to remember. Who was that invented by? Gutenberg? She tried to put dates to some of the science Donnelly taught at Frank Moores. When was Copernicus? He said the earth went around the sun, she knew that, but when did he say it? She remembered other names, other scientists, Bacon, Lavoisier, Boyle. There was a Boyle's Law, she was sure of that. Maybe in the end she wanted to know that stuff. She thought she would keep the book.

It did not occur to Cathy that taking the book was theft until she was out of the building and well down the alley. She unconsciously assumed that the store and the apartment above were abandoned and so its contents salvage. Rosenkrantz was dead; he wouldn't miss it. Clutched in her arm was a dead man's book. She and Chuck had helped themselves to his booze, disrespectfully trespassed his home. She wasn't generally superstitious but felt anxious now. Then there was the law. What if Rosenkrantz's Chicago relatives knew about the book and were expecting to inherit it? But then, if it were that valuable someone would have already come looking for it. The bookcase hadn't been disturbed, there had been no inventory taken. She would keep the book. It was how she would initiate contact with Chuck in September. She would tell him that they had to meet in private to discuss something ... she would show it to him once he vowed to keep the secret. He had shown her the way into the building. He was a conspirator. She went home.

Her father shouted after her as she started up the stairs for her room. She walked into the kitchen to answer his call, forgetting until it was too late that she still held the book.

Dad did not look well. There was a Cellophane sheen to his brow. He was seated at the kitchen table, crutching his weight with it.

"Where were you?" he asked.

"Down to the Regretta," she said.

"Too hot for me today," he said.

"Are you okay, Dad?"

"Back," he said.

"Did you want something?"

"Didn't know who it was, that's all."

She waited for him to say something else but he remained silent. He seemed stuck there, unable to get out of the chair. Cathy went upstairs to her room.

♂

Marty's sleep was fitful. He was a boy, one of the awkward teenagers he saw and detested at his school, hopelessly inarticulate—cramped.

Lying there anticipating being alone with Jackie, what poise he possessed left him. Over and over he made detailed arrangements in his head. It would be a picnic. He would take a basket with some sandwiches, some fruit and maybe some cheese—not anything smelly—a bottle of wine. He supposed Beaujolais was apropos a picnic. He'd buy a wicker basket first thing in the morning. He'd remember to gas up the car, have a full tank. Was Jackie fixed? She was childless. Would he need condoms? No, of course not. They wouldn't have sex right off, first time out. Would they? Maybe they would. They were having an affair, that's what it was all about. And how few stolen moments would they be able to share, what with Ted's problems and Marty's busy work schedule? How few moments were there left to be stolen? If they were going to do it, then they'd best get on with it. If they did have sex would it be out-of-doors on the spongy cover of the Perroqueet Downs? Fucking out-of-doors was problematic—the ground could be hard, there might be bugs, you'd get sand up you. He noted to bring an especially large blanket on which to spread their alfresco lunch, just in case. It had been so long since he'd had sex with anyone besides Sophie. Everybody had their own particular way of making love, particular needs, areas to which special attention must be paid, zones of exclusion, and he would need to learn Jackie's. There were things you could tell … without looking as it were … and it was in such a way, an intuition—no, a more profound sense—that he divined Jackie's taste for … No, it wasn't true, he didn't know that at all, *that* was merely a projection of his desire. He'd see. She'd see. Together they'd discover each other. They'd both been around, they could make it plain what they wanted so as not to waste time. He lay in bed, trying not to think about it.

4

He regretted having worn jeans. He was never comfortable in casual dress and the day was proving too hot for denim. Even in short-sleeves, the windows down, he was overheated as his car approached Jackie's house. Shorts would have been more comfortable, but Marty thought men looked ridiculous in short pants, as they did in ball caps, in running shoes, with ponytails, or, most repellently, earrings.

He discovered, too late, that the store at which he intended to buy the wicker picnic basket did not open until 10 A.M. To make the best use of his time, he had gone to the liquor store in the interval to get the wine only to find that it held the same hours. In the end, pressed, he packed the basket in the store, carrying his plastic shopping bag of sandwiches, fruit, and chocolate from the trunk of his car to the cash. This gave his enterprise a shadowy character, his hiking to take a lunch by the sea a transparent act of imposture. The clerks eyed him judgmentally as though someone so late to the picnic game didn't deserve such a lovely basket.

He rushed to Jackie's. And now, approaching, he was sweating and at the last minute concerned that Rex or Meredith might spot him. They lived just around the corner. How would he explain himself if he were seen? How close was Rex to Ted? Shit! Didn't Jackie say that Ted was "in group"? *Group* was Rex's speed. There was no reason why Rex should have shared with Marty that he was in therapy. But then, if Rex were in group therapy with Ted he wouldn't be around to see his brother sneaking off with his friend's wife. Where, Marty wondered, would Rex's loyalty lie, with his brother or the new pal, the fellow loser? And was Rex so pussy-whipped that he would begrudge another man, any man, some skin, so feminized by Meredith that he would think his own brother a cad?

Marty realized he was being irrational. There was no evidence to suggest that his brother was in therapy with Ted Spurell, that the two men were even close friends. All he knew was that they'd taken the same stupid cooking course at the vocational college and they attended the same AA meetings. Besides, it was Meredith he really need worry about. Though he was in good stead since pretending to counsel the knife-wielding Cathy, he doubted that beneficence was enough to spare him reproach in the matter of banging the married neighbour. If Meredith came aboard him Marty would remind her that it was she who had introduced the adulterous pair, perhaps unconsciously encouraging their sinful act. She hadn't pulled the trigger, but she'd put the gun in his hand.

He could see Rex and Meredith's house now, snapdragons, pinks, and lobelia—easy plants—in the window box, half spent and slouching from the heat, recyclables next to the front door. He turned the car onto Alderdice Street, coming to a stop opposite Jackie's place. Marty pulled on the hand brake. He needed to sit still for a moment, slow himself down. He wanted a cigarette but would wait until later, share one with Jackie.

Then, as if reading his mind, came Cathy's voice.

"Cigarette?"

She gave him a terrible fright. While he was looking through the passenger window at the lemon-cream house on the other side of the street, Cathy stuck her head in the driver's side window, bringing her face close to his.

"Sweet Jesus, Cathy!" He wondered what she was doing there, forgetting for a moment she lived not fifty yards from where he was parked.

"Sorry," Cathy said. "Do you have a cigarette to spare?"

She could have cadged money, keys to his house, he would have given her anything to beat it before Jackie Spurell, perfumed and guilty, came out the door.

"Sure," he said, taking the pack from his breast pocket and handing her three.

"Are you going to see Dad?"

"Rex. No. Yes. Yes, but then I remembered something." Marty turned away from Cathy and looked across the street. Jackie, in tan shorts and a white, sleeveless T-shirt, was standing before the open door. She looked at Marty and gave a shrug. Was it a signal, now that they were in peril of being caught, to call off their date, to bail out?

"Okay," said Cathy. "Do you have a match?"

Marty tried to fish the lighter out his pants pocket, but the seat belt was in the way. He scrambled to unfasten it.

"Here, take it," he said, passing the plastic lighter, slippery with perspiration from his fingers, to Cathy.

"That's okay," she said, using the lighter and handing it back.

Marty snatched it. He looked across the street. Jackie was approaching. A step behind, his beleaguered noggin safe in a Tilley hat, was Ted.

"Hi, Mrs. Spurell," said Cathy.

"Smoking?" answered Jackie.

"Uncle Marty gave it to me."

Jackie leaned in the passenger window. She grimaced.

"You ride up front," said Ted.

Marty couldn't see his face, only his midsection through the rear passenger window. The fly of his corduroy pants was down. Out the rear window Marty saw Cathy walking away, down the hill toward her house, puffing out a trail of smoke.

"Okay, honey," said Jackie. Ted climbed in the rear, Jackie in the front.

"Hi, Ted," Marty said.

"Hello, Marty," said Ted blithely.

If he suspected that he was a cuckold he showed no sign of it. These new antidepressants were reputedly powerful agents. Maybe he knew, knew all about it and didn't care. (Marty had just assumed Ted was clinically depressed, but it could be something worse, a dangerous psychosis, sexual depravity, homicidal rage.) Maybe

Marty had gotten it all wrong, maybe Jackie had simply assumed Marty's intentions were noble and invited the husband along.

"Where's Rex?" Ted asked.

"Yeah," said Jackie, "did you reach him?"

Now Marty saw it. Somehow Jackie had been trapped and fabricated some story to account for Marty showing up. She couldn't say anything to Marty in front of Ted, only indirectly lead him.

"No," Marty said, "I didn't."

"I wonder, is he home now?" said Ted.

"Actually, no ..." Marty said, and then to add a strand of verisimilitude to the lie, "I was just talking to Cathy."

Marty didn't say about what. He gunned the car, getting out of the neighbourhood as swiftly as possible.

ኀ

The three shared some idle banter, how it was great to finally be going out to the Downs, what with it being in the news and all, and especially on such a grand day, and how hot the weather was lately and was that maybe this global warming thing and wasn't that wonderful for the Regatta but now they'd had enough of the heat since Ted and Jackie's bedroom, being on the third storey of the house, was unbearable at night and they'd taken to sleeping on the Hide-A-Bed in the guest room on the second floor but how that didn't seem all that much better? By the time they were out of the city and on the highway, Ted was a-snooze.

Marty and Jackie were silent as they drove. He stole a glance at her legs. The thighs, bigger than he'd expected, filled the legs of her shorts. They were deeply tanned, enough that her knees looked a little dirty. The toffee gilding of her areola was visible beneath the points her nipples marked on her shirt. Her breasts were small and tight to her body, each wanting to be a single handful. She caught him looking at her. She brought her hand slowly to her mouth and put her finger to her lips.

"It's his medication," she said. She was telling Marty that they could talk but not freely. She needn't have said anything for already, just a few kilometres beyond the city's southern limit, the landscape—barrens, oily bogs, evergreens, the scattered shacks—again and again, entranced one to hush.

Marty took a left at an unmarked junction onto a road that led through a gap in the hills and out onto a long peninsula. They were doubling back, returning toward the city from the rear.

As they descended toward the coast the air stuttering in the open windows cooled. The peninsula was wide enough at its base that, though the ocean was occasionally visible through the conifers, you did not at first have a sense of riding a spine thrust into the water.

The road was a scant two lanes, the bleached pavement crumbling at the edges. Out the driver's side window the land began to rise more steeply, creating the jagged barrier that separated the wild from town. The brambles visible through the passenger side window diminished and, more and more, there was the sea, until they were driving in reach of its spray.

Beyond berry-picking Marty knew of no reason to come here so he was perplexed by a bustle ahead. As the road rose and fell, the commotion came in and out of view. When the car's angle of approach was just so, a bright light was visible.

They arrived at some flats, meadows between the salt water and the hills, and the activity was plain to see.

"What's that?" wondered Jackie.

They were amidst it, slowing to a crawl between lines of semis, pulled over on both sides of the road, territory marked with blaze-orange pylons, their mass testing what little shoulder there was. A regiment, all fitted with two-way radio headsets, were working from the backs of the trailers. Racks of torn and soiled clothes were wheeled down ramps. A high priest and attendants blessed and anointed a bulky black machine, a block of steel in a leather and moulded plastic caul, affixed with tubes, cylinders, and wires all mounted at the end of a resting jib. And everywhere people were getting Styrofoam cups of coffee, picking over tables of pastries and sandwiches. Cinema was evidently hungry work.

Down a cart track to the shore, pallets of prefabricated despair and depravation were being unloaded and assembled. Hollow shells of rough timber houses and spindly flakes for drying salt fish were being slung together, the carpenters moving with the enterprise of ants. Of most interest to Marty was a woman in a protective mask working behind the builders. She was spraying the wood with an atomized smut that instantly aged its appearance. One side of an eighteenth-century fishing settlement was growing out of the ground.

"It's a movie they're shooting," said Marty. "Lauren Walker's in it."

Marty stopped the car to let an Amazon cross the road, a shrink-wrapped bale of plastic replica split cod hoisted on her shoulder.

"Lauren Walker! Wow," said Jackie, "I just saw her in a video the other night, *The Chief.* She was awesome. She played this retard. I think she got like an Academy Award for it or something."

Marty lifted his foot from the brake. The film disappeared in the rearview mirror as the road continued on, away from the shore and into the hills.

They reached, what seemed from below, the crest, only to discover another range beyond. Here the road turned sharply. The prospect opening before them, sheltered to the north and east by treed hills, was of a bowl of green and blond, a valley that rolled slowly to the south. It spilled into the sea in beaches and dunes. A far spit rose out to a headland. Beyond this, shrouded at their bases by mist, were two soaring island spires capped in velvet. At their ken, softening the arced line of the horizon, was an endless fog bank.

The road came to an end. Marty drove the car up onto the sod and stopped.

"This is it, I guess," he said.

"Emflompf . . . ?" asked Ted, waking.

Marty turned off the ignition and got out of the car. At a distance he could hear the sea churning, a wet machine idling away, booming and banging where it collided with the land like a never-ending accident. At his auditory limit there was a cranky piano of industry, the city hidden over the hills.

"Ach-laaaach," went Ted. He stood next to Marty, pulling his pants out of his crack. "So this is the Perroqueet Downs."

"Look," said Jackie. She pointed ahead to a square doorway ornamented in the fashion of a pagoda, erected over a centuries-old footpath.

"Door," said Ted, sounding for all the world like one of the Telletubbies.

Marty got the picnic basket. Jackie reached out to share the load, taking the blanket. The closing of the car's trunk flushed a partridge that had lain unseen in scrub not ten feet from where they stood. With one clap of its wings, the bird pitched itself into the air. It caught a zephyr, which conveyed it over the valley. At a distance Marty lost sight of it. The company of three set off toward the strange marker.

The construction was an entrance to the Perroqueet Downs as envisaged by Gerry Hayden and crew. On the lintel above were the words "THE NEW FAR EAST" and in smaller letters below "A new way of community."

"What does that mean?" asked Ted.

"I don't know," said Marty. What he did know, now as not before, was how desirable a location the Perroqueet Downs was for a development. They had not driven more than twenty minutes, easily shortened with a few well-placed roads. Expropriate a pasture here, dynamite a cut through the rocks there, drain some wetlands and this Arcadia was close to downtown. The plans to blast were probably already drafted. Moreover, the spot, while on the sea, was nestled in protective geology. The hills cradled it in a giant's arm, shielding it from the nor'easters. The trees here at the head of the valley were straight, tall and mixed, birches and larch breaking up the impenetrable stands of spruce. The grasses and peat, which took over closer to the point, were not, as they appeared on television, featureless, but a plush carpet. The variety of the low-growing plants was astonishing: leaves delicate or leathery, sporting berries, seed heads, and pods. But this, at ankle height, was only the canopy. Below was fibrous growth, a thatch of runners and then farther down interwoven mosses, emerald foam—a fairy forest of redheaded matchsticks. It seemed to Marty that if you reached your hand in there it would be cool as a well. In those spots where boulders cut through they were festooned with lime and mauve lichen. Gerry Hayden knew what he was doing, but Marty saw, to his dismay, that Hank was right.

Marty and Jackie walked around the faux Japanese entrance. Ted passed through.

The pillowy downs were encroaching on the footpath. It had become so narrow in places that the three went single file. Marty then Jackie then Ted. It headed in the general direction of the point until it met a brook running from the hills. Here the path turned and followed the freshwater course.

They tried picking their way through an area of nettles but finding no path turned back and went around. The flora changed as they passed. They were soon amidst purple staffs of monkshood and patches of cow parsnip. Closer to the water there were roses gone wild and ancient lilacs.

The stream did not run directly into the sea but formed a barachois, collecting behind a leaky berm of stones and, farther up the shore, into a brackish slough. Marty remembered the drawings Hayden showed him in the restaurant and saw that the marsh was where the environmentally friendly sewage treatment plant was to be situated.

Tidal action was pushing the beach rocks up and sucking them back with a clattering, as if the landwash were breathing with consumptive lungs. At the top of the sculpted ridge there was a line of desiccated seaweed and kelp.

At the beach they separated. With a cane of driftwood Ted idly poked at the detritus near the high-water mark. Jackie went down closer to the water's edge, daring the surf. Marty hung back on the grass and found a spot for their lunch. He supposed the day wasn't entirely wasted, he'd seen the Perroqueet Downs. Sharing the drive with Ted had denatured his desire, not merely because the opportunity for its fulfillment had been stolen from him, but because proximity to the victim of his planned action had given him a twinge of conscience. Besides, he had other, more pressing concerns. An affair with a married woman was, at this moment, foolhardy.

Marty spread out the blanket Jackie had left with him and began unpacking the basket. He would have to eat sparingly so as not to point up the fact the meal was set for two. Ted was using his scrawny stick to lift a shrivelled plum-coloured sack, a devil's purse, from the beach.

The natural splendour of the surroundings was wearing on Marty. It complicated matters that he could not dismiss Hank's cause as a reflex, an automatic opposition to anything involving a bulldozer. But progress came at a cost. The preservationists were advocates of doing nothing. They were men and women of inaction. Marty resolved not to become squeamish, to put doubt from his head, and once the picnic was done give the area a critical recognizance—his ostensible reason for coming after all.

From his vantage point he could see a wide sweep of beach. Dotting it were abundant jellyfish, wet patches with a jade petrochemical sheen, stranded as the tide receded and now roasting in the sun. More could be seen in the water riding the swells, umbrellas of slime just beneath the surface. Marty couldn't remember them ever being so plentiful.

He watched Jackie and Ted, like all finished couples keeping their distance but unable to break free of each other's gravitational field. They would forever tumble, twinned, through space.

Marty checked his watch. It was going on two o'clock.

"LUNCH!" he yelled.

Ψ

Ted ate like a pig, pushing sandwiches in his chops, gobbling olives and chocolates, pouring mineral water into his mouth until it overflowed and spilled on his chest.

"What a great idea this was," he said, cheeks puffy with ham and cheese.

"Yeah," said Jackie.

Marty uncorked the wine. Pouring himself and Jackie a glass he felt Ted's gaze. Ted was chewing more slowly, mulling something over. Did the count of glasses start him to wondering?

"I assumed ..." said Marty, "that you and Rex wouldn't want any wine, being in AA."

"No," said Ted. "I'm surprised you drink."

"How's that?" asked Marty.

"Alcoholism runs in the family, you know."

"I didn't know. But then Rex is the only one on either side to ever have a problem. I always blamed the arts."

"No, that's not true," said Ted.

"Then the critics."

"No."

"Drove him to drink. A little joke."

"No, I meant about your family. Your father was an alcoholic."

"My father? I don't think so."

"Rex said so during meetings. That's how your father died, right? Drunk driving."

"No," said Marty, draining his glass. "He was avoiding a moose, or a caribou, or something."

"Rex said he was probably drunk."

"No. I've never heard that. Rex probably just ran out of hard luck stories for the meetings and had to make one up. Sometimes I think he enjoys telling the tales more than he enjoyed the boozing."

"Whatever," said Ted.

How dare he? thought Marty. He looked at Jackie. She was busying herself with the food, fussing over the jars and plastic tubs, avoiding having to look at either Marty or Ted.

"Did you bring my pills, Jacks?" asked Ted. Looking to Marty, he added, "Got to take them with food."

"No, I thought you brought them," said Jackie.

"Oh well, I'll take 'em when I go home. Or maybe I won't."

"What are you talking about?" asked Jackie.

"I was reading this thing, this pamphlet that the Mad Pride people put out, and I was thinking ... maybe ... about not taking my pills. They say it's a conspiracy put together by the big pharmaceutical companies."

"Mad Pride?" Jackie's tone betrayed that she didn't really want to know.

After Ted had eaten three cookies, several hundred grams each of Gouda and cheddar, and drunk a Thermos of coffee, he announced the need to relieve himself. Lunch was over. Taking a small packet of facial tissues from the basket Ted wandered off to a shallow depression not far from where they were eating. His head was still visible when he crouched. Marty decided he didn't want to watch Ted taking a shit and went for a stroll. Jackie followed.

"It turned out that his group therapy was moved back a day because of the Regatta," Jackie said the moment they were out of earshot. "I was in a real panic. There was no way to warn you. He was just hanging around the house, and I knew you were coming ..."

"It's all right," said Marty.

"He's going to make me as crazy as he is."

"I can see that," said Marty. He looked around. Ted was still going about his business.

"It's a nightmare."

"I'll bet," said Marty.

"I still want to see you," she said. "Alone."

There it was, stated as candidly as manners would allow, but it might as well have been a plea to be fucked there on the spot, dirty talk in his ear, so suddenly was it registered in his trousers. Needing to be yet farther from Ted, Marty quickened his pace. Jackie kept up.

"I looked up your number, on Michener Crescent, right?" she said.

"Yes."

"I'll call you."

"Yes."

She glanced downward. Something caught her eye. She spun around, still looking at the ground.

"What's all this?" she wondered.

They were standing amid a series of ridges in the earth, parallels ten or fifteen feet apart, occasionally cut by other, perpendicular lines. They were only inches high, maybe a foot and a half wide, and marked the turf like vertebrae beneath the skin of the back. The side of one mound had weathered away and showed them to be stacks of flat slate over which the Downs had grown.

"They're foundations," Marty said. "There used to be a town here, Dunchy Head. The houses must have had slate foundations."

Marty saw that he was within one of the largest of the rectangular enclosures, at least twenty feet by thirty, too big to have been a family dwelling, too far from the water's edge to be a twine loft or store. He thought for a moment it was a church, but then saw evidence of a still grander structure, in better radio range to God, on a rise farther up the valley. Then it occurred to him. He was standing were once there had been a school.

"HELLO?" called Ted.

"Over here, Ted," Jackie shouted over her shoulder.

"Come on," said Marty. "Let's get to the point."

♅

Any trails from Dunchy Head to the point were now lost. The distance to land's end was roughly the same as the trio had already come, but without sure footing or a clearly defined route it took more than twice as long to travel. They crossed the sand spit and climbed a wedge of scree to the closest tower.

The earth was raw here. The crushed layers of sediment that had formed the stone columns over millennia were exposed. The strata ran not on the plane of the world but were hove and tilted. The place was geological wreckage.

Marty heard the birds on the islands before he saw them. Whether pecking at nests in the cliff face, or riding thermals, or flying out to dive for fish, they complained incessantly in hundreds of seabird dialects, none possessing the beauty of their woodland cousins.

A ring of turf circling the promontory suggested a tonsured skull. The crown was covered with more marginal flora than was found on the Downs, just a skin of something like moss, though oilier, a proto-plant, organic and mineral. The environment was harsher here; the ammonia of guano stung your nostrils. The fog was almost upon them, you couldn't look around or over the bank, and the chill from the adjacent sea had a qualitative difference. It was a colder, saltier, wetter cold.

Coming this far it felt an obligation to go to the edge and look at the birds. There were several species using every part of the island pillars; turrs and gulls and tinkers finding improbable purchase on the vertical face; chubby harlequin-faced puffins—the Frenchmen's sea parrots or "parakeets" from which the place took its name—emerging from burrows in the band of shaggy sod. The air about the islands was dizzy with their comings and goings. Marty knew it was supposed to be majestic but found that the avian activity—in all directions at once—stripped the world of its top and bottom, making it senselessly multidimensional. It induced in him something like motion sickness. Still there was the sense that he should stand there for a period and marvel.

Finally Ted said, "I'm freezing."

They headed back.

It was dusk by the time they reached the car. The slope of the valley was so gradual that it went unnoticed on the way down but had made the return more arduous than Marty expected. He could feel the climb in his calves; the familiar band of pain was forming in his knee.

The fog had overtaken them. As patches of varying density went by you could judge how hurried was its passing, but could feel nothing, no wind, driving it on. He wondered what force propelled it with such urgency. When Marty put on the headlights they had little reach.

On the road they again came upon the movie set. The power of the film lighting was such that a corona formed over the landscape. A traffic marshal in a reflective vest stepped in the road and waved them to the side with a luminous baton. Marty rolled down his window. A fresh-faced young woman leaned in to offer an explanation. She opened her mouth but was cut off by a squawk from a walkie-talkie strapped to her chest.

"Complete quiet, please."

She complied with the order, smiling at everyone in the car.

"Cue effects. Roll sound," said the radio. Ahead the village they'd seen being put together earlier burst into flame. "Roll camera. Mark it. Roll playback! Playback!" Amplified song filled the air. "Action!" Victims, mouthing the incomprehensible words, streamed from their burning shanties. The traffic girl looked into the car and smiled again.

Marty heard laboured breathing. He turned and saw Ted, jaw in a palsy of either terror or mirth, it was impossible to tell which. Marty remembered Ted had been asleep when first they'd come this way. And, of course, there was the mention of him forgetting his pills.

"It's okay, Ted," said Jackie. "It's only a movie."

seven

" … AND ESPECIALLY TO WELCOME the grade nine students to The Red Pines. For you young men and women this is going to seem like a whole new world …"

The appearance of the "whole new world" usually marked the mid-point in Hank's address to the opening assembly. Marty would stay tuned for other posts like "greater sense of responsibility," "you are a Red Pines student even when you leave the school grounds," "the high expectations of your parents and teachers," and, in conclusion, something vaguely spiritual or uplifting, often an anecdote about a former student who, with the unheralded help of his parents' money, had overcome some sort of adversity. Marty was not listening closely, just monitoring Hank, in case he went off on some ecological tirade. Marty's vision was similarly detached, looking past Hank's back at the gymnasium full of students without really seeing anything. He was seated on stage between a Korean United Church minister whose name he'd already forgotten and the mayor. Marty was the only one up there who would not speak. He thought of Jackie Spurell, whom he was to meet later that day.

Setting up the rendezvous with Jackie took some doing. He'd called once, got Ted, and done his Felix Smith routine. Jackie, waiting for some sort of sign, guessed it was Marty. She hadn't been able to call back until the next day, leaving a whispered message on his machine. It went on like that for seven or eight days. Finally they spoke, Jackie calling from a pay phone at a pharmacy downtown. They set a time to meet for drinks at Marty's place … and … and talk some more? Marty wasn't sure.

"Become whatever you want …" Hank was saying, "even, I suppose, mayor of this city …" there was some laughter, "or prime minister."

Marty tried to resist fantasizing about the pending encounter with Jackie. It would happen soon enough—there was no sense making himself crazy with anticipation—but the drone of Hank's voice over the PA, the system's accompanying electric hum, forced a retreat into his own head. Jackie and he would sit side by side on the couch. They would say how hard the wait had been, but how denial only stoked their desire. Jackie would say how she could bear it no longer, how she needed and would have … Marty would crawl …

A bustle from out in the gymnasium interrupted Hank. Marty scanned the crowd for the source. Hank continued, "… Dorothy Chan, a former student of The Red Pines, who despite having lost over ninety percent of her vision now works at the United Nations …"

Marty spotted the culprits. Four or five boys toward the rear of the gym, shifting in their seats. He saw their heads were bowed, their faces averted so their backs, in a line, made the fingers of a gloved fist. Who were they? Which teacher was responsible for them? Marty could see Abe Summers seated two rows ahead wilfully ignoring the fracas.

"… And we hear more recently of Lucinda Gomez, who, though a paraplegic …"

Now there was laughter, an eruption of hoots, a short suppression and then barking guffaws. The boys couldn't contain themselves.

Pitts was in the aisle, summoning them with an impatient jerking of his arm, an imperative hooked index finger at its end. Buckled in fits, snotting themselves, they staggered down the row of chairs, snagging legs and banging shins along the way, making a holy show of their surrender. It was Russell Malan and posse, probably all smoked up, an assembly being as good an excuse as any to blow a fatty. As quickly as he could, Pitts herded them out of the assembly. Summers did not deign to turn and watch.

The mayor spoke. He seemed sane. Litter was the theme. Before a brief and tepid prayer, the Korean minister managed to say positive things about the Muslim, Jewish, and Hindu faiths. Hank had done well to find this one. The speakers gave Marty time to calm down, to put away his rage and come up with a reasoned response to the boys' outburst. He would not deal with Russell, but with Russell's father. Marty saw this giving him leverage. Marty would insist that if he were ever to entertain revisiting Russell's grades, the boy's behaviour must cease to be an issue for the remainder of his final year at The Red Pines. Dirk Malan would gather from this entreaty that Marty was a deal maker, a man willing to do a … Marty couldn't really characterize it as "good" … a man willing to do *one* deed for another. He might use the call as an opportunity to broach the subject of Dirk Malan investing in The Red Pines franchise. A stated interest from Dirk might light a fire under Gerry Hayden, who had yet to respond to the proposal Marty sent him more than a month ago. Marty would call the other boys' parents as well, but he knew Russell was the cause of the trouble. The clergyman was saying something about Mahatma Gandhi.

The miscreants were in the office, crowded onto a bench. (Marty had picked up the carved piece for five or six bucks at an auction. It was from a nunnery that had closed. Its discomfort was singular.) It was where all wrongdoers waited to see Marty and, less frequently, Hank. It was Marty's intention to make them sit on their bony young asses for a good half hour, stew and fret after telling them he was going to call their Deputy Minister dads and Head-of-the-Radiology Department moms for whom their conduct was a black mark on the family name.

He was about to speak when Mrs. Norris stepped between him and the boys.

"Yes?" said Marty.

"There's someone in your office. Mrs. Caddigan."

"Where's Hank?"

"He's showing the mayor the damage to the trees out back."

"Tell Mrs. Caddigan I'll see her shortly. Gerry Hayden or a fellow named Singh haven't called, have they?"

Mrs. Norris did not answer or move but stood in place until her eye caught his. She was telling him, without saying it aloud, that Mrs. Caddigan could not wait. Marty nodded that he understood.

"Go to class," he said to the boys. "I'll be calling your parents about this."

It worked, not as well as if they'd been left to dwell on it, but it worked. All of them, except Russell, looked at one another in disbelief. Mr. Devereaux was not playing fair. This kind of infraction didn't merit such extreme measures. There were no hard-and-fast rules, no official infraction/punishment equivalencies, but everybody had a general understanding of how things went down. Russell didn't react at all but rose hastily and left without looking back. Marty wondered if Russell was frightened of his father.

Mrs. Caddigan was seated with monastic poise, back straight, feet flat on the floor, still. Her hands were stuffed into the pockets of a muted-gold raglan with a synthetic gloss and brought across her lap so that the unbuttoned coat wrapped her as tightly as bandages. Approaching her from behind, Marty could see, through the legs of the chair, her white stockings and shoes. He was grateful she had left her lachrymose husband at home. There was a faint smell of hospital coming from her, rubbing alcohol maybe, aldehydes, ill breath.

"Mrs. Caddigan, what can I do for you today?" He remembered, with disgust, the envelope of money she'd left.

"It's serious, actually."

"Serious?"

"Yes."

"It happened," she said, "June past. But I only became aware of it last week. My daughter, Audrey, was pregnant. She was counselled to have an abortion by your music teacher, Mrs. Zwitzer."

"Oh dear," said Marty. It wasn't the kind of thing he ever said, so fey.

"Yes," said Mrs. Caddigan. "I'm not a pro-life nut or anything. I'm not sure I wouldn't have suggested Audrey do it myself. To be honest, I know that's exactly what I would have suggested … it's just … it just doesn't seem appropriate that a teacher …"

"No, it's not appropriate, Mrs. Caddigan, not at all."

"I think I'm hurt, too, that Audrey didn't come to me."

"Of course you are. You have every right to be."

"So … I'd be … I'd … if I had my choice … I'd leave it alone. Put it behind us, assume you would severely reprimand the teacher, even let her go, and leave it at that."

"Right?" Marty could not see where she was going.

"But … and I'm still trying to convince him otherwise … but Rick, that's my husband, Rick says he's going to sue."

She let her words hang there, let Marty weigh them.

Marty knew the thing to do was to stop speaking with Mrs. Caddigan immediately, to terminate their conversation as politely as possible and promptly call his lawyer. But feeling that he was running out of time, he couldn't help himself. Running out of time to do what, he didn't know.

"Is that a wise thing to do? It would mean putting your daughter ..." he searched, "putting Audrey through quite an ordeal. And we would have to respond ... with our lawyers. She'd be required to testify if there were a civil proceeding." Marty realized he was threatening her.

"I agree with you, and I'm still trying to convince Rick not to. It was a mistake to tell him about it. He's very angry now, about a lot of things."

Marty thought of Audrey, remembered her getting out of Russell Malan's car, thought of her lashed to the post in the school play. Joan of Arc! If push came to shove he would assert the girl was some sort of hysteric.

"And," Mrs. Caddigan continued, "I don't know why, or if it'll do any good, but maybe if we spoke to the parents of the boy ..."

"The boy?"

"The boy that ... might as well say it ... the boy that knocked her up."

"You know who he is?"

"No," she said, "and Audrey won't say much ... but I read between the lines it's a boy from school. Do you have any idea?"

"I don't," Marty said too quickly, "but then I'm not in contact with the students as much as the teachers. I'm mostly an administrator. I could make some inquiries."

"Maybe that's the thing to do. If Rick could speak to them, to the parents ... and the teacher, this Mrs. Zwitzer, if ..."

"It's Miss. *Miss* Zwitzer."

"Sorry, yes, if this Miss Zwitzer, if she was disciplined, then maybe ... I don't know ... really."

"No, neither do I, but let's make an effort."

"I'm not sure about this, but I'm worried that for someone of Audrey's age they … the clinic that is … they would have required a signature from some sort of guardian."

"Honestly, I don't know. I don't know how it works," said Marty.

"I've spent every waking hour … no, every minute asleep or awake, every moment of the last sixteen years worrying about Audrey, worrying over her breathing because some nights when she was laying in her crib it seemed funny, irregular or shallow, about how, when she was a baby, she didn't seem to want to walk, seemed happy to crawl, about the colour of her poop and snot, Mr. Devereaux, about whether her scarf could get caught up in something and choke her, about falling on the ice, nut allergies, bullies, not having friends, having the wrong friends, drugs in school. Fires everywhere. About disappointment. I've worried. I have been so tired with worry and with all the rest of it, the unwashed laundry, the violin and the soccer and the forgetting to buy the goddamn Cheerios and having to get back in the car and drive back to the supermarket, all of it. I've been so tired that I wanted to weep. That tired, Mr. Devereaux, that I wanted to bawl. Now this."

Mrs. Caddigan said no more but did not get up to leave. She took her hands from her pockets and let them hang, limp, from the arms of the chair. Her raincoat fell open, letting Marty see her nurse's uniform, a hard plastic name tag pinned to the breast. Gail Caddigan, RN, looked impassively out the office window.

♀

Marty waited by Sophie's desk until the last student shuffled from her final class of the morning. Her hair was still Heidi, but set against her usual workday outfit was less eccentric, more severe. The two didn't bother with any small talk.

So that it didn't end with the spectacle at her Regatta party, Marty had visited Sophie three times since. The meetings were cordial. They once went to lunch. An opportunity to discuss the clumsy dissolution of their relationship hadn't presented itself. They knew anyway.

"Did you encourage Audrey Caddigan to get an abortion?" It seemed to Marty that Sophie anticipated the query, had been waiting for it.

"Of course not. You know me better than that, Martin."

"What, then?"

"She came to me, told me her situation, told me what she was thinking. Fair to say I didn't discourage her."

"Shit, Sophie, no."

"And I made a phone call for her. It was the right thing to do. She's sixteen, Martin."

"Her father is going to sue the school."

"For what?"

"I don't know. He's a crazy, a bitter crazy … it's not good … for the school's reputation."

Sophie shook her head, either in disbelief or disgust, and turned her attention to some needless paperwork.

"I don't think you appreciate the seriousness of the situation, Sophie. Her father is …"

"Let's not make too much of it. It was early. They might have used that new pill for all I know. We're talking about a tablespoon of pink jelly."

"Please don't characterize it that way in court."

"Remember, Audrey came to me." Sophie stopped and huffed. "The father! It's absurd. I didn't fuck his daughter. That pleasure, I believe, went to that vile Malan boy."

"I gathered that."

"And surely, this talk of a lawsuit, it's the Malans' money they want."

"They don't know it was the boy. And I'm working on something now, a project, that ... suffice it to say I don't want to antagonize Dirk Malan. I'm hoping he's going to be involved. He's a potential investor and ... he's got a certain profile and sway in the business community."

Sophie drew the deep breath of a singer, her chest filling, her bust rising, and with a suddenness that made Marty jump, slammed her open palm onto the desk.

"You sound like my father. You should move to Austria, Martin, really."

♁

Marty consulted the computer and found that Russell Malan's timetable dictated the boy be in Room 226 for math with Mr. Slocom at 1:20.

So as not to betray his intent, Marty pretended to be making a routine patrol of the second-floor corridors. He'd lately wearied of the once-habitual exercise. His presence sent a whispered alert up and down the long hallways, a hush falling as he passed. This time of day this part of the school was scheduled for the grade twelves. They seemed younger to Marty than they were the year before, and the year before that. They were miniatures of the men and women they would become. Their vanities and insecurities irreversibly in place, and already, navigating the real estate of their lockers, formed into the packs that would become neighbourhoods, self-help groups, and district associations.

He saw Darcy Slocom ahead, ploughing through the crowd with text, teacher's guide, and register clasped in hand and hiked up into his armpit, the skirting of his jacket trailing him in mockery of an academic gown. He was another one, like Abe Summers, whose brief stint here was turning into a lifetime. Like himself if he didn't watch it, thought Marty.

Slocum disappeared into 226. Then Marty saw Russell, dissolute, trudging the same trail. Marty caught up with him just before he got to the classroom door.

"Like to have a word, Russell."

Slocom approached the door from within to close it.

"I'll have him back shortly," said Marty, taking Russell's arm and leading him away. The bell rang and in mere seconds they were alone in the hallway. Marty put Russell's compliant form up against the lockers.

"You get Audrey Caddigan pregnant, Russell?"

"I dunno," the boy answered, looking more interested in his ill-kept shoes than anything Marty said.

"Then you don't know much, do you."

"I know enough, sir."

"No, no, I don't think you do. Her parents are off their heads about it." It occurred to Marty now that he didn't really much care about Audrey Caddigan's parents and was, in fact, bored by their girl's story. But he was angered that the consequences of someone else's mistakes might fall, like a teetering rotten tree, within the ambit of his business.

"She had an abortion, what's the big deal? She can't get my money now."

"Your money? You mean your dad's money?"

"Whatever."

"You stupid ..."

"HEY!" Russell dropped the pretense of inattention. "Don't call me stupid."

"Why not? You are stupid, Russell."

The boy had heard enough and went to move away. Marty's hand shot out, the flat of it taking Russell in the shoulder with such force that the boy came off his feet, colliding with the lockers, his head following his trunk so that there was a double pump and bang from the impact, a *va-boom* of timpanic flourish. Marty'd not measured the strength of the blow. It was a reflex and he was surprised it was so hard. Russell was winded. Marty made himself continue speaking, though he knew by the flutter in his bowels that he had crossed a line.

"Don't move until I'm finished talking to you."

Russell was catching his breath. He looked Marty in the eye and smiled as though he'd just won a prize.

"Why? If I try to go back to class will you hit me again, sir?"

No, not so stupid after all, not where it mattered. Russell smirked and walked away, past the door of 226, down the length of the corridor to the front stairs, which he descended with theatrical languor.

Teachers or vice principals were no longer to hit, even jostle, students. Marty wasn't too worried that anything would come of it. He was sure there were no marks on the boy, no bruises or lesions to convince investigators that something serious had taken place. But the question was enough, and it had yet to be asked of anyone on The Red Pines staff. Russell could, Marty supposed, take it upon himself to up the stakes, cutting or bashing himself to make it look worse. The boy was capable of such an act.

Marty assumed that in one brief lapse he'd sunk the prospect of Dirk Malan investing in his project. He could no longer hesitate in calling Gerry Hayden and asking about the proposal, whether he would sign off and Marty could submit it to City Council. He was going to have to shore up that end of the deal before there were any rumblings from the Malans. Most likely Russell wouldn't say anything to his father, wouldn't risk taking shit over knocking up Audrey Caddigan, and everything would be fine. But Marty couldn't be sure.

Marty walked to the rear staircase at the end of the corridor, opposite the way Russell had gone. Through the large windows in the stairwell he descended he could see, across the soccer pitch,

Hank returning from the pine grove with the mayor. Marty had warned Hank of the risks of bringing attention to that situation, but Hank and the mayor looked to be chatting amicably. Maybe Hank had found a solution to the problem.

This early in the school year there should have been many things to attend to, but Marty was ahead of himself. He decided to check up on Pitts's planetary paintings. If Hank and the mayor came in the rear door of that wing he might learn what was up with the trees.

Pitts had promised Marty that his student assistants would return a few weeks before school started so that the project would be completed in time for the first day of classes. Such was not the case. The depiction of Uranus was completed, a blue orb rung with diaphanous threads, just fitting—trapped really—within the confines of the section of wall provided it. Saturn, the planet Marty most eagerly anticipated, was like the other giant, Jupiter, only partially revealed, a mass of moody orange bands. It was shown in an oblique approach, as a sash, with large and small moons woven within or worn on the surface of the rings like badges. At this point Neptune existed only in outline. The panel that was to be home to Pluto was black. The students, as Marty understood it, had not let Pitts down but took some time repairing the mess he'd made of things during the summer. Considerable improvements were made. The features of the Jovian surface were better defined; the great red spot was imbued with active fury instead of inarticulate rage. The lifeless white specks that were Pitts's stars were replaced with twinkling charms. Marty was happy enough. The project finally seemed like a good idea.

The rear exit did not open. Hank and the mayor must have walked straight on to the parking lot.

♂

Marty arrived home early, planning to shower, but closing his car door he saw Jackie, cutesy knapsack slung over her shoulder, walking down the street toward him. It appeared she had been lying in wait. He waved and smiled, aware of tension in his face and neck. He needed to swallow. Jackie jogged the rest of the block to the driveway.

"Beautiful day," she said. "I know I'm early. I walked."

Her cheeks were rosy and there was painted colour around her eyes and on her lips. The makeup was inappropriate somehow, suited to the night and clothing more formal than her sweater and jeans. Maybe she was at a loss as to how one dressed for such an occasion. Marty certainly had no idea how the game was played.

"Let's go in," he said.

4

Whenever anybody entered his house, let alone a prospective lover, Marty always felt a generalized anxiety. He supposed he'd grown used to Sophie's comings and goings, but otherwise ... When he threw a Christmas party for the Red Pines staff a few years earlier he had to fight back a panic attack. It felt as though there was something awful, something shameful, hidden somewhere in the house that the visitors would find. But Marty did not know what that thing might be, or where it was concealed, like it was evidence planted to incriminate him in some crime.

Jackie sat unnaturally upright on the couch. Her knees were squeezed together. Her tiny backpack was at her feet. She sounded as if she had not yet caught her breath. Nerves didn't become her. This woman was not the same creature he'd met those months ago at the vocational college. Marty took off his jacket and laid it on the back of a chair in the dining room. He loosened his tie and then worried that it looked as though he were tactlessly preparing to disrobe.

"Drink?" he asked.

"Yeah, sure," said Jackie.

Of course, that's what they'd said, wasn't it, drinks? What else was he to say? Care for some adultery now? Could I interest you in a tawdry affair? Jesus, he wasn't much good at this. "What would you like?"

"Oh?" Jackie hadn't thought about it. "Scotch or ... something ... Scotchy."

As he mixed the drinks in the kitchen, a glass almost slipped from his fingers. He noticed that the veins in his wrist were visibly pulsing. He could feel that he was flushed and kept needing to swallow. The sound of ice dropping into the tumblers seemed loud, as if the glass would break. The quiet of the house was making it all worse. The stereo? God, no. He needed to say something.

"So ..." he said, his voice raised so Jackie could hear him in the next room, "when you were in nursing did you know a ... a Gail Caddigan?"

"Gee ..." Jackie said, "I can't remember. Which hospital does she work at?"

"I ... I don't actually know," said Marty, carrying the drinks, a gin for himself, a Scotch for Jackie, back into the living room.

"Why?" asked Jackie.

Marty sat next to her on the couch. He raised his drink. Jackie followed suit.

"She has a daughter at my school. She was in today."

"Yes?"

"And ..." Marty now regretted bringing it up. "Well her daughter got pregnant and had an abortion." He was talking about teen pregnancy and abortion! What kind of precoital chitchat was that?

"Right. What does that have to do with you?"

"She claims that her daughter was encouraged by ..." Now he was really in it, he swallowed what felt like a ping-pong ball of thick saliva. "By a teacher at my school."

"Oh, that's serious."

"Yes."

"Are there going to be repercussions?"

"I don't know," said Marty.

It was Jackie's turn to fill up the silence. "I want a cigarette," she said, handing her drink to Marty and grabbing for the bag at her feet. "You want one?"

"Sure," said Marty.

She lit the first cigarette and, after taking a deep drag herself, went to give it to Marty who, holding both drinks, didn't have a free hand. She brought the cigarette toward his face; a fraying strand of smoke got in his eyes and he closed them. Feeling the featherweight touch of the cigarette on his lips, Marty closed his mouth, getting a salty taste from Jackie's fingers. The smoke was very strong. Flecks of tobacco leaf were peppery on his tongue. He looked at the package and saw they were smoking unfiltered Camels. Jackie must have noticed.

"When he was still flying, and we would get passes, Ted and I ... we used to go to Florida or Arizona and I developed a taste for these." She took her drink from Marty. There was an empty oversized ashtray on the coffee table. Jackie moved it closer and repeatedly tapped her cigarette to summon ash.

"Did you," she asked, "clean up on my behalf or something?"

"No, not really... I'm ... I've been faulted for being too fastidious." It was something Sophie accused him of.

"I'm a real slob," said Jackie. She was still trying to get a handle on her racing breath. "Whoa. Isn't this very weird?"

"What is?"

"Us, meeting like this?"

"Yes. I find it ... strange."

Jackie nodded her head before tipping up her tumbler and downing her double Scotch.

"Could I have another? I enjoy a drink. That's what my mother-in-law would say, 'I enjoy a drink.' But at home … well, you know …" she said, holding out the glass.

In the kitchen, pouring Jackie's Scotch, it occurred to Marty that the two would soon have to eat. He didn't have anything in the fridge, just some frozen, processed low-calorie things in the freezer. Given their situation, or, more precisely, Jackie's situation, they would not be able to go out. There was a half-decent Chinese place that delivered. He didn't think he had any wine. Wine was called for. He polished off his first gin, thinking that his having a fresh drink would make Jackie more comfortable having asked for one herself.

"Do you like Chinese food?" he asked as he returned to the living room. But the room was empty. She was in the bathroom, he thought. Her knapsack was gone, too.

He sat, holding the two drinks, listening for her. He could hear kids playing outside in the street and Murphy's gas mower. He sniffed one of his armpits and regretted not having had a chance to shower. Condensation was forming on the tumblers. There was dust on the mantel. If the housecleaners were only going to come every two weeks he'd have to give the place a once-over every other Tuesday. He listened for the sound of running water, the taps, the toilet flushing. He listened closely, for the hiss of a woman pissing or just some movement. Had she run out on him? He hadn't heard the front door close. It would almost be a relief.

He put the two drinks on the coffee table and walked to the bathroom. Standing outside the door, he asked, "Jackie?"

"Marty?" came the answer, not from the bathroom, but from down the hall, from the bedroom. "Marty?" She bent the sound of his name so that it was a call to be found, a call from someone after the lights had gone out.

She was lying on his bed. She had taken off her sweater to reveal a tight short-sleeved jersey with a busy floral print. One knee was up. The other leg, crooked, lay flat on the covers. He could see from the doorway that the top button of her jeans was undone, the waistband open and loose like peel coming away from fruit. She was almost hyperventilating, her anticipation the verge of dread, as if she was expecting some sort of invasive medical procedure.

He was on the bed next to her. He took the two flaps of her pants, one in each hand, and pulled. The zipper came apart with a gentle *buzz*. Jackie's hips rose to let Marty more easily draw the jeans off. She was wearing panties that looked almost boyish, like briefs, laundry-fresh and white. On her feet were peach-coloured ankle socks.

She was not moving to undo Marty's trousers or unbutton his shirt, and he had to stand and undress himself. She looked from his standing sex to his eyes. She took her shirt and pulled it up to reveal her breasts, pulled tight against her ribs by the arching of her back, the nipples as hard as Marty's cock. He could see her heart rattling its cage.

She gave way, offering no resistance to any force put upon her, mouth opening to his, tongue a soft host to his, arms yielding, thighs impassively fanning. He went for her breasts and she watched him.

It was all give, no take. He lay on his back, working his arm round her shoulders as he did so, pulling her on top. She ran down him like water. He felt the wet of her mouth, her hands lying on the muscles of his upper leg. He could come, but stopped himself, taking her face in his hands and guiding it to his lips.

She kissed his mouth and his ear and then his neck and so drew him back on top. He just about fell in, her legs spread so wide.

"Do anything, Marty. Just don't ask. Please don't ask," she said.

It was nothing like what he'd dreamed of.

He acquitted himself well, and only when it seemed certain Jackie wasn't going to come did Marty let himself go.

Lying on his back with his eyes closed, he could sense Jackie looking at him as she ran her fingers over his shape. It wasn't long before they'd found their way to his crotch, kneading him to another erection, one bloodier, more punishing, more hard headed and purple than his first of the afternoon.

Marty went at Jackie from behind with such ferocity that shudders ran up her back with each thrust. This time she came, and with a wail that told of the kind of pleasure only found in the truly sinful act, with an adulteress's yelp. Marty's grip left white handprints on the cheeks of her ass.

♄

Marty was one of those for whom there were moments of melancholy after having come. It left him mute. But having been given a good fucking was licence for Jackie to talk, to empty herself of words, was the start of a story she'd been longing to tell.

Jackie had been thinking of leaving Ted for some years, she said, but the domestic situation had degenerated to the point where she was finally ready to act. There was even a hint of menace in the air. She had a livid mark on her bicep, the consequence of having been pulled aside by Ted, rather too ardently, for a reprimand. Ted sloughed it off as an accident but … Besides, Jackie figured there was this one flight attendant from Moncton he had definitely been banging. She had brought it up before, that it might be over between them, just one time—the night before he drove the Airbus off the runway.

Then there was the AA business. When Ted quit drinking he put all the behaviour down to the booze. Jackie didn't buy it. He was an asshole, not an alcoholic. She was determined to get out, not right away, but as soon as possible. Marty heard the implication: part of getting out meant … coming here? She didn't announce it, but she sure-as-shit didn't say where else she planned on going. No sister's or mother's or girlfriend's place figured in the scheme, no "place of my own." And she was kissing him a lot, between thoughts there'd be a peck on his forehead, familiar nibbles and licks. Marty again mentioned dinner.

"It's not too bad, no MSG, or so they say."

"I can't," said Jackie, lifting Marty's alarm clock from the night table. "I gotta go."

Jackie called a taxi and dressed. Marty pulled on his pants and shirt and waited with her by the front door, sitting on the carpeted steps that led up to the living room. Jackie's hair was mussed. Her makeup was smudged. Her lips had the plumped and overripe look of having been pounded with another's. Marty wanted to say something about it, warn Jackie that Ted, if he had any wits about him at all, would take one look at his wife and guess that she'd been off screwing someone else, but he couldn't think how to put it. The taxi blew its horn. Jackie opened the door, started to go, and then turned back to wrap her arm round Marty's neck and haul his mouth to hers. As she let go Marty could see Something Murphy watching from his lawn across the street.

Jackie left. Marty sat on the steps for a few minutes, thinking of Sophie.

The next day and the next Jackie was back.

ψ

In the two days since school started Cathy still had not seen Chuck. She couldn't very well go up to his friends and inquire as to his whereabouts, get his email. If she did they would ride her. They would torture her for the rest of the year. They would hound her with a question for which she simply did not have an answer, "Whatcha want Chuck for?" She didn't need them to be humiliated; she could accomplish that on her own. Quite a feat, really, managing to embarrass yourself in solitude. Cathy did it, though. Lying in bed at night or first thing in the morning, imagining being with Chuck, she would flush with shame. She'd dreamed once of actually biting into him. What could that mean? Jesus, swooning like a girlfriend was pathetic enough, doing it without actually having a boyfriend was beyond. Before school started she toyed with the idea of just dealing with it, of putting all the awkwardness behind her, of going up to Chuck and saying to his face, "Come on, Chuck, kiss me." But she didn't have the courage. She had to face it: she had a schoolgirl's crush. She was a schoolgirl, which, really, was reason enough to kill yourself.

Not knowing what else to do, Cathy passively searched the hallways, drifting from drinking fountain to locker to cafeteria, lingering in the exits and stairwells in the hope of seeing him.

Today was the first of Donnelly's physics classes. She was confident Chuck would be there. She was quick to take a seat at the back and watch the students arrive. There was the regular parade of losers and geeks, but no Chuck. Maybe he was sick. Maybe his family was late coming home from Ontario.

Donnelly explained the material they would be covering in this, the final year of high-school physics. There was electricity and electromagnetism, more mechanics, there was to be some nuclear physics. They would start with a brief survey of some astronomy and astrophysics.

Perhaps Chuck had transferred to another school. He'd said his mother's family was well-to-do, maybe he was at The Red Pines this year. How many Curtises were there in the phonebook? Cathy wondered. There were only so many places he could live if he were attending Frank Moores. Maybe the family had moved house, gone off to one of the new western suburbs, Paradise, the Pearl, CBS, the distant grids that were beyond even Cathy's orbit. Chuck would then be at Valdmanis Collegiate or Calvary High, parts unknown.

For some reason Donnelly had written "cosmic rays" on the blackboard. Cosmic rays?

"… Pions in the upper atmosphere …" he said.

There were bus routes out there, Cathy thought, long drives to the malls and big box-stores and farther to the breeding grounds, the pens. If she had a car it wouldn't be so far. She was going to sign up to take Young Drivers of Canada later this semester. She would need the approval of the parentals.

" … But the muons have a half-life of 1.4 microseconds, so how is it that they reach the surface of the earth? Miss Ford-Devereaux?"

Had Donnelly said her name?

"Miss Ford-Devereaux?"

Yes, it was Donnelly and he'd asked her a question. "I'm not sure I understand the question, sir."

"We were talking about cosmic rays." He knew she hadn't been listening. "The protons from outer space, when they collide with the upper atmosphere they produce a shower of particles, right?"

"Yes, sir," Cathy said.

"The pions decay into muons. But the muons only have a half-life of 1.4 microseconds, so how is it that they are raining down on us right now? Most of the muons would have decayed. How can we account for the numbers of muons we measure reaching the surface of the earth?"

Pions and muons? Was he being serious? From their vacant looks Cathy could see that her classmates didn't have a clue what he was talking about.

"I don't know, sir."

"The Special Theory of Relativity," said Donnelly.

If it was meant to be an answer to the question it was lost on Cathy.

"Einstein's theory says that as we approach the speed of light time slows down. The muons are travelling at a speed very close to that of light. Time is passing more slowly within that frame of reference."

"Time is passing more slowly?" asked Cathy.

"Yes. At the speed of light, time stops. In theory anyway."

She laughed.

"Something funny about that, Miss Ford-Devereaux?"

"No, sir. It's fantastic."

Donnelly continued. If he were to be believed, there was a torrential rain of cosmic dust falling forever on our heads. The stars in the night sky were an ancient record of bursts and blasts from distant space. There were nebulae that served as stellar nurseries. Dream foundries. There were binary systems, neutron stars, and pulsars. The sun in the sky was a yellow dwarf, an expiring star, which would become a red giant and then a white dwarf. At the centre of our ten-billion-year-old galaxy was a black hole. Cathy wasn't surprised. It felt like it.

Cathy didn't think about Chuck again until class was over. She let everyone else leave before approaching Donnelly.

"Yes, Cathy?"

"You don't know what happened to Chuck Curtis, do you?"

"No, why should I?"

"Sorry, I …"

"I think, maybe …" He looked out the window, trying to remember details. "Because …" he squinted, "yes, I had to confirm his marks for Mrs. Sexton, she was sending a transcript to Ontario somewhere."

"What does that mean?"

"I don't know for certain, but if I were to guess, I'd say he was going to school there. He's not on my register. He's not attending Frank Moores this year."

Swarms awaited their yellow bay buses, bees nuzzling their fat queen. Clusters of the idle-stunned hung about the exits unable to imagine, again today, what to do in the interval between the end of school and the feed trough. A few of the chosen made their way to nicotine-infused beaters. Cathy passed invisible. She could almost step right through them.

She walked home via the university, a seven-kilometre detour. The sheer size of the place, the dozens of buildings over acres, was a puzzle to her. She wasn't stupid, but it was unfathomable that there could be this much to be learned. Could be that it was mostly bullshit, just posturing. The kids on campus were only a year or two older, but seemed much more so. And they were dirtier, more careless with their appearance, as though preoccupied with important thoughts—but this too might have been an affectation.

It was after four o'clock when she got home. Right away she caught a whiff of something burnt in the kitchen. In the sink there was a scuttled fry pan with a charred bottom. Scorched lumps of some unidentifiable foodstuff—sausages perhaps—were tossed on the top of the garbage. There was an ashtray with a stinking roach on the kitchen table.

"MEREDITH!" It was her father bellowing from the second floor.

"No. It's me!" she shouted back.

"CATHY!" He sounded unusually pleased to learn it was her, as if she'd been away for a time and her return was a grand surprise. "Come up and see your father."

His office smelled of pot and something fruity, tropical like pineapple or banana only sweeter. He was too big a man for his chair, its arms pushed into his flabby flanks. His knees were a hazard, forever knocking with a warbling boom the cheap metal of the desk. One of his eyelids was drooping. He was within his rat's nest of books, stacked and wrapped around him, teetering towers of shit nobody was interested in hearing him cite. If she hadn't stolen it (if that was what she'd done), she supposed she could show him the old tome she'd taken from the bookstore. He'd know what it was, but he'd go on and on about it, she knew. He was hurriedly putting something into one of his desk drawers, hiding it, as she found her mark on the office threshold. The computer, its plastic housing yellowing with age, ticked and wheezed.

"How's my girl?" he asked with a stupid grin. He hadn't called her anything like "my girl" in years.

"Okay," she said.

He nodded in response, first to signal affirmation and then as if dropping into sleep and coming round again.

"Your mother down there? She downstairs?"

"I didn't see her," Cathy answered. She looked at one of the books on top of a pile. It was open to a page of illustrations. She recognized them from her schooling, in junior high, she thought, as having been made by Shanawdithit, the woman they said was last of her Beothuck race. There were drawings of their conical dwellings, the mamateeks, and of spears and ceremonial staffs topped with bones or horns, instruments for spells. The picture she remembered most vividly was a simple rendering of a female figure with shoulder-length hair. Said to be dancing, she raised her arms more as if in prayer or surrender—giving up anyway—whether to a gun, the poxy gods, or blindsiding history, no one would ever know. This drawing her father had defaced with a pen, with a furious blue business, more in anger than idleness, like arcing electricity emanating from the eyes masking the shock and the sorrow.

"So, what I want to know is … what happens?" said her father.

"What do you mean?"

"In a day, in a life. So much happens that doesn't seem important, doesn't seem to mean anything, and that's most of what we do. That's mostly what we are. And you know, in a play or in a movie or on TV there's never any of that. And when anybody ever tries it's just pretentious and boring. I'll ask for … what's this? … for the sixteen-thousandth time … what did you do today?"

"Nothing."

"See! Nothing!"

"People don't want to see that stuff anyway," she said, thinking of her day and its heartbreak and disappointment and wonder, of it bringing her here to this arsed-up interrogation by her fermenting dad. She couldn't answer that question. Nothing happened and it overwhelmed her.

"Why not?" Now he sounded peevish.

"They don't need to, they see it every day."

"Good, 'cause I'm writing some sensationalist pap about a dead Indian woman. Your mother's friends will love that." His mood swung, he cheered, starting to snicker. "Talk about your appropriation of voice! This is out-and-out grave robbery." Laughter shook him and he was reaching for his back. He seemed to read her mind, answering a question she wanted to ask. "Went to the doctor about it this morning. Finally."

"What did they say?"

"Tests."

"Dad?"

"Yes?"

"Can you teach me to drive?"

Over the next weeks Jackie kept Marty informed of her efforts to leave Ted on an almost daily basis. At first Marty found this disquieting but soon took comfort in the fact that progress was slow. Jackie, it turned out, remained quite fond of Ted's family, was happily anticipating a visit from his sister, Helen, who lived in Edmonton. Leaving the broken-down brother before Helen arrived was out. Marty learned that Ted's mom's place was one of Jackie's regular haunts, that the two were gal pals who spoke almost every day, though not, he trusted, about her infidelity. Marty realized, with unease, that his fucking Jackie was not, for her, an isolated act but part of a much larger complex of community and family relations, a small cluster of cells in a giant organism, one akin to those vast fungi that stretched for miles beneath the surface.

Jackie's comings and goings, and Marty's professed schedule, made it easy for Marty to avoid her. Only twice in the next three weeks did they manage to come together for brief after-school trysts. A pattern was quick to emerge. Jackie would get four or five ounces of whisky down her before giving her body to Marty. The candour of her capitulation, the kind of filthy pleading that Marty himself found impossible, precluded any other approach to the act. She was, as he wished he were, a beggar for it, a sexual supplicant, a bottom who would not get up. Only in the moment when Marty first hovered over her splayed form did she carry out her sole act of authority, taking his hips in her hands and pushing him inside as if performing seppuku.

As much as she gave of her flesh, she took territory. In short order she had captured Marty's house, underwear and stockings planted like flags by an advancing army. He wondered if it was him with whom she was having the affair or his space and the sanctuary it offered. She made herself instantly familiar with the place, and every time she went home Marty needed to go around putting ashtrays back where he liked them, rearranging toiletries, sticking the Scotch in the cupboard, re-staking his claim.

Marty was going to say something about this, a gentle suggestion, the last time Jackie'd been over. She was in the kitchen, naked but for a T-shirt of Marty's she casually pilfered from his dresser (risking a telling slip-up with hubby), eating soft Port Salut cheese off her index finger, sticking the finger into the cheese like a knife and then scooping it in her mouth. As she stood there eating she left the fridge door open. Just let it swing open as she ate, a tiny fog bank forming in the air around the exposed compartment. It was the open door that prompted Marty to consider saying something, couched, maybe, in terms of being environmentally conscious, energy efficient, concerned about CFCs or something, but before he could formulate exactly how he'd put it she'd gotten on her knees. He had felt the cold air from the fridge on his legs. He couldn't speak. It was as if it had been *his* mouth that was full.

Jackie could call his office at any time, first thing in the morning, four in the afternoon. She would call several times in one day. Marty instructed Mrs. Norris, if he'd already spoken or, more precisely, listened to Jackie already that day, to say he was away from his desk. This day he didn't need to manufacture an excuse. Ken Singh had, after a number of calls from Mrs. Norris on Marty's behalf, finally called back and asked if Marty was available to see Gerry Hayden that afternoon.

"So what's that about?" Jackie asked.

"The project I mentioned."

"No?"

"Yes, the school for the development."

"Right, yes, I remember, the Perroqueet Downs thing."

"Yeah."

"How long will the meeting go on?"

"I don't know," said Marty. "It's late in the afternoon. If we're going ahead with the project maybe we'll have a drink or something to celebrate, so I couldn't say."

"You should give me a key."

"What key?"

"A key to your house," said Jackie. "I'd be there when you got back. I could even make us something to eat."

"Sure. Right. Remind me. But, like I say, tonight I don't know how long I'll be."

"Well, maybe I'll call later."

Sophie was outside Marty's office. She was saying something he couldn't make out to Mrs. Norris. Sophie laughed, as if Mrs. Norris had told a joke (an impossibility), and sauntered into Marty's room.

"Yeah, look, I've got someone here, I gotta go," he said to Jackie.

"Right, okay, so maybe I'll come later," said Jackie.

"Yeah, call and make sure … gotta go."

"Bye," said Jackie, hanging up.

Sophie sat in the chair on the opposite side of the desk. Marty caught himself about to officiously ask "What can I do for you?" Instead, he said, "You look very nice today."

It wasn't flattery. She was in a tapered white blouse with lacework about the collar and a knee-length skirt that hugged her tall legs, dressed like a music teacher really, an eager, young music teacher. Her hands were powdered with the chalk that rained from the blackboard, giving her a formal bearing. Since parting company with Marty, Sophie looked younger every day, younger and more vital.

"Thank you, Martin. I'm swimming. Every day."

"That's wonderful," said Marty, thinking that the very public nature of the pool made it an unlikely haunt for Sophie. People changed, he supposed, though Rex, a lifelong student, said they didn't.

"I have to apologize about the thing with the Caddigan girl. I'm willing to take the blame."

"Oh, I … I haven't heard anything more, so maybe that's the end of it." In truth Marty sensed that it wasn't the end of it. Mrs. Norris reported that young Miss Caddigan's attendance was becoming uncharacteristically spotty. Normally Marty would call the parents. Not so now.

"I know you, Martin, and I know you'd try to protect me, but there isn't any need. I'll take it on."

"I'm not as noble as all that, Sophie."

"Another thing. There are … there are items, personal items, of yours at my house." Sophie said this with a forced smile, a disproportionate, toothy display. "I considered bringing them in, but there is … it would be a couple of garbage bags' worth … it seemed tacky to me."

"You're right." Marty saw that Sophie was uncomfortable but not downcast.

"So you can come and pick them up. I've put them all together."

"I'll come by. I'll call first," said Marty.

"No need to call, Martin."

"Okay."

"How are you doing, Martin? You look tired."

"Lots on my plate now."

Hayden's headquarters were downtown in a five-storey Edwardian brick building that once surveyed the harbour with proprietary pride and now, with the change in the nature of business conducted within, was re-oriented to face the street. A formal main entrance was now a service bay. Once-coveted space on the waterfront apron was now used as a parking lot.

Marty was disappointed by the interior. It hadn't seen any work since the late 1960s or early 1970s. It was modernist and spare, with small futuristic flourishes, atomic-model patterns, orbiting balls ornamenting the metal banister of the stairs. Above the lobby, hung like a mobile, was an enormous light fixture resembling an old levered metal ice-cube tray. The floor was terrazzo. Like most efforts to envisage a future, the design shortly became a collection of tacky artefacts. In time it might become a museum piece.

A receptionist, hair up for the period, sat at an elevated station trapped in a wraparound desk. She was scowling, as was every person passing. When Marty stated that he was there to see Gerry Hayden she sniffed loudly, as though she didn't believe him, and then stressed the "Mr." when she said she would call "Mr." Hayden's office. To her evident satisfaction, she reported to Marty that there was no such appointment with any Mr. Devereaux. She sat there smugly, waiting for Marty to leave.

"Mr. Singh, then," said Marty.

She repeated the procedure.

"He's with Mr. Hayden," she said. "You can just go up."

"Where's that?" asked Marty.

She blew more air in exasperation and, pointing to an elevator, said, "406."

The hallways of the fourth floor were bedecked with architectural drawings and watercolours celebrating the company's material achievements. The old Haydens, with small-scale shipping around the coast, a couple of sawmills, and a distribution deal for some patent medicines—kidney pills and the like—were well off. They existed on fringes of the St. John's merchant class, invited to the grand houses for their soirees, people with whom one would do business, but into whose family the names would not marry. They commenced their building after Newfoundland's confederation with Canada. Seeing the pictures of the air terminals, the fish plants, the public housing and hospitals, Marty remembered that political connections to the Smallwood autocracy became the foundation of the family fortune. Not many of the structures endured, almost all on display were now derelict or had been demolished. The airports were renovated beyond recognition, the hospitals to a lesser extent. Most of the industrial buildings had gone the way of the half-baked schemes that spawned them. (It was Rex's observation that Smallwood the mountebank was his own mark.) Only the couple of schools and the public-housing projects were still serving their original purpose. Further along came the fruits of this generation's labours, a prison in Ecuador, a resort in Mexico, fish plants in Indonesia. The world was now their oyster or, more accurately, their flash-frozen farmed prawn.

The Hayden worker bees kept their heads down. They followed an unofficial dress code, adhering to decades' old white shirt and tie, skirt or dress strictures. The place smelled of methylated spirits and the baked dust of forced central air.

A secretary was standing waiting for Marty. She greeted him with a perfunctory smile and ushered him in.

It was the largest individual office Marty had ever seen, taking perhaps an eighth of the floor space of the fourth storey. It was a corner suite, two full walls of windows providing a commanding view of the harbour and the narrows, a low ceiling exaggerating the sweep of the place. The furnishings were not in any way extravagant. The boss's desk was modest. The sectional couch and chairs were leather but showed age. There were three large tables on which were spread blueprints and the like. The lot of it was functional.

Gerry Hayden was in motion, the forward head, taut muscles in his neck and shoulders giving him a rapacious aspect. His shirt was patterned with perspiration and his tie was loose. Ken Singh was sitting on the corner of the desk. Two elderly men Marty didn't know, both with the countenance of morticians, were seated on either end of the couch.

"Way to fucking go, Marty. Thanks," said Hayden, only bothering to glance Marty's way.

Marty didn't understand. "What's the problem, Gerry?" Marty asked. But Hayden had snatched a phone from its cradle.

"Debbie, it's like a furnace in here. I thought the maintenance people had dealt with this."

Ken Singh was coming to Marty holding out a copy of the local newspaper. It was folded to show the top half of page 3 or 4, near the front anyway. He handed the paper to Marty.

"I don't believe that prick for a minute." Hayden was again talking to Marty, but about whom, Marty did not know. "It's a payback is what it is, because we dropped the sewage treatment thingy. Like we had a choice. This isn't a charity, Marty. I don't run a charity, I run a business. It's a business. And another thing, can somebody tell me what is wrong with a golf course? Isn't golf good? Participaction, right? It's grass—isn't grass good? Kenny, tell me when grass became like fucking cyanide?"

Marty looked at the proffered page hoping to find the cause of Hayden's animus. It was a photograph of the mayor, holding a bullhorn, speaking to a crowd. It was outdoors at some park. There were chestnuts and beeches in the background. A balloon on string was caught bouncing against His Worship's head. A clown stood at his right. Hank stood at his left. Marty tried to scan the article below but was distracted by Gerry Hayden's continuing screed.

"That why he's cozying up to these Green types. Like he could give two shits about the Perroqueet Downs. Fuck him, just fuck him."

Marty didn't need to read. Hank had made a convert of the mayor. He'd taken him down to the river and dunked him in.

"You said he was … the mayor, you said …" Marty worried whether he should be speaking openly in front of the two men on the sofa. "There were some psychiatric issues."

"He's hiding behind that," said Hayden. "I think now that's a put-on. He probably read some polling data showing that seventy-six percent of St. John's voters are nuts, so he figured, you know, if you can't beat 'em … No, he's not crazy, he's a double-crossing prick. And you know, Marty, I thought you were going to help us on this. I thought you were going to shut your friend Lundrigan up for us. I thought we talked about that. Didn't we? Jesus, I thought we had some kind of an understanding."

"An understanding for sure," said Ken.

"An understanding," said Hayden.

"You wanted me to go to City Council. I sent you guys the proposal."

Gerry stopped his pacing. He threw his arms wide in mock celebration.

"The proposal! Right. We got a copy handy there, Kenny?"

"Got one right here."

"Right," said Hayden. He went to Kenny and plucked the document from his hands. "This one is really a beauty. You must have spent hours on this, Marty?"

Marty knew better than to respond.

"What are you talking about, Marty? The something of something tradition or something. Remind me, Kenny, what the hell was that?"

"The Common Sense of Tradition," answered Ken.

"*A* Common Sense of Tradition," corrected Marty.

"Wow," said Hayden. "Even if I could make any sense of it, why would you send me that? Did someone … did I or did Kenny … give you the impression that we wanted to invest in some school scheme? I'm sure we said we looked into it and decided against it. I'm sure we said something like … we'd give you the first opportunity to bid on the lot, on what is, you know, land with tremendous retail potential … I think we said first right of refusal or something to that effect … and that in return you would shut your friend up."

"I misunderstood," said Marty, reaching into his jacket and taking out his cigarettes.

"What are you doing?" asked Hayden.

"What?"

"There's no smoking here. No smoking."

"Of course, sorry," said Marty, putting the cigarettes back in his pocket.

"This network of schools you're proposing . . ." It was Kenny, his tone pacific. "Maybe you're getting ahead of yourself. You've run a single school in what is . . . a small city."

"Check that, Kenny," Hayden said. "In what is: a rinky-dink backwater with a tax regime that is fucking hostile to business." He now looked toward and jabbed his finger at the old men on the couch. "One that is going to be in my fucking rearview mirror the day my father is put in the ground."

Kenny tried again. "Not to say you haven't run the school well. It's a model, Marty, a model. But what you're talking about, to do it properly, it's a large investment. For anybody. I'm not talking about us here, because we are definitely not interested, but for anybody. And if you went into those markets that are already served by existing private schools, you'd have to be very seriously capitalized to take them on. It could take years to get the share of the market you'd need for profitability." Kenny stopped for a breath. He shrugged, as if he'd searched for an upside and been unable to find one. "Besides, there are serious issues regarding productivity. Your costs will always and forever be climbing, but there's nowhere to find efficiencies, you can't make classes bigger or hire less staff. You're trapped. You've got to continually increase fees. And then demographics. By 2004 half the North American population is going to be over fifty years old. They're going to need hips, not homework. Like Gerry said, we looked into it and . . ."

"You're not the first person to think of this, Marty," said Hayden. "There are some large concerns in the States. They see you coming after even a tiny, insignificant portion of their market share," Hayden meant to indicate the small size of the market share by holding his thumb and finger slightly apart but was so overwrought that he was squeezing the digits together with such force that they were turning white, "and they'll stomp you. People are hearing about this guy and that guy making boodles overnight on tech stocks or with derivatives. Those are fairy tales, Marty, the fairy tales of the eighties and nineties. Realistically, it takes years, years of hard work, perseverance, a good product, and a lot of political contributions. It's pay-as-you-go down there in the States. Pay-as-you-go."

"I think," Ken said, "you'd want to come to the table, just to talk, you'd want to come with, I don't know, serious cake."

"You want to talk to the Ontario Teachers' Pension Fund is who you want to talk to. Serious cake, Marty," said Hayden, "and that's what I'm going to be out if this Downs thing goes south, okay?"

"But. But who knows, Marty, maybe it can happen for you. People are thinking," Ken continued, "… and the banks are encouraging this with their lending practices, but people are thinking, some well-placed people are even saying it, that this period of prosperity is a permanent condition. But. But … when the economy contracts …"

"*When,* Marty," said Hayden, "but … *when.*"

"Yes, I see."

No one had yet asked whether Marty wanted to sit down. He guessed he wasn't supposed to stay.

"Your daughter, Sarah, I believe her name is," Marty said. "You never got back to me about enrolling her."

Hayden was already on his way to forgetting Marty was there. He was taking a seat facing the two silent figures on the couch, whether to grant audience or take instruction it could not be said.

"The wife wanted her in French immersion," Hayden answered without looking around.

eight

A LONE YOUNG MAN, fourteen or fifteen years of age with a sloucher's hump, a tireless self-abuser's tuck, walking down the street with a face full of nails was Marty's first indication. A shivering huddle of unconvinced and unconvincing pirates and princesses at a bus stop made it clear. That Halloween was approaching must have been all over the tube—candy advertisements, plugs for late-night monster flicks, parental cautions—and Marty'd done little else but watch television for the last few weeks. Was he so disaffected and dull with drink that he failed to notice, failed to register even the simplest facts flickering before him? It was possible. He had caught himself watching, uncomprehendingly, a badly dubbed American film on the French channel and thought at the time he must have been doing so for some minutes.

Temperatures had dropped precipitously in the night, producing the first killing frost of the season, late in the year for St. John's. The grass and the branches of trees and shrubs were bent under icy rasps.

As he rounded a corner on his route to The Pines, Marty's car tires struggled to grip the pavement and he'd nearly run over a Spider-Man.

Marty was usually well ahead of the kids heading to school and so wasn't used to seeing them along the streets making obstacles of themselves. But today he'd overslept. That wasn't entirely correct. He hadn't been sleeping so much as lying in bed, lacking the motivation to move. His clock radio's alarm was tuned to CBC Radio 2, a classical music service (Sophie set it years ago, Marty never thinking to change it), and at 6:15 this morning it had come to life near the beginning of a piece he was later to hear identified as Benjamin Britten's String Quartet Number 2 in C Major, Opus 36. Sophie would have been able to identify it after the first notes, that it was, to be precise, the first movement: *Allegro Calmo Senza Rigore*. She would know when it was written and what was going on in Ben's life at the time, what aesthetic currents were influencing his composition (or what the BBC were buying those days), what the critics didn't like about the thing, the parts that interpreters found a challenge. Having to guess, it seemed to Marty that Mr. Britten was, despite a brave face, in despair. Marty could do no more than open his eyes and, paralyzed, listen to the entire movement. It was full of a coruscating anxiety, tense with conflict between desolation and the divine. It did not so much come to a resolution as to an acceptance, and made Marty think how hopeless it was if those were one and the same. It was the function of art, according to Rex, to articulate for the audience that which they could not. But surely there were things best left unsaid. Programming that kind of music at that hour of the morning, Marty thought, was irresponsible. Better they had someone on telling jokes. A chirruping Mozart number followed, but the damage was done. Marty had a smoke going before he had even put aside the covers.

♀

If Britten wrote the music for "Morning Was a Cigarette" then Alan Pitts was its librettist. He accosted Marty in the parking lot of The Pines. Marty wasn't yet out of his car. Deep lines in his forehead, Alan was distraught.

"Marty, can you come with me, round the back way? There's a problem with the planets."

Now when one entered the school via the science wing, one stepped into an illumination. The effect, of levitating above worlds, was finally achieved with the recent completion of Neptune. The large planet was rendered in blue bliss, a meditation on impossibly turquoise tropical waters. Surely this was more to do with the God of the Sea than the methane truth of that remote place and showed uncharacteristic lassitude, giving in to the kids, on Pitts's part.

"They seem to glow, Alan."

"I put some radium in the paint."

"Is that all right?"

"Oh yeah, no big deal."

"What's the problem? Everything seems fine. I've got to confess it's better than I ever imagined." Marty had told him this already but sensed Pitts might have been fishing for sanction—he appeared in some kind of need.

"Pluto."

"What about it?" said Marty, looking at the final panel, the one nearest the door they had come in. In the middle of the starry night sky there was … maybe? … a pinprick black spot, a yet darker, less reflective moment at the centre of the dark rectangle. Perhaps Marty saw something only because he expected to, maybe there was nothing there at all.

"It isn't a planet, Marty."

"Sure it is."

"No, it's not. There's no way to dance around it."

"What is it then, Alan?"

"It's a trans-Neptunian object."

"Right. I'll go with that."

"Well it is."

"But everybody calls it a planet. So it doesn't matter. You're not saying this is an issue, are you?"

"It's a very big issue. The International Astronomical Union says it's a planet when they know it's not, just to keep everybody happy. Don't make waves, right? Little white lies to spare feelings are one thing, but Marty, this is science. What are we telling the kids? What will they take from that? It's all models, models, models. Just to make it easy for everyone to understand. That's bullshit, Marty. We've even cheated the scale to make the paintings more easily understood. And in the depiction the planets are equidistant. What the hell is that about? Pluto? That's just going too far."

"You want to tell them, what? That this fundamental truth we have taught them, that there are nine planets, isn't true?"

"Yes."

"No."

"I think it's important. They'll see how knowledge advances, how mistakes are made, how the truth changes."

Oh for a salary man, thought Marty. Some regular guy who showed up, taught his class, coached a hockey team, and spent his summers *up to the cabin*.

"That's all very noble, Alan, but the nature of truth … it's big stuff and, as far as I know, not part of the curriculum."

"But you …"

"I shouldn't be flip but … this is high school. They can find out what they don't know in university."

"You think?"

"And who defines what a planet is anyway? What's it mean, *planet?*"

"Traveller. Wanderer."

"And Pluto does that, right?"

"Yes, of course, in a big way. The orbit, though, is … it's unlike the other planets, it's just Kuiper Belt stuff, that's the …"

"I'm late, Alan. Let me think about it."

"That would be fine."

"But I tell you … I'm inclined to say finish the goddamn thing and be done with it. Models are fine for our purposes."

"Right."

"That's all then?"

"Yeah. I … and I'm getting divorced."

"Shit. I'm sorry to hear that. What happened?"

"No need to feel sorry. I'm not going to waste any time being surprised by this. Jill just said she'd had enough, you know, and told me to get the hell out. In fairness to her, I haven't been the easiest person to live with, what with my depression."

"You're not depressed, Alan."

"Oh, yes, I am. Clinically depressed."

"I didn't know."

"It's being treated."

"Well … good," said Marty.

"That and the age difference maybe … and for the last number of years, you know, it hasn't been a real marriage."

No, thought Marty, that was obvious, not a "real" marriage—probably a trans-Neptunian one.

"I'm sorry, Alan," he said again, and then, "I'm late," before heading to his office.

♁

She was, through the veil of sleep, aware of a presence in the room. She stirred. Maybe a shadow, an interruption of the early light setting off the hundreds of Barbies patterning the curtains, fell over her still-closed eyes. Maybe it was the time-telling aromas of toast and coffee. When she woke she saw a glass of orange juice on her night table. When she placed her feet on the floor she detected hard filaments of autumn air. The integrity of the wooden structure was compromised. The outside got in. It was always that way with these old Victorian houses. It was the first frosty morning of the year. On her shin she noticed another mark of her ungainliness, a mustard-stain bruise. On her knee there was another, a tiny scar, a "C" for Cathy. She stood, lifted the loose-fitting pyjama top over her head and tossed it. She pulled her underwear out of the crack of her ass. The briefs, once a pale pink, were now faded almost to white. The elastic waistband was losing its tensility and hanging slack. She fingered a threadbare spot in the cotton-blend fabric and felt flesh. She peeled them off and tossed them in a Backstreet Boys trash can. From a tangle of undergarments in a dresser drawer she selected a clean and newish powder-blue pair, also an ill-fitting brassiere, heavy grey woollen socks, flat black tights with a ladder-like run at the top of the left thigh, and a T-shirt emblazoned with the fading and flaking image of a shit-eating blue-bottle, once belonging to her too-fat dad, promoting the world tour (two nights at The Ship Inn) of some band called Larger Than Flies. From the closet she withdrew an old navy tunic she'd nabbed, for like twenty-five cents, at the Goodwill. It was part of the uniform for a Catholic girls' school, Our Lady of Fatima, which had closed down years ago. It was made of some stiff ageless synthetic and featured wide pleats, like those on a kilt, and broad shoulder straps. On the bib was a school crest. On the crest there were naïvely rendered heraldic symbols—a lily, a scroll tied with ribbon, an image of the Virgin Mary—gilded by heavenly rays and below it all a rippling banner with a Latin motto. Cathy could never put the tunic on without speculating about the girl who had once worn it, and imagined that they, by sharing the garment, had a kinship. Cathy could not, though, picture the girl as the woman she must now be, maybe with babies hanging off her, maybe with a daughter Cathy's age. After stepping into the panties and putting on the bra, fastening it like a belt around her waist before turning it around and pulling it up over her shoulders and breasts, she stopped and went to the ghetto blaster. After shuffling through a few CDs and deciding against Patti Smith, or Lizband, or Wilco, she put on the radio. Her two favourite stations, the only two she ever listened to, were the student station from the university, M.U.N. Radio, and V.O.W.R., a service operated by volunteers. Her decision to tune to the Voice of Wesley Radio was rewarded by Hank Williams. *"When you and your baby have a fallin' out ..."* he sang. Already the bra was aggravating her, digging into her flesh. Already she was reconsidering what she would wear. But what difference would it make? But there wasn't time. She didn't know who Hank Williams was but was loving the song. She drank her glass of juice and went downstairs.

Her mother was in the kitchen, sitting at the table turning a cup of coffee around and around with her fingertips.

"Thanks for bringing me the juice," Cathy said.

"That must have been your father."

"Where is he?"

"He was up early and went off somewhere in the car." Meredith glanced at the clock on the stove. "He should be back soon. He's got to see the doctor at ... Are you going to make your bus?"

"No. I was going to ask for a drive."

"Well."

"Where did he go?"

"I have no idea."

"I'll walk."

"You'll be late. I'll give you money for a taxi."

"I was going to have a cup of coffee."

"Go on. You'll be late."

"I'll miss homeroom, so what?"

Cathy took a mug from the cupboard. It had a logo for some fair trade supplier of coffee beans on one side and a Spanish slogan, *"Hasta La Victoria Seimpre!"*, on the other.

"I suppose you think you're too old for a Halloween costume, do you?" asked Meredith.

"No," said Cathy, pouring herself a cup of coffee. "This is it."

♂

The halls were clogged with students, many in some sort of disguise, if only a mask. Already, as they headed to their homerooms, much of the face paint was smudged or runny, the grease fertilizing fields of budding zits.

Marty didn't think they should be allowed. They were too old for this sort of thing. A costume was an excuse to misbehave, to make a show of things, to not take the day seriously. In the school's first year even teachers had shown up in regalia. Marty quickly put the kibosh to that. The following year Cloris Foley had defiantly donned a pirate's eye patch. Lacking depth perception, she had walked into a sharp protruding corner of an easel, badly gashing one of her pretty cheeks and saving Marty having to say a word more about it. This was school, private school, the day's education paid for and so entitled to more regard. But there was no stopping the kids. It was because they let the kids in the public system dress up that Marty had no choice. His guts boiled.

He was drinking a lot of gin—gin and tonics, gin and sodas, gin with orange juice—enough gin to have developed a juniper berry acuity that enabled him, he thought, to identify Bombay Sapphire or Tanqueray or Gordon's by nose. This did not mean that he became a connoisseur. He was satisfied with gin X and lately settled for an economical Canadian brand that possessed curious malty notes beneath a high nose of gasoline and underarm deodorant.

His stomach was protesting with eruptions of corrosive belching, sulphurous blasts that just about burnt his mouth and lips in passing. In the past few days it was inducing chest pains, a feeling that he had swallowed a length of pipe. In search of remedy, but to little effect, he was wolfing fistfuls of chalky Tums and Rolaids every morning. Rex took a superior product called Santex or Lopex or something that Marty resolved to look for. The enzymatic calamity in his liver was starting to show in his eyes; a yellow flag, for caution, was being raised. With his expansion plans thwarted there was nothing with which to occupy his time. If he managed to avoid servicing Jackie (sexually insatiable and emotionally inexhaustible) by fabricating some appointment, it seemed better that he dull his mind with booze and television than revisit the rejection of his proposal. Drink and the tube shared a capacity, much needed now, to slow the moment and yet quicken the night.

Devils slowed his passage. They shouldn't be allowed.

He'd read them wrong, Hayden and Kenny. They'd played him, imagining they might employ him in some chicanery to advance their plans for the Perroqueet Downs, cutting him loose when he proved useless. He wasn't any different from that hapless loser from the Minor Hockey Association they were stringing along. Their actions were without malevolence, it was just business. Thinking back, which was what he was trying not to do, Marty saw that they'd never lied to him, they'd never made anything like a promise, they'd sucked him in with vague blandishments, they'd seduced but never lain down with him. That's how it was done. A chapter of his life was over and it had ended badly. He would fulfill his obligations for this school year but all the while hatch an exit strategy. It was necessary that he move away. St. John's was the scene of his comeuppance and would forevermore have that association. He was getting that feeling ... what was it Sophie called it? ... *Weltschmerz.* The Germans possessed such a rich lexicon for anguish.

He needed out. Yes, it was essential he get away from Jackie, from Rex and Meredith and Cathy, from Sophie with her funky new friends, from the insect clatter of Something Murphy's whipper-snipper, from the dust accumulating on the mantel, from the hopelessness of another stillborn spring, from the mauzy Junes, the fogs of the capelin scull, from Newfoundland's twinned fatalism and frivolity, from its colonial inferiority complex (they actually crowed about the British Empire starting here!), from its village cronyism and envy. His poor countrymen were auto-mesmerized, put half to sleep by their retarding nostalgia for the bad old days. The place's very name was rolling over in his head, impossible to turn off, a snot-nosed corner boy's imbecilic refrain, "Noofhunlan an Labador, Noofhunlan an Labador." Sink, island! he thought. Drown, Newfies! Drown! Sailors drink the sea! To live in the oldest part of the New World was to miss the point. Perhaps the West, mountains and cities without a history, a Calgary or a Kamloops, better suited Marty's nature. "Fly da fuck," they said in town. Well, he would.

Mrs. Norris, clutching a sheet of paper, was bearing down on him. What was so important that it couldn't have waited another couple of minutes?

"Mr. Summers dropped this," Mrs. Norris said, handing Marty a typed letter, "and then he left. I've called for a substitute but there's no one to take his first class."

Left? The letter was addressed to The Deputy Minister of Education, a Mr. Fred Bonia-Coombs. Marty was copied. "I'll take the class," Marty said while scanning the letter for what he knew would be damning words. The boy's name, "a student in my class, Russell J. Malan," jumped out, and a date, "conversation of June 6 … Mr. Martin Devereaux, the Vice Principal, instructed me to alter Mr. Malan's grade so that …" and Summers's craven retreat, "I refused to do so but it would appear that Mr. Devereaux took it upon himself to falsify the record and so enable Mr. Malan to pass." Marty looked to the top of the page; it was dated Tuesday, October 28. Summers, the gutless wonder, had given it three days to wend its way through the system so that Marty wouldn't have chance of calling in a favour from someone in the bureaucracy and intercepting it. By now it had probably been read, and pushed around the desk and forwarded and re-read, by a half dozen Department of Education apparatchik and irreversibly deemed actionable. Close behind his head a wall-mounted bell rang. The surrounding crowd's pace quickened. Mrs. Norris waited for the sound to subside. It was not her nature to shout.

"You've also had some calls, just now ..."

"Sure, sure."

"Mrs. Spurell called twice."

"Thank you."

"This letter from Mr. Summers is very serious, isn't it?" asked Mrs. Norris.

"Yes, it is."

"And Mrs. Foley, well ... naturally she's gone, too."

"Cloris? Why?"

"Well ... it's been an open secret, everyone knew but tried to be discreet so ..."

"What are you talking about?"

"They're lovers, Ms. Foley and Mr. Summers, have been for a while now."

"Abe Summers is a homosexual."

"I don't think so, Mr. Devereaux. Something of a lady's man ... or so I've heard."

"And you're telling me that Cloris Foley has left, too?"

"Yes."

"Oh fuck. You'll have to find someone to take her class, just for this period, until I think of something. Just let them ... draw ... or something."

"They're doing video and web-based work now."

"Video? Why?"

"It's part of the curriculum," she said.

"Okay." Marty now remembered Cloris hectoring him to buy her some sort of newfangled digital video camera last year and relenting just to shut her up. "Then ... whatever, let them make a video. What's this class I've got to teach?"

"Mr. Summers's English 239, that's the new one."

4

Literary themes were absent in the costumes of Summers's advanced English. The students evidently preferred the moving image to books, the majority of them done up to look like intergalactic warriors—part Galahad, part Gila monster—from some Hollywood special-effects extravaganza or, most likely these days, a computer game. Marty didn't keep up with popular culture so the specifics were lost on him. It was hopelessly atavistic, dressing up as bogeymen to shoo them away, another stage in the lifelong battle with fear. They would soon think they'd conquered it, only to see it return with a vengeance in the middle years, a more mature, more capable incubus visiting their king-size beds as it had their cribs. There were a number of "punks," their spiked-hair and studs an unwitting mockery of rebellion. There was a single obligatory vampire and six Buffys to slay him. There was a kiddie-porn ballerina. There were four or five churlish, druggy fucks at the back who wore nothing, resolutely refusing to ever participate in anything and imagining people noticed. Most notably, at the front of her row, just a yard from Summers's desk so that it was difficult to avoid looking at her, was Audrey Caddigan as an expectant mother. She had affected indolence in her appearance, pinning up lank hair in loose buns like teased sacs of spider eggs. An absence of makeup left her sallow. She looked too baffed to bother. Beneath a pale blue maternity muumuu patterned with chunky citron-and-pink flowers, a mound, like to burst, rose from her belly—the baby she wasn't having. There was enough stuffing to prohibit her closing her legs. No matter how cold-blooded Russell Malan might be, thought Marty, this getup would scare the living shit out of him.

"Mr. Summers is unable to be here today," said Marty, rooting through the emptied desk (for what precisely he did not know). "I'll be taking today's class. Now, what were you ...?" He'd straightened and directed the question to the entire group, to no one in particular. Audrey Caddigan answered.

"We are doing a story. 'Araby,'" she said.

"'Araby.' Right. Could I borrow someone's ...?"

A stout myopic lad, one of the movie characters in a green bodystocking with bulbs of plastic armour at his joints, came forward and handed Marty a thin paperback, never seeming to take his eyes from the floor while doing so.

Dubliners. Joyce story. Summers had said, hadn't he? Marty knew this book, or should have. It had been in an English course he'd taken. The cover was different. Now it was an old photograph of streets in the Irish capital; then it was virtually featureless, a white band over dull orange, title and author, suggesting a package of rations, a week's worth of British letters. Now they were putting some effort, however flawed, into selling it. "Araby"? "Araby"? It was familiar. It would come to him. He'd fake it until then. Was it something to do with a horse? Was it the one where snow was general all over Ireland? He flipped through the book and found the story near the front. "North Richmond Street, being blind ..." The first line told him nothing. Then there was mention of a Christian Brothers' school. Was this a tale of thrashings and buggery? Was there a burning fergusing of some laddie's "O"? No, Marty would have remembered and Summers, new to the Roman fold, wouldn't have dared. Further down the page words were italicized, *"The Memoirs of Vidocq."* What did that mean? Joyce: illusions Marty couldn't fathom (you wanted your laughing and grief to get it), and the stories so heavy with R.C. morbidity and colonial shame they could have been set in St. John's. It was coming back now.

"So, James Joyce …"

He remembered giving *Ulysses* a go. When did Marty Devereaux take it upon himself to test the wide spine of the masterpiece? Back when he himself was a queasy undergraduate scratching his pimples it had been suggested "additional reading" for a course, perhaps the one in which he'd read, and also failed to remember, the book now in his hands. "Anglo-Irish"—no, was it "Modern"—English, three-thousand and something or other? During his term at the academy Marty had assiduously avoided anything from these optional lists, but the supposed ineluctable literary greatness of *Ulysses* (which he'd first misheard as "Ill At Ease") moved him to purchase a copy at the university bookstore in the hope it would spur theretofore absent intellectual passion. The story was said to occur during a single turn of the earth. Dublin days were long, said the volume's girth. He'd given up on it early on, around a morning bowel movement. It was in a box in his basement, probably rubbing right up against nervous Mrs. Woolf, with much else he'd forgotten.

"A modernist, yes?"

Nobody said anything.

"Now in 'Araby,' the protagonist … what's his name?"

"I, sir," said Audrey Caddigan.

"I?"

"It's in the first person, sir."

"Of course, right you are … and everything since … anyway …"

That was bad. He turned the page and scanned the next two.

"O love! O love! many times …" and then just below, "Araby." "She asked me was I going to Araby." Yes! he said to himself. Yes, that's it! The bazaar! He, the "I" of the story, means to buy the girl a present. And the uncle half-pissed at the supper table like a Rex. He was remembering it now.

"Almost a love story on the face of it, wouldn't you say?"

"Totally," said Audrey.

No one else was going to speak voluntarily. This was Summers's elite grouping, his grade twelve English *schutzstaffel*. Surely "totally" was not the best they could do. Were her classmates afraid of Audrey? Were they aware of the terminated pregnancy and thus so uncomfortable in her presence that they wouldn't breathe a word lest it come out sounding like "baby" or "mommy"? Maybe the young mother-to-have-been just dominated the class, was so likely to have the correct answer that no one else bothered. That it should be a girl was more evidence of a worrisome development being reported by his teachers, the sudden and steep decline in the academic performance of boys. Grrrls, it seemed, thunk as much as they rocked. Boys, for reasons unknown, were losing their way.

"Can someone other than Ms. Caddigan elaborate?" Marty said, recollections cascading now, propelled by the weight of the load, that the Joyce story was theorized to be heavily laden with symbols, that Marty'd thought the proposition dubious and said so to his prof (who'd spent the rest of the class scoffing at his presumptuousness), that there was a raven-haired girl from around the bay, older than he, who thought the same and told Marty so in the hallway afterward (and he, knowing from class how much smarter she was, being flattered), and how they'd ended up two or three hours later, after drinking enough coffee to make them shake, back (because her roommate had a biology lab that afternoon), back at the tiny basement apartment she rented just off campus, together like long-time lovers, their bones balletic. She had a thick melodious accent. He remembered now, but she (what was her name?), but she didn't make a big deal of their tryst, didn't make anything of it. They'd met once more a year or so later at an improbably crowded English Society beer bash, and again after they'd talked and laughed (she covered her mouth with both hands in a failing effort to contain startling whoops), and he'd just listened to her voice. They'd gone back to her new place, a room with peeling wallpaper in a shared pile downtown and again made love, and it was like he was miles inside this woman. What was her name? What kind of self-centred pig would forget her name? If he could not remember it now he was in jeopardy of losing her. This was, he sensed, the memory's last chance, the facts might remain but the colours would drain, the touch go out of it.

She was deliciously negligent in her dress, this girl, wearing any old thing from the Sally Ann or, as the song went, *"a big check coat from John D. Snow's and a woolly hat for my head."* Her hair was a tar-black tuckamore. If Marty knew where she was he would track her down, just to call and say hello, maybe admit that he was afraid of her back then, that he'd not called her because he realized he had nothing with which to impress her, no knowledge, no wit, no mystery. That same year a vicious wind, the inconsolable remnant of a hurricane, ripped up an aged dogberry tree and threw it atop Lloyd Purcell's Dodge Dart, and when the boys emerged from a party, in a place not that far from Sophie's, and saw the car crushed they had nearly pissed themselves. And the same week Rex, outside a bar downtown, had talked back to some troglodyte from the Constabulary and had his jaw broken, and Hank won a big meet, surprising a heavily favoured Yank wrestler. And in a week Marty, his bum Bobby Orrs beginning to fail, ran poorly in a race in Wolfville, Nova Scotia, where the autumn air had the tang of rotting apples. And in a year his parents were dead.

What was her name? He could imagine a name he supposed, invent one, that's what Marty did, but he knew it wouldn't do him any good at all.

"The narrator," said a girl, "is in flove with his friend's sister." She was in a mouse costume—no, it was a rat, a rat costume—whiskers painted on her cheeks, hairless tail dangling from her seat. "Or he finks he is." Her prosthetic buck teeth were giving her trouble. "Fhat's why he wants to buy her fhe gift."

"Thinks?"

"He's too young to know what flove is ... he's fust a boy."

"Perhaps," said Marty, realizing now that scholars imbued the story with symbols so they might have something to say in trying circumstances such as these. "Does the gift symbolize anything?" What was it the boy had bought at the bazaar? It was jewellery, Marty remembered. He knew that much. A brooch?

"I don't know that it symbolizes anything, sir." It was Audrey Caddigan again.

"No?"

"I mean, it just is. He even says it. It represents his vanity."

"The brooch?"

"What brooch, sir?"

"Isn't that the gift?" Marty now thought it might have been a vase.

"There's no gift, sir."

"Sorry?"

They were looking at him with suspicion now, beginning to deduce that he might not know of what he spoke. He looked to the fat-faced clock on the wall above the door. He remembered picking the clocks up, twenty-six of them, at a liquidation sale. Assets of a medical supplies wholesaler that had gone up the spout. Twenty minutes of class remained.

"The narrator," said Audrey Caddigan, "goes to the bazaar and it's too late and the stalls are closing and he doesn't end up buying anything for the girl."

Marty looked down at the book and flipped to the final page of the story. "Gazing up into the darkness," it read, "I saw myself as a creature driven and derided by vanity; and my eyes burned with anguish and anger." Marty didn't remember that bit at all. What kind of an ending was that for a class of grade twelves? Summers was a pretentious asshole. Marty should have known not to entertain his proposal. Perhaps Marty, having acquiesced then, gave Summers the confidence to fire off that letter to the Department of Education. Marty should have just told him "no," should have kept him in his place, a subaltern.

"Yes," said Marty as if he'd known it, "this thing he doesn't get …" He looked at the clock, the pulse-taking tool, and there were still twenty minutes left, something was wrong, a doctor must be summoned, a code called. "I have to check something at the office, why don't you …" Marty looked down at the book, "start reading 'Eveline'?"

In the empty hallway he felt his shirt had bunched and woven into ropes under his arms. He was like a rabbit in a snare. He wasn't old enough to have problems with his memory, but it seemed as if he'd never before read the conclusion of the Joyce story. Maybe it was a new edition based on recently discovered author's notes. Maybe he was a touch hungover. He'd go to his office, get a drink of water, and return to the classroom without his blazer.

Something brown and sticky, Coke or Pepsi, had been spilled halfway up the front stairs and been left long enough to run all the way to the first floor. He noted to call Mr. MacNaughton to have it cleaned up and wondered why someone hadn't already reported it. They'd miss him when he was gone, Marty thought.

Passing Hank's office Marty saw that Hank was talking to two suits, young buzz-cuts. He was crossing the threshold of his own room when Mrs. Norris rose and frantically waved to him. Her face was flushed, not rosy but angry-red in blotches. She was beginning to show her age lately, thought Marty.

"What is it?" he asked.

She hurried to the countertop separating her workspace from the entrance area and leaned over it on tiptoe, the other leg lifted, so that she could almost whisper. "They're the police," she said.

"And?"

Mrs. Norris shook her head.

"Okay," said Marty. "Okay." He continued into his office.

"And Ms. Spurell called again. And your sister-in-law, Meredith."

"Sure, sure," said Marty.

He disentangled himself from his jacket. The fabric of his shirt was clammy against his skin. He knew why the cops were there. Russell Malan had no doubt mentioned to his parents his being shoved up against the lockers by Marty. An investigation by the police was the last thing he needed. If it were ongoing he wouldn't be able to leave town, lest he appear guilty. He wished there was a door on his office. He needed a moment to himself.

It was possible, of course, this was to do with Summers and his letter to the Department of Education—though it was unlikely that the law would be dragged into it, unless they were proposing what Marty had done was somehow criminal fraud. Marty resolved that he would make Summers pay. He would argue that the boy was treated unfairly by Summers and that he had no choice but to intercede. If perhaps he'd been overzealous then it was just an indication he wished to err in the boy's favour, it was a mark of his generosity, his big, soft heart, nothing more. First he would have to check and make sure Summers hadn't taken copies of Russell's tests as evidence.

But he had just been at Summers's desk and it was empty. Meredith had called. What did she want this time? Had Cathy overdosed or been arrested for shoplifting or mistaken a real wiener for the tofu variety and had an adverse reaction, had Rex gone on the booze? Were they so helpless down there that they must forever call him? If it weren't for Rex's dumbfuck cooking class he wouldn't have met Meredith's friend Jackie and would now be free of that encumbrance.

The cops could be there because of the Caddigans' complaint, he supposed. But again where was the criminal aspect of that business? Was Sophie's counsel, as it involved a minor, illegal? Was the girl a minor when Sophie had spoken to her? No?

Sitting behind his desk he loosened his belt. He was no longer able to comfortably use the well-stretched third hole and moved to the more accommodating fourth. He wasn't going back up to that classroom. He'd send Hank. Hank, who was going to be seriously pissed off when he learned what had happened to Summers and why.

No, Marty realized, what the police visit most likely concerned was the circumstances of the pine grove. Hank had taken the mayor out there after the opening assembly to apprise him of the situation. The City looked into it and, as Marty suspected, the evidence of illegal activity, the drugs and whatnot, necessitated the involvement of the Constabulary. Marty had warned Hank this could happen.

There were papers on the desk that required his attention: several plumbing contractors' quotes ranging from the higher-than-expected to the plainly shocking, a troublesome note from his insurer concerning changes to his policy with regard the French class's annual excursions to Saint-Pierre and Quebec City, an absurd request from Cloris Foley for a financial contribution toward her attending the Documenta Art Exhibition in Kassel, Germany (if she hadn't left Marty would have reminded her that it was not unknown for teachers in the public system to pay for rudimentary supplies out of their own pocket). It was all trivial and aggravating. There was a long letter, a semi-coherent tract denouncing Western decadence (Yeah, and? thought Marty), in a barely decipherable hand from Dr. Abousaada. Marty gave it only a cursory read, skipping to the end to learn that the doctor was withdrawing his two children from The Red Pines and demanding that a refund of fees be forwarded to his new address in Rawalpindi, Pakistan. No!

Of greater concern was the cost estimate of readying the school's computers for the catastrophe that was to befall them at the turn of the millennium, this "Y2K" thing. They wanted twelve thousand bucks and were telling Marty that by rights he should be upgrading the systems every three years. A toaster oven had a longer life. That they planned the obsolescence of an information technology had unsettling implications. Three years! They could go fuck themselves.

He saw now that his and Hank's mistake had been in opening a high school. They should have applied the same principles to earlier grades when the students were less self-assured and more easily managed. They could have charged the same fees. Or, like Kenny Singh had observed, the elderly. Maybe that was the ticket—not education at all but caring for the ailing mothers and fathers of the baby boomers. They needed to be warehoused, to be cleaned and scrubbed, and their yuppie children weren't nearly as fussy about how they treated their parents, who were becoming unsightly and infirm, as they were their high-performance kids.

He looked at the school's furnace oil bill. It was almost three times as large as the previous month's. It didn't make any sense.

Out the window he saw the cops leaving, getting into their car and driving away. They were so young. Marty went to Hank's office.

But Hank was grey, possessed that repellent pallor one usually saw in the dying. His hands were laid flat on his desk in front of him and he was looking at them as if waiting for them to perform, as though they might act on their own.

"What was that about?" asked Marty.

"They … I'm going to be charged," Hank said, looking at Marty for the first time since he'd come in.

"Charged with what?" A potted African violet atop one of Hank's filing cabinets was precariously close to the edge. Marty reached to push it back and in doing so put his weight wrong, felt the weakness in his knee, and had a fleeting sense of listing.

"Sexually assaulting Russell Malan. Indecent acts."

The statement detonated with magnificent brutality. It was a militant blow to Marty's chest, stomach, and head. A crash. A high-speed collision where you'd seen the oncoming car and you'd braked but it was too late.

"What?"

"That's what they said. It's not true, Marty."

"No, of course not, Hank, of course," Marty said, lowering himself into a chair facing Hank's desk. It was still warm from one of the cops. "When is this supposed to have happened?"

"I gather back when I was tutoring him. That's what it seemed like. Their questions had to do with that. Maybe … I guess they didn't want to give any details away … or to check me out … or something."

"The boy, Hank, he's like …"

"He's a bug, a maggot. Someone should step on him."

"Obviously you can't say that now, Hank. You're going to have to not say certain things. People are going to be listening for everything. Watching. So like, hush, right?"

"It didn't happen, Marty."

"Of course it didn't."

"Really, it didn't."

"I know! I know it didn't."

Marty knew Hank was telling the truth, but the visage he presented in denial, shaky, crestfallen, would persuade no one. The more adamant Hank became the less he would be believed. It was the kind of thing that one had only to be accused of to be seen as guilty, a vessel for the village's dark thoughts, the reflection of everyone's potential venality.

Marty saw how it was just management, how it was so perfect a solution to everybody's —excepting Marty's and Hank's—problems as to be irresistible. Who had first proposed this *auto-da-fé,* this fatwa? Kenny was the brains. Most likely, he'd refined some vulgar notion Hayden had spewed in rage. Was Dirk Malan in on it, or had he simply made it possible? It was problem solving. It wasn't cowardly on their part to have the police do the dirty work, it was just the way they were. They always got the help to do that sort of thing. They paid more than their share of taxes, they should be afforded some special service. Their property was worth more and so was more closely guarded. It was the same thing.

Hank would be fighting this thing for years and could never win. He was for the stake. He was so closely associated with opposition to the Perroquect Downs development that a gambit to stop the bulldozers now would be akin to sanctioning child abuse. Marty realized another active element: Summers's letter. Dirk Malan was no doubt informed of the contents by someone he knew in government. Any shortcomings in Russell's academic performance could be put down to the traumatic effect of having been molested by the principal of the school he was attending, and Marty's attempt to alter the record a natural part of a cover-up. A letter to this effect would accompany Russell's application to a top school and he would be granted entry; to deny him such would be to continue the victimization. The Caddigan girl's troubles could be put down to dysfunction in Russell born of the tragedy that had befallen him. It would be as if Hank had knocked up the girl.

Yeah, Kenny put this together. People demanded a root cause these diagnostic days, some scarring event that was responsible for those parts of themselves that didn't work. Now Russell had his. If

Russell were at all articulate he'd no doubt end up being some sort of advocate or spokesperson—shit! Dirk Malan's talk about his son faking a degree in literature was the perfect prelude to rich, spoiled Russell having some hush-moneyed ghost write his redemptive "my triumph over adversity" bio. The boy would be popping up on television chat shows to plug it, selling his story to some movie-of-the-week pimps. Who knew how it would go, except that it would end badly.

There was a caste division in victimology. Russell wasn't walking into a world of the wounded like some underclass loser. He was going to "get help," to "see someone." He was entering a protected realm, a somnolent asylum. The Malans were probably happy to see him go, even if Russell had done his part for the business, had stepped forward and taken one (in every sense) for the team.

What was Hank saying now?

"God, Marty, Beth and the kids …"

"Beth will understand. This kind of thing has always been a risk for us."

"No."

"Yes, Hank, it has," Marty said forcefully enough that Hank, diminished Hank, turned away. "What exactly are you alleged to have done?"

"Jesus." Disgust showed on Hank's face. The corners of his mouth dropped and he drew his lips in.

"It's going to come up. We might as well …"

"They didn't specify. They were just asking questions. Maybe they don't want to give away the details of their case, but I gather it's … touching and stuff."

"Touching is not that bad, is it?"

"Marty!"

"I mean in the scheme of things. I mean there must be a scale."

"My God, Marty." Hank's panic was revving up.

Of course there was a scale, only it was unsaid, like everything about the business. The same people who decried its aberrance claimed it to be shockingly commonplace. It needed to be brought out into the open yet never spoken of.

"They haven't actually charged you yet, though, have they?"

"No. And they try to keep this private, right? They try to protect the identity of the ..."

"Yeah," Marty said, knowing full well that it didn't matter. The news would travel via whispers, its progress hastened by every entreaty to secrecy.

Hank would be prosecuted with the extra zeal reserved for violators who were said to be in "a position of trust." How unfair this was, to demand that the Martys and Hanks be so certain, so sure, that they were always to be in a position of trust. It would better serve everyone, it was more honest, to say up front that their teachers and principals, that their parents, priests, doctors, police were, in fact, in a position of profound doubt and uncertainty. The greatest sins, said the new Pharisees, were between those of unequal power. (Was then God the ultimate abuser?) No odds that a sexual encounter might be consensual and between adults—only that it was later regretted. The jails, thought Marty, would surely burst. This case, a headmaster and a boy in his charge, was so good an example as to be almost a caricature of impropriety.

Transgressions by those of rank were now so commonplace, so run-of-the-mill, that the public no longer paid attention to the details of the case. One who had risen to lofty heights must necessarily fall. That Hank was a seemingly well-adjusted family man, a convert to environmentalism, a quintessence of modern virtue only the more doomed him to judgment, so conditioned now was the public to be counterintuitive in its suspicions. It was always the last person you suspected these days. Everything everybody did was likely a masquerade, a way to put you off the trail. You could never be too careful—evil lurked everywhere. Believing that you had been lucky and escaped harm was no comfort, for recollection of horrible events disappeared into a foggy realm of repression, only to pop up later like a demented jack-in-the-box. (Marty's experience was otherwise. While his fond memories were steadily dissociating, the painful ones lingered with diamantine resilience.)

Indeed there was a general state of public apprehension. Marty reasoned that some agenda was being served, that this condition had been induced. There was money, somewhere, in fear. Maybe that was the next big thing.

"You think, you know, and then … then you're unprepared. Marty, this … if we don't nip this in the bud, if we don't do something fast, this could ruin us, the school."

"Nah, this is a problem, a serious problem that requires management. We'll deal with it," said Marty, though he was, in reality, unsure. "First thing we've got to do is get you hooked up with a good lawyer. You probably should have called one before you even talked to the cops."

"Yeah, but you think to yourself, this is a mistake or some kind of mix-up, I'll clear it up … I should have …"

"It's a risk of this business, Hank."

"I've done nothing to deserve—"

"Stop. Stop, okay? That means nothing. Who deserves anything? Everything is everybody's fault."

"Everything is everybody's fault? You should put that on T-shirts."

"I'll have to do something."

"Beth …"

"She'll know the difference. I'll tell her. Listen, I'm with you on this thing, okay. I'm there."

Marty meant what he said and it must have shown because Hank seemed to take some comfort from it.

"I was just thinking," Marty continued, "about a bunch of stuff, and I remembered when you beat that heavily favoured Yank in that—"

"Krauss."

"Hmmm?"

"His name was Krauss, Earl Krauss. He was from Wisconsin."

"Yeah, I was remembering how you beat him in that competition."

"What's that got to do ...?"

"Nothing. It's just that I remembered it this morning."

"He was beating me. I was finished and I was trying not to be pinned, just trying to survive, and it was hopeless. He was so good and extremely strong. Beef fed, you know. He had me and ... and my thumb, I don't know how this happened, it felt like it went between his ribs, or under them or something, and I could see it in his eyes when it happened, this pain shot through his face, it was like fireworks in his eyes. Then all his weight went against him and he was through." Hank drew a deep breath. He was settling down, glad to have been able to think, if only for a moment, of something else.

"Now, a lawyer? You know anyone? I can think of some commercial guys but ..." it was too late for Marty not to say it, "we'll need a criminal lawyer. Know anyone?"

"The only lawyers I know have got kids here at The Pines so ..." Hank shook his head.

"You go home, Hank," said Marty. "I'm fine here. Call me later."

"Okay."

"Promise you'll call me."

"I will."

♆

The cultural divide at Frank Moores was marked today by those who came costumed and those who did not. Those who had not dressed for Halloween made a point of not participating in anything. They did not attend hockey games to root for the school team. They were not members of any school clubs. They shunned all extracurricular activities with the exception of school dances, which they would attend only so they could marvel at and jeer, in their superior way, the prancing or the needy who had come to shake it. In their view the world, at least the one made and inhabited by their parents, was total shit. The people that joined in, those that participated, were endorsing all that was wrong with this total crap world. Play in the shit and you get shit on you. Cathy once wanted to belong to the non-belongers but now found their rules more stifling than those of the tit-heads in the drama society or of the thick-legged girls of the soccer team. The longer she lived, the more isolated, the lonelier, she would be.

She'd missed homeroom and her first class, English. She hated the English class. The teacher, Miss Hennessey, would exhaust herself trying to draw comments from the class about assigned stories or essays that none of the students had read. The old bag would then sulk over having wasted her time on the little ingrates. The class was made even more unbearable these days by the collection of Newfoundland stuff they were supposed to be reading, a flimsy volume entitled *Diddle Dum This One*. In this book was a scene from a play written by her father, something boring to do with Joey Smallwood and Confederation—like, get over it! Thankfully, probably because of her double-barrelled name, the Ford in front of the Devereaux, Miss Hennessey hadn't made the connection. Today, Cathy knew, they were going to be looking at excerpts from some sealing disaster thing. She'd heard it all before: the heartlessness of the captains and merchants in feudal Newfoundland, the sudden and blinding storms on the ice floes, the bodies of the departed swilers frozen and stacked on deck like firewood as the ship sailed into St. John's Harbour.

Cathy would make the next class, physics with Donnelly, and then, she thought, it being so nice out, pip-off the rest of the day, walk downtown. During recess she'd go to "the park," a patch of grass just outside the chain-link fence that delineated the school grounds, where students smoked. She would look for Jeanette, see if she was interested in joining her.

It was necessary that Jeanette chain-smoke, so they ended up in a crummy doughnut place. The coffee was the worst Cathy ever tasted. Jeanette drank watery Pepsi.

"It is so pointless for me to stay in school," Jeanette was saying. "I'm never going to pass. And I'm not interested anyway. It's just a waste of my time."

"What would you do?"

"Shoplift."

"Like shoplift a car and an apartment?"

"I don't know, get a shitty job. Junior handjob trainee at Wal-Mart."

"What's the point of that?"

"I should do like a webcam thing, just stay at home and like have perverts pay to watch me watch television ..." Jeanette tossed her head sideways, swinging her cape of hair away from her face and back over her shoulder.

"They pay to watch you get undressed and like masturbate and pee and stuff, not to watch television."

"Fine, I'll watch television naked. I'll pee. I don't care. I'll bet there are like Japanese men who'd pay to watch me watch television, even with my clothes on. They have like people who are into everything over there. Thing about the web is that nobody knows who you are or where you are, so people aren't necessarily anybody any more and the people that like go on the web looking for stuff, they don't want you to be anyone anyway. It's like amnesia, only like in the present. Is there a word for that?"

"I don't know what it is."

"I'm doin' a webcam."

"Good for you."

"Maybe if I could move in with some guy …"

"Like Scott?"

"No, not like Scott. Some older guy, who like had a place. I don't know."

"You gotta do something you love."

"What are you, like a guidance counsellor? I love sleeping in. I love watching the story. That's the truth. That's being honest with myself. And don't tell me you want to be like a nuclear brain surgeon or something."

"Something interesting."

"You should learn how to like clean up oil spills and save birds. You should be like a seabird scrubber."

"Fuck off."

"The education part is the only thing I don't like about school."

♅

Summers's substitute arrived just as Hank was leaving, and Marty sent her straight to Summers's classroom. When he explained the situation to Mrs. Norris, as he knew he must, she clutched the back of a chair for support.

"This is an inherent risk of our occupation, Mrs. Norris," he said again. "We take precautions, but …"

"There's no truth to it then?"

"I'm disappointed you would even ask."

"I'm sorry, but … you hear about it so much, like it's always going on."

"That's the media, they're parasites. It makes a great story and it's easy. I don't think it happens as often as people think. There's a certain measure of hysteria." Marty was not interested in having this conversation.

"It happened to me," said Mrs. Norris.

What to say?

"I'm sorry to hear that," was the best he could offer.

"When I was a teenager, an uncle."

"There you go, hey. Terrible."

"Not that it has anything … any bearing on Mr. Lundrigan."

"No," said Marty. "Now, when I came downstairs there was Coke spilled on the steps. Could you please tell Mr. MacNaughton to clean it up?"

"I've paged him, Mr. Devereaux. Twice," she said.

"Goddamn it."

Marty soon realized that he hadn't the faintest what MacNaughton got up to in the course of a day. His caretaker was, or had been, so reliable that Marty never had to call on him. MacNaughton anticipated problems or dealt with them so promptly that there was never a need to ask him to do things. He was the one person on whom Marty could always count.

Marty gave no thought to the route of his search and simply went marching about.

If they saw that Hank might beat the charge they would just stop the procedure. The damage would be done, their cause served. In fact, the more Marty thought about it, the more he became convinced that the matter would never go before a jury. He knew enough of this crowd now to see how they operated. They had sent their message. They would, at the eleventh hour, withdraw in the name of good taste and propriety, to keep the names out of the papers, to spare Russell the ordeal of testifying. Should Hank decide to parry, to counter that he'd been defamed and needed to win back his good name, they would simply threaten him with an epic legal battle in which he would be ludicrously outmatched. And did it matter now what turn events took? Marty could spend an eternity imagining one scenario or another. He and Hank were fucked anyway.

Marty resolved to clean up the stairs himself. He checked two utility closets and found them in surprising disorder. The second room, a complete shambles, was possessed of a sinister chemical odour. An industrial cleanser had been spilled on the floor. Collecting in an iridescent pool it was eating into the linoleum. There was a cardboard box of stained, volatile rags, a virtual fire bomb, kicked into a corner. In neither of the rooms was there a mop or bucket.

He used his master key to unlock the door to the basement.

Before he could see anything, he was struck by the dankness of the air rising to meet him. When he flicked the light switch he saw that it was snowing down there.

Indeed, it looked like fat flakes of wet snow gently falling to earth. The stuff was accumulating in undulating sheets, hanging like lace sheers from the ceiling or rising up from the concrete floor like submarine flora. It was all white, all luminous white clusters of spores.

To varying degrees it covered everything, collecting where the listless subterranean air currents dictated. It draped a wobbly pillar of broken chairs that looked to have been stacked by Dr. Seuss. It appeared as gauze on exposed wires. An old soccer net, repairs to which were forgotten or abandoned, was a monstrous pupa.

Marty saw the orrery on its side, leaning against a wall. The strands formed a silky web over the solar system, the sun at its centre the host spider.

The mops and buckets he was looking for were at the bottom of the stairs, but he forgot his purpose for the moment, going farther into the basement to see if he could discover the source of the fungal bloom. He supposed the foundation might have given way to ground water. He worried that the spores might form a health risk, he'd heard of that.

"MacNaughton?" he shouted, knowing there would be no response, his janitor hadn't been down here in some days.

Marty could hear dripping, and across the large space saw an effluence from an open door at the top of a small rotting staircase. The light made it plain that the room was full of steam.

The door was to a high chamber, drum shaped, where Marty could not remember having ever been. Here it was almost raining, so thick was the steam. It was perceptibly warmer. A metal ladder ran up the wall to yet another opening, from which the hot cloud was billowing like a vent into a Turkish bath. Marty climbed the ladder.

He was in the skin of the school, between the exterior and interior walls, backstage, behind the flats. Pipes and cables and electrical wire ran the length of the small gap. The exterior walls were coated with a hardened lustrous fibre, like an insect carapace, a beetle back. Some sort of sprayed-on insulation or sealant, he supposed. It was flaking off in patches.

Turning sideways, Marty entered the narrow passage and advanced, foot sliding to foot, closer to the source of the steam. He could tell now from the sound, an insistent hissing, that a hot water pipe had ruptured. He wasn't particularly claustrophobic, but inching along between walls that just about pressed on his shoulder blades and chest was a trial. A horrible thought occurred to him. MacNaughton must have done exactly as he was doing and become trapped and somehow perished, asphyxiated or maybe electrocuted.

Marty came to a junction. The passage continued in two directions; not five yards down one route he saw, at head height, the leaking pipe.

As he got closer he saw that these pipes too had once been sprayed with some sort of coating. He was breathing in the tiny particles they were shedding. The adhesive substance was completely absent at the point of the pinprick breach from which the steam was escaping.

He was as near the hot issue as he dared. To examine the leak from the other side would mean putting his face into the stream and scalding it.

He retreated, going back the way he'd come, managing in the process to hook and tear the cuff of his right trouser leg.

He grabbed the bucket and mop on his way up from the basement. He might as well get used to it; he would be cleaning up until Mrs. Norris tracked MacNaughton down. The situation in the basement was an outrage. This degree of negligence, it had clearly been let go for weeks, merited dismissal. He remembered the oil bill.

There was a fine down of spores on the bucket and the mop, so Marty rinsed them in the sink of the least noxious of the two utility closets. He poured a generous dose of the cleanser, Floronax Pren-7 Institutional, into the bucket and topped it with hot water. The fumes coming up off the mixture burned Marty's throat. He'd like to pour Floronax Pren-7, undiluted, down Summers's throat, down Hayden's, down young Russell's. He'd like to watch them choking on it.

After sloshing the cleaning solution onto the steps, Marty realized he didn't have anything with which to wring out the mop. He used his hands, twin trickles of the squeezings ran up both arms under his shirt sleeves. He could feel it aggravating the skin.

The fire alarm sounded.

On another day Marty would have been pleased to see how rapidly and in what good order the students came down the stairs. Today, waving them past the still-wet and slippery section of the stairs, he caused two well-planned and executed columns to merge and so fall into disarray. This jumble of masked and costumed bodies, the intergalactic army, then intersected and disrupted the neat lines streaming down the corridors of the first floor.

Evacuation took fourteen minutes, not the six provided by Marty's scheme, not the seven and a half that stood as a drill record. Whether it was the chaotic state in which they exited the school, or that they were in costume, the kids standing around outside were impossible to keep in ranks. The head count, undertaken by the teachers, supervised by Alan Pitts (who came forward and volunteered), took another ten minutes. After another ten minutes a senior officer among the firemen who responded informed Marty that it was, as usual, a false alarm, that a search of the building revealed that one of the kids had pulled a wall-mounted alarm on the second floor. A prank. Marty apologized and the fireman said it was nothing, it happened all the time. Marty pointed out that it had only happened once before at The Red Pines. Marty summoned Pitts and asked that he pass on the all-clear.

Though cold enough to see your breath it was a clear day, a sterling autumn day, so the kids were uncooperative when being corralled to class. Marty needed to sit but stood, as if in review, watching them file into the building.

Sophie stopped to talk to him.

"Where was the fire?" she asked.

"There was no fire. Somebody just pulled the alarm outside 246."

Sophie looked him up and down, perplexed. Marty looked too and saw that he did appear as if he'd been putting out fires (which, in a way, he had). His pants were filthy from his basement expedition, his white shirt was stained with something slick and bituminous. The students could only have drawn the same conclusion as Miss Zwitzer or would otherwise have been snickering as they passed. His undoing looked like heroics.

"Is everything okay, Martin?" she asked.

"No," said Marty.

"No?"

"Not here. Later."

"When?"

"Can't say. MacNaughton's gone too, so I'm going to have to stay after and clean up some, just for today."

"Gone too? Who else?"

"Can't here. Later."

She shook her head as she left, as if Marty was being unnecessarily cryptic, carrying on, like men did, as though they were keepers of state secrets.

When Cathy got home there was no sign of life in the house. It was cold inside, the thermostat untouched since being turned down before bed last night. Cathy reached for it but then decided against moving the dial higher. The chill was quieting. There was no note. There were no smells of cooking. Perhaps the parentals had another fight and both fled the house in a rage. These used to be grand operatic clashes, with bawling and foot stomping and door slamming. Disputes over matters of principle, about politics and art. Of late their battles had lost energy, were over bills unpaid or fences unpainted, and just petered out after a brief interval of recycled insults. Her mother was heading off to Seattle for some protest in a few weeks, and Cathy sensed that both her parents were looking forward to being apart.

Though it was only four o'clock it was already getting dark. Cathy went straight to her room.

From the bottom of a box in the back of her closet she retrieved the book taken from Rosenkrantz's. She noticed for the first time that the edges of the pages wore a blush patina; they were freckled. She sat on the bed, placed the book in her lap, and opened it.

She swept the flat of her hand across the page. The paper possessed a dampness that made it feel cool. In black ink—full, true black without a hint of blue—there were drawings of simple forms, like you would see in a geometry primer. There were circumscribed star patterns, mandalas.

All the text was in taunting Latin. The shapes grew more complex as she went along, among them multifaceted three-dimensional forms, stones cut like jewels, occasionally with inexplicable drawings—a fire, a lobster, a singing bird—on the exposed faces. This made Cathy think, almost hopefully, that the book was somehow involved with the practice of magic. She was almost a third of the way through when she noticed musical notation printed in the margins. Atop the page were the words "DE PROPORTIONIBUS." Now the shapes were imprisoned in cages, seemingly to be measured. What were surely stars were shown at the centre of great circles and circles within circles. And finally there were the planets, Cathy knew that much, *Saturnus, Iupiter, Mars, Telluris Et Luna, Venus, Mercurius.*

It postulated, she guessed, that all these things, the shapes, the harmony of music, the orbits of the planets round the sun, conformed to some similar set of rules, that there were inescapable proportions, a governing rhythm to the universe. It made sense, she supposed. Did she tick, did she chime?

She closed the book. She regretted taking it. It was unfathomable. She'd put it back where she'd found it. Maybe it would fall into the possession of someone who could make use of it.

♀

A plumber was summoned to repair the broken pipe. Marty contacted the government's employment office to post a notice for the janitor's job. He arranged through the company that cleaned his house to have people come to the school until the position was filled, but they couldn't provide anyone until Monday evening. Mrs. Norris failed to reach MacNaughton despite several attempts. It being Friday there were few after-school activities. The girls' soccer team pounded the half-frozen pitch, possibly their last outdoor practice until spring.

The drama club was to have a meeting, but with Summers absent it was cancelled. Some of the members hung around nonetheless, practising either their burning-with-creative-intensity or their disengaged-narco-tubercular looks until Marty kicked them out.

Marty started cleaning the building at four. It took him twenty minutes to unclog a toilet full of paper towels. A cursory mopping of the second-floor hallways took him another hour. He'd have to come in tomorrow and possibly Sunday to finish.

As he drove home his arms were shaky with fatigue.

He fixed himself a drink: gin with, in the absence of anything else, instant iced tea made from crystals. The doorbell rang.

There were three young kids, not yet school age, in animal costumes—a leopard, a lion, and an elaborate bat with fun fur and translucent plastic wings—accompanied by their parents.

"Twick ow tweat!" said the tiny lion.

Marty looked to the mom and dad, kempt breeders straight out of the L.L. Bean catalogue, she in a woollen lumber jacket, he in canvas with corduroy on the cuffs and collar. A ridiculous honey-basted moon was over their shoulders like they'd brought it along. Marty thought he recognized them, from up the street. On another day he would have seen them as potential customers and put some effort into playing his part.

"Give mwe somphing good to eat," said the leopard.

The parents were beaming. They were, and all like them, joy junkies, intoxicated by adoration, addicted to the angelic aural champagne that was a child's laughter. The more rational knew that the sound, with its direct conduit to the heart, was only the siren call of their greedy genes and not heavenly music ... unless, it occurred to Marty for the first time, unless those were one and the same thing.

"I am so sorry, but I've just come home and ... I tell you what ..." Marty fished in his trouser pockets and came up with a few nickels and dimes and a lint-covered Rolaids tablet. He laid his drink on the floor by his feet. It looked as if he were toting around a urine sample. He took out his wallet and gave each of the two cats five-dollar bills and the bat a tenner. "Now you have to buy your mom something nice," he said to the bat. The parents looked displeased and hurried the children from the house.

Marty closed the door and then rushed to turn off all the lights so the place looked unoccupied. His car was in the driveway, but the kids wouldn't put it together.

Halloween was always Sophie's thing. She made a big deal of it, always putting on a costume, making a fuss of the few kids that came to her door, being too generous with the candy. In recent years, after running out of the Diabetes peanuts he'd been obliged to buy at school and the caramels he'd grabbed at the drugstore on the way home, Marty would close up his house and drive over to Sophie's.

He walked to the phone via the kitchen so he wouldn't be noticed passing the living-room window. He sat at the dining-room table to listen to his voice mail, anticipating the call from Hank, the bad news from the homefront. He had seven new messages.

"Marty, it's Jacks. Give me a call, would you?"

His drink tasted awful. Iced tea worked with vodka, didn't it? What did they call those? He drank it anyway. The next message played.

"Marty. Jacks. I left a message with your secretary at school, but ... well ... she's useless ... Call me." She sounded pissed off. Marty thought about the parents of the trick-or-treaters and their dirty looks. What, in the name of God, was so offensive about giving the kids money? Too precious by half, these people.

A long tone indicated a caller who did not leave a message. Long Island Iced Tea! Vodka and iced tea was called Long Island Iced Tea.

"Marty, this is Meredith. Could you give me a call, please?" No, I won't. Not tonight, thought Marty, hearing the brittle fragility of the voice. He preferred the old strident Meredith to this uncertain woman.

"Marty, it's Jacks. Call me the moment you get in. It's important. Ted knows."

Ted knows. Ted knows about us? Ted knows I'm banging his wife?

They were knocking at the door again.

Ted knows what?

A strident boom startled Marty and he jumped in his seat, spilling some of his cocktail. The noise came from the other side of the living room, from the window. Egg and shell were oozing down the glass. The pane continued to warble.

"Marty, Jacks. He's very upset. His mother told him. I suppose I shouldn't have said anything. Anyway, he's left, he just stormed out of here, so watch out. Anyway, I'm glad he knows … I mean this is just … just ridiculous to be carrying on like this, in secret. God, we're adults."

Whatever that meant, thought Marty.

"So I guess tonight's out."

Yeah, I guess.

Next there was a clumsy hang-up, the sound of a handset bouncing and rattling around the cradle as if it were dropped. Probably Jackie again.

The doorbell rang. Marty did not move. They would go away. Then there came heavy knocking. Marty slipped off his shoes, padded through the kitchen, and looked from the top of the stairs to the front door. Through the small frosted glass in the door Marty could make out not children at his door but a single adult.

Marty was aware of pressure building up inside his head, in his sinuses. He needed, urgently, to blow his nose but could not for fear of the trumpeting giving him away.

The person rang again and then turned their back on the house. For the longest time they didn't move, stood there as if on guard before walking away. Marty went to his bedroom. The window there provided a broad view of the street.

It was Ted, of course, and he was going nowhere. He'd only moved down to the end of the driveway. He was considering the presence of Marty's Saab. Whatever pills he took probably slowed his reason. Chump was wearing Florsheims and track pants. Across the back of the pants were the letters M.U.N. for Memorial University of Newfoundland, Jackie's alma mater. The seat was loose and droopy, containing as it did Ted's much less substantial ass. It looked like he'd shat himself. His head was covered with a ball cap, some promotional giveaway with a large cloth crest. Against the October air he had pulled on his old pilot's jacket. Marty could see the Air Canada wings pinned to the breast. Ted was the scariest looking thing on the street.

He was clearly beyond embarrassment, was functioning on the other side of abject humiliation, a place without consequence where there was nothing left to lose, no dignity to preserve.

And Ted was deranged, of that there was no doubt. Most likely he'd come to talk, to hector/lecture/plea, to wail, to blame. He was so into his own head, so treated and coddled, that he was probably a deadly whiner, a suffocating weight of lament.

In answer Marty could only say that he didn't care how Ted felt, but if it were a consolation he no longer had any interest in seeing the fellow's wife. He could have her back. Ted would never believe him.

This was a full day and very bad one. Marty didn't have the fortitude to deal with any more so, taking a page from Hayden's book, the phone still in his hand, he dialled the police.

"No, I've no idea who he is," said Marty, seeing now that sentinel Ted's presence was discouraging the youngsters from coming up to the house. They were just skipping the address. Next year some kid would dress up as "the crazy man that murdered Mr. Devereaux."

"He's not from the neighbourhood, that's for sure." Marty continued, "It's the children I'm thinking of, the trick-or-treaters. I mean, what's he doing out there?"

The cops were, thankfully, older than the blue-boys that had come to the school. They were definitely heavier set, built for nights in the city. When they got out of the car they did not rush Ted with a club or spray him straight away with mace or pepper. They looked to be indulging his need for therapeutic conversation.

They blabbed long enough that Marty finished his drink, which, on further consideration, he felt was a worthy experiment in mixology—not a complete success but an investigation he would repeat as soon as Ted was dealt with.

The end came with a hand, in a latex glove, laid on Ted's upper arm, a gentle coax in the direction of the cruiser. Ted showed that he didn't like being touched by yanking his arm from the cop's grip. And when the cop again put his hands on Ted, more insistently this time, implacable Ted shoved him back. He was shortly bundled in the other officer's arms, unable to raise his own, and then roughly stuffed, for transport, into the car. The police brushed themselves off, radioed a call—probably to the lock-up—and departed with the cargo. Marty toasted them with his empty glass.

Even with the curtains drawn the glow of the television would alert the outside world to the presence of Marty within the house. He could do no more than shuffle around in the gloom. He fixed himself another iced tea and gin and dubbed the concoction "St. John's Piss." Without the lamps he'd figured into his design, without the sun coming round the blinds, without his stage lighting, with only the dissipated blue of the streetlamps and moon, the furnishings of the house looked misplaced, dead, drowned within a sunken ship. It was a problem when one so carefully planned things, when all elements were considered in relation to one another and so well tied together. If one tiny part failed to fit or stood out as artificial, it revealed the wire forms, the otherwise invisible bindings, the glue and tape and string holding the world together.

He changed into a clean shirt and trousers. He put his shoes on. He'd had too much to drink but was going to drive anyway, see what Sophie was up to.

He heard his phone ringing as he closed the front door behind him.

♂

Befitting the date, the cries of the city were more manic than usual. Behind the ventilators' thrum, the shuttering and bolting, the creaks and contractions that rose from the stands of office buildings were heavier. The far shrieks of the night—those indecipherable calls that might be either ecstasy or distress, love or assault—were giddier.

A quartet of gals, office workers in what remained of the costumes they'd donned that morning, swayed as they tacked their bagged happy-hour asses up the hill to the cheap parking or the bus west or the one-bedroom place almost downtown. They were, Cathy saw, the good sports of wherever it was that they worked, the organizers of the going-away parties, the baby showers. They were the ones who collected for the disease. They were clerks or secretaries. Bosses didn't dress up for Halloween. Would she be a secretary? Of course not, she thought, but then … why not? Was she too precious? Her marks weren't that great. It was wage slavery, though. Lecherous idiots lorded it over you, drove you like a pony. Yes, it was a bad deal. Yes, all that endless, boring, Jurassic-age feminism that her mother got on with … it was all true. But then what, what did you do? Apparently, despite your obvious qualifications, you couldn't just *be* a rock star—to start with you had to stick with those retarded fucking piano lessons before your parents would even consider buying you an electric guitar. She wouldn't follow in her father's footsteps, that was for sure. That was a road straight to a particular sort of hell. And her mother for all her efforts, all the best intentions, was doing the same thing now—fighting the same battles, trying to fund the irrigation of the same patch of desert—that she had been doing forever.

The foursome were laughing; they knew where happiness was found.

Cathy had secreted the book home from Rosencrantz's, but now, returning it, felt no compulsion to conceal it and carried it openly by her side, bumping it off her hip as she went, like it was just another school book.

She was relieved to be getting rid of the thing, to have made the decision. There was something about the book that demanded attention she wasn't prepared to give.

Cathy could smell wood smoke on the evening air. There used to be a fire in the hearth at home almost every cold night of the autumn and winter, but now it was rare. There used to be company and chatter, but that had fallen off. Her parents were losing their enthusiasm for life. They were just getting through it. Her behaviour wasn't helping, she knew, and she experienced a pang of guilt. She'd make an effort to brighten her disposition, even if she didn't actually feel any happier. What was served by being so sullen all the time?

She was cagey entering the lane behind Rosencrantz's, approaching it obliquely, gravity accelerating her cross-legged trot down the slope so that the passage seemed to scoop her up.

It reeked of cats.

She knew not to hesitate, to get to that back door and get in, so she was thrown as if she'd missed a step in her sleep when she saw it was gone. Her hands, and the book, came up in front of her face in a shielding reflex. The sights and sounds of the busy street beyond rushed up at her. There was a hole where once there'd been a bookstore. On the walls of the buildings to which it used to be attached you could see lines left by the scorched beams and blocks. It was like a cut in a cake. Otherwise it was as if it had never been there at all. There was no rubble, no inky waters, no pages blowing around. It was like they'd vacuumed it up.

4

Sophie's door, the back door that faced onto the pavement, was the only one still lighted on the crescent. Despite the temperature it was wide open. The other houses appeared to be self-consciously dimmed, not blacked-out like Marty's, but discouraging to would-be trick-or-treaters nonetheless. You'd say that Sophie's beckoned but for the apparition that awaited one at the threshold. As he approached, Marty tried to guess what or who it was she was trying to be, her face was a painted mask the colour of paper, her hair was combed up and back to show either electric emanations from her skull or perhaps a halo. She was wearing a gown the shape and trim of a wedding dress, only more silvery-grey than white. It was spangled like a cheap theatrical piece. She was seated on a chair, slumped, her arms resting on the thighs of her wide-open legs, a large bowl of choice bonbons before her.

"Trick or treat?" asked Marty.

"Oh, *scheisse,* I don't know … is there a difference?" She'd had a few drinks.

"What's the costume?"

"Elizabeth Regent, dummy. *Die Erste*. Not the German one. The Virgin. Newfoundland's first Queen."

"Many kids come by?"

"Hardly any. It's ridiculous, *Maahten*. This part of town's become a graveyard or at least its waiting room. Without kids, what's a street?"

"I would have thought you would have had enough of kids during the day?"

"They're almost adults. Just as bad as adults in any case. Besides, why do you think I stick with your shitty job? One can never have enough of children. Life is its own meaning. Drinky?"

"Yes, pleasey."

"Nobody else is coming anyway."

For a queen Sophie made a singularly indecorous picture, flat on the couch, her dress gathered up about her middle. Her legs and feet this way and that. She couldn't much care. She had poured them each a generous glass of white wine.

"I should tell you what happened today … at The Pines," said Marty.

"About Hank and the boy?"

"Who knows?"

"Oh, just everybody."

"I shouldn't be surprised, I suppose," said Marty.

"No. People love to spread bad news." Sophie pulled herself up so that she could the more easily drink her wine. She waved her glass in Marty's direction, half a toast. "How's the new girlfriend?"

"Over."

"That wasn't very long, *Maahten.*"

"I'm quite embarrassed over the whole thing, actually. Don't particularly want to talk about it."

"Poor baby. Now tell me you didn't come over tonight right after she turned you out."

"Something like that, only way more complicated. I knew you'd be dressed up, it being Halloween."

"You won't get a pity fuck here, honey."

"Hadn't even crossed my mind."

"I hope it's not my costume. Or am I too old and respectable?"

"No. You know what I want to say?"

"What?"

"That we should get married."

"Oh, Martin," Sophie cackled. "That's really pathetic."

"I know."

"We definitely shouldn't."

"I know. Can I sleep on the couch?"

"Yeah, sure."

nine

EXCRUCIATING PRESSURE in his sinuses woke Marty at dawn. Spears of pain radiated from somewhere behind his face, applying force on his eye sockets. He was muddled and yeasty as he made his way to the bathroom. When he blew his nose there was a quake within his skull, a shifting of wet matter followed by series of gurgles and pops. A whistling noise, a chirping from a part of his anatomy he'd rather have remained unknown—passages and membrane walls—went on for seconds after he'd emptied the cavity. It was the spores. They were colonizing his head.

He briefly considered fixing Sophie breakfast, but it was too early. She liked to sleep late on the weekends. He left the house as quietly as he could.

Dishevelled and in need of a shave, he shouldn't have gone for breakfast at MacNamara's diner. A man with Marty's profile in the community had to keep up appearances, but he could not make himself go back to his own house. He had a sense that somebody, Jackie or Ted or Hank or the cops, somebody would be there waiting for him. Worse still, that there might not be anybody there at all.

As he sipped a third cup of coffee he watched the fresh couples arriving. The girls were always flushed and the boys uncombed.

They grinned at each other like fools. You never saw the wasted evenings for they'd said their goodbyes in the wee hours. Breakfasts together spoke of hope.

There were other patrons, of course, the businesspeople, owners of the one-off retail outfits, or the small contractors for whom Saturday meant nothing more than another day's work. There were those who could not sleep for fear of what dreams brought and came, with relief, to join with those beginning the day. There were, as always, a couple of tradesmen, a couple of shift workers. And there were those, like Marty, whom the night's tempests had washed ashore.

Marty decided to answer Meredith's call from the day before. He wasn't being magnanimous, merely delaying returning home or going to The Pines to continue cleaning the place. He did not want to get on with things. "Things" were so very unpleasant and growing more so as he thought of them. The Pines was in very serious trouble. They might have been able to live down one of their staff being accused of sexual improprieties, but this was the principal and co-founder. There was, Marty saw clearly, a chance that they would be put out of business. Yesterday this possibility seemed remote. Recalculating, he saw that his earlier worst-case scenario was not the worst case at all. The fact was they stood to lose everything. The school, if it failed, was worthless; there was no equity in the operation save the building itself if the brand was shot (the banks queued ahead of Marty and Hank for their share, so the two partners could lose their original investment). If the shit really came down and there was civil action, Marty could lose his house. He was facing ruination and heading to his brother's house to deal with what would no doubt be petty troubles, inconveniences, scrapes and itches.

The low sun on this first day of November, while bright, was cheap with its heat. The blacktop of the streets, the carbon polish, kicked the rays back up so that the light was not illuminating the world but erasing it. The shimmering shaved corners and consumed the delicate lines of the world, chewed up the filigree and tracery. It was all glare. Driving to Rex's, he saw people walking the streets reduced to shapeless, amorphous grey-black cores, rippling posts of presence.

"Bring in other partners," Hank had said. Like who? Nobody wanted to take those kinds of risks, they wanted their numbing jobs and their middling paycheques, they wanted to go home on Friday and forget about it. Jesus, he thought, what if Hank ended up behind bars?

Marty was out there by himself. There was no one to catch his fall, no one on whom he could rely for comfort or support. At least Hank had Beth and the kids, some sanctuary to which to return in the dark.

Marty had only Rex and, he supposed, to a lesser degree Meredith and Cathy, but what use were they, so needy and weak? Here he was, up against it, a man trapped, and he was driving over to their place to help them sort out their lives, to throw them a line. They could all, all three of them—and he was going to say this, finally say it to their faces—they could all just fuck right off.

He pulled up in front of the row house. Opening his car door he noticed a figure, back-lit, standing on the corner ahead, the corner of the street on which Jackie and Ted lived. Jackie and Ted. Whether it was either of those two he could not tell as, crossing the street, they disappeared. It was an illusion, he knew. He'd blinked as they'd dashed or turned back and rounded the corner out of sight, trick of the light.

But Jackie and Ted would always be around, the town wasn't big enough that he'd avoid them forever. They'd have put the sordid business behind them, tried and succeeded not to think about it—ever—kissed and made up and then they would see Marty, at the gas station, at the mall, at the airport, and they'd have to relive the betrayal all over again. Marty needed to get out of Dodge.

♆

The stark sun was streaming through the windows of the house, exposing areas meant to be in shadow, revealing dirt and chips and nicks. Cathy's legs had vanished in the shine reflecting from the floor of the hallway so that she appeared to be hovering there, as if in anticipation of his arrival, waiting for him to do his redemptive dance again. But he had nothing left.

"What is it this time?" he asked.

"Terminal cancer," she said.

"Come again?"

"It's something called multiple myeloma. His blood is dying."

♅

It was, Meredith told him as they sat in the living room, a malignancy of the white blood cells.

"It's treatable, it responds to chemotherapy, but … it's invariably fatal, they can't even tell him how long …" Meredith said. "The back pain is from … from lesions in the spine."

"Old people get it," said Cathy.

"Your father isn't old," said Marty.

"That's what I meant," said Cathy uncertainly.

Marty sniffled. His nose was runny. Meredith, assuming this was to do with his response to the sad news and not, as was the case, an allergic response to the growth in the basement of The Pines, placed a comforting hand on Marty's shoulder. With her other, she offered him a tissue from a box. The two women looked to have been wrung dry of tears. Their eyes were branded with raw rings.

"Is he at the hospital?" asked Marty.

"No," said Meredith, "he's in the yard."

He was hugging the tree, actually embracing the big maple. This kind of thing was to be expected, thought Marty. There were supposed to be stages, and some sort of namby-pamby total earth-love experience was, no doubt, one of them, rushing around nosing flowers, squinting at the sun, taking it all in one last time. This was going to be rough, thought Marty. He felt like turning and running.

"You heard?" asked Rex, letting his arms drop.

"Yeah, I … I mean … God, I'm sorry."

"I have 20/20 vision, Marty. I've still got all my hair."

"Yeah?"

"It doesn't seem right."

"No, it doesn't."

"The blood's off. When I wrote that episode of *All Heart* for Lloyd Purcell, they gave us a little—I shouldn't say little, it was the size of a phone book—anyway, they gave us this bible that tells you about the show, how to write to format, the main characters, all that. At the back of this thing they included a long list of medical conditions, diseases and stuff that could be used in the scripts, along with the symptoms and shit. They had put red dots, sticky red dots, next to the diseases that had already been used in previous episodes. It was so fucking tasteless, so television, but I tell you I read every one and then worried about getting them all. I'm sure I remember each one and there wasn't any multiple myeloma. It's not even a good way to end a story, Marty."

Rex looked up at the tree.

"But when the doctor said it, it just immediately had that ring of something nasty, maybe prefacing it with 'multiple.' You get 'multiple' anything and you know you're good and fucked. I don't know. Do I know anything? There are some things you are going to have to do for me, Marty."

"Sure."

"First, you've got to help me get rid of this tree."

"How's that?" Marty heard him. It wasn't what he expected.

"Like chop it down. Driving me to distraction for years."

"If we chop it down it'll just fall into the house."

"I know. We'll have to do it in sections, with slings and stuff. Rent a chainsaw. I was always afraid to use one, afraid I might cut my hand off or my foot off and … now … well, it won't matter."

"Yes, it would, Rex."

"I don't intend to saw my leg off, Marty, I'm just saying … that …"

"We'll need scaffolding or something."

"Exactly."

"But … I mean … how long is that going to take, chopping the tree down like that?" asked Marty.

"I'm not supposed to be dead within the week, if that's what you're getting at."

"Rex, come on …"

"I'm terminal and you're trying to get out of helping me cut down this tree."

"Not true."

Rex knew it wasn't true, he only wanted to play with Marty. He looked up again now, considering the maple, making a study of its shape so that he might take it apart, an iniquitous backward architecture.

"Those branches are always bigger on the ground, once you get them down," Rex said. "Everything looks smaller when it's above you, when you have to look up at it, did you know that?"

"I don't think so."

"No, it's like a real phenomenon, like the moon when it's rising, when it's on the horizon, it looks huge and then later in the night it seems smaller. What's that called, that?"

"I don't know."

"Did you see the moon last night?"

"I did."

"Spectacular. Time of year," Rex said. He was so matter of fact. No, he was almost chipper.

"You seem … good …"

"I guess …"

"I mean … emotionally," Marty clarified.

"I don't know, it hasn't hit me. I have waves of … sort of meaningless fantasies of violence and revenge. Revenge for what, I don't know. There are people from all the years, from school and the theatre and on that dumb television show, who I didn't like … stupid fucks and bad actors who have done reasonably well, who seem relatively prosperous and happy, who I haven't thought about in years, and I just want to fucking murder them. And this mook at the bank who turned me down for a loan, years ago, must be fifteen years ago, Marty, I want to kill him. Nobodies, like everybody who deserves this more than me, which is, of course, everybody. Everybody is nobody 'cause they don't have my problem. I'm almost certainly going to be told that it's an unhealthy attitude."

Rex squeezed himself against the cold. Marty kept his mouth shut.

"I have to see a counsellor tomorrow. I took a pill, too, an anti-anxiety thing. I asked for it. Truth be told, I wasn't surprised because I was feeling, you know, not well … No, not true, I knew there was something wrong, but … When I left the doctor's office I thought I'd have a drink … but I can't. I'm afraid, you know, that if I go on the beer I'll … I'll … well, I don't want to embarrass myself. Not now."

"No. No regrets."

"What?"

"Regrets," repeated Marty.

"People say that, don't they? They say that all the time. 'I have no regrets.' How the fuck can that be?"

"I don't know."

"That's just such bullshit. I have a lot of regrets and remorse. How could you have lived without having regrets?"

"You're right." Marty noticed anger welling in Rex, a rage born of frustration that he hadn't seen since they were boys. Fair enough.

"Who would have guessed that all my anxiety was justified, only misplaced? Worry, Marty, but make sure you're worried about the right thing. So …" Rex was checking himself, keeping hold. He looked upward to the leafless crown of the maple. "Can we get on this tree thing right away, like tomorrow?"

"Absolutely."

"Good. Now the other thing is … " Rex flinched for the first time, an involuntary muscle contraction in his cheek like he'd been stung. "See, if I were to be perfectly honest with myself …" now a chuckle, manic and plaintive, "which is just as well, given the circumstances. Completely honest. I'd say that ever since the accident, ever since Mom and Dad died, and that's a long time now, doesn't seem long, but … ever since they died I've been … constantly … what? … uneasy, in a sort of state of unease. I was trying to think what it was, how to better characterize it, like anxiety or what, and I realized that … closest I could come was simply … 'scared.' Except when I was drinking, I've always been kinda shit-baked. It's unbecoming, cowardice. A little scared of everything and nothing. So. So I do not want the same thing to happen to my girl, to Cathy."

"Okay," said Marty.

"I don't know what it takes, what kind of lies that it requires, but that's what you got to do. You have to be some sort of emotional anchor, I guess. Reliable. Grace under pressure thing. And that's you. It's not a stretch. And love her."

"I love Cathy, Rex."

"Yeah, more though, like care … till it hurts."

"Right. I will."

Rex shrank with a sigh. "And you know, over the years, Cathy and Meredith, they've grown entirely ambivalent about me. I've become … furniture. And I don't blame them 'cause I'd grown ambivalent about myself … but now there's going to be all this guilt over it … shit … and Meredith's Seattle trip … she'd really been looking forward to that …"

"I'm sure that—"

Rex cut him off with another thought. "And, naturally, if anything happened to Meredith—because her sister, Lily, is a mental case—naturally you'd be the one to take her, to take Cathy."

"Naturally," said Marty.

"And teach her how to drive. Like, not … but now, she wants to learn now."

"That's easy."

"It's funny … because lately I've really been thinking that I've been a terrible parent, that I totally cocked-up being a dad, you know, and yet … I, for the life of me, I don't trust anyone else to do it. Not that I don't have complete faith in you, Marty, it's just the way I feel."

"I understand. Perfectly."

"I have to stop talking about this now," Rex said. "I wish I had faith … that I could bring myself to get on my hands and knees and crawl into The Temple, but you know I can't bear the just and the righteous, so to try now would be a lie. And goddamn it, death is such a fucking cliché, Marty. Is that what you're left with?"

"No. This is a bad moment, that's all."

"People worry about how they'll be remembered and it's weird but ... I take comfort in knowing that eventually I'll be forgotten. It seems a relief, somehow, like it's a load off. Not to say that ... well ... truth is ...mostly ... I don't want to die." Rex paused and then asked, "How are you?"

"Me?"

"Yeah, you."

"Rex, I'm ... what can I say ... I'm devastated."

"No, I mean besides this."

"I've got a few things on my mind. Nothing major. Just the usual day-to-day stuff."

"Right. I got to get my shit in order, you know, papers and ... just my shit. I keep waiting for a profound thought, you know?"

Marty wasn't sure what he meant. "Yeah," he said all the same.

Marty must have shivered—he was cold—because Rex said, "Go on inside. I can't right now."

Meredith was nowhere to be seen. Marty wandered into the kitchen and found Cathy sitting at the table.

"Wow," he said, immediately feeling stupid for having said so.

"Yeah," said Cathy.

"I ... need ..." No, he didn't *need*. "I want something sweet. Is there anything sweet?"

"There are some molasses cookies Mom made on top of the fridge. They're really good," she said. "And there's ice cream, I guess."

Marty opened the freezer drawer. There was a cardboard tub of vanilla ice cream. Inside the fridge he found a plastic bottle of ginger ale.

"Ever had a float?" he asked.

"No," she said.

"Do you have like … a scoop, for the ice cream?"

"There's one in the drawer by the sink."

Marty opened the drawer. The ice-cream scoop was there, as was the bread knife with which Cathy had slashed her mother's hand. The scoop was an old relic, heavy construction metal with a thumb lever that turned a curved bar inside the cup. Marty got two big pint glasses (so like Rex to have the proper glasses with which to serve a porter) from a cupboard on the other side of the kitchen. Into each he put two scoops of ice cream. The mechanical action of the scoop brought to mind the workings of the orrery. He thought again that he should get the device from the basement of The Pines and have it repaired and give it to Alan Pitts as a token of appreciation for the work he'd done painting the planets on the walls at the school. He topped up the big glasses with ginger ale; the blobs of ice cream rose to the top. He got two spoons from the cutlery drawer.

"A float," he said placing it in front of his niece. "We used to have them all the time when we were kids. Me and Rex."

♀

He was doing the best he could, she thought. He was, however awkwardly, trying to be like an uncle to her. She spooned some of the float into her mouth.

"It's good," she said, though in truth she couldn't, right now, tell one way or the other. Uncle Marty would keep trying to be especially concerned for her now, she supposed. He'd have to. He and her father had probably just now been talking about it, making arrangements. She should do her best to appear grateful for the attention. Maybe she genuinely would be. Uncle Marty was a fool, for sure, but he wasn't such a bad guy. He was eating his float like a little kid, one spoonful fast after another, without pausing, looking down into the glass. He gave no sign of being upset other than there were tears, ludicrously plentiful tears, coursing down his cheeks.

Most of life was a pose. You went from one to another as a way to get by. You struck them for your own benefit as much as for others. Uncle Marty was sitting there, weeping into his ice cream, having a brief moment of truth. What would it take to live one's entire life so honestly, to never wrap yourself in the blanket of your own myths? A person would have to be so brave to do that.

She was about to cry again, she felt it.

People died. Everyone did. But in her heart she secretly held that they did not, they simply went on forever. To do otherwise was too lonely a thought. Sadness could not be so central to existence. What was the point of living if only to die?

She was going to cry. To think of herself now, in the face of this news, was wrong, was selfish, but it seemed that it all had to do with her.

So much time and thought, all that religion and science, was dedicated to the great mysteries, and it would always be for nothing. What did anyone know? The belief that it was heroic to ask questions to which there were no answers was foolish and vain and wishful and, probably, all anybody had.

She started to cry again.

The stuff in the heavy glass in front of her looked primordial, white and slow churning. There was a gentle effervescence so that it whispered a *shush*. The bubbles were of what? Carbon dioxide, she knew. An exhalation, which, escaping from the liquid, commingled with the oxygen and nitrogen, the noble gases, argon, and the stranger, xenon, the breath of prophets that carried the dust of empires, of Napoleon's bones, that filled the room, the house, the street, the sky. And through all this there was forever falling a blizzard of rays and particles, blast marks radiating from the beginning of time, the muons and pions, raining down from the sun, from the stars dead and alive. And she was in it, they all were, at the command of the waves that streamed to and from eternity, travelling the sweet invisible air.

Acknowledgments

I THANK Irena Murray, Chief Curator of the Rare Books and Special Collections Division of the McGill Library, for arranging access to the Kepler. I am grateful for the scholarly assistance of Rod Donnelly in maths and Simon Avis in some questions of disease. The insight and encouragement of Meg Taylor, Mike Jones, Suzanne DePoe, Lisa Moore, Anne Troake, and Steve Palmer was timely and vital. Especially thanks to Cynthia Good and Tracy Bordian, sages of Penguin.